This is a shocking, powerful, courageous book. Once begun, it cannot be put aside. Once read, it cannot be forgotten.

It is the story of men and women who live and work behind the locked doors and barred windows of a state hospital. It is a story of people trapped in a world where emotions fester and tensions explode into murder and violence.

The chief of staff whose harsh, unyielding devotion to his profession destroys a vulnerable colleague; the two pretty student nurses who become involved in a dangerous romantic triangle; the dedicated attendant who brings humanity to her menial job; the corrupt doctor who takes brutal advantage of his patients ... the strong and the weak—these are the "caretakers." Their actions may shock and surprise you but you will not be able to deny or dismiss them.

"The author has a definite talent for creating and sustaining tension and conflict."
—*Denver Post*

" ... her obvious sincerity (in what is fundamentally a polemic attack upon society's handling of one of our greatest social problems) is more convincing than the slick platitudes of professionalism. And her rough-drawn characters may well be more true to life because drawn from fact." —Frank G. Slaughter, M.D., in *The New York Times Book Review*

Other SIGNET Books of Special Interest

- ☐ **LISA, BRIGHT AND DARK by John Neufeld.** Lisa is slowly going mad but her symptoms, even an attempted suicide, fail to alert her parents or teachers to her illness. She finds compassion only from three girlfriends who band together to provide what they call "group therapy."
(#P4387—60¢)

- ☐ **THE STORY OF SANDY by Susan Stanhope Wexler.** The moving true story of a foster parent's courageous fight for the sanity of a deeply disturbed little boy. (#Q4517—95¢)

- ☐ **I NEVER PROMISED YOU A ROSE GARDEN by Hannah Green.** A beautifully written novel of rare insight about a young girl's courageous fight to regain her sanity in a mental hospital.
(#Y4835—$1.25)

- ☐ **ONE FLEW OVER THE CUCKOO'S NEST by Ken Kesey.** A powerful, brilliant novel about a boisterous rebel who swaggers into the ward of a mental institution and takes over. (#Y5148—$1.25)

- ☐ **THE AUTOBIOGRAPHY OF A SCHIZOPHRENIC GIRL by Marguerite Sechehaye.** The classic case history of a young girl who retreats completely into a world of fantasy, and her slow recovery.
(#T4117—75¢)

THE NEW AMERICAN LIBRARY, INC.,
P.O. Box 999, Bergenfield, New Jersey 07621

Please send me the SIGNET BOOKS I have checked above. I am enclosing $_____(check or money order—no currency or C.O.D.'s). Please include the list price plus 15¢ a copy to cover handling and mailing costs. (Prices and numbers are subject to change without notice.)

Name_____

Address_____

City_____State_____Zip Code_____
Allow at least 3 weeks for delivery

The Caretakers

DARIEL TELFER

A SIGNET BOOK from
NEW AMERICAN LIBRARY
TIMES MIRROR

COPYRIGHT © 1959 BY DANIEL TELFER

*All rights reserved including the right of
reproduction in whole or in part in any form.
For information address Simon & Schuster, Inc.,
630 Fifth Avenue, New York, New York 10020.*

*This is an authorized reprint of a hardcover edition
published by Simon and Schuster.*

TWENTY-SEVENTH PRINTING

 SIGNET TRADEMARK REG. U.S. PAT. OFF. AND FOREIGN COUNTRIES
REGISTERED TRADEMARK—MARCA REGISTRADA
HECHO EN CHICAGO, U.S.A.

SIGNET, SIGNET CLASSICS, SIGNETTE, MENTOR AND PLUME BOOKS
are published by The New American Library, Inc.,
1301 Avenue of the Americas, New York, New York 10019

PRINTED IN THE UNITED STATES OF AMERICA

PROLOGUE

IT WAS NOT A LARGE TOWN.

In the beginning, the only reasons for its existence were the flour mills, the railroad terminal and a main street lined with the usual stores, movie houses and banks.

It was Canterbury that set the town apart from thousands of others like it and gave the townspeople a feeling of uneasiness and a sense of unwelcome responsibility. They resented their town's being automatically identified with a famous mental hospital. Yet, with an incongruous about-face, they were grateful for the money spent in their real-estate offices, stores and bars by the influx of strangers who came to the institution to find work there. Prosperity helped them to tolerate the hospital. Nothing could make them like it.

The appearance of the hospital itself was not offensive. The buildings were clustered in a group, surrounded by lawns and tall trees and graveled paths. The original structures were aged and gray, but spectacular architectural changes had come later—a towering rehabilitation center, the great, beautiful geriatrics buildings, surgical and convalescent wards, minor and major surgeries, drug-rooms, classrooms, therapeutic and clinical laboratories, even recreation halls, cheerful dining rooms, a bakery, a laundry, canteens both for employees and patients.

Everything was modern and complete.

The food from the hospital kitchens was good and plentiful. There was no shortage of bed linen or clothing. There were enough soaps and disinfectants and mops and scouring powders. That was obvious from one look at the floors of the untidy wards, gray from fierce, constant scrubbing. The water supply was excellent, the plumbing first-class (one or two female patients had even been known to rid themselves of infants secretly stillborn behind a pile of laundry bags by flushing them down the toilet).

And, perhaps most important of all, the hospital had the most modern methods of treatment and rehabilitation, the newest medical and surgical discoveries and devices.

But despite its appearance of strength, Canterbury was weak—and its weakness lay in the men and women who worked there. Many of its physicians left as soon as their residency was completed. Most of the affiliates—the young, eager girls who came to the hospital to finish their training and become registered nurses—went on to serve in private hospitals where the pay was better. The majority of the attendants gave little thought to the patients and worked only for their pay checks.

And the patients grew in number. Their beds spilled out of the rooms and the dormitories into the halls. They overflowed into the annexes, they pushed out into screened porches and verandas. From the beds the patients went to sit in dull, pathetic rows in hard chairs placed arm rest against arm rest, or to stand with their noses against the steel mesh of the windows, staring at God knows what. They were always waiting.

They plodded in to meals, they came back to the chairs and the windows, they went to bed. Otherwise, they waited. If they waited long enough, something might happen. Visitors, perhaps, or a fist fight in the ward.

Or they might even die.

Part One

CHAPTER 1

WELL I'M HERE, Kathy Hunter thought, glancing around from her vantage point beneath a tall tree on one of the green slopes overlooking Canterbury.

She had arrived at the hospital the day before to begin the six-month psychiatric training that would complete the cycle of her professional education, and these were the last few moments she had to herself before it would be time to walk down the hill to her first class. She could not decide whether she was frightened or merely overanxious.

A small girl, she believed that she looked stocky, and had developed the habit of sitting with her feet tucked up underneath her skirts. She sat that way now as she stared down at the buildings, her hands clasped in her lap and a dark-blue cape over one arm.

In nursing school she had often thought ahead to this time, wondering how she would feel when she actually began to care for the insane. Would she feel the way so many people do in the presence of the crippled or the deformed—eager to look and yet embarrassed and ashamed? She realized that if she had to ask herself such a question, she must be lacking in something. But what? Maturity?

The Canterbury brochure had said: "Research, Training, Rehabilitation, Custodial Care." But there was more to it than that, she knew. It was learning to understand people—patients, but still *people*. Like her father and mother, her neighbors back home, clerks in stores, the cop on the corner, like the kids she went to school with.... Like herself, even.

I'll be late for class, she thought, but she did not move.

As far back as she could remember she had wanted to be a nurse, holding firmly to the desire all through grade and high school. Then, a few days before leaving for the hospital where she was to spend the next three and a half years, she had become terribly depressed. She felt homesick even before she had finished packing her clothes. She was sure her parents didn't care that she was leaving home. She loaded her phonograph with the most melancholy music in her record collection and even let the dog sleep on her bed across her feet every night.

On the last day, her mother came into the room and sat down on the bed.

"Kathy," she said, "we've been so proud of you. We want you to remember that we love you dearly, and that as long as we live we'll be here when you need us. Will you remember that?"

Kathy saw that her mother's eyes were red-rimmed, that her mouth was smiling but that her hands were clutched together tightly; and she realized that her departure was going to be much harder for her parents than for herself.

"I'm not going away forever," she whispered.

"Of course not. You're just growing up."

"How—how did you know, Mother?"

"Know what?"

"That I—I wasn't sure any more—about anything?"

"Darling, I felt the same way the first year I left your grandmother and grandfather and went away to school. As if my whole world were coming to an end. Oh, I wanted to go —until I started to pack. Then I just knew I was making a terrible mistake."

"I'll never make a good nurse," said Kathy, almost wailing.

"Why not?"

"I don't know enough."

"Not yet. You may never know enough. But just knowing things isn't the whole answer, Kathy. It's something inside that counts. The desire to help, to put the needs of others before your own. There's a big gap between the word 'goodness' and—well, the word 'efficient,' for instance. With all the knowledge and efficiency in the world, you can't be good at anything unless you really want to be."

"I know that," Kathy said.

"I'm moralizing," Mrs. Hunter said. "But it's because you mean so much to me. I wanted you to know how much you're loved and how much you'll be missed."

After that everything was all right, and when Kathy left the next morning she cried only once on the train.

The training at the hospital was not easy. She scrubbed units, emptied bed pans, measured urine, stood by while accident victims were sewn up and while babies were born. She learned how to prepare a dead body for consignment to a mortician. She studied chemistry, drugs and nutrition, flesh and blood and organs, diseases and symptoms. She learned the proper attitude of respect to maintain in the presence of doctors and supervisors.

She didn't go home often because there wasn't enough time unless she traveled by plane, and she couldn't afford the fare. But because of the hard work, after a few months she was not too lonely. She was not beautiful, with her dark hair cut short and caplike, her fine brown eyes and cream-colored skin, but there was something in her look and manner that made her first interesting and then attractive. She made friends easily among the other student nurses and met a few boys she enjoyed going out with, and a few she could have done without, those who seemed to think that there was no finer sport than chasing probationers up and down halls or maneuvering them into utility closets. And eventually the hospital became a second home, a place of busy routine and of security. Now she was far from that security and about to enter a strange and complex world, one she did not understand. She had never felt so alone.

She did not like to think that she feared the unknown. And yet, she thought, why couldn't she be like other girls, fall in love, get married, have a home? This was the most beautiful time of the year, with cool nights and balmy days, the good smells of spring everywhere. I wish I could fall in love, she thought, a little crossly. This is the weather for love. For a brief moment she was sure it wasn't the weather for nursing sick people and being afraid. Immediately she was contrite, remembering how much she had always wanted to be a nurse. If it had turned out to be somewhat dull and prosaic, more hard work than satisfaction, at least she had chosen the career herself. As for being afraid, wouldn't that disappear as soon as she learned all about Canterbury? Of course it would!

I'd better go, she thought, glancing at her watch. She was about to stand up when she noticed a group of people strolling along the slope beyond her. There were several men and a woman looking down at the buildings. She waited until they had passed out of sight before she jumped up and ran quickly down the hill.

The path led through a thick clump of bushes at the bottom of the slope, and as she stepped between them she suddenly came face to face with a stout, middle-aged woman who completely blocked her way. Kathy was suddenly terrified. She had been trapped by an insane woman! To escape, she would have to turn and run back up the path.

But before she could make a move, the woman, as startled as Kathy herself, said, "My, but you gave me a turn! I sure didn't see anybody behind that bush. My goodness!"

Kathy pulled herself together. If the other woman was really a patient she must be harmless or she wouldn't be outside and alone. Anyway, she didn't look like the kind of person who could possibly hurt anyone. Her weight, her obvious age, her neatness, were as reassuring as if she and Kathy had accidentally bumped carts in a supermarket.

Still, the fear had been there, Kathy realized. Buried, but not too deep. Disgusted with herself, she turned sideways to let the woman pass.

The woman did not move. She seemed unaware of Kathy's first reaction of fear. Her own face was pale and strained.

"Maybe you can help me," she said. "I don't know a thing about this place. My husband—well, I'm a widow and I got to have a job. My next-door neighbor told me to come out here. You happen to know which one of them buildings a person gets hired at?" After a deep breath she added, "God, I'm scared!"

She isn't a patient after all, Kathy thought. She's a stranger to this place, just like me. And I let myself be frightened by her.

"You want the main office building," Kathy said, pointing to it. "That one in front with the glass bricks around the entrance."

The woman looked. "That one? Don't—" she hesitated—"don't seem like that could be the right one. My, ain't it nice looking? Almost like a library or something. You sure that's the one I'm looking for?"

"Yes," said Kathy. "And don't be afraid," she added impulsively, almost as if she were telling it to herself. "I was told that all the patients outside on the grounds have paroles and are perfectly harmless." Yes, and she had forgotten it until this moment.

The woman did not seem to notice the little flush that came and went on Kathy's face. She was absorbed in studying the building. "Oh, I'm not afraid of the patients," she replied abstractedly. "It's the job. Getting it, I mean. Me with my eighth-grade education facing all those big wheels in there. I probably ain't got a chance."

Kathy's feeling of shame gave way to sympathy. The woman wasn't afraid of the patients; she was simply nervous about applying for a job. She needed a job. She needed help.

"How do you know until you've tried?"

The woman turned back, her expression uncertain. "I told you. I never went past the eighth grade in school."

"So what? You're as good as anybody else, aren't you?"

The woman's plump face turned white, and her hands came up to her throat in an odd, despairing movement.

"What kinda thing is that to say?" she whispered.

Kathy reached out and touched the woman's arm. "Of course you are. You're just as good as me or anybody, understand? Maybe you did only go so far in school, but if they need you down there, they'll hire you. And if they don't—why, you'll get a job somewhere else. You'll see. Just keep telling yourself that you've got something somebody wants and don't ever let anybody think differently. Do you see?"

She remembered her class and looked at her watch. "My class! I'll be late if I don't run!" She eased past the dumpy figure. "Good luck," she shouted over her shoulder. "Goodbye!"

She ran off down the path, her starched skirt and blue cape flowing back, her feet making quick sounds on the gravel.

A fine thing! she thought as she ran. It took somebody like that to make me realize how insecure I must be to be afraid of people just because they're sick in the head instead of in the stomach or the lungs. A fine thing! There's a woman who looks as if she's never had much of anything, and all she wants is a job, while you, you've had everything. What kind of nurse are you going to be?

She was thoroughly disgusted with herself, and when she walked into the classroom she was much too sober for a girl of twenty-one.

CHAPTER 2

THE OLDER WOMAN watched Kathy running down the path. As good as anybody else? she thought to herself. Well, I kinda thought I was once. Don't know where I stand right now. I don't rightly know.

She looked unhappily at the now empty path, then her shoulders lifted. But I still got to get me a job. That's for sure, regardless. Thanks, lady. Thanks for the good luck. I sure need it.

Reluctantly she turned and gazed in the direction she had to go. Good as anybody else? Oh, no! But who would ever know? Besides, they weren't her judges, those people who hired and fired down there. None of their business what she had done in the past. She hadn't wanted to do it, had she? But she'd do it a million times over, she told herself fiercely, if she had to burn in hell for eternity. If God couldn't understand what she had done, then she didn't care. She simply didn't care.

She tried to think about the job she had to have instead of remembering about Harry. She wouldn't tell anything private to those people who hired for Canterbury. She would just try to make them see her predicament.

Because remembering about Harry—and really, when did she ever stop?—brought him back, clear as day. The moaning that tore at her until she was almost frantic. God! Help me, Jesus! Help me, Jesus Christ!

Three months and five days ago the doctor had cut Harry open, then sewed him right up. A matter of time, he had said. Only you didn't believe that when you loved somebody. You said no—politely, of course. And got busy. As though you could do something to stop what was happening!

Jesus Christ! Sometimes screams, but mostly moans.

Sweat on her upper lip, Millie Higgins jogged toward the doorway faced with the glass bricks. But she was not there; she was back in her house the day Harry died.

Helplessly, she remembered. Naked except for a very short, thin cotton gown, Harry lay flat on his back. The day before, Dr. Travis had made an incision to let the accumulating fluid drain out before it drowned his heart. Afterward, Millie was constantly nearby, checking and replacing the soaked, foul-smelling pads or making new ones, opening the gauze, cutting it to create large, substantial squares. When not doing this, she bent over Harry, gently wiping his sweating face with cloths dampened in cold water. She dropped the discarded pads into number-ten grocery sacks, and when she had to she rushed outside to burn them, then hurried immediately back to Harry's side.

She concentrated on the clock, waiting for the times Harry had to have his medicine; she thought of nothing but helping Harry.

The doctor had not said in so many words that Harry was dying, but Millie knew. The knowledge had come swiftly and surely when Dr. Travis had come into the room the day before for his daily check, taken one long look at the bladder-like abdomen, then muttered something about edema and paracentesis.

"Para . . . what? What did you say, Doc?"

But he hadn't answered—just opened his case, taking out instruments wrapped in sterile packages. When he did speak it was "Water. Boil some water." Then she knew the score.

Yesterday, she thought. Yesterday she had still hoped. Today she knew. It had been no good, none of it. The surgery three months back, for instance. So much wasted time and effort, so much more for Harry to endure. Dr. Travis should have been honest. He should have let her know that the surgery wouldn't help, that it was far too late to help, that nothing could be done any more for Harry.

She was terribly angry for a moment, then she felt ashamed. After all, how could the doctor know before he opened Harry up and took a good look? Most of that kind of stuff was guesswork anyway. A person had the natural strength to get well and live or he didn't.

She remembered now that Dr. Travis had cautioned her against being too hopeful. And he had cut his bills almost in half, knowing how poor she and Harry were, how every cent they had was going into Harry's treatment, including the small amount left over after her mother's funeral expenses, as well as the house-tax money she had managed to accumulate out of Harry's disability checks. Good old Doc. He must have realized how much she had depended on her mother's old-age pension. When it stopped coming in, she and Harry had really been pinched.

Honesty forced her to recall that she, herself, had insisted on the surgery. She had willed herself to believe it would be successful—banking on it until Harry started to swell, until he was literally gasping for breath from the pressure. Why get mad at Doc? He wasn't to blame.

She changed the packing again. She took a bit of cotton and used it to spread carbolated vaseline all over the inflamed area.

Harry moaned without letup as she worked, but she knew her touch was not responsible. He had not been without pain for weeks, the pure, white-hot agony radiating through his body from the area of his bladder. Yesterday's cutting had made no difference one way or another, apparently. Either he couldn't feel the sharp instrument penetrating his stomach or else the new hurt was swallowed up in the ever-present old torment.

She glanced at the clock. Almost time for the morphine. She turned to the tray on the night stand. The morphine bottle was about the length and thickness of a matchstick. She picked it up and carefully counted the tiny tablets. There were quite a few left, and she was fiercely grateful, since they were so vital to Harry—and vital to her, because without them he would be screaming most of the time. She went wild when he screamed.

Abruptly she was aware that the moaning from the bed had stopped. She swung back to find Harry's eyes open and fixed on what she held in her hand.

"Millie. Sit here by me, huh?" His voice was heavy, panting.

She placed her broad bottom on the edge of the bed and smoothed back his matted hair. "Yes, Harry. I'm right here. I'll always be here, Harry. You want something, doll?"

"Millie, how are things? How you making out?"

He had been out of his head with pain so long that she was surprised that he could ask a sensible question.

"I'm doing all right, Harry. Perfectly all right. What makes you ask?"

"Millie, my insurance. There won't be much left."

"God, Harry! Don't talk that way. I don't want your insurance. I want you. My old man. You hear? You hear me?"

"No, Millie, I gotta talk. Listen. Listen now. You got to figure this out. Bury me as cheap as you can. Real cheap. No fuss, no nothing. You understand, Millie?"

She held back the tears with a harsh effort. "Harry, didn't you hear me? You got no call to talk that way. Just be quiet and try to sleep so's you'll get better. Try to sleep, doll."

His breathing was shallow, almost no breathing at all. His arms lay away from his distended girth, his hands plucking at the sheet.

"Millie, I got to talk about things. I know there ain't much left. What'll you do? What'll you do, Millie?"

"Do? Why, I'll do all right so long as I have you, Harry. Could you drink a little juice, honey? It's pineapple mixed with orange. I got it right here in this pitcher. There's cracked ice in it so it's real cold. Just a little to wet down your throat, Harry."

But he could not swallow the liquid, even when she took a spoon and fed it to him in small sips. Finally she gave up, putting the glass and spoon aside with a sigh, and sat watching him, her face drawn and anxious with her effort to hide her emotions.

"Millie," he whispered in his cracked, panting way, "you been awful good t' me, and I never did a thing for you—not a thing. No nice things, this cheap house—not even any children. Not one kid. Why couldn't I do that, Millie? Why? I sure tried. Now here I am, getting ready to leave you in a fix—"

"Harry! It's all right. You sound as if you got yourself sick on purpose. What kinda crazy talk is that? You know you couldn't help it. You been the best husband a woman could ever have. I wouldn't trade you for the fanciest rich guy in the whole world!"

"Millie, let me say what I got to say. Jesus Christ, it's hard to talk. What you going to do after? Huh? How you gonna manage, Millie? Is the money all gone?"

Her hands tightened until the knuckles were white, but her voice was controlled. "Now, Harry, of course if ain't all gone. I got plenty left—enough to take care of us both for a long time—a long, long time."

His fingers plucked a little harder. "No, Millie. It's gone. You know it is. My operation—it took it all. I know. You ain't telling me different. It took all your mom's insurance money. You won't have anything left at all. You'll have to go to work. Godamighty, I never did a thing but leave you trouble, Millie."

"If you don't hush and save your strength, I'm not gonna sit here. I'm gonna leave and go out in the kitchen and whip me up a cake or something. I don't have to listen to that kinda talk. You been a wonderful guy, Harry. You know what you been to me. You know."

Briefly the fingers lay still. "I—I guess there was a time we had some fun, huh? Huh, Millie? We had some pretty good times, didn't we?" For a very brief moment his eyes brightened. Then the pain was there. "It ain't gonna be much longer, Millie. We got to figure out what you can do. Why don't you let the house go and you live with Ralph and Emily? They'll be good to you, Millie."

She snorted. "Your brother and his wife? You think I want to be a first-class baby-sitter for them two? Kids all over the house. Where would I sleep? Under a bed? Anyhow, nothing's gonna happen, Harry. You're going to get better. You gotta make up your mind. Make up your mind. Harry, you hear? Make yourself get better. I want my own house and my own man. I want you, Harry."

Her held him for a little while, then he slipped away. "No, Millie—you know how it is. You know." He stopped, his breath shuddering in his throat.

Tenderly her hands mopped the perspiration on his face. "Take it easy, doll. God's sake, take it easy. Try to sleep, why doncha? Whatever happens, I'll make out all right, so you gotta stop this worrying. God above, what's there to worry about but you?"

From some source he retrieved a little strength. "That's it, Millie. That's what I wanted to say. It's not me. Now, look. You won't go to Ralph's house, maybe Ruth'll help you. Jesus Christ, I never figured my old lady'd ever have to go to work. I thought I had it all worked out so's you could have enough to live on and still make the payments and the taxes on the house. It was that damn operation messed us up and for what? It never did no good!"

"Harry, doll! We didn't know. None of us. We didn't know until we tried, did we? We waited too long." She stopped, dismayed. But he had known the score, too. All along.

"That's what I been telling you. And that's why we gotta do some figuring right now. Ruth'll help you, Millie. She'll tell you how to go about it—getting a job, I mean. And don't put it off too long. Not that I want you to work, Jesus Christ. Only, you'll be better off than being here alone all day. Millie, look at me."

The tears held back so diligently began slowly to spill

down her cheeks. "God, Harry, ain't I looking? Ain't I always looking? You got to sleep and rest and not wear yourself out like this, doll. You're gonna be better tomorrow, or the next day. You wait and see."

"No, Millie, no!" He gasped. "You know how it's gonna be. Just worse and worse. Jesus Christ, don't seem like it could get any worse. That's something else I wanted to talk about. Listen. Look at me, Millie. Why—why doncha help me, Millie? Jesus Christ, if you loved me, you'd want to help me. You know what I mean, Millie? You know?"

They had been over this before. She thought he had forgotten, but now she saw that he had not. "Harry, you mustn't ask me. You know I love you, honey. I love you so much I'm all twisted up inside with it. If I could take all your pains outa you and stick 'em inside my own guts, I'd do it right this minute. But that other—you know I can't, Harry. You know I can't. What if you was gonna get better, maybe swing the other way? You think I'd be fool enough to spoil that if there was any chance at all of it happening?"

"Jesus Christ," he moaned. "It ain't gonna be but one way. Godamighty, help me, Millie! Help me! Don't do it to me, letting me hurt like this. You know I ain't got no more chance than a snowball in hell. Help me, Millie. Goddam it, help me!"

Her hands wiped the sweat from his face. The tears flowed steadily now.

"You shouldn't push at me about it, Harry. A woman's gotta hope as long as she can. A woman just can't up and throw something away until she knows, really knows. It wouldn't be right. It would be murder, Harry. God don't like murderers. You know that. The Good Book says He don't."

"God ain't mean. God wouldn't let a person suffer like this. What if God were down here, sitting by this bed? You think He wouldn't do it fast? I tell you, Millie, he'd put out His great big old hand and I'd be outa my misery right now. This minute. Don't you ever believe God would be as mean as you are."

She made a little sound, a strangled kind of noise. "God don't have to give up all He's got. He's got plenty others beside you. But you are all I got. How can you say I'm mean? Harry, Harry—my God, how can you say such a thing?"

"I'm sorry," he panted. "I didn't mean it, Millie. You know I didn't. It's just that I—Jesus Christ, I hurt, Millie. I hurt so."

Of course he didn't mean to hurt her. How could he, hurting so bad himself?

She began to give way. "I—I could step it up. The doctor says I could give it every three hours 'steada four."

Travis had told her that when the morphine stopped taking

hold, the end would be very near. Still she fought against acknowledging how close the time was.

Harry was silent then and she relaxed, the tears checking as she thought of all she faced.

Afterward—a word she hated and dreaded. Sooner or later she would have to give it recognition.

"Millie," Harry said. His voice had turned thin. "Remember that week we spent in the mountains right after your mom died and you wanted to get way from the house for a little bit? Remember?"

Did she remember! She was only amazed that he could.

"Oh, yes," she said softly. "We didn't have the cats then. We just gave the key to Ruth and asked her to water the plants and we headed out. You and me. That was a nice little cabin we found. Cheap, too."

"We hardly put our clothes on once while we was there."

The delight of it all came back to her. "Yes, I remember. We never had no time for clothes unless we went outside, and then only on account of the mosquitoes."

"I wanted you all the time, Millie—all the time."

"You never minded because I got so fat, did you, doll?"

He was holding the pain back like a curtain. She knew he was.

"Jesus Christ, what a question! You were still Millie, weren't you? You think I married you on account of you had a figure like a movie star, huh? I loved you no matter what. You think getting old and all stops a man from loving his woman, huh? If it does, he never really loved her in the first place. A man really loves a woman, he can go to bed with her if she's sixteen or sixty, thin or wide as a door." He stopped to gasp and pull at the air around his mouth, then he went on, even more thinly. "He sure as hell don't wanta leave her in a fix like I'm leaving you. No money, the house ain't paid for, all the bills—Godamighty, Millie, I hope you'll see fit to forgive me for not seeing ahead better'n I did." Again he stopped to suck in air.

"There you go. Why, I'm planning for you to outlive me, Harry. You'll be getting married again and I'll have to come back outa my grave to take care of that."

His face gleamed with sweat. "Millie," he moaned, "take it away. I can't stand it. Help me, Millie. Don't let me hurt any more. Please, Millie. If you love me—if you love me, you'll do something. Remember, Millie, you said—up in that cabin. Whatever I'd ask you to do—anything—you'd do it. Remember, Millie?"

He had been trapping her. All this talk! "Harry, not this. Not this! You know what I mean. We was talking about sex, Harry. Sex!"

17

"Millie, Millie! A man goes crazy! He can't stand so much. You want me to go crazy, Millie? God, God, if it was you in my place, I'd never let you suffer, Millie. Never. I couldn't do that to you."

She put her head down, gripping her hands together. "Men are stronger'n women, maybe," she whispered. "Some women ain't got any guts. All they can do is love somebody and get hurt. They die by inches, too, Harry. Believe me, they do."

"Millie, Jesus Christ, have mercy! Nobody'll ever know. Not Doc. He won't care. He'll say it's a blessing. Hell, that's why he lets you do it."

"Harry, doll, try to rest. You're making yourself worse. You don't hush, I'll go outa this room. I will, Harry."

He became frantic with his effort to make her see. "I'm not making myself worse. I *am* worse. Cantcha see? Every minute I'm getting worse. Goddam it, Millie, you was lying to me all the time, wasn't you? You didn't mean what you said a-tall. You'd do anything for me, anytime! You can't love me and do this. You're selfish, that's what. You want me to suffer. Goddam it, Millie, you *know* I ain't gonna make it. You *know!*"

"Oh, Harry!" She began to shake.

"Jesus Christ, Jesus Christ," he mumbled, unable to move but trying to shake his head against her and the fury of the pain. "Wish I could reach that goddam tray. I wouldn't hurt not one second more, not one." His voice went into a long, steady groan.

She lifted her face, looked at him fully, seeing the marks of his terrible suffering. Her own features were damp with sweat. Because he was right. He wasn't going to make it, and she did know that. Why was it so hard for her to admit what she was doing to him? After all, she did have the power to do something else. So that made him right about her being selfish; that explained why she refused to help him. She didn't want to lose him, all he had meant to her, or give up the order of her daily existence. She was hanging on like a dog with a sour bone, while he was going through hell!

She had been fearful, too, she thought contemptuously. Afraid that if she did help Harry as a really loving wife would do, she'd be caught and punished. In the face of Harry's dreadful need, how could she have been influenced by such a cheap emotion? Hadn't he said he would do as much for her? For a moment she felt quite humble, thinking how strong and great his love for her was, and how poor and ordinary a thing she had given him.

Suddenly she knew a great scorn for herself. She clung— how she clung—while Harry used what little strength he had left to worry about her future! She sat rigid, a suffocating tightness in her throat.

Now she could look at the tray on the nightstand and study the items there—the rubber-capped bottle of sterile water, the forceps standing in the zephiran-chloride solution, the covered jar of alcohol sponges, the pan of needles and syringes immersed in more alcohol. And finally the morphine, the precious morphine.

It was settled. She had made up her mind. It would not be too hard to do, really. She would just pretend she had gone out for a walk and someone else was taking her place. A nurse, for instance, a real, honest-to-God nurse.

She stepped into the tiny bathroom to wash her hands, thinking how funny it was that she should still feel a need to be as sanitary as possible. When she returned, she listened for a moment to Harry's steady moaning, then took the lid off the pan of syringes and the cover off the sponges. She slipped the forceps out of the zephiran chloride, drew a sponge out of the jar and placed it on the tray. Next, she selected one of the syringes, taking it from the alcohol with the forceps and placing it between thumb and first finger of her left hand. She used the forceps to retrieve a plunger which she inserted into the syringe, testing to see if it slid easily back and forth, and then went back for a needle, working it firmly onto the base of the syringe.

I'll dig a hole in the back yard and bury all this, she thought disjointedly. God help me to do it.

Carefully she took the plunger she had just tested out of the syringe, placed it on the alcohol sponge, uncorked the tube of morphine tablets and dumped all of them with deft precision into the syringe, replaced the plunger and picked up the bottle of sterile water. She rubbed the cap firmly across the sponge, then inserted the needle's tip through the cap into the bottle's contents, withdrawing enough water into the syringe to dissolve the tablets completely.

The syringe in one hand, the sponge in the other, she leaned over the bed.

"Harry," she said softly, gazing intently into his face. "Harry, you awake?"

Saliva bubbled in a little froth at the corners of his mouth. "Jesus Christ, Jesus Christ, how can I sleep! How can I—"

"Harry, open your eyes. Doll, look at me. Look, Harry."

The lids of his eyes lifted heavily to let him peer through. "Millie," he whimpered, "there's a bunch of knives in my guts, cutting 'em all to pieces. A bunch of knives, Millie."

"Yes, doll, I know. Harry, I love you, doll. You won't forget, will you, Harry? You'll wait for me, huh? Wherever you go? Huh, Harry? I gotta know, doll. I gotta be sure."

His eyes brightened a small bit, just a flicker really. Perhaps not at all. Perhaps she imagined it. "Millie, you—you gonna help me? Millie, Millie—"

"You'll wait for me, doll? You promise, Harry?"

"Godamighty, yes! You know I will. Right there—where-ever it is—Godamighty, Millie—help me. Help me."

She dropped her mouth to his, shutting off the animal distress. When she raised her head, her face was warm, enormously warm and tender.

She found a spot on his arm which did not already have a telltale dot and wiped the spot well with the sponge. Deftly she inserted the needle, drawing the plunger back a little to make sure she hadn't touched a vein, then slowly pushed it home. Afterward she placed the syringe and sponge on the tray, covering everything with the clean towel. Then she returned to the bed, kneeling laboriously.

She did not pray, just knelt there, her eyes never leaving his tormented face, her hands clutching one of his. She hoped it would be easy. Just drift off, Harry, wherever you're going. Easy, easy, doll.

"Sweetheart," she whispered, "don't forget me—all we've had together, what it was like. Doll . . . doll, it was wonderful. Wasn't it, Harry? Wonderful, wonderful, every minute of it. You and me, doll—eating together, sleeping, not sleeping . . ." She stopped, seeing the change beginning, the shadow creeping over his face. She swallowed and held his hand tighter.

"I'm right here, Harry," she said steadily. "Right here, doll. I'll be right here by your side forever, Harry. You hear?"

His lids lifted; his eyes peered out through a deepening glaze. He said nothing, but she could feel the relaxation taking place in the hand she held, could almost tell when it reached his wrist and started up his arm. Slowly his mouth went slack, almost comfortable. She brought the hand she held to her lips.

"Harry . . . Harry!" she whispered, the tears beginning, a great hot flood of them pouring down her cheeks and over the hand now convulsing and jerking against her mouth.

After a long, long time she raised herself to her feet, straightened the sheet and shuffled to the telephone in the hall.

"Dr. Travis, please," she said and waited. "Doc? This is Millie Higgins. It's Harry, Doc. Only—you don't need to hurry. Take your time. . . . Huh? Oh, about five minutes ago, I guess. . . . Okay, Doc. Thanks a lot. Thanks. Just walk in. The door ain't locked."

She went on out into the kitchen and stared at Georgie and Jennifer waiting by the refrigerator to be fed. Jennifer was pregnant. By the looks of things, it might be any time now.

Confused, Millie stepped around the two cats. What had she come to the kitchen for? Oh, yes, to feed the cats. Best be doing it. They were always hungry, especially Jennifer. She put down canned fish and milk, then slumped into a chair at the kitchen table, dropping her head onto her arms. She was more tired than she had ever been in her life. And suddenly very lonely. God, how quiet the house, how terribly quiet!

"Harry!" she said and jumped to her feet, running back into the bedroom. "Harry!" she shrieked. "Speak to me! Don't leave me, Harry! Harry!"

When Dr. Travis came in she was sitting quietly at the foot of the bed, her face expressionless. Before he spoke, he examined the tray, confiscated the morphine bottle, snapping it neatly as he dropped it into his pocket. He did not comment on the fact that all the tablets were gone.

CHAPTER 3

MILLIE WALKED THROUGH THE DOOR with its border of glass bricks and glanced around nervously. She was surprised, seeing the tiled floors, the marble counters and fine woods, the buckets of potted plants, chrome ash trays, everything clean and gleaming bright. It was like a bank, she thought. She had supposed it would be dark and dreary, like an old jail. She had to make herself remember her neighbor's words. Canterbury is sure to be good for a job, Ruth had said.

She edged forward uncertainly. As if to give her courage, the first door she came to had NURSING PERSONNEL painted on its window in strong, black letters. All she had to do was step up, knock and go in. Easy. About as easy as taking off her clothes right there in front of everybody. And the longer she waited, the worse it would get. But she had to have a job; it always came back to that.

She adjusted the straps of her slip over her plump shoulders, hitched her dress up in the front and down in back and opened the door. She looked into a huge place so full of people that she filled with panic. She would have fled instantly, but she was caught in a tide of people coming in right on her heels, and she was powerless to move against the current.

Without quite knowing how she got there, she found herself standing in front of a desk, being questioned by a girl who looked hardly old enough to be out of school. In a pleasant, impersonal voice, the girl wanted to know all about Millie. First, was she a high-school graduate? No? Just one year, then, of high school? The eighth grade. Did she say the *eighth* grade?

Looking at her oddly, the girl cut off her rambling explanation; she merely pointed out that graduation from high school was a requirement for anyone who wanted to take the aide-training course offered by the hospital. Miss Terry *preferred* high-school graduates, but sometimes . . . The girl hesitated. Did Millie need a job very badly, and had she had any experience in taking care of sick people?

Millie's heart sank. She managed to say something about the seventeen years she had nursed her mother. Batty as a bedbug, too, Mama had been. Somewhere on the application form the girl wrote the word "senile."

Millie added, And Harry in bed eight months before he—

The girl lifted her head. This Harry, had he been senile also?

Millie stared. Senile?

Oh, that meant aged, sort of. Incompetent mentally.

Millie shook her head violently. Harry died of cancer. Eight months it took.

"Well, now. Well, now," said the girl, not looking at Millie's face. That was quite a lot of nursing care, after a fashion. Yes, that certainly would all be called good experience, every moment of it. The girl made hieroglyphics on the form and was finally satisfied.

"Now, Millie, please sit down over here at this table. We have a little test for people who want jobs. Oh, nothing to worry about. Just fill in these papers—you know, put your answers on the blank lines following each question. . . . No, don't start until I tell you to and be sure to let me know as soon as you've finished. . . . Yes, right here. That's fine. Here is a pencil and an eraser. You may make corrections, only work as fast as possible. Thank you, Millie."

Millie sat down on the edge of the chair, accepted the pencil and began chewing nervously on its tip. When the girl said "Begin," she started to write. She worked steadily and made no erasures. Ruth had told her about this test. Erasures count against you, Ruth had said; just take your time and you won't make any mistakes. The girl had said to work as fast as possible, but Ruth ought to know something about it, thought Millie. She worked out here, didn't she?

When Millie lifted her head, she was triumphant. The girl looked at her watch, made a few more notes on the application form, then took it with the test papers into another office. She was back presently, a pleased glint in her eye. She acted as if she were personally responsible for Millie's success. She beckoned. Millie got to her feet and was led to the other office and firmly pushed through the door. At this point the girl returned to her own desk and Millie realized with some confusion that she was now facing someone new, another woman seated behind another desk.

The woman was Lucretia Terry. She was middle-aged, tall and very thin, with dark, hot-looking eyes and a sour, annoyed expression. She was the final authority on almost every phase of hospital routine. Even Dr. Herrington, the superintendent of Canterbury, had been known to back down before her lashing assertiveness. For fully a minute she looked at Millie over a large ash tray piled high with cigarette butts.

"What makes you think you know enough to work out here?" she barked suddenly. She knew what she was doing; she did it deliberately. She wanted people to know from the very start that she was law in Canterbury. Her word must never be questioned. If she made mistakes, she would find out herself and right them. But she seldom made mistakes.

Millie's mouth fell open. She could feel her heart thudding against the weight of her breasts.

Miss Terry looked at Millie with contempt. "Sit down!" she said. "Sit down! Don't stand there like a fool with your mouth open."

Millie sat down suddenly in the nearest chair. She closed her mouth, swallowing, hating herself bitterly for feeling so frightened and inferior. What in God's name had she done to make the woman look so mean? She'd barely come into the room. Anyway, she had a right to come looking for a job. They didn't have to give her one, but that didn't mean she had no right to try.

Lucretia Terry knew almost exactly what Millie was thinking. She had spent years determining the thoughts in the minds of those who came to Canterbury looking for jobs, and she could judge and condemn or approve with uncanny accuracy. This ability gave her power and helped to keep her on her pinnacle of importance. She relaxed slightly, lighting a cigarette and keeping silent, until she saw that Millie was almost ready to get up and run away. Then her sharp glance stopped Millie on the edge of her chair.

"Sit *down!*" she said. She sat back herself and blew out a cloud of smoke. "We don't usually hire people who haven't graduated from high school, Mrs. Higgins. But we need people. Badly. We have a wonderful aide-training program for new employees, but the individual must be a high-school graduate before he or she can enroll and receive the benefits of the program. However, with our employee turnover that great, we are forced to hire people of your limited qualifications, whether we like to or not. We have no choice in the matter.

"You seem to have had some experience," she went on coldly. "I hope you realize that the work in this hospital is not easy. We give no favors. I am referring to time shifts and wards. You must expect nothing except hard, exacting work. Never ask for anything. I am the one who decides which ward is best for which employee. Also, you will never take time off unless it is absolutely necessary. Further, you will solemnly agree to be completely subject to all hospital regulations. Do I make myself clear?"

Millie gasped. She stared stupidly. "You mean you're giving me a job? I thought . . ." Terribly confused, she stopped.

"You thought I was giving you hell just for the fun of it?" Lucretia said tartly. "We need people like you, Mrs. Higgins. Everyone we can get. Don't misunderstand me. You will—I hope—make a good employee, but I wish you could be better. Now, let's not get insulted all over again. I am director of nursing personnel and I am personally responsible for the welfare of a great number of patients. I can't afford to be polite. You understand?"

Millie nodded.

"Keep in mind that my word is law as far as you are concerned. If you do your work well and I get no complaints from the people who will make out your merit ratings, you will find you have a very good job. When you work for Canterbury you are a state civil-service employee, and a rating system is used to let us know just what kind of an employee you are. The supervisors and ward charges determine these ratings. Now take these papers back to that girl you first talked to and she will finish putting you on. We have a bulletin board in the foyer of this building where the weekly schedule for all hospital employees is posted. You must remember to check it to find where you are placed and what shift you will work. That is all, Mrs. Higgins."

Millie tried to stammer a thank-you, but nothing came. She clutched the papers in a wad against her stomach, got herself off the chair and backed foolishly out the door. A hand touched her elbow; the girl had been watching for her. Wordlessly, Millie followed her back to her desk and handed her the papers.

The girl sat down and smoothed them carefully. "Good. I knew she'd take you. After scaring you half to death, of course. You made eighty-four on your test."

Millie's dry lips parted. "But . . . my age and everything," she stammered.

The girl said, "Doesn't mean a thing. If you're healthy and strong and really want a job and pass the test too, why, it's a cinch. Wanta know something? They can't keep enough help out here. They just don't pay enough. Well, let's get busy, shall we? Now let's see. These are for you, Millie. This booklet tells you all about the institution, how it's operated and everything. This one explains what the hospital expects from you. Fundamentals, that is. You'll learn actual procedures on the wards. This brochure gives salary rates, pay raises, retirement plan, vacations, sick leave and so on. The employees have their own union." The girl looked closely at Millie. "Am I going too fast? You *are* following me, aren't you?"

Millie nodded dumbly. The girl hesitated, then went on. "Don't quote me, but be sure to join the union. And by all means sign up for the insurance. It's cheap and some day you may need it. I had a friend working on Hydro who got kicked in the chest by a patient. She was ready to go off duty, so instead of getting the ward charge—that's the person who is boss on the ward—to write up an injury report, she let it go until the next day. You can guess what happened. The office wouldn't accept the injury report because it was a day late. So my friend had to pay for her own mastectomy. That's removing a breast by surgery. In her case it was both."

Millie found her voice at last. "No!"

"Can you beat it? She still works out here, but like I tell her, she's a fool. She ought to sue the staff, only how far would she get? And where would she find another job afterwards?" The girl looked wise. "The office has it all figured out. They know most of us will take anything to keep our jobs. They play favorites, discriminate, use unfair tactics — God, what don't they do! The reason I'm telling you all this is that I'm getting married next month, so I don't have to be careful and watch what I say any more. I'm going to quit and this place can burn to the ground before I'll ever come back."

She said it matter-of-factly, without rancor. Millie shifted her feet. "Oh, I won't tell anybody what you said. I never was one to gossip," she said earnestly.

The girl smiled. "Bless you. That's a good rule to follow. Especially here." She finished her work, placed it all in a large folder marked with the initial H and looked up again. "Now you come in Saturday and see the schedule. It's posted every Friday night late and shows the whole next week, beginning Monday morning. You'll find your name somewhere, Millie. When you go home today, study these booklets, especially the part about uniforms and so on. And one more bit of advice. Buy the very cheapest uniforms

25

you can find to begin with, because new employees are started on the untidy wards to see if they can take it. Wait till you see what the score is before you invest too much. Those nylon uniforms are nice but they're expensive and the laundry out here won't do them, while you can get five cotton uniforms done a week for nothing. It's all in your booklet. Goodbye, Millie, and good luck."

Millie walked out of the building, staring dazedly at the papers she was holding in her sweaty, iron-tight grip. She looked up. How sweet the air was, now fresh. The day that had begun so thinly, so little like spring, had turned magically bright.

"God be praised, God be praised!" she almost cried aloud. She had a job. Money—steady, stable, reliable—coming in regularly every month. She could pay her bills, keep the house, rid herself of worry. She would sleep.

She turned in the direction of the parking lot where she had left Harry's dilapidated, elderly coupe. Uniforms, she thought. Five or six cheap, white cotton uniforms and a comfortable pair of white oxfords. White stockings, too. All the attendants wore white stockings, just like the nurses. Nylon, probably. You could hardly get cotton stockings any more. And then she would be all set for work.

That word brought back the interview inside the building. What had that Miss Terry meant about not being afraid of hard work? Millie's nostrils expanded in a little snort. Why, hard work had been her middle name since the night her mother had her first stroke more than seventeen years before. And then the dirt was no more than settled on her grave when Harry began . . . All that bedding to wash and the cleaning and always waiting on someone. Who would know better than she the meaning of hard work?

She shook herself loose from thoughts of Miss Terry. The woman had been rude and mean, but probably that was just her way. Lots of responsibility made some people act peculiar, Millie reasoned philosophically. So forget the woman! The important thing was that now she could pay bills and feed the cats and eat a small steak herself once in a while.

When she drove through the great archway that separated Canterbury from the town, she headed for a butcher shop, steering with one hand while the other got the purse open and fumbled through its contents.

"Let's see now—thirty-seven dollars and sixty cents. That oughta be enough to buy uniforms and shoes and what else I need and some left over. I'll get a steak, a little steak. And pork kidneys for the cats. A can of milk, too, and maybe a can of that cheap mackerel. We'll have a picnic, Georgie and Jennifer and me. We won't think about anything. We'll just eat and enjoy ourselves. That's exactly what we'll do."

In the middle of her joy, her vision blurred. Five or six tears suddenly welled and rolled down her face. Thank you, God, for letting me get the job. You ain't holding it against me on account of Harry? You know I had to do it, don't you? You know. Don't tease me, God. If it ain't right and fit for me to help take care of those sick folks, don't let me even get started.

But He hadn't interfered. Evidently, He was not going to punish her now. Maybe later, but not now. She wiped her face with the back of one hand and groped for a Kleenex.

"Now, look here," she said aloud and strongly. "You just got to use common sense, Millie Higgins. You found that out the other day when you thought about killing yourself and Ruth came in and got it out of you. Did she ever tell you off! When your time comes to die, it'll come, but until it does, you being a strong, healthy person, you got to do what you can for others. Suicide's wicked when a person can be helping out somewhere. Maybe you did wrong about Harry, but it's done and you can't undo it. Now you start behaving yourself and don't you ever be a cry-baby again."

The car picked up speed. Her shoulders straightened. She did not have a guilty conscience, she told herself resolutely. What she had done, no matter how you looked at it, she had had to do.

"I'd do it again," she said, closing her purse with a snap.

CHAPTER 4

DR. JUBAL HERRINGTON, superintendent of Canterbury, led the group that Kathy Hunter had seen on the slopes above the hospital buildings. Behind him came Walter Sturgis, the hospital's business manager; Margaret Rich, who was Lucretia Terry's assistant; a senator and his friend from the state capital; and finally the man they had all agreed should be hired to write a series of articles for the hospital's benefit. His name was Michael Stewart, and he was a well-known young journalist, recommended by no less a person than the governor.

Dr. Herrington frowned, thinking how much easier and cheaper it would have been to have got a competent hack writer. He was sure that Stewart was not a man to write lies at any price. Stewart must be convinced somehow that Canterbury's needs were more important than its all too obvious shortcomings and faults. There were so many unpleasant things to be seen that if they were revealed to the people of Dakota, the publicity would be both sensational and embarrassing. But how to show Stewart that his task was to make the public indignant at the hospital's lack of funds, not at the hospital's management?

We can't help some things, Dr. Herrington thought defensively. We do the best we can with what we have, but on our budget our best may not seem very good to outsiders. His frown deepened. More doctors, he almost said aloud; we must have a bigger staff.

Mike Stewart trailed slowly behind the others. He had arrived at Canterbury two days before, been assigned a room in Nurses' Residence, given a meal book to use in the employees' cafeteria, and turned over temporarily to Dr. Larry Denning, who shared offices on one of the upper floors of Surgery with Dr. Donovan Macleod, Chief of Staff.

What he had seen so far was disturbing him deeply. So much misery and suffering was almost unbelievable. He had been told the figures. Over half a million Americans, many of them probably not much different from himself, were in such places.

A slight movement on the hill above caught his eye. A girl sat on the grass under a tree, looking down at him. From her size he would have guessed her to be a child, but her uniform and cap and blue cape proved otherwise. When she realized he was watching her, she looked away. He turned his attention back to the people around him.

He was a little annoyed that his thoughts should be so contradictory about them. They were hiring him to write about the hospital because they wanted to put over a fund-raising campaign. He was fully aware that all institutions did this at one time or another, and Canterbury's needs were obvious enough. Further, this part of the hospital staff—in fact, the whole staff—was no doubt as competent and trustworthy as that of any similar institution. The staff of a mental hospital couldn't have an easy time, he was sure; there were bound to be great difficulties and overwhelming responsibilities. Why, then, should he feel the way he did?

There was Margaret Rich, for instance—a short, plump woman with heavy coloring, wearing a spotless, carefully tailored uniform. She nodded automatically with each thrust of Walter Sturgis' arm as he pointed out various wards. Why didn't he like her? Mike wondered, scowling. Was she too correct, too faultless, too—unctuous? A hell of a word, he thought, but it did fit. He could see himself as an employee under her thumb, and instantly he was squashed, flattened to nothing, humiliated. That was it. That was what came through. He looked away from her and turned his attention to Walter Sturgis.

Sturgis was talking quietly in a careful, controlled way. It was clear that he was always careful. With each frugal sentence he was trying to convey to Mike—without offending Jubal—that Canterbury's greatest need was for buildings. Cautiously he mentioned crowded dormitories and the lack of proper recreational and clinical facilities. When he spoke of beds that pushed out onto porches and stood side to side in halls because there were more patients than space, Dr. Herrington turned, spreading his hands impatiently.

"Buildings!" he snorted. "That's all you ever think about, Walter. Well, we need more than buildings. Let's emphasize that point immediately. But we also must have a larger medical staff."

"Of course," Walter agreed instantly.

"Therapists, aides," Margaret Rich murmured, "and attendants."

"We have plenty of attendants. Plenty, plenty. That's the least of our problems." Dr. Herrington sounded harassed.

Mike noticed that Margaret flushed. Probably did it every time she thought she was being corrected, he guessed. It made her look raw and angry.

Jubal Herrington turned to Mike. "Higher wages," he said gloomily. "We'll never have an adequate staff here until we can pay at least a reasonably adequate salary."

The senator and his friend concurred. They knew the problems: the doctors who left as soon as their residency training was finished because they could get better pay elsewhere; the high turnover among the attendants for the same reason. They were well aware of the crowded conditions on the wards and the limited facilities for clinical work and therapy treatment. To them it was simply a matter of presenting the facts to a voting public. Dr. Herrington and his staff would not be held responsible for a state-supported mental institution's being overcrowded and understaffed; a budget could be stretched only so far.

"Well, there's your job," the senator said. "Think you can do it, Mike? Staff as well as buildings?"

They all looked at him. After a moment he said, "Yes."

His face held such a determined expression that they all nodded.

"Good," said Dr. Herrington. He looked as if he wanted to add something to that but couldn't decide exactly what.

He wants me to see what they're trying to accomplish and what they must have, but he doesn't want me to see anything else, Mike thought. Why? Why everthing good but nothing bad? Didn't Herrington realize he had already discovered two kinds of people working in the hospital—the ones who gave everything they had and the others for whom it was just a job, a pay check? Couldn't Herrington understand how shattering it was to be thrust into the terrible world of a place like Canterbury?

He thought back over what he had seen in the past two days and suddenly recalled what had been his most painful moment. He had stood with Dr. Denning while a young woman named Mary Elsie Blayton was brought into the female receiving ward.

Mary Elsie was the wife of a flour-mill worker. The Blaytons lived in a new house in a group of many others just like it. Their lawn was always nicely trimmed; the house was kept freshly painted and the windows sparkled. The brightness stopped at the front door. Inside was Mary Elsie's vodka.

Before being committed, she had been drunk for nine weeks, starting on the night she ran shrieking into the street, stark naked, screaming that she had just been raped by a Mexican.

The police found the fellow, a scared youngster hardly old enough to know which side was up on a girl. They hustled him off to the precinct station, where, in a stammering mixture of Spanish and American, he swore that Mary Elsie had seen him going home one night down the alley—he went down the alley to keep from being caught by his old man for being out so late—and had stood naked in the kitchen door and invited him in. *Naked!* he said, his Adam's apple bobbing wildly. What's more, she had invited him in a number of times afterward, when her husband was working the night shift. This time—this time—he went in but he couldn't do anything. You know? He was tired or something, thinking maybe he ought to start coming down some other alley. He shrugged. He couldn't please the lady every time, could he?

When Jim Blayton was notified, he told his boss about it, was given the rest of the night off to straighten things out, and hurried down to the station. Evidently he knew his wife better than the police had given him credit for, because the young boy was released and Jim took Mary Elsie home.

The next day she stayed in her house. She ordered vodka from the corner liquor store and went on a bender. One night three weeks later, Jim came home from work and discovered she had piled every stitch of clothing she possessed in the middle of the basement floor and set fire to the pile.

He called in a doctor. The doctor came and studied the situation. Give Mary Elsie a little more time, he advised. Her vanity had received a crushing, brutal blow. Give her time. Be gentle. Be loving. Do not reprove. That, along with massive doses of Vitamin B complex and tranquilizers, should do the trick. And taper off slowly with the vodka. Going too fast would constitute another shock. It was a tricky problem, the doctor said, but not an insoluble one.

Jim and the doctor stayed with it for six more weeks. By that time Mary was climbing the furniture like a monkey and playing with herself constantly. When Jim finally let them come to take her to Canterbury, she still looked as beautiful as a doll, her soft, smoke-colored hair rippling to her shoulders, her big, blue eyes looking at him through a puzzled glaze.

"It won't be long," he promised raggedly. "You'll be home again just as soon as they can clean it out of you, sweetheart. I mean it."

She hiccuped daintily. "Clean wash out? Clean wash out?"

"That goddamned liquor!" he said, then groaned and caught her tight. "Darling, darling," he muttered incoherently, his lips on her hair.

She struggled fastidiously. "Go 'way. You're messing my new dresh. Don' wanna be cleaned out anyhow. Don' wanna." She pulled her head free and back to stare up at him with an owlish expression. "You don' like for me to be drunk," she said with immense dignity, waggling a finger in his face. "I know what you want. You wanta screw—thash what you want."

"Mary Elsie! Don't start that—"

"Hard 'n' fast as you can. 'N' alla time. Alla time."

"My God!" he said sickly.

She put her finger on his chest. "Screw, screw," she said, leering prettily. "Only I don' like it. You know why? On account of you *kill* me."

"My God!" he said again.

"My God, my God," she mimicked. "Make you mad, don't I?"

He slapped her. Tears welled, her chin quivered. "You think you're so smart. You think that ol' doctor doesn't know what you try to do, huh? I'll tell him. That's what I'll do! How you're always screwing me only you can't never do nothing. I'll tell that doctor, I will. You wait and see."

Jim went back into the living room. "I can't do anything with her," he told Larry Denning and the nurse who had come to help get her to the hospital. Then he covered his face with his hands. "God help me!"

Larry and the nurse stepped into Mary Elsie's room. She had removed her clothes and was standing over them, voiding unconcernedly.

They carted her off, wrapped in two stout bed sheets and well tied with a rope Jim carried in his car.

Her chart in his hand, Mike had seen this bundle being set on its feet, had seen through the sheets that it was small and shapely, the exposed face like that of a lovely doll, the hair long and silky and thick. And the incredible air of dignity. The blue eyes stared around, filled with enormous tears; the mouth trembled. What had she done to deserve this?

"Not only an alcoholic but schiz as well," Larry said as he finished telling about Mary Elsie.

"But she's only a kid," Mike whispered. "And beautiful. Look at that hair. What happened to her?"

"Who knows? It might be a long story. It might have happened fast, just like that. Eventually we'll find out."

"Can you help her?"

"That's what we're here for, isn't it?" Larry said cryptically.

That's no answer, Mike thought. "Take care of her," he said after a moment without knowing why he said it.

"Of course." Larry's face showed nothing.

No one paid much attention to Jim Blayton. Mike thought about that as he handed Mary Elsie's chart back to Larry.

Poor devil, he almost said aloud as he looked at Jim's expression. If Jim had been the worst criminal in the world, he couldn't have looked more miserable, more guilty, more despairing.

The guided tour finished, Mike broke away from the group and walked slowly down the path to the class he had been invited to sit in on, Dr. Macleod's first period of instruction to a new batch of affiliates. No wonder he felt hostile and antagonistic, he thought. What a far cry from the Blaytons to the people he had left. They were free—*free!* The Blaytons were trussed and tied by the chains of their trouble like animals ready for butchering. It did no good to tell himself that the hospital and its staff were not to blame or that Mary Elsie had been brought to the right place for help; he was too upset by what he had seen to be rational.

CHAPTER 5

THE CLASSROOM WAS IN THE BASEMENT of Nurses' Residence. There was a dais for a large desk, blackboards and charts hung on the walls. Near the dais at one side stood a hospital bed neatly made up and holding a recumbent life-sized mannequin, and directly in front of the dais were several rows of chairs arranged in semicircles.

Kathy found the place easily, since all the young nurses she saw were going in that direction. Surrounded by a buzz of conversation, she went to the nearest empty seat, settled quietly, opened her notebook, placed two well-sharpened pencils in the crease and glanced around. The girl in the next seat looked vaguely familiar; after a moment she recalled where they had met.

"Hello," the other girl said. "Why, I remember you. We came into the station on the same train yesterday."

"That's right," returned Kathy, thinking how different the girl looked now. The day before she had worn a hat and a loose coat with a collar high around her face and had seemed very ordinary. Now she had on the uniform and cap of her school and was quite beautiful, with high breasts, long, slender legs and a face of rounded cheekbones, delicate pink-and-ivory coloring, heavily fringed eyes almost purple in color and full, warm lips. Her pale-yellow hair was twisted neatly back into a netted bun.

Kathy pushed her feet under her chair and out of sight. "My name is Kathy Hunter," she said, feeling awkward and mousy.

"Althea Horne, room fourteen upstairs, second floor."

"I have room twelve upstairs, across the hall from you. We're neighbors."

"Hi, neighbor. Come over whenever you feel like borrowing something. I always have plenty of cigarettes on hand, and white shoe polish, and white thread."

Kathy laughed. "I've got a hot plate which doesn't give me away by smoking and a year's supply of jasmine bath crystals I inherited from a former roommate and never use. You use that stuff? No? Well, how about stockings? I can always lend a pair in an emergency. My mother dipped into her savings and bought me twelve boxes, three pairs to the box. I didn't want her to, but she insisted."

Althea grinned. "Swell. It's a deal. You and me against this house of horrors. It won't keep us from sleeping at night, will it?"

"Now, that's a good question." Kathy looked at the other girl. "Frankly, I don't know. I've never been around insane people and I just don't know. Right now I'm frightened. I feel like sleeping under the bed, not on it. Tell me they're just people."

"Of course they are—I was only kidding," Althea said. "I mean, my sense of humor gets out of hand sometimes. Of course they're people. We'll probably learn to like them better than the ones who are sane. I've got a relative out here."

"A relative?" Kathy stared.

Althea looked quite composed. "A cousin," she said, nodding. "She's ten years older. Her father and mine were brothers. I never knew my father. He and my uncle were killed on a fishing trip. A sudden storm and a capsized boat. That started the whole trouble."

"But . . . I mean . . . well, what happened?" Kathy hesitated. "Or do you dislike talking about it?"

"No, not really. I suppose I should. It isn't that I'm callous about it or anything, but it happened so long ago that it's almost as though it happened to someone else. I was three and my cousin, Edna, was thirteen. Our fathers were dead, so we lived together—Edna and her mother and my mother and I. There were other relatives, but not where we lived, and my mother had a good job—she was secretary to the local postmaster—and our home was paid for, so Aunt Nodie kept house and did the cooking and we all got along fine. At least I thought we did. Actually there was something wrong with Aunt Nodie. Uncle Jake's sudden death must have done it. Anyway, she picked on Edna all the time. That's the only part I remember and only vaguely. Luckily for me, or I'd be so full of complexes I'd be locked up right beside Edna. But you wanted to know—"

Sombody behind them said, "Be quiet," loudly.

"I'll tell you later," Althea said out of the corner of her mouth.

Kathy picked up a pencil, nodded looking straight ahead and watched a man cross the space between the outside door and the desk. He shuffled some papers on the desk, felt in his pockets, and finally pulled out a drawer, closing it with a sharp snap when he didn't find what he was looking for. Finally he gave up the search, left the desk and stepped off the platform. Then he looked at the affiliates who were now absorbed in his actions. *Dr. Donovan Macleod*, Althea wrote in her notebook.

He deliberately made himself think of uniforms instead of girls as he stared at them. He felt the old familiar distaste rising in his throat. Every class affected him the same way. They preened like birds in mating season, flirting and trying to catch his eye, doing everything under the sun to attract attention. As a lot, he always loathed them the first few days. They all looked alike—bright, eager, hungry, ovals of flesh for faces under various caps and colors of hair, with red slashes for mouths and predatory eyes. He began talking, letting his mind drift to his latest book while his lips moved automatically.

"Ladies," he said clearly, "we are here to study the behavior patterns of Canterbury patients, why they act as they do, what has been done in the past for such patients, what we are trying to accomplish today and what we expect to do in the future."

Pencils went down on paper and heads bent a little. He put his hands into his jacket pockets. "You will see many distasteful sights in this institution," he went on dryly. "You will shudder and wish you were elsewhere. You will wish to God you had never set foot in Canterbury. But you will stay. If you are dedicated, you will stay and learn why you are here and what you can do about it. Today," he said softly, "we will not talk about the mentally ill in terms of their various afflictions. We will not discuss aggression, withdrawal, projection, deviations, personality conflicts, motivations. No, ladies, these are not what we will discuss." He frowned.

"We will talk about life," he said. "Not just this organism which must have breath and flowing blood to exist, must eat and evacuate, must have shelter and clothing. You are already acquainted with the mechanism of the human body. You are trained in nursing care, the administration of medications, the proper attitude to display in sickrooms. You know what will be demanded of you by your physicians and superiors. But you have not yet come face to face with this thing, this life that the mentally ill give up when they enter institutions or for that matter when they first begin to experience the different phases of their illness. And we will discuss this, because without an insight into what they are deprived of, you as their nurses will never fully understand their problems."

He sauntered down a row of seats. Abruptly he paused. A child! he thought, staring. Was someone playing a joke? Then he realized that the girl in the last seat was merely a very small person and sitting in some fashion that made her seem even smaller. He scowled.

"What's your name?" he asked, addressing her directly.

She straightened herself quickly, her face flooding with color. "K-Kathy Hunter," she stammered.

"You are inviting tuberculosis with that posture, Miss Hunter. If these chairs are not comfortable, bring a pillow next time."

There was some hastily suppressed laughter. Dr. Macleod glanced around carelessly.

"If you do not wish to be dismissed in a body, you will remember that levity is not encouraged in this class," he said coldly. He waited until the room was deathly quiet and then he went on with his lecture, calmly, as though there had been no interruption.

"How many of you know what life really means? Imagine yourself locked in a closet. It is dark, small, you are there, you cannot get out. There is a door but no doorknob. You see a slit of light at the bottom of the door, so you sit down on

35

the floor to run your fingers along that slit. And you pray that someone will come and open the door because you feel there isn't enough air, you will suffocate before long. You want to get out, out into light and freedom and blessed, sweet air." He looked at their intent, still faces and shrugged a little "But no one comes. No one. So you cry, finally. You cry and beat on the door. You even scream. You are so frightened. Your fingers begin to bleed because you pound so hard, you skin your knuckles. And still no one comes. Well, ladies that—generally speaking—is the lot of the mentally ill."

They seemed absorbed but not too horrified, yet. He knew the reaction. It took a little time to make them see what he had been watching for years.

He saw Michael Stewart ease himself quietly through the door and come forward to a chair, lumbering like a bear in his awkward effort to avoid making any noise. He twitched his brows at Stewart in recognition, waited again until the absorbed faces had swung back from this minor disturbance and took up where he had stopped.

"Figuratively speaking, Canterbury patients are locked in mental dark closets. They have lost what you and I have and often regard with indifference, even contempt. The freedom to make decisions, to live what we like to assume is a normal existence. For instance, the right to go into a store, buy or reject a piece of merchandise; the right to belong to a civic organization, a garden club, the PTA, the Elks or Masons or Knights of Columbus. They are not Democrats, not Republicans. They may be classified on their case cards as Baptists, Catholics or Jews, but it is all meaningless."

He passed a hand over his face. He was tired. He had been working on his book half the night. He stepped up on the platform and sat down behind the desk, thinking rather disjointedly that the affiliates now had finally become a class to him instead of faces and caps; and would this stock lecture, which he knew so well and could recite forward or backward, mean anything to Stewart? The man seemed interested but stern, almost antagonistic. Donovan wondered why. Was it part of his nature, or had he seen something that had upset him?

"Life," he continued. "The right of a man to take a woman, the woman to bear children. The right to receive mail, to send it, to be Mrs. Jones, a good neighbor who will share in a car pool to deliver a group of children to school. Or Mr. Smith, who owns power tools and will gladly lend them to do-it-yourself friends. Or Mr. Brown, who can buy a fine rifle and go deer hunting in the fall. Even the Breens, who belong to a square-dance club and will attend weekly sessions dressed in the clothes ranchers wore at the turn of the century. Do you see what I mean, ladies? Today there are more than half a million Americans committed to institutions or under private care for mental illness, and we have chosen to become their caretakers. It is an enormous responsibility. We must handle it in the best manner possible, alleviate where we cannot cure, and always remember that we are free and they are not. They are the living dead who know only how to die, and we must not forget for one instant that this is an appalling national waste, a spiritual waste, if you like. We must do all we humanly can to be the right kind of custodians. Perhaps, then, we can help to turn the tide."

The caps bent, pencils and pens scratched busily. A girl came in the door, went slowly by the rows of chairs and up to the desk. She handed a note to Dr. Macleod, then waited silently, watching the affiliates. She was thin and flat-chested and not too young, but her hair was neatly waved and her sweater and cotton skirt were very clean. The affiliates did not know that she was a patient, but they would eventually, because they would be given her case to study. She was trusted with a ground parole and had the privilege of using a small cubicle which connected Dr. Macleod's office with that of Larry Denning's. In her cubicle were a desk and a typewriter. She had been a good typist once and could still do a fairly adequate job when not upset, and she was always doing errands for someone. Like the rest of the patients, she was locked up on a ward at night, but otherwise she was reasonably free, although she could not leave the grounds. She never tried to leave. There was no place to go. She was the joint responsibility of Drs. Macleod and Denning, since she did office work for both of them.

Some of the affiliates glanced up as she left with her return note. She did not look at them but went out quietly, her head bent. Dr. Macleod went on with his lecture.

CHAPTER 6

OUTSIDE, THE GIRL STOPPED for a moment. Calmly she opened the note, read it, refolded it and put it into a pocket. Then she sauntered down the path. She was in no hurry. When she saw a convenient bench she sat down, spread her arms back across the top of the bench and crossed her legs. She tilted her face up and unexpectedly laughed. She was about to begin a secret conversation with herself, a device she often employed to keep from getting lonely.

"Dora, you shouldn't have gone away."

"I had to, I had to. They made me. What are you gonna do when they *make* you, huh?"

"You should have thought of something. You're smart. I guess you really didn't care."

"Didn't care? Are you crazy? You know better than that."

"You're just saying that."

"All right. I'll say it again. You know better."

"Don't go away, Dora. Don't go away."

The girl on the bench looked around and repeated to herself: Don't go away, don't go away, don't go away. Then she listened, her head tilted. Her name was Madge Henderson and she had been in the institution a long time. She always remembered it as though reviewing the case history of two total strangers, a girl also named Madge and another one named Dora Martin.

Quite by accident, they had arrived in Canterbury at the same time, right out of business college, to apply for office jobs, and were put to work the same day at adjoining desks. Impressed by this coincidence, they decided to get an apartment together. Shortly they were sharing everything they had except clothing, Madge being short and dainty while Dora was large-boned and gawky.

Their association worked out very well until one of the young resident surgeons noticed Madge and decided that he and Madge could have a good time if Madge only would. She was on the brink of giving in when she made a stunning discovery. She was in love, all right, but not with any intern. She was in love with Dora. She learned this by accident.

She was getting ready to go out with the young doctor. She had just stepped out of the shower and was standing nude in front of the bathroom mirror, removing bobby pins from her soft, brown hair. She was nicely molded, with rounded thighs, a flat stomach and small, firm breasts. Suddenly she was aware that Dora stood behind her, staring into the mirror over her shoulder, looking avidly at her.

There was a long moment of silence in the little bathroom. Dora was undressed and had slipped on her bathrobe, catching it carelessly at the waist with the tie belt, and Madge noticed that one of her breasts was exposed also.

Madge felt as though she had plunged into a great void. She turned slowly, resting her small hips against the cool rim of the sink, her eyes going to Dora's face.

Softly she said, "What's the matter, honey?"

Then Dora looked up from what she had been eying so intently. There was hunger in her face—hunger and torment and fear.

"God!" she whispered. "Don't go, Madge. Don't go out with him."

"Why not, Dora? Why not?"

"I'm going to cry," Dora said, still whispering. "Don't look at me. Please don't look at me."

"You're not going to cry. Don't you dare!" Madge said fiercely.

She put out her hands and untied Dora's belt, letting it drop. As the bathrobe sagged open, she raised her hands and pushed the garment away from Dora's shoulders, reaching to do it because the other girl was so much taller.

The bathrobe dropped beside the belt. Madge looked at Dora's body, slowly, all over.

She placed her hands like small shields over Dora's breasts. "Yours are lots bigger than mine. They're beautiful!" Then she sighed. "We might as well face it, honey," she said gently. "I'm glad I found out before I made a mistake."

She held her hands on the breasts a second longer, then pulled them away and seized Dora's arm, propelling her out of the bathroom.

"You've got a date with that damned Lester," Dora panted, standing where she had been pushed, her legs a little apart, her stomach heaving spasmodically.

"I know it."

"What are you going to do?"

"I'll show you what I'm going to do." Madge darted to the door of the apartment, slipped the bolt home and flipped off the light. The apartment did not become completely dark because there was an old-fashioned transom over the door and a hall light burning outside. In the dim glow, Madge's naked body came toward Dora's. She reached out and pulled Dora to her.

They lived together for two years before the office put a stop to the affair by dismissing Dora outright and warning Madge of the consequences should she carry on with Dora outside the institution. Madge might have quit and gone with Dora, but almost immediately Dora found another friend, a small, brown-haired girl who resembled Madge somewhat. After that Madge resigned herself to staying on as a typist for Canterbury.

But she began to do considerable drinking alone in her apartment. When she switched to barbiturates, forging her prescriptions and trying to have them filled in the hospital's own drug room, Lucretia Terry had her committed as a patient and turned her over to Dr. Macleod and Dr. Denning for special treatment. After many cold sheet packs, much shock therapy—both insulin and electric—and heavy doses of tranquilizers, she was put on a more or less permanent parole.

The parole meant she could never leave the institution unless someone was interested enough to petition the staff for her release. But no one ever did; there was no one who cared. She was a good typist, the hospital needed her, being always short of competent help, and her wistful glances at young affiliates never bothered anyone.

She was always asking herself which she liked best, Dr. Macleod or Dr. Denning. When she became upset and hysterical, Dr. Macleod would send her over to Hydro for the hated shock therapy, but Dr. Denning would get a pass from the office and take her out to his mother's home in the country where she was fed all the fried chicken and cold milk she could stuff down and was encouraged to toast herself in a sunsuit on a blanket in the sun, and was taken for long walks in the woods by a garrulous, elderly hired hand who kept up a running stream of conversation about the farm and the seasons and the new batch of whatever had been born recently, kittens or pups or even calves. And at night she could watch TV, eating apples and popcorn with everyone else, never a question asked, never an unkind or careless comment dropped to bring on the horrible, choking hysteria, the scorching floods of tears, the twisting in her muscles and tendons which she simply could not control.

When she was well, however, she rather preferred Dr. Macleod. After all, he didn't have a mother on a lovely farm. He had to use the facilities afforded by the hospital. And he was so dignified, so sincere, while everyone knew what a chaser Larry Denning was, always going to motels on weekends with this or that nurse. She had no cause to be jealous because neither of the two doctors meant a thing to her, really, but she felt a physician, a professional man, should have a moral code and stay with it. Sodom and Gomorrah were all right for her kind, but not the others, the people who counted.

Madge stopped talking to herself and explored her pockets. The note was there, but her fingers went past it to something else. Furtively she looked around, then brought the something out, holding it closely so that only she could see what it was. It was a ring of keys. She had gotten it out of one of Dr. Macleod's desk drawers in his office, picking the lock with a bobby pin and a paper clip. The keys would unlock any door in Canterbury except the elevator doors in the new rehabilitation building. She knew, because she had seen the chart that had all the key numbers on it and what doors were opened by which numbers.

Her fingers caressed the keys. They gave her a feeling of special power. With them she could roam at leisure, providing she did not get caught. She could leave her ward at night if she were very careful, because there were only two employees on at night—the ward charge and an assistant—and they always managed to sleep some, although that was something they were never supposed to do. But she saw them, putting their feet up on the desk, their heads back against the wall, their snores giving them away. She could sneak past them, get the heavy door open, remembering, of course, to lock it afterward, and be as free as a bird. She could even run away.

Her eyes turned cloudy. Where would she run to? There would be a description of her in the town, so she wouldn't be able to get a job. Without a job there would be no money. Without money where were you?

She shook her head. She wouldn't run away. There was no place to go. But she would keep the keys. They would never be missed. There were three other sets left in the drawer and Dr. Macleod carried a set besides. It might be months before anyone checked the keys. It was Dr. Macleod's desk and his office and he had been in it a long time. No one was going to embarrass him by asking to count his keys.

She put the keys back in the piece of toilet tissue she carried them in to keep them from rattling and returned them to her pocket. Her main concern now was where to hide them. During the day she could keep them under her typewriter, between it and the case. It was a portable and always sat in its case. No one ever disturbed it. The keys would be safe there. During the night—she would have to think about that. It was hard to hide things on the ward. Sharp eyes all around and the charges ready to jump a person for no reason at all. No privacy, no place to keep little treasures.

She stirred uneasily. Maybe she had better put them back. She couldn't hide them on the ward. There wasn't any place. For a moment she felt quite upset. Her leg muscles began to twitch. Then it came to her. Of course! Why hadn't she thought of *that* before? Some of the other patients did it and so could she. Would it be big enough? She might have to rupture the hymen a little more, but so what? They'd just think she was menstruating again. She'd get the keys in there and plug herself up with paper or something—anything to keep the keys from falling out. No one would ever guess.

Pleased that the problem was solved, she got up, brushed the back of her skirt with one hand and moved off down the path.

CHAPTER 7

DR. MACLEOD'S CLASS moved out into the sunshine. "We're going on a tour," Althea said, catching up with Kathy.

"Who's conducting it?"

"That supervisor up in front. See her? She's short and has white hair." Althea pointed and Kathy nodded.

"Her name is Leslie—Elizabeth Leslie. She's our counselor."

"She looks nice."

"She is very nice, everyone says."

"Where are we going?"

"I don't know. It depends on what they want us to see the first time, I suppose."

"I hope it's not too long. I'm starved."

"Didn't you have any breakfast?"

"Yes," Kathy said cheerfully. "I had two eggs and toast and half a cantaloupe."

"My," Althea said, staring at her. "Do you really eat all that? I can never get anything down but coffee and juice."

"I'm always hungry for meals. My mother trained me. She's a wonderful cook."

Althea looked away. She was obviously thinking about something that bothered her, but she didn't say what it was. Someone else turned and said to them, "Do you think we'll have specialing to do? I'm hoping we'll get way from that here."

Both Kathy and Althea shrugged. "It's a hospital," Kathy said. "We'll probably do everything we've ever done anywhere else."

The girl behind them said, "God, I hope not! I just came from a TB clinic and if I never wear another mask, it'll be too soon. Look at my hands." She held them out for inspection, cracked and seamed from green soap and disinfectant.

"You're probably the first one they'll send to a TB ward," Althea said coolly.

"Oh, no!" the girl said, putting her hands into her pockets.

"I'll take babies," Kathy said. "You suppose they have babies in this place?"

"I don't see how," Althea said. "They're locked up on wards. They don't let the men in with the women."

"But what about paroles when the patients are taken home? There should be babies," Kathy said stubbornly. "I've done more in OB than anything else."

"Ladies," Elizabeth Leslie said, stopping in front of a two-

42

tory building and turning to look at them. "This is an arthritic ward, female. These patients are all bedfast. You may ask questions, but please stay with the group and be as quiet as possible. Anything unusual can make some of these patients worse."

She unlocked the door, ushered them in and relocked the door. They found themselves in a long hall, the floor covered with linoleum scrubbed beyond recognizable pattern. Near them was a desk with a lamp and several chairs. Then started the beds, a row on each side. At the far end of the hall were two tall, narrow windows. Three women dressed in uniforms came to meet and escort them down the hall. They passed arched openings with no doors and looked through into large rooms with the same pattern of beds in rows with barely enough space between them for anyone to get by. They saw carts loaded with huge piles of linens and a row of ancient wheelchairs. They inspected the linen room, which also held cabinets for medications and drugs. Kathy could not help observing all the ash trays in this place and she saw, too, that it held the only chairs in the building that looked comfortable. No doubt this was the hideaway and retreat of the employees, the three regulars on each shift and the five who were chosen from a rotating list of substitutes. If their patients were not specialed at least three times during a shift and checked faithfully every two hours for wet beds, they developed ulcers, decubiti. At Elizabeth's request, the charge showed them what was meant, uncovering a nearby patient. This one lay in the fetal position, bound immovably by her regression and her disease. She weighed possibly seventy-five pounds. Her eyes saw nothing; she could not talk. She was bones encased in paperlike skin drawn so tight there seemed to be no padding of flesh anywhere. On one knobby hip there was an ulcer the size of a saucer, raw and angry-looking in spite of a heavy dressing of surgical powder.

"That," Miss Leslie said, pointing delicately, "is the hip bone. You see? It is completely exposed."

The charge replaced the bandage and the rubber ring which would keep the ulcer from rubbing against anything and deftly turned the stiff skeleton. On the other hip was a similar sore.

The girls shuddered. Was this thing living? Stirred because it had been turned, the skeleton jerked its lips. The sound was soft, a moan, a whisper of pain, nothing more. They turned away sickly, all but Kathy and Althea, who kept staring at this tiny creature who might once have been a pretty girl and later perhaps a married woman and a mother.

Then they looked at each other and shook their heads a little, their pity identical.

"At least her bed is clean," Kathy said, almost fiercely, as though, since this was all that was left for the patient, it must never be neglected.

"What makes them keep on living?" Althea whispered.

"Not God," Kathy said. "God wouldn't do such a thing!"

They turned away and caught up with the group. They were being shown another patient, one who still could protest her pain. Twisted and swollen, she could move only her head, but she kept it going with ceaseless motion, back and forth, back and forth. "Please, God!" she panted, saying it without letup until it ran together—pleasegod, pleasegod, pleasegod. All the hair and much of the skin were worn off the back of her skull, although her head was fastened into a frame which would permit the slow rub, rub, without anything touching.

"Why don't they do something?" one of the girls said.

"They tried to," Miss Leslie said, "but nothing has helped." She covered the patient and they went on.

They paused by the bed of a patient who looked quite sprightly, sitting up in a reclining position. "She can't lie flat any more," Miss Leslie said matter-of-factly. "Her spine is twisted."

"Is she psychotic?" someone asked.

"Goddam right I'm sottic" came in a dry cackle. "You bring me a bottle, dearie, and I'll show you a first-class sot."

They all started, not knowing whether to laugh or simply stare. The charge said crossly, "Behave yourself, Anna. You know better'n to talk that way to company."

"Don't know nothing, nothing. Gimme a bottle, you hear?"

Her voice rose shrilly and they all moved off hurriedly. They had been told to be careful not to disturb anyone.

"How is Barbara?" Miss Leslie asked.

"She's clean right now," the charge replied.

They went to see Barbara. She was a victim of syphilis with general paresis. The charge explained the restraints made of old cotton stockings tying Barbara's wrists to the edges of the springs under her mattress.

"She's a BM eater," the charge said candidly. "Don't seem to hurt her, but she sure makes a mess."

Barbara looked at them brightly. "Hello, Martha, how are the girls?" She was a Vassar graduate and had gotten her syphilis honestly from her own husband. Martha was her sister, the girls her own, now grown and married. Barbara called everyone Martha and always asked about the girls.

The group shuddered and pulled back fastidiously, but

Kathy and Althea looked at each other, then turned back closer to the patient's bed.

One girl looked faint. "The smell . . ."

Miss Leslie held her mouth firm. The girl who looked faint said, "I won't have to work on a ward like this, will I, Miss Leslie? I won't be a bit good because I'll be vomiting all the time."

Miss Leslie went ahead to unlock the door. "You'll get a checkup, Miss Miller, from a staff doctor. If you can't tolerate certain odors, of course you won't—" Her voice was swallowed up by everyone crowding out into the fresh air.

"They're horrid," Kathy said, holding back with Althea and walking a few steps behind the others.

"They think we are for not getting overwrought about it all."

"But we'll take care of people like Barbara and they'll try to get out of it. They'll do everything they can to get the easy assignments."

"Oh, I don't know. I think they'll have to take their turns right along with us on these bad wards."

"Well, I hope so. I should certainly hope so."

"But really, wouldn't it be better if they didn't work on a ward like that?"

"Why?"

"Because they'll sluff off. They'll say they've done certain things, like cleaning up beds and dressing those terrible ulcers, and they won't have done it at all, actually. I wouldn't trust some of these nurses to take care of a house plant."

Kathy nodded. "I see what you mean. And then they'll rationalize. They'll say they've got an allergy when all the time it's just because they don't like to get their hands and uniforms dirty."

Althea looked grim. "And we'll probably joke and make fun of what goes on here because that will be the only way we can stand it, seeing these poor people and what they're going through."

"Yes," Kathy said. "It's terrible, just terrible what happens to people. Why does it have to be this way?"

"I guess even the experts wish they knew all the answers. I don't even begin to know a few." Althea straightened her cap. "The main thing for me, I'll be satisfied if I can get married some day and have a home." Her eyes came around to Kathy. "But not because I want to get out of here. I'm just the type who needs to be married."

"Needs to be? Is there such a thing as that?"

"I mean—"

"Isn't it natural for a girl to think about marriage and a

home? And children?" Kathy looked curiously at Althea. "I think there's something wrong with a girl who doesn't—"

Up ahead, Miss Leslie turned around. "Ladies, let's keep together, shall we? Our next ward is a male detention ward, a maximum-security ward, as it's called, and we absolutely must stay in a body. These patients can be very dangerous. Most of them are in irons or restraints and they usually behave better toward visitors than the patients on Female Detention, but there is no excuse for being careless."

"They behave better because they're male and the visitors are female," someone whispered. "Try taking some men into a female ward—"

"Naturally," said the girl who didn't like smells. Already she was brighter and more cheerful. A male ward? She could take this.

"Look at us," Althea muttered to Kathy. "Watch us strut."

"She wiggles, too."

"Unfortunately," Althea said a little gloomily, "we have something in common."

"What do you mean?"

"I'll strut and wiggle for a man too. But it's got to be the man I want to strut for, not just any man."

Kathy laughed. "With your looks you'll have plenty of chances to do that. Now, take me. If I strutted, I'd waddle like a pigeon because I'm so short."

"You might at that," Althea agreed candidly. "Don't strut. Just sit in a chair some place and blink. That will work wonders for you."

"But not on these patients. No strutting, no blinking. It wouldn't be fair. It would be cruel."

"God, yes. Think what it must be like for some of them. Wanting a woman and knowing it's as hopeless as wanting to be the first man on the moon."

"I wonder what they do."

"What can they do? Dream about escaping, if they've got any sanity left. Or they masturbate or crawl into bed with each other. What else can they do?"

Kathy pulled back. "I don't want to go in here. It's not fair. How would we feel if people paraded by us as though we were in cages?"

"We're supposed to be learning something, remember?" She looked at Kathy. "Let's hope to God we do. If we hesitate now, you know what they'll think, don't you?"

"What?"

"One, you're sentimental, and being sentimental out here is as misplaced as trying to milk a cow on a living-room rug. Two, you're neurotic yourself and need psychiatric help. Three, you're displaying signs of perversion—you don't like men, you like women."

"My God, I believe you mean it," Kathy said, staring at Althea.

"Mainly because it's so."

"You mean we've come out here to learn all this stuff and yet we are being watched, too? Now, Althea!"

"All right. Don't say I never warned you. These supervisors and doctors watch us all the time. They do it almost unconsciously because it's their profession. You should see the sheets of data they file on each student. They never look at someone and just say, That's a nice person and I'd like to get better acquainted. Just wait. You'll see how this thing goes. It's almost contagious. After a time, you'll be doing it, too. You listen to somebody with a real honest-to-God beef and right away you think, That person's taking the chip off his shoulder and putting it on somebody else's."

"All right." Kathy shook her head. "Just so they don't chase me up and down halls. But there's one thing. They don't need to think I'm going home and look at my parents with rank suspicion just because they still sleep together in a double bed. I think it's wonderful that they still love each other that way, you know, that it'll never get too old for them, or they get too old for it. When they die . . ." She shook her head again, her eyes dark. "I hope they die together. If they don't, the one who is left will anyway, and that will be terrible. I can't tell you how terrible. Anyway," she said, breaking off, "how do you know all this?"

Althea shrugged, looked moody. "Did you forget? I've got a relative out here. I've had to learn about these places."

Ahead, Miss Leslie was unlocking another door. "Now, remember, ladies, these men are dangerous. Some of them are sent here from the state penitentiary, for rape, for assault, for murder. They have at times gotten loose from their restraints and broken milk bottles stolen from their dining room to mutilate each other and the attendants as well. So please stay together, all of you. And don't talk to the patients, don't act friendly. They won't care, believe me. But they will become excited, and after we leave the ward the attendants will have a bad time getting them calm." She was small and dainty, but her glance went over the group like a sharp knife.

The giggling subsided. When the girls were completely silent, she led them in to see men shackled in irons and strapped to chairs. Then she held back a little in order to watch their faces and their reactions. Later, she would note on her report how each affiliate behaved, and the hospital would begin to have a picture of these nurses and where

47

they would best fit in. Obviously, they could not give management of a male ward to a girl who wiggled when she walked.

It had been a long, hard day, full of new and frightening things to be seen, and understood, and studied. The girls dined in the cafeteria—those of them who had managed to keep their appetites after their first look at the wards of Canterbury.

After dinner Kathy and Althea sat together in Kathy's room and discussed the day, each one glad that she had found a friend.

Poking at a box of chocolates, Kathy capriciously lifted the top tray in the box and examined the bottom layer.

"Why do I do this? It isn't good for my teeth and it's fattening, too."

Althea was sitting before Kathy's dressing table, experimenting with a new hairdo. "You just need something to do when you don't want to think. Why don't you take up smoking?" Her own cigarette lay on an ash tray beneath a blue curl of smoke.

"Is that really it? I don't want to think?" Kathy turned over on the bed to lie flat, her face toward Althea, her hands under her head.

"Of course. It's a compulsion. You don't really want the candy," Althea said calmly. "Anyway, what do you mean, fattening? You're not fat."

Kathy moved restlessly. "I look fat. It's because I'm so short."

"Wear heels, then. You can add a couple of inches that way."

"I can't. They kill me."

Kathy watched Althea for a moment, then raised herself on one elbow. "Althea, you never did finish telling me about that cousin of yours this morning. You know—Edna."

"Oh?" Althea frowned into the mirror. "Didn't I? Where did I leave off?"

"You said it was a good thing you didn't remember everything when it all happened or you'd probably be locked up with her. What did you mean?"

The brush Althea was using slowed a little. "Edna killed her mother," she said after a moment.

"What?"

"Aunt Nodie was always tormenting Edna. For no reason at all. Like burning her with matches. Really. Or making her hold her hands under the hot-water faucet until Edna . . . That's the part I remember. Edna screaming and Aunt Nodie doing some of those things. Once she made Edna put her hands flat against a unit on the kitchen range and then she turned it on and held Edna so she couldn't take her hands away."

"But why, for heaven's sake?" Kathy asked, appalled.

"I don't know. She was always telling Edna that if she punished her in this life, she wouldn't have to burn in hell when she died, and that she only did it for Edna's good, to make her a better girl. As I remember, I don't think Edna had to do much to set Aunt Nodie off. Just a look on her face would do it."

"Oh, how horrible! It makes me sick to hear it. No wonder she did what she did. Edna, I mean."

Kathy looked at Althea. She wanted to hear how it had been done, but she hated to ask, it was such a terrible story. She felt a great pity welling up for Edna and for Althea, who had been there, who must have shrieked in terror when all this was going on, a baby forced to be a witness.

The brush slowly stroked the pale-yellow hair. "Edna broke Aunt Nodie's neck," Althea said simply. "Her hands were all twisted with scar tissue, but she got them around Aunt Nodie and squeezed until the bones cracked. That's in the records on file here."

Kathy shuddered a little. She thought about a thirteen-year-old girl putting deformed hands around a mature woman's neck and choking until the neck cracked.

"Where was your mother, Althea? Didn't she try to stop Edna?"

"She was working. I was crying when she came home, so she didn't notice what had happened. She came right to me without even taking off her coat, and then she heard something and turned, but it was too late. Edna had been waiting for her."

Kathy's voice trembled. "You mean Edna did the same thing to—your mother?"

Althea turned and looked at Kathy steadily. "That's exactly what happened. Edna killed my mother too. I suppose she didn't hate me. I was like a puppy or a kitten or one of her dolls. She could hold me and love me and I loved her back. I never told her she was wicked and bad. I never hurt her. Little as I was, I knew why she didn't kill me, but I couldn't tell the cops who came first or the doctors who came later. I think I distinguished myself by screaming hysterically most of the time and demanding that Edna be returned to me. I can't recall ever asking about my mother from that time on. Shock, I suppose. I probably didn't want to remember how she looked after she had been choked to death." She looked at Kathy. "Relax," she said. "It could

49

have been worse. I might have been old enough to *really* remember it all."

Kathy shook her head. "Where did you go to live then?"

"Believe it or not, I was adopted by the next-door neighbor. She was a widow with a substantial income, and she promised the court faithfully that she would shower me with devotion, spank my bottom when I was naughty, feed me well and leave me all her money when she died. The court was so happy to settle the problem of me that they overlooked the fact that she was middle-aged and had no husband to be a father to me. But I'm not complaining. She was wonderful. I loved her dearly and still do. When she died there was just enough money to pay for my nurse's training, but she didn't plan it that way, I know. She wanted me to have the best of everything always. As far as I'm concerned, when she took me under her wing I got the best."

Both girls were silent a moment.

"Althea," Kathy said, "I do so hope you'll be happy. You *deserve* to be happy after all that." Shyly, she reached out and touched her friend's hand. Althea smiled at her.

CHAPTER 8

WHEN MARY ELSIE BLAYTON ENTERED Female Receiving, she was dressed in a sacklike denim garment with holes for neck and arms and no fastenings of any sort. She was placed in a small room which contained nothing but a narrow cot, a bare, striped-ticking mattress, a narrow, barred window and a door with no doorknob, only a very small opening in it which was too high for her to see out unless she pushed the cot against the door and stood on the cot.

After she was left alone, she thought about the cot and looking out the door's tiny window, but decided it would be more fun to examine the denim garment. She slipped it off her head and discovered it was just like a pillow slip, no seams anywhere.

"Tubing," she said, chuckling, and looked up to see two eyes staring at her through the tiny window. She sat motionless, staring back. Then the door opened slowly, and she realized the doorknob was on the outside.

A slender man, quite dark, stood in the doorway, his eyes going over her naked body thoughtfully. "I am Dr. Andreatta," he said, enunciating carefully so she would understand. His lips crinkled in a smile, but his eyes were wary.

"Andreatta?" she repeated, and suddenly tossed her head back and laughed.

His smile grew warmer, less wary. "That fonny, no? I am Portuguese. You know—from Portugal."

"Portuguese?" she said, blinking. "Is that Mexican?"

"Oh, no. Mexican is from Mexico, across border in thees country. Portuguese is from across the ocean. Many doctors come to thees country to study deef'rent methods. I choose thees hospital because they are using Reserpine. I do not like lobotomy. It makes people vegetables. You onnerstan thees?"

Her hands held the denim sack loosely. Suddenly, she dropped it and put her hands back on the cot, leaning on them and bringing her feet up at the same time to cross them on the cot's edge. The maneuver threw her breasts high and spread apart her thighs. He glanced out the door, then moved swiftly to the cot and placed his hands on her breasts. Almost immediately he released her and stood watching her thighs twist sensuously.

"Put back the dress," he commanded quietly. "I weel be back later. Tell no one, you onnerstan?"

On his way off the ward, he passed two affiliates near the ward station. One of them gave him a slow, heavy glance which he ignored. She was always available, while this other . . . He began humming as he unlocked the door to let himself out. At the curb he saw a battered convertible with a young fellow sitting in it. Stepping over, he said courteously, "I am Dr. Andreatta. I weel be psychiatrist to your wife. We hope to accomplish much. She is very young, no?"

Embarrassed, Jim Blayton kept his face averted for a second. He had been crying. The doctor felt an instant, deep, warm sympathy. He did not consider it shameful to weep; shame lay in a man's sterility or his inability to give delight to his woman. Whether weeping could be classified as an unstable emotional outlet did not concern him at the moment.

"How old you say? I have not studied the chart as yet."

Jim fumbled for a cigarette. "Twenty-two," he muttered.

"Ah, I thought perhaps fourteen, fifteen."

"Twenty-two."

"How many little ones? Children?"

Jim found his cigarette but just held it, not trying to light it. "No—no children."

"Ah," said the doctor wisely. "Part of the trouble perhaps."

Jim dropped the cigarette, wiped his hands on the sides of his pants and reached over to turn on the ignition. "I wouldn't know," he said tightly. "Guess that's your problem, Doctor."

He stepped on the starter, and pulled away abruptly from the curb, leaving the doctor staring.

When Jim reached home, he finished off the almost empty bottles of vodka he had found tucked away in odd places—the clothes hamper in the bathroom, her hat box on the shelf in the closet, in the empty space in back of the TV set. Then he threw himself across her bed, on the frivolous ruffled spread she had made herself. Suddenly he was crying again, great sobs shuddering up from his stomach as he listened to the silence in the house.

"Mary Elsie!" he gasped, pounding the silly spread with his fists. "I'm so sorry—so sorry! Don't forget me, sweetheart. I'll make it up to you, honey. Honest to God I will. Don't forget me, honey—don't ever, ever forget me. I love you so. God, God, why did this have to happen to us!"

She had accused him of things he could not do. He hadn't been able to do anything since shortly after they had been married when she had gone west to Denver for a month's visit with her folks. He had held himself in as long as he could, then gone out and got plastered, thinking it would give him some relief. Instead, he had ended up in a cheap hotel with a frowzy bitch who yelled every time he made a plunge. Right then he should have known something was wrong, but he was too drunk. If he had only used some sense! Before he knew what had happened Mary Elsie had come back and that very night he gave what he had to her. His excuse was that he didn't know, not until he began to run a fever and went to the doctor. Then she began to get sores, so painful that she couldn't go to the john without crying. Now everything was ruined, his marriage shot to hell, every cent he could beg or borrow going into the expensive treatments, finally Mary Elsie losing her mind. God, why had it happened? Other fellows stepped out on their wives all the time, while he had done it only that once. And drunk at that. Would things ever be right again?

He cried himself to sleep.

A week later, four women sat in rocking chairs just outside the arrangement of counters that created the ward station on Female Receiving. It was midnight and they were comfortably protected by a well of radiance from the hall night light, while beyond lay the gloom of corridors and shut doors and sharp turns leading to invisible parts of the ward. They heard the outside ward door open and close and looked up to see Dr. Andreatta approaching. Respectfully they began to drag themselves out of their chairs, but he motioned them down.

"No, no, ladies. Please. I only check a little, by request of her husband, the Mary Elsie Blayton. Do not come with me. I know the way quite well."

Mrs. Shell, the ward charge, night shift, began to show every evidence of knowing her duty as charge, but he insisted. "No," he repeated emphatically. "Not necessary. Too much noise. It weel disturb other patients. I let myself out the back way. *Tenho pressa, faz favor.*"

"Nice little man," she murmured, watching him step lightly away into the gloom on the balls of his feet. Briefly, she wished her feet would work as well as his. "Nice," she said again. "So considerate. Wish all the docs out here were like him."

Millie Higgins sat in one of the chairs. This was her first assignment, a surprising one because she had fully expected to be placed on a bad ward. Female Receiving was so pleasant that she didn't even mind working nights. She did not see the patients being brought in; they were settled and usually asleep when she came on duty.

"Smell him," she said conversationally. "He musta bought up all of Woolworth's perfume."

Mrs. Corry, elderly and experienced, said, "Dr. Andreatta always smells good."

"That ain't dime-store perfume, believe me," Mrs. Richards said. She was younger and inclined to be flighty. "My niece works in Morris' department store at the cosmetic counter an' she says he buys all his stuff in there. Expensive stuff. Didja see his hands?"

"No. What about 'em?" Mrs. Shell held her newspaper still a second.

"Fingernail polish."

"No," said Millie, enthralled.

Mrs. Shell looked indulgent and Mrs. Corry snickered. "Most of these doctors out here get manicures. Why not? They got to keep their hands looking nice."

The women giggled, all but Millie. She looked a little embarrassed and withdrew to her magazine while Mrs. Shell began the languid movement of her newspaper fan again. "God, it's hot," she said.

"They got the heat on. Didja ever see it fail? When it's winter outside, we freeze to death on this ward. Now that it's spring we get all the heat we shoulda had three months ago."

"It's so still. There ain't a bit of circulation in here."

"Feels like maybe we'll get a storm. Most likely a lot of lightning and thunder and no rain."

53

"We'll get rain," Mrs. Shell decided torpidly. "We will certainly get rain. My feet tell me so."

"Hope we don't get nothing. We get rain, we'll probably get hail and my lilacs are just beautiful. You planting a garden this year, Mrs. Corry?"

"No, I'm not, Mrs. Richards. I got that lumbago, you know. Hits me right here in the small of my back and I can't stoop worth anything. Once I get down on my knees I can't get up. I gotta holler for help. Or else be near something so's I can pull myself up. So I just ain't gonna bother. Anyway, by the time I got things fit to eat, I figure they cost me twice what I can get 'em for in Safeway. Radishes, lettuce, tomatoes, whatever you name."

"God, yes, you're sure right about that. Only, do they *taste* as good, huh? You think they do?"

"Probably not. But with lumbago you can't be choosy."

Mrs. Shell's fan slowed, jerked into movement, slowed again. Finally it dropped into her lap and her chin settled solidly upon her chest. When her upper lip began to twitch spasmodically with a little bubbling sound, Mrs. Corry and Mrs. Richards lost interest in the merits of home gardening. They slipped their feet out of their shoes with soft sighs of relief, leaned their heads back against the edges of their rockers, and joined Mrs. Shell. Millie was left all alone to listen to the multitudinous little noises of night on Female Receiving.

Down the hall, Dr. Andreatta turned away from the light and the four women. He found the door, raised himself on his toes and used his flashlight for a glance through the window. Mary Elsie was lying naked on the cot. He let the light feel its way over her body while the tip of his tongue wet his lips. When the light reached her face, he saw that she was awake and staring straight into the beam. He unlocked the door and stepped in, pulling the door shut by means of a twisted handkerchief he had ready in his pocket.

Quickly he undressed, folding each garment neatly. Against the small sounds he made, he heard her rapid breathing and a swishing noise as though she were moving her hips restlessly on the bare mattress. When he was ready, he placed the flashlight on the window sill, the light turned to the cot. Then he looked at her, feasting his eyes on what he saw. With a groan he came at her, plunging down, down, down, until he was lost in an excess of copulation.

After a time, when he was finished with her, he cleaned himself carefully, dressed as quickly as he had undressed, picked up the flashlight and stood for a moment by the cot. She lay exhausted. Her thighs were flat, innocently relaxed, almost more tempting than before, her small face sleepy and drained of all emotion. He glanced at his watch, dropped his mouth to her stomach and tenderly kissed her navel. She stirred and moaned as he raised himself and left the room, locking the door softly and walking off the ward as quickly as possible. Outside, he lifted his face to a rush of cool night air and patted the front of his trousers, making sure the fly was closed.

How wonderful it had been, he thought; how wonderful he felt. Rejuvenated, remade, a man reborn. Astounding that he never lost one bit of his precious ability or his enormous capacity. Mary Elsie had proved a delicious treat. Best of all, it could be repeated again and again. If not with this one, then with another. But he would not leave this one until another just as tempting came along.

Dr. Andreatta did not know that before he got off the ward, Millie had left, and then returned to, the circle of light. The other women were still dozing.

She settled herself quietly in her chair and clutched the chair arms to keep herself from shaking. At the moment she could not remember what had made her go down the hall alone into the darkness. She had been told that to go anywhere alone on any ward at night was a violation of one of the hospital's strictest regulations, but out of the darkness something had reached and touched her curiosity with stirring fingers, some out-of-the-ordinary little sound. So she had gone, softly and alone, down the hall and around the corner. Then she had noticed the faint glow coming from one of the little door windows and reasoned that this should be investigated. Only after she lifted herself on tiptoe to look into the room, she wished to God she had stayed where she belonged and minded her own business. It was terrible to be a witness to anything so shocking and revolting as what was taking place in Mary Elsie's room.

She debated whether to arouse Mrs. Shell and tell her what was going on. Uncomfortably she remembered Mrs. Shell's comments about Dr. Andreatta. Very possibly the charge would not believe her. Anyway, if Mrs. Shell—and Corry and Richards, too, for that matter—were the kind who could go to sleep on duty, they probably weren't about to go to the office with a nasty story about one of the resident doctors. They'd have to admit they had been sleeping.

Millie was positive they would call her a liar. She decided she would tell Ruth Ellison about it. Ruth had worked for the hospital a long time. She would know what to do.

Somewhat relieved by her decision, Millie stopped shaking. She picked up her magazine and found the place at which she had left off in a story about decent people and real love. Several minutes later, to her confusion, she found that she was still in the same place. Either she had read the same page over and over or she had dozed. She gave up, letting the magazine drop in her lap and putting her head back as the others had done. She listened to the stillness and thought about what she had seen, wondering about a doctor who could behave so horribly! He oughta be arrested, she thought, but who would do it? Someone had to tell on him first.

An hour later she was amazed at the ease with which the other three women aroused themselves, straightened their caps, put on their shoes and managed to appear brightly wide awake when Elizabeth Leslie, the night supervisor for the whole hospital, made an unexpected ward visit. How did they know she was coming?

"Time for ward check," Mrs. Richards said out of the corner of her mouth, showing this was their normal procedure, a matter of training, being able to waken themselves before they could get caught.

"Don't often get Leslie—supposed to get Mixon. Leslie must be looking for something. Straighten your cap," Mrs. Richards hissed.

Millie shoved her cap back and stood at polite attention with the rest while the ward records were checked, and later trailed along to help peer into rooms and corners. She liked Elizabeth Leslie. The woman was little and white-haired and sweet-faced and very serious.

Then why can't I tell her? Millie thought, with something like panic. Somebody ought to know what's going on with that Mary Elsie.

It was her job that held her back. She was sure she would lose it, the job that meant so much, the house and the cats and the bills, because the other women would get mean and furious and call her a liar. She shook her head despairingly. She couldn't do it; dear God, she couldn't. She'd tell Ruth and then she'd have to root out of her mind what she had seen, just never, never think of Mary Elsie.

"Why, the dirty sonofabitch!" Ruth Ellison exclaimed. She was Millie's next-door neighbor, a wiry, flat-chested woman with prematurely gray hair. In 1944 she had been married sixteen months when her husband was killed in the Battle of the Bulge. Since then she had worked continually at Canterbury. She was a careful person and had managed on her salary and Bill Ellison's insurance to pay for her house and other property as well. She could have quit her job any day and gotten by, but no one knew this except a lawyer in town, one of Bill's buddies. She never gossiped, never had much to say to anyone except Millie. She considered Millie her only friend; she was a faithful and conscientious employee. Her one passion was for the rose hedge at the back of her house, a thing of real beauty when it bloomed. People would go out of their way to walk down the alley and look at her hedge.

"Then what did you do?" she asked.

Millie's fat shoulders moved uncomfortably. "I didn't know what to do. I was afraid I'd get fired if I said anything. You know how it is, Ruthie. I gotta have my job. And them women weren't about to let on they'd all been sleeping. I was in a real hole, believe me. That's why I waited to tell you. No use aking what I should have done. It's what to do now."

"Seems to me you're still in a hole," Ruth said judiciously. "You go to the office now, they'll wanta know why you waited so long." She frowned, thinking about Millie's problem. "They won't fire that doctor, Millie. They need doctors. Doctors are important and that girl's just a patient. She don't really count. Now if she was rich—I mean, if she had rich people in back of her—you could go to them and beg 'em to not mention your name. Then, they could get busy and make a stink. On the other hand, if the girl had money, what would she be doing in a state hospital? Seems to me there's not much you can do. I know how you feel. It's terrible, just terrible. Something oughta be done. But not you, Millie."

"Maybe I could write a letter," Millie said, a little stubbornly. "But not sign my name. Just say it happened on so-and-so night, which they can prove by looking in the record book, because I saw that Mrs. Shell write it down."

"Oh, Millie!" Ruth was exasperated. "Don't you know that'd be a dead giveaway? Who was on duty that night? You and three other people. You'd all be called into the office and in five seconds they'd know who wrote the letter. Besides, it ain't good to send letters with no name. Lotta people won't even read 'em. They figure if a person can't sign a name, they haven't no business writing in the first place."

There was a silence. "All right," Millie said. "What do you think I oughta do?"

Ruth got up from the kitchen table and brought back the coffee pot. She poured coffee, took the pot back, lit herself a cigarette and returned. "You seen the schedule for next week?"

Millie blew on the coffee, took a sip and shook her head. "Didn't stop at the office this morning. I came straight home. Jennifer had her kittens, the first batch. I didn't want her to have no trouble and me not there to help. Figured it might be like the first baby with a woman, kinda tough."

"Oh, that." Ruth tapped ashes off the cigarette. "Well, they took you off Receiving."

Millie leaned forward, her chin falling. "They did?"

"Yeah. They put you on days."

"Days?" But something was coming. Millie stared at Ruth.

"You're on Stationary."

There was another silence. Stationary was one of the most untidy wards in the hospital, where all day long the patients, dressed in denim sacks with holes for necks and arms, sat strapped to chairs and benches in rows around a huge, barren room; the noise, bedlam, a continuous racket of groaning, weeping, screaming or raging, some of the women talking without ever stopping, others singing and hardly stopping to breathe.

"Well," Millie said uncertainly, "I figured I'd have to work there sometime. Receiving was nice, all but for that one thing. Anyway, it'll be nice working days. I haven't been sleeping so good . . ." Her voice trailed away. There was no point in not being philosophical about this, but being taken off a good ward to be sent to a bad one seemed rather unfair, like being punished for no reason. She wondered vaguely what she had done or not done.

Ruth guessed her thoughts, having been through it so often herself. "You know it don't mean a thing, don't you? When you first went to work I couldn't understand why they gave you such a good ward. Usually they start everybody on the very worst ward they got. Honest, Millie. I suppose they needed somebody on Receiving just when they put you on, so that's why they sent you there."

"We didn't do a thing," Millie said, shaking her head. "We just sat and chewed the rag. Mrs. Shell counted pills when the morning shift came on and we all went together to check the rooms a coupla times, but the rest of the time we just sat. And slept. They did. I . . . maybe I dozed a little, sometimes."

"All right. Now you're changed. You probably won't ever go back to Receiving. They'll keep moving you until they place you somewhere. Wherever that is, you'll stay. You won't see that Andreatta again nor that girl. So just forget it. If there was something you could do, I wouldn't say this, Millie. But there isn't. Believe me. You'll just get canned and then what'll you do?"

"A good question, Ruthie. A very good question. Starve to death, probably."

"You could eat your cats. Long-tail rabbit."

Millie could not laugh. "Ruthie!" she said, shocked.

"I was just kidding. Listen," Ruth said, "don't say anything. Promise me?"

Millie sighed. "Okay. You oughta know, Ruthie. You certainly have worked out there long enough." She finished her coffee and got up. "God, I'm tired. I gotta go to bed. Just think, one more night and then tomorrow night off. Seems like six nights in a row ain't right. Why don't we get forty hours a week like other working people do?"

"It's coming. Our union's working on it. Maybe a raise, too." She went with Millie to the door. "How many kittens did Jennifer have?"

"Five," Millie said, beaming through her fatigue. "Little dolls, Ruthie. Fat as butter. All calico but one, and he's Georgie all over, black with white on his nose and white boots. You want him?"

Ruth shook her head. "You and your family. What would I do with a tomcat under my feet?" Her rejection was emphatic but her tone was affectionate.

"What shift you working next week?" Millie remembered to ask.

"They changed me back to days, too," Ruth said. "Wish they'd make up their minds. And I got Hydro. That means I'll be there a month on account of they usually leave you through a series of treatments."

"Good. We can go in my car."

"No, let's take the bus. It's cheaper. When we go back on nights, God forbid, we'll use your car."

She shut the door and Millie went down the sidewalk to her own house. What does she do with her money? she wondered briefly, then was rather ashamed of herself. Ruth was the best kind of friend a woman could have and it wasn't for her to question what Ruth did with her money. Probably what the rest of us do, Millie told herself; just get by.

The following Monday she went to Stationary. She looked at the women strapped continually to their seats and her stomach heaved. Then she looked at the drudges who were sent in from other wards to do the dirty work of cleaning and mopping. They were morons and epileptics. They spent the whole day pushing huge wheeled buckets from mounds of excreta to pools of rancid urine and the stench did not seem to bother them. It wasn't that the patients could not be taken to the toilets; there just was not enough help. Over a hundred women on the ward and all of them so potentially dangerous or disturbed that it required the combined efforts of the whole shift to herd each one down, twice a week, to the shower room for a vigorous scalp-to-toe scrubbing.

"You think we got time to take each one of these women to the john when they want to go?" the second-in-charge said, seeing Millie's face. "Fighting all the way and then she just sits there and screams at you?"

The attendants on Stationary were tough, scrappy women. They had to be. They had to force food and medication into these patients' mouths while sidestepping kicks which would have maimed a mule. Their days were spent subduing violent women. Millie was baptized promptly.

Lois was a twelve-year-old patient, so vicious and unmanageable that she was kept in continual restraint in a private room. Her case card stated that she was seven when her father first violated her, that at the age of eight her services were being peddled around the neighborhood. When she was eleven, she was delivered of a stillborn infant, was found by the attending physician to be both alcoholic and syphilitic, and was subsequently committed to Canterbury. Penicillin cured the syphilis; it did not halt the mental degeneration. The wary efforts of two attendants were required to feed her, and it took six women to give her a bath.

That first day on Stationary for Millie Lois got loose during her bath. With pure venom, snarling and shrieking filth, she tore into everyone, sending caps sailing and buttons popping off uniforms. By sheer force of numbers the attendants regained control of the situation. They dragged her small, naked body down the hall and held her flat while the charge slapped and kicked without mercy until she was reduced to a gasping mess of bloody welts and bruises and was silent for a change.

Millie almost quit. She had studied her booklets. They plainly stated that any mistreatment of patients was to be reported to the office. But how to go about this was not explained. Again she was in a dilemma. Should or should she not tell? She helped strap Lois back into her hard, bare chair. The charge did not apologize for what had happened. The second-in-charge looked at Millie.

"Little bitch, ain't it? Just like an animal. Almost killed a 'filiate we had come on the ward once. Knocked her down 'n' jumped on her stummick. God, she menstrated for a month."

So they didn't tell. They never told on each other. It was unthinkable, disloyal, being a traitor.

CHAPTER 9

THE OFFICE GAVE MIKE STEWART a cubicle. It had an outside window, a desk, a chair and a typewriter, and it was sandwiched between Lucretia Terry's office and a lavatory for the stenographers. Sitting at the desk, he could hear the toilet being flushed. On the other side he could hear either Lucretia's sharp, unpleasant voice, or Margaret Rich, her assistant, soothing and placating in an undertone. Lucretia's voice was irritating, but Margaret's made him want to rush into the office and kick her.

"God's sake," he would mutter. "What in hell are you afraid of? Give it right back to the old witch."

On the third day he crammed his briefcase with everything he had taken out of it, ran his hand through his crew cut, making it stand up even more than it had, and walked over to Surgical.

In Donovan Macleod's office he explained his predicament. "I'm a writer," he said unhappily, now trying to smooth down his hair. "I can't work over there with all those women around me. I'm used to a newspaper office, maybe twenty men and two women. This business of all those rubber-soled shoes slipping around and toilets flushing and that personnel director screaming her head off—man, I can't take it. Maybe I'm neurotic, but I've got to have a little peace. Another thing. I can't stand everything so clean. Sometimes I forget to get cigarettes and it's a hell of a note hunting for a butt when somebody is always dumping out my ash trays."

Donovan laughed. "That's patient help," he explained. "They go overboard because it means privileges for them."

Larry Denning had come in from his office to join them. He was wearing a new sports shirt. Donovan whistled. "Madge seen that?" he wanted to know.

Larry fingered the material. "This is in honor of the first day of June. Anyway, I'm not a senior staff doctor. I am only a lowly junior. I can afford to be a little informal." He looked at Mike. "How about using my office? I'm not in it very often and Madge never touches my ash trays. She'll do a little typing for me, some filing, and she's good on errands, but that's all. Otherwise, she never bothers me. And I always keep an extra carton of cigarettes in the left-hand bottom drawer of my desk."

"And he never locks his desk even when he knows better," Donovan commented dryly.

"Who's going to take what I've got? I don't keep anything in my desk the way you do in yours."

Donovan lifted an eyebrow at him and turned to Mike. "I'll be in my office more than occasionally, but you're welcome to come in with me. I can get the office to put in another desk. There's plenty of room. By the way, Larry, I have a new typist. I haven't told Madge about her, because this girl's helping me at night in my apartment. She's one of the affiliates, the March beginning class. Althea Horne."

"Your secret's safe with me," Larry said, smiling.

Donovan frowned. "No secret. I just didn't mention it to Madge because from all the signs she's ready to have another bout and I didn't want to be the one to trigger it. But I've got to get this book finished. I've got a deadline from the publishers, and Madge is actually more of a hindrance than a help. I have to do over most of her typing. You know what she's like."

"Sure, sure," Larry said, still smiling.

A strained smile, Mike thought, sensing something and wondering what it was. What lay between these two, the dark, thin older man and the young one who looked like a football star from some university? What gives? Mike wondered. They did not like each other, obviously. They were courteous because they worked in the same hospital, but the antagonism between them was thick in the air. Jealousy? But which way? Why should Donovan Macleod be jealous? He was head of staff and dear to Canterbury. But what did the other have to be jealous about? Young, healthy, a big fellow, topping Donovan by a head, did he resent Donovan's faintly patronizing air of know-how and know-better? Could be, Mike thought, his nose for news quivering.

"I saw her," Larry said with a little smile. "Believe me, you couldn't have made a better choice."

"She's a good typist," Donovan said shortly.

"Of course. A good nurse, too. I looked up her record. With a figure like that, what is she doing in Canterbury? She could be a model or some rich man's mistress. She wouldn't have to *work* for a living."

"She's a nice girl, a lady. You should get married, Larry. I sincerely advise it."

Larry shrugged. "It's a lot more fun playing the field. Besides, on what I make I can't afford to."

"Your father could help you out."

"Look, Donovan, I'm twenty-eight. I quit going to my father for help some years ago. He'll die some day and leave it all to me and then maybe I'll settle down—that's the word you're thinking, isn't it?—but until then I'm strictly on my own and I like it that way. Now, this affiliate, this Althea—if she could do some typing for me, I might forget how poor I am. She certainly sets off bells every time I see her. Maybe I should write a book." His insolence was faint but definite. He looked at Mike, grinned and went back into his office.

Donovan's eyebrows moved. When he does that he's not quite so handsome, Mike decided. He looks stuffy and prosaic, pedagogic. God forbid, I think he's going to give me a lecture.

"Women," Donovan said. "They don't have to possess

minds, talents or standards. All they need are bodies, preferably beautiful ones, nice faces and not be too old."

"That's what Denning sees?"

"That's all he sees, all he's interested in—except professionally, of course. I'm sorry. I shouldn't talk about him."

But he irritates you, Mike thought. He's young and full of the animal. Come off it. You're not so old yourself, Donovan!

"I'll take him up on his offer," he said aloud. "Then you won't have to go to all that bother of having a desk moved in. The office staff is going to be disturbed enough when they discover I moved out."

"They'll get over it." Donovan was agreeable. Plainly, he was relieved at not having to share his office. "You know," he said, "sometimes we get just as confused here as the people we're looking after. Now, don't quote me on this. It might be embarrassing."

"That should be the least of your worries. After all, I'm being hired to encourage the public toward freer spending on state institutions, not to expose the mildew on the staff."

Both men laughed. "You won't find any mildew," Donovan said pleasantly. "A few old-fashioned theories on my part, perhaps. I just don't happen to believe in hieing myself off to bed with every woman who takes my fancy on every possible occasion. I like to spend my energy on my work."

Mike felt a little uncomfortable. How had Macleod guessed what he was thinking? But this was a psychiatrist. It was his business to follow the way people's minds worked.

"But I'm not old-fashioned when it comes to research and the latest methods of treatment for these patients. Anything that can be done for their welfare is my territory, believe me."

Mike rumbled sheepishly in his throat, cleared it and grinned. This was chief of staff; naturally he was concerned with the patients solely. According to what Mike had learned, Donovan lived and breathed for what he could do for them. He was an exceptional man; if he couldn't take a little ribbing from a junior staff member, it didn't have to mean he was pompous. He was honestly sincere in not wanting to be the reason a patient named Madge might go into an attack of hysteria. It made sense, and who was he, Mike Stewart, to smell out trouble between two men he knew about only because the office had permitted him—in view of the nature of his project—full access to all records, a vast assortment of them stored in the vaults under the office building? Hell, if the office knew the hodge-podge of stuff that ran through his mind sometimes, they'd lock him up on the spot. No, he had money. They'd put him on a couch and send in an analyst.

"I'll tell you what," Donovan said suddenly. "How would you like to witness some therapy first hand? We're not supposed to let anyone in on Hydro except bona fide practitioners, but I can give you a gown and a stethoscope to dangle from your pocket and no one will know you're not what you seem to be. Except staff members, of course."

"I'd like to. You know I would."

"I think I can arrange it with the office," Donovan said with his own little smile. He glanced at his watch. "I'm due there now. This is what we call shock day, a twice-a-week procedure. Twenty patients or so are due for treatment, some of them for the first time and the rest repeats. The ward's capacity is thirty patients and it's always full." He stepped to a drawer in a wall cabinet and took out two surgical gowns. "We can get these on the ward—I usually do. But this time we'll go prepared. We can leave these behind us on the ward afterward." He handed Mike a stethoscope. "Put that in your pocket just so." He demonstrated, stepped back to look. "Very professional. I'd swear you were the real thing. Come on. These ward charges get very disturbed when they have everything set up and you don't show up on time."

"Just a minute. Let me get rid of this." Mike picked up his briefcase and went with it into Larry's office. Larry was busy with a box of case cards. He looked up with an absorbed smile. Mike placed the briefcase on a corner of the desk and hesitated.

"Say, about this Madge. What happens when she flips?"

"Madge? You mean, how does she act, or what kind of treatment does she get?"

"Treatment. I've got an idea how she acts."

"Well," Larry said, sitting back and rubbing a finger over his chin, "it depends. Donovan sends her over to Hydro for shock, sometimes wet-pack therapy, and increases her thorazine dosage. When Donovan's busy and I take her case—" He stopped and stared at Mike. "Why did you want to know?"

Mike shrugged, his expression innocent and beguiling. "No reason. Just curious. What do you do?"

Larry remembered Mike standing with him on Receiving and watching Mary Elsie Blayton being brought in. Mike had looked more than shocked; he had been angry, although he had never said why or at what. Surely not at the hospital, Larry thought. The hospital wasn't to blame because people went crazy. There had to be some place for them to be sent to, a place like Canterbury, and then Canterbury did its best to help them get well—if they could; it wasn't Canterbury's fault when they couldn't get well. But he liked Mike and was prepared to be agreeable. After all, Mike probably didn't give a damn what Donovan thought and said about Larry Denning. Larry was sure Donovan had said something. Not that he cared. He liked women, so why lie and be a hypocrite about it? As far as he was concerned, women were God's gift to men and he was not one to reject the Creator's bountiful and lavish dispensations.

But he hated to look like a do-gooder. After a slight hesitation he said, "Actually, I don't do anything important. I get a pass for the old girl and take her out to my mother's place. It's a big, old farmhouse and my mother has plenty of help, so she doesn't mind. She's always nursing something, kittens or a calf or baby chicks, and there's no question of expense because the old man's well heeled."

"I know," Mike said. "I gathered that from Donovan." He grinned his thanks and went out.

Larry's frown was puzzled. He looked after Mike. What jolly thing did I say to bring on that grin? he wondered. Maybe he thinks I play around with the patients. He hoped to God Mike didn't think he took Madge out to his parents' farm to get into the hay with her. The first one to object to that would be—after himself—Madge.

He set to work on the case cards. Finish them and get over to number-fifteen unit, he told himself. It would take him all day to check the male wards, but if he hurried he might finish in time to circle back by Hydro and take another look at that typist affiliate.

CHAPTER 10

"What do you think of Macleod, the Great White Chief?" Althea asked Kathy one night during one of their gossip sessions.

"Dr. Macleod?" Kathy looked surprised. "What brought that out?"

"I just wondered."

"Not much, frankly. He's so—stiff or something. I don't think he likes us." Then she shrugged. "Oh, he's a good doctor, I guess. I worked on Male Surgical last week and didn't see him once outside of class, but I heard plenty. The charge thinks he's next to perfect and the supervisor, Mrs. Beck, couldn't talk about ward problems because she was so full of Dr. Macleod."

Althea nodded. "I worked on Geriatrics and saw him every day. He's going to let me do some typing for him."

"I didn't know you could type."

"Took it in high school and got pretty fast. Sixty-four words a minute."

"But how——I mean, did this just happen out of a clear blue sky or something? When will you have time to type? And type what?"

"He writes books. Didn't you know? And I'll help him evenings. Not every evening, of course, but when he lets me know. Some patient's been doing his typing, but she's flipped, right in the most important place in this new book. I heard about it from Beck and went over and offered to help. He's going to pay me a little. Not as much as a regular typist would get, but I'm so thrilled at getting to do it I'd gladly do it for nothing." She turned and stared into the mirror. It wasn't a very good mirror and it distorted her reflection somewhat, but Kathy could see it in how her eyes darkened and her mouth turned soft.

"My goodness," Kathy said suddenly. "How long has this been going on? I mean, I certainly didn't notice anything."

"I haven't been trying to hide it," Althea said dreamily. "Oh, Kathy, isn't it strange how it happened? The first time I saw him—well, you were there, remember? He walked in and stood in front of us and I fell in love. Crazy, crazy. I told myself it just doesn't happen like this, only in stories. I scolded myself like hell. I took pills every night to get to sleep. And I didn't let anybody know, not even you. I thought I'd get over it, honest I did. It was something silly, like a cold or a toothache. It would go away. That's what I told myself, Kathy. Can you imagine?"

Kathy shook her head in puzzled wonder. "Well, I certainly would never have guessed. Are you sure it isn't something like infatuation? I mean, we're not kids in high school any more."

Althea said strongly, "I'm not sure of anything except that Donovan Macleod is in my mind all the time. I even asked Miss Leslie about him. She told me everything. He's thirty-eight. He's been here at Canterbury six years. He comes from Baltimore and he's supposed to be tops in his field. He's written several books besides this one I'm going to help him with, and the office is scared to death he'll decide some day to accept one of the fabulous offers he's always getting from other hospitals and leave Canterbury. They just know they could never get anyone to take his place, anyone as good as he is. He shares an office setup with Dr. Denning in the Surgical building——" Althea brought her brush down through her hair as though she were caressing something—"and he's never shown any interest in women here, as far as Leslie knows."

Maybe he's queer, Kathy thought, but she said aloud, "Well, that's nice. That's a break for you, isn't it?"

She felt a little lonely, not really jealous, but faintly envious. She suddenly missed her parents and the shabby little house in Dayton. When she graduated, she would go home for a good visit before she accepted any placement offers and sleep until noon at least one day with her dog across her feet again. Her mother always mentioned him in her letters. Kathy looked at the box of chocolates on her night table, took one and popped it into her mouth.

Althea put down the brush, made a rope of her hair and started pinning it up with bone hairpins almost the same color as the hair. She suddenly became sensible and blunt.

"Right now, to be honest, he hardly knows I exist. I'm just a machine and he's going to take advantage of my ability, not me. Worse luck. He's been run to death by females, Kathy. Affiliates, supervisors—even attendants. They all love him. He's scared of women. He only likes patients. So I was careful. And I intend being careful until I get my hooks in." This was her view of feminine assault upon any male ego. Hooks in, unremovable, final. "I shall wear blouses and skirts, very plain, you know. And no perfume, no fingernail polish. I'll be strictly business, down to those loafers I keep for walking!"

"He'll be blind if he doesn't notice how beautiful you are."

"Thanks, pet. You really think so?"

Kathy was not embarrassed. "Of course you are," she insisted warmly. "You are—well, if I were a man I'd say you were out of this world. You have such unusual coloring and your figure is wonderful." She was not envious. This was her friend and she was glad to point out what any man would be a fool not to see. Perhaps in some way she could help Althea to "get her hooks in."

Althea laughed. "Honest to God, Kathy, the man just stares at me. As if I were some kind of strange animal. Probably because I've been so careful. You know, not made up to him or flirted or showed him what a pushover I could be." The skin around her eyes crinkled. "The funny thing, it's all I can do to stay careful. I want him so badly. Sometimes it frightens me, the way I want to go to bed with him!"

Judiciously, Kathy considered this. "You mean it wouldn't matter whether you were married or not?"

"Sure, I'd want to be married. It's so much safer. Oh, not because I'd be afraid of pregnancies. You know as well as I do that nurses don't have to get caught that way. But because with marriage a girl has her man. He's tied to her. He may step out on her, but he's still her property. If Donovan Macleod and I were married, he wouldn't want to step out on me, because I'd keep him so busy, so satisfied, he'd never think of another woman." Her breath caught. "But, if he wanted me and didn't want marriage—just me—I'd never say no, Kathy. Never. That's how I feel about him."

"Oh, Althea!" Kathy said, looking at her friend, her dear, kind friend whom she felt so close to. "Don't get hurt." She felt quite angry with Donovan Macleod for a moment. She sat up, her face serious, her dark eyes stern. "You make him marry you, Althea. Don't go to bed with him until he does. Men have every advantage. They get all the breaks. Do you know what I mean? Don't make it too easy for him."

"Can't help myself," Althea said softly. "I'm crazy about him. I'll do anything I can to get into bed with him. Besides, he's a great psychiatrist. He's too smart for me to make him do anything."

She picked up the pins that were left over and dropped them into a pocket. "Thanks for letting me do my hair in here, pet. Guess I'll run along. Time for me to get busy."

Kathy sighed and got off the bed. "How about going to the movies with me tonight? My mother sent me ten bucks just to throw away."

Althea felt a gentle pity. The child was lonely. She had her enormous, rich, wonderful love and the chance to do something about it, while Kathy had no boy to go out with yet. But go to a show? Take time away from the thing that possessed her, watch make-believe passion when she was swelling, ready to burst, with the real thing? She shook her head.

"I'd love to, Kathy, but not tonight. Donovan's expecting me to start typing as soon as possible, so I thought I'd give him a buzz. You know, loafers, no perfume, just me?" She looked at Kathy a little anxiously, hoping she would understand.

"So it's first names," Kathy said with a maternal frown. "Okay, some other time."

Althea reached the door and hesitated, her hand on the knob. "It's like this, Kathy. When a girl's in love she isn't accountable to anything but that love. I love Donovan so much that I dream about him at night and wake up still thinking about him. When a girl gets like that, she's like a cat in heat. She starts doing something about it. It has to come first. I know. I look like a porcelain figurine. Too fragile to handle. But I'm not. If I ever get a chance to go to bed with our Dr. Macleod, he'll never forget it, believe me."

"Okay, okay," Kathy said. "Just so it's not contagious. I can't afford to get in heat. I've got to pay my folks back for my education first. All I'm saying is, be careful, for Pete's sake. You'll be the one to get hurt, not the good doctor."

Althea opened the door and turned back with the expression of a mischievous gamin. "You know something, Kathy? In spite of the way I talk, I've never been had. Won't Donovan be surprised?"

"For God's sake," Kathy exploded. "All the more reason for you to be married first. That's worth a license. And stop bragging. There are still a few virgins left in nursing."

Althea laughed and went out. Remembering something, Kathy stuck her head out the door. "We're working together next week," she said after Althea. "On Hydro, no less. It's already posted."

She shut her door then and went back to the nightstand and the box of chocolates. She studied it for a moment. Dr. Donovan Macleod. She said it aloud. It had a solid, respectable Scottish sound.

Doesn't mean a damn thing, she thought. He's probably a stuffed shirt, even a heel. He didn't like the way I sat in class. So that means he probably picks on people. Doesn't notice women. Hah, I'll bet! We probably don't know the half of it. He'll break her heart and then she'll commit suicide or something.

She was positive he would do nothing but harm to Althea. Resolutely she put the lid on the chocolate box, got out her textbook on materia medica and found a pencil. I'll watch him, she told herself, chewing on the pencil eraser; I won't take my eyes off the old goat. He just better not do anything to hurt Althea or he'll certainly hear about it from me. Even if I get kicked clear out of Canterbury!

She remembered what Althea had said. Well, what was wrong with it? A woman in love *should* feel that strongly. Kathy thought about men, tall and thin and short and fat, alcoholics, prudish men, self-righteous men, young, eager men, older ones just as eager but not so vital. She wondered briefly if she would ever meet one who could make her feel the way Althea was feeling right now.

She settled back on the bed, opened the book, took the pencil out of her mouth, and got busy. All this business about heat and men and Althea's safety would not help her pass the test coming up in the morning. If she did not pass, she would have to make it up on her own time. "And alone with the monster—oh, save me, who will save me!" she said dramatically, pointing one foot into the air and throwing an arm out wide. Immediately she relaxed and looked a little sheepish.

Why didn't I go on the stage or something? she wondered.

It might have been such fun. That's what's the matter with me. I need to have some fun.

Suddenly she dropped her pencil and book and got off the bed, going to kneel at the open window with her elbows on the sill and staring out into the darkness. She sniffed at the fragrance that came from some tree blooming nearby.

Why couldn't she be in love, too? That's what she really needed.

What would it be like to be in love, deeply in love, crazy, crazy with it? A nursing career was so cut and dried. If you turned out to be good, reliable, you could always be sure of getting a good placement. But wasn't there anything a nurse could plan on except dedication?

I want to be in love, Kathy thought, hurting inside with something she couldn't explain.

I want to be silly in love and not responsible for what I do, she told herself. I'd like to run barefoot across grass and stay up all night the next time there's a new moon, just to watch the way it goes in a little arch across a corner of the sky, so thin and the sky so black. I'd like to be drunk once, really drunk—vodka, maybe—and the next day have someone tell me what I did.

She dropped her head on her arms and looked out into the night. What would it be like to sleep with a strange man? she wondered. One you'd never seen before and never would again? Would you feel unclean, spoiled, or would you feel nothing at all? She explored the thought carefully but reached no definite conclusion.

She wondered, too, if most girls fell in love with love first, before they fell in love with some man.

Reluctantly she went back to her book.

Kathy and Althea stood in front of the charge's desk, trim and precise in spotless uniforms and caps, waiting to get acquainted with her. There were eight women assigned to Hydro, two affiliates, two aides and four regular attendants, one of them the charge. She had been a practical nurse in a general hospital and had been accorded the status of aide on coming to Canterbury. She was a tall, heavy woman with a placid, benign face. Everyone agreed she was ideal for Hydro since she was impartial and gentle with the Hydrotherapy patients, who came there only because they were highly disturbed. She was also diplomatic. The affiliates left Hydro after their training period and still liked her, as did the aides. Her name was Molly. She had been day charge for sixteen years.

She introduced everyone, the aides to the affiliates, and the affiliates to the attendants. She even introduced a patient standing near the desk. Then she explained the routine of the ward.

"Our patients are here for treatment or therapy. They are, ordinarily, patients assigned to other wards. Usually they are pretty good, they eat well, do ward work and can have visitors and enjoy recreation of some sort. When they become disturbed, their ward doctors send them over for a course of treatment. The doctors decide whether sedative tubs will be enough or whether they need shock or sheet packs. Today is shock day and we have twenty patients to shock. The attendants on this ward have worked here a long time. They will show you the procedure and after that you may help with the treatment. We have our own dining room for Hydro. The office feels that highly disturbed patients need the very best in food and that eating in a dining room, at individual tables, is therapeutic. Next to the TB ward, we have the finest kitchen in the institution." She looked at the new help. "I want to warn you ladies that you are never to attempt handling a patient alone. You must either have another aide or affiliate or an attendant with you. These patients are not like the untidies who are kept strapped or in seclusion all the time. At times these women can think and they can be very dangerous."

Ruth listened indifferently. She had heard it all so many times. Caution, caution, caution, and then they all went right ahead and took the wildest chances. Molly meant what she said, but she couldn't be everywhere at once. Just so the office never found out. They probably know a lot more over in that office than we think they do, she thought.

Kathy and Althea looked at the aides and then at the attendants. Everyone smiled a little. This was not a ward in which you held someone off at arm's distance because your status was higher; if you got into trouble and needed help fast, it was nice to know someone would come speedily because they wanted to, not because they had to. The records told of pitched battles almost every day on Hydro between employees and patients, so a league between employees was a comforting thought.

The breakfast cart was trundled onto the ward. "For the patients who get treatment," the charge said. "They are allowed only coffee and toast. Then if they vomit after shock, there's not so much to clean. Two of you ladies will take the other patients to the dining room. We have three patients who will get trays."

She indicated the huge tubs used for sedative tub therapy. Two were in use. Kathy reasoned that the other patient must be in sheet pack. The patients who were to receive shock were gathering around the desk. There was no apprehension on the part of the regular employees. It might have been a family gathering, Molly speaking almost affectionately to this or that woman, her voice gentle. Two of the attendants began to set up trays. The patients helped themselves to coffee and toast and looked longingly at the big pan of scrambled eggs, another of crisply fried bacon. There was everything on the cart to make a well-rounded breakfast—hot cereal, cream, two kinds of juice, stewed prunes and coffee cake.

Molly helped herself to coffee and toast along with the patients. "We don't eat on the ward, you know," she said, a twinkle in her eyes. "But I've been up since five o'clock and there's still a long day to go." She covered the toast with scrambled eggs and several strips of bacon, placed it all on a paper napkin and sat down at her desk.

Kathy noticed that the two women who had filled trays had also included extra coffee, toast and eggs. Now they moved off to the tubs, placed the trays on the canvas tops near the heads out in view and began spoon-feeding these patients, stopping occasionally to take a bit or a sip themselves. The charge had a swallow of her coffee and glanced up directly at Kathy and Althea.

"After you've had some coffee or whatever you want, will you feed the patient in room four? She's in sheet pack and may not want anything, but you can try some of that hot cereal and a glass of milk. Put plenty of sugar on the cereal, maybe a pat of butter."

Althea and Kathy looked at each other. They had meal books which cost them very little and which they could use in the excellent cafeteria set up by the hospital for employees. But they had yet to work on a ward where the employees did not eat at the hospital's expense if it could be done. So far they had steered clear of this mild chicanery, but now they were part of a small, intimate group, intricately and closely allied. It would not hurt them to conform. They poured coffee and drank it and nibbled at coffee cake while they prepared a tray for the patient in room four.

The patient in sheet pack was Mary Elsie Blayton. She was strapped to the narrow bed in room four, her shrouding of tightly wrapped wet sheets giving her a formless and impersonal appearance. Her sunken eyes and pallid skin made her look almost dead, but there was perspiration on her face, the only part of her exposed, and a constant twitch at one corner of her mouth.

The girls unlocked the door, went in and placed the tray on the foot of the bed. They had read the case card on Mary Elsie.

"Hello, Mary Elsie," Althea said, just as she would have said it to anyone, another affiliate or a friend or someone at the door. "How are you this morning? Did you notice the sun's trying to come out? It looked like rain for a while but instead we're going to have a really hot day."

"We brought you some breakfast," Kathy said, and she too was speaking to a friend or someone very ordinary, certainly not a girl who had been wrapped like a mummy in a number of sheets taken directly out of a bed of cracked ice and who had been like this now for some sixty hours. "A nice breakfast. Hot cereal and coffee and juice and some delicious coffee cake. It has brown sugar all over the top. You eat all this good stuff and then we'll take you out of your pack and let you go to the bathroom."

They prepared to feed Mary Elsie. They tucked a clean towel under her chin, the ends on either side of her face. They found a pillow, worked it under her head. They brought the tray up close and stood, one on each side of the bed. Kathy took the spoon for the cereal and Althea was ready with the coffee. Mary Elsie did not open her eyes, did not indicate she had heard anything or knew they were present.

Kathy dipped into the cereal. "Here, honey," she said coaxingly, her voice a little sad. The girl seemed so dreadfully young. She put a little cereal between the lips, saw it disappear, dipped up some more cereal. Several spoonfuls went in. She looked triumphantly at Althea. "I think she likes it," she whispered.

"How about some coffee now?" Althea whispered back.

Kathy leaned over to wipe a spilled drop off Mary Elsie's chin. "Okay," she muttered and then it happened. Mary Elsie made a round circle with her mouth and blew. From the amount of cereal that shot out, she must have collected all that Kathy had fed her, storing it in her cheeks like a squirrel. Neither Kathy nor Althea could duck in time; their faces received the full impact. Kathy got most of it.

Aghast, they looked at each other. "My God!" Kathy said. "Look at us!" They dripped cereal and saliva.

They grabbed for Kleenex and finished with a corner of the bedspread. Then they began to giggle. "You should have seen the look on your face!" Althea gasped.

"You mean I didn't look as though I'm accustomed to starting off the day like this?"

There was a sound from the bed and they stopped laughing and turned to stare at Mary Elsie. Her eyes were open, brightly blue and full of venom for the added insult of being forced to eat. But her voice cajoled. That was the first approach; be sweet, say please, act like a lady. Then if nothing happens, tell them off.

"Undo me, will you? Please, please, please. I have to go to the toilet. I can feed myself, really I can. I'm sorry I spit at you, but I was just trying to get that cereal out of my mouth. I never eat cereal. Please, Nurse, if you don't let me out, I'll do it right in the bed. It's number two and I don't want to do it in the bed. Please, Nurse. I'll go right down to the stoolroom and come right back. And then I'll feed myself. I'll be real good."

They looked at each other, down at the bed, then up again.

"We're supposed to feed her first."

"But why not? We have to repack her anyway."

"And give her a bath and oil her before that."

"She'll feed herself. I'm sure she will."

"Okay, then. Let's do it."

They started untying the knots in the canvas straps. Their voices turned professional, a little stern. "Now, remember, honey, you're going right down to the bathroom. Then we'll give you a nice warm bath and rub oil all over you. Then you'll come right back here and eat your breakfast. Okay, huh?"

"Please don't give us a bad time because this is our first day on this ward and we don't want to get any demerits just because we were nice to you. Will you remember that?"

"Oh, I won't do a thing, honest to God I won't. Just hurry, hurry, because I gotta go, I gotta go right now. You're so sweet, both of you, just like my best friends, Beverly and Mildred. They live on each side of my house—you know my house on Cedar Lane, you know that street? Beverly and Mildred are taking care of my violets while I'm here getting well. I am getting well, you know. Oh, my goodness, hurry, hurry. I can't hold it in much longer."

They had the straps undone and unwound. They stood the cocoon up on its feet after sliding it off the bed and began unwrapping sheets. A rank stench came up at them. Over Mary Elsie's emerging body, they looked at each other.

"I think she went several times," Althea said finally.

"You're not kidding," Kathy said as the last sheet dropped to the floor.

Mary Elsie staggered. Her skin looked puckered and aged and raw in spots. Her hair was matted and lifeless. She regained her balance with remarkable speed and suddenly was gone, flying out the door and down the hall, shrieking with laughter. Althea and Kathy bent down, gathered up the foul sheets, and were after her.

"Will we ever get told off!"

"We were supposed to repack her."

"But not let her run naked all over the ward."

"Oh, shoot. Who's there to care?"

"Just that charge, that's all."

"But the kid has to go to the john."

"Oh, now look. You really think she can do any more?"

With the help of two of the attendants, they finally caught Mary Elsie, gave her a bath, oiled her body thoroughly with sweet oil and returned her to a clean bed. Then she was repacked, the sheets coming frozen right from the locker. Mary Elsie wept hysterically as she was rolled and turned and deftly encased in the icy, wet shrouding. As soon as they finished, down to the straps which would hold her flat and motionless, heat would rise in her body and she would begin to sweat; but this first cold contact was devastating.

The two attendants took the tray and left Althea and Kathy to take a pulse reading. If the reading became very high, Mary Elsie would have to be removed from the pack.

"Be sure to lock the door when you come out," one attendant cautioned, "or some patient might get it into her head to undo those straps for Mary Elsie."

Kathy pushed a wisp of hair back into place. "Think of doing this every day for two weeks," she said, her breath short.

"And the day's barely begun," Althea agreed.

They looked at Mary Elsie. She had become silent and drowsy. Althea put two fingers on the pulse in her throat, timing it carefully.

"I'll bet she's really cute when she's all right and fixed up, her hair clean and all, don't you?" Kathy murmured.

"Poor kid," Althea said, finished with her count.

They were told about electroshock therapy. The patient receiving it was placed on a high surgical cart. The three attendants and the charge planted themselves strategically on either side. They held the patient, demonstrating the proper spots and explaining how——not too tightly because a bone might be broken in the convulsion, but enough to keep the patient on the cart, enough to prevent the patient from throwing something out of joint. The attending doctor would place electrodes on temples already oiled with a special formula for better contact; he would set the controls on his machine according to what he believed the patient should have or could endure, and then hold the chin and neck firmly in order to prevent a broken neck. A thick pad was always placed between the teeth. Afterward, the patient would be wheeled into a receiving room and put to bed and strapped down until full consciousness returned. Sometimes the patients were quite wild, coming out of shock, and the restraints were to keep them from hurting themselves. The aides would stay with them during this period because often they vomited and could choke to death if unattended.

"What good is it really?" Kathy wanted to know. "This shock therapy?"

"You should ask the doctor," Molly said. "I'm not supposed to say. I can only tell you how I look at it."

"Well?" the girls waited.

"The shock or the convulsion, something, makes a break in the patient's thinking circuit. After enough shocks, he's regressed back past the focal point of his present trouble or whatever made him get high. If he receives the right kind of therapy after shock, someone who understands and will talk to him and take an interest in his case, the shock course seems to be very good for him."

"You sound as though you aren't too sure."

"We don't have enough help for that. We give 'em shock and that's all we can do."

"Is it true that shock is sometimes used for . . . punishment?"

Molly looked at them. "You won't quote me, of course, but it's like this. Say there's a charge and two attendants on a big ward. Some little old lady gets up, doesn't feel too good, but not sick either, and doesn't want any breakfast. Maybe she's thinking about her kids, or her dead husband, or how nobody ever comes to see her and why in God's name is she in Canterbury in the first place. So she gets cranky, she won't make her bed, she won't help with the sweeping. A thing like that mushrooms. The charge and the attendants have their hands full. They've got to give medications, see that everyone gets cleaned up, hair combed, the beds made. When the supervisor comes around for checks, the ward's gotta look nice, a hundred or so women have to be dressed and presentable. They haven't got time to fool with this old lady and her tantrums. So right off they call in and say Mrs. So-and-so is off again and they get an order to send her over to Hydro for a course of shocks. What can I do about it? I wish it were different because I hate to see that, but I just work out here, too. On the other hand, when a patient—an up-patient—gets really violent, there's nothing like shock to tame him down."

Both Kathy and Althea were silent for a moment. "What about tranquilizers?" Kathy asked. "Don't you believe they'll take the place of this kind of therapy some day?"

"This off the record?" Molly asked with her twinkle. When they nodded, she said, "Someday, yes. But right now they're still experimental. Did you notice those patients drooling down their fronts, slobbering and snuffing and shuffling like they were almost paralyzed? They are on heavy tranquilizer dosages. If a patient has catarrh, and he gets tranquilizers, he fills up with mucus until it seems he'll choke to death. God, that's a mess. It scares me, watching what happens." She looked placid enough but her eyes stopped twinkling. "I think everybody in the hospital is getting tranquilizers now, more or less, because we don't begin to have the number of patients to shock we used to have, and that's fine, it's wonderful. I understand a lot of patients even get to go home when their people want to bother with them. And someday they'll have medicine that'll do the work without any side effects. They're working on it all the time. That'll be the day. But until they do, we have this to put up with. It's a job, you know."

A voice said something. They turned around. A small, elderly woman stood in the doorway with an anxious expression on her face. "That's Lillian," Molly said. "Her father was a big judge in town and her husband was head of the school board. She's seventy-four and weights ninety-eight pounds. She threw her cereal at the charge on Ward Ten in the second unit this morning, so Dr. Macleod decided she needed a few treatments. Come on in, Lillian. How you feeling, honey?"

"Oh, no!" said Kathy in a small voice, looking at Althea. Althea said nothing but put her hand on Kathy's wrist. Staring at the fragile face, the crown of soft white hair, both of them were thinking the same thing. Is this fulfillment, the final blossoming, the answer to the expectancy of things to come? Why, then, bother to live at all?

But Kathy was thinking even further. So that's your precious Donovan! Making this little thing go through shock! She wanted to stand in the center of the institution and shout out her indignation.

CHAPTER 11

Two WEEKS went swiftly by and Althea bloomed. She not only did Donovan's typing but she saw him every day on Hydro.

"He lets me make coffee now in his kitchenette," she told Kathy. "I make it the first thing and we drink it all evening. Last night he had doughnuts."

"Is that supposed to mean something?"

"It means he was thinking about us, doesn't it?"

"It means he was hungry and likes doughnuts."

Althea looked at Kathy. Something was different about Kathy, but what? She was changed somehow, a little strange, as though something she could not understand was disturbing her. Perhaps it's this ward, Althea thought. She's lonely, too. She keeps talking about going home to see her folks.

Maybe she should ask for a few days off and go home.

But she did not say anything to Kathy. She had noticed Mike Stewart several times on the ward with Donovan, and Donovan had told her about him. Mike was nice, she thought. As tall as Donovan but broad-shouldered, which made him look stocky, and that funny haircut and the way his chin jutted, and his sharp eyes kept looking at everything. He had noticed Kathy right away. Althea felt that his stares at Kathy were special. She wished Kathy would respond in some fashion because, really, the fellow was nice. It would be wonderful for Kathy to have someone interested in her; it might make all the difference in the world in Kathy's life. She was so happy with herself that she wanted something nice to happen to Kathy as well. She believed, too, that with so many affiliates in Canterbury, a girl had to be on the lookout for available men. There weren't too many of them. Most of the doctors were married, even if their wives weren't with them. But there was Donovan and Larry Denning and several others and now this Mike. Larry had been coming on Hydro more than was necessary, but not to see Kathy. She knew why he came, but she disliked even thinking about it when she was so wrapped up in thinking about Donovan. She had seen Donovan first and that was it. No one else could count now.

Kathy realized that Althea was disturbed about her, but she could not explain why she felt as she did nor when it had started. Sometime on Hydro, she supposed, but that was only a guess. They were all so close, the employees and the patients, like a family. What hurt one hurt everybody. When the therapy did not succeed or a jaw was dislocated or there was a knock-down, drag-out battle, trying to get someone undressed and into pack, everyone suffered. Neither she nor Althea nor the aides, for that matter, had a decent uniform left after the first few days, and every morning she felt she was girding herself for something new and unexpected and devastating. It wasn't easy to force one's will on someone else even on doctor's orders, not when that someone was so terribly afraid and resistant. Then there were the patients who were foul-tongued and obscene, and that hurt, because quite often they had once been schoolteachers or mothers of large families or important women socially, and well educated. It was painful to listen to their invectives and endless tirades and watch what they did to themselves and know that when balance returned, they would cry and sob and beg to go home to their families, not realizing that the families either were no more or would not or could not handle the situation their condition created. Sometimes they even knew, and that was the worst of all to Kathy, those lost, lonely faces staring out the windows of Hydro between treatments. She knew what they wanted: death or oblivion. They could have nothing else.

She told herself that she was getting depressed by Hydro and she honestly tried to believe that. But when Mrs. Beck, a counselor for the affiliates, came around to check what the charge had said in the records about her and Althea's work, she could scarcely force herself to stand at attention. She despised Mrs. Beck and the authority she represented. In Kathy's thoughts it became petty tyranny, and all her sympathy went out to the patients. She knew better, but she began to feel that they were getting a dirty deal and that something should be done about it.

She tried to rationalize this extraordinary feeling by telling herself that Mike Stewart had started it all, coming on the ward with his pugnacious air and pinning everyone down with his endless questions. She did not particularly like him, but she could not say she disliked him, either. He was clever with words and sometimes brutally honest, and somehow he had singled her out as his main target. When he gets through with me, I feel stripped, she told herself. She remembered the time Madge had been brought in and had bitten Molly during pack. That had been a real ordeal for everyone because it took all of them, the whole crew, to subdue Madge. She never stopped screaming and jerking from the time she got inside the big outside door of the ward until she was finally and firmly strapped into pack. And clamping her teeth into Molly's arm like that. They had had to call for help from Male Hydro, and even with two husky attendants from there, Molly had lost a chunk of flesh on the inside just below the elbow. And she didn't do a thing, Kathy thought with wonder. She seemed to take it for granted. She placed a Kotex pad over the hole to soak up the blood and took herself over to Emergency for a tetanus shot and first aid. Could Mrs. Beck have kept from slapping the hell out of Madge? Or Althea? Or me?

Mike Stewart and Donovan Macleod had heard about the fight immediately. Macleod knew what Madge could and would do, of course, but Mike was startled. "What did you all do?" he asked, bristling at the nervous, shaking group collected around the desk after Molly had left.

But he looked directly at Kathy with his hard, bright glance and she felt the hackles rise. "What do you think? We did what we had to do. We fought and held on. She was like springs, like steel springs. We weren't hurting her, but we had to get those sheets wrapped just so, because they cut off the circulation otherwise and that's not good when a patient has to be in pack seventy-two hours." She stared indignantly at Mike. Did he think *she* made the rules?

"Seventy-two hours wrapped in wet sheets strapped flat? My God!" Mike slapped his forehead with his hand. "It's medieval torture, the Dark Ages all over. What are you trying to do, kill people?"

Donovan frowned at Mike. "Not at all. It's excellent therapy. It elevates the temperature and produces a form of sedation without drugs. The patient isn't always kept in pack for seventy-two hours. Sometimes the desired result is achieved earlier. We use it when and where we can't use insulin therapy. It's safer and more humane and sometimes will do more for a patient than electroshock."

"You mean when a patient is just plain mean and you want to take the fight out of him, right?"

"Well, it certainly takes the fight out of them," Donovan said, hedging. He sometimes found it difficult to explain to laymen that certain procedures were still in use because Canterbury was a little behind certain foreign hospitals that were experimenting with revolutionary new techniques. He did not like to have to apologize for what was being done when there was nothing he could do about it anyway; Jubal Herrington was head of the hospital and determined all its policies. Donovan was only chief of staff, as Mike knew. Any hospital was bound to be a complex structure, and mental hospitals more complex than most, since they included surgery and general care as well as all the rest—research, rehabilitation, custody and so on. Frankly, he was going to be relieved when Mike finished whatever he had to do and went on his way. Then he could concentrate on getting the book to his publisher.

He glanced at Althea. She had been more than helpful, and he was grateful to her for what she had done.

A day or two after the incident with Madge, something else happened. Kathy got hurt this time. A new patient had been brought in, sent directly to Hydro without the formality of going through Receiving; nothing had as yet been done for her. That meant she would have to be given an enema, her TPR taken and a blood-pressure reading made in order to start her chart. She still wore her own clothes.

"When they skip Receiving, it means they need treatment fast," Molly murmured.

But the girl stood in front of the desk quietly, making no fuss of any sort and waiting to be told what to do. She was a tall girl, rather pretty, large-framed and competent-looking. Her hands were clean and manicured. The case card said she was a professional prostitute, sent in to the hospital because she had gone berserk and tried to kill somebody.

"Look, honey," Molly said to the girl, "why don't you go into the day room and have a chair? We'll get to you just as soon as we fill in these papers."

Another patient came up. "I'll show you where to go. You just follow me."

Obediently the girl went. Ruth and another attendant set up the nearest bed for an enema—rubber sheets, towels, enema can with soapy solution and the rest. Althea went to the cabinet for the tray with its thermometer and various jars, and one of the aides brought out the baumanometer. Molly sent Kathy into the day room for the new patient.

"We're ready," Kathy said pleasantly.

The girl got to her feet. She looked fixedly at Kathy for a moment. Suddenly her fist lashed out, catching Kathy squarely in the face. Without a sound, Kathy went down and two patients ran shrieking to the desk. They converged instantly, Molly moving with amazing rapidity, considering her weight, the rest close behind—Althea, the aides, the attendants. Kathy was flat on the floor, her eyes open but dazed, blood beginning to seep from her nose, and the area between her eyes already starting to swell.

The new patient stared at them. Her fists unclenched. "I wanta use the phone," she muttered. "I gotta use it. I gotta call somebody."

"Come on," Molly said quietly. "You aren't very well. Let us help you, then when the doctor gets here, you ask him about using the phone."

The girl looked at Molly. "You sure about that? I gotta know. You don't know how important it is for me to call somebody."

"I know," Molly said, calm and gentle, "but I can't help you myself. Everything we do, we have to ask the doctor first."

The girl let herself be led, then. She submitted to the enema, to all they did to her, and finally to the bed in the private room, where she was strapped loosely but securely. "Don't forget," she said tonelessly. "I gotta use the phone."

"We won't forget," Molly said, almost adding, "We'll wait for you to forget." Because the girl would, eventually.

Dr. Macleod came to examine Kathy. Mike was with him. Kathy was seated, holding with one hand an ice pack to the back of her head and, with the other, a wad of tissue to her nose. She looked a little defiant but not frightened, not even too disturbed. She was a little apprehensive that her nose might be broken, and her head ached slightly; otherwise she was thinking about the girl, about why she had to do such a thing, and the fine way Hydro had moved in to help her. Not much could happen with people around like Molly and Althea and Ruth Ellison and the others. That was real teamwork.

Althea sat nearby, watching anxiously as Donovan probed and felt. She winced when Kathy did, almost feeling real pain in her own face. She noticed how gentle Donovan's hands were, how carefully they moved across Kathy's skin. If she had not been so concerned over Kathy, she might have felt resentment or envy. Instead, she could only remember how her heart had pounded when the fracas first began and she had rushed in with the others to see Kathy flat on the floor. What if that girl had killed Kathy! It made her heart still pound hard to think how close a thing it had been and how different the outcome might have been.

Kathy had her head against the back of the chair as Donovan made his examination, and at first her eyes were closed. The touch of his finger tips was quite light. She hardly felt them as they searched. She was thinking how odd it was that she should be submitting to their pressure when she had so resented their owner, and how sensitive they must be if they could discover anything with so delicate a probing. There was an odor not at all unpleasant about them, cologne or hand lotion and soap and, very faintly underneath, a male, tobacco smell. Donovan's face was there, too, but his breath was light and pleasant, with the same tobacco smell tinged with clove—his toothpaste or mouth wash, perhaps. She was almost hypnotized, and yet there was a strange awareness of feeling, so that she could have sat there for hours, letting his fingers pry around to see if her nose was broken. Abruptly she opened her eyes. His face was so close she could see the close-shaved stubble on his chin and the fine hairs in his nostrils and the delicate webbing of lines at the corners of his eyes. For a moment she studied all this, and then she became aware that his eyes were fastened on hers, were studying her as intently as she studied him. Confused, she closed her eyes again, but now she felt her heart pounding in her chest.

"Nothing broken," he pronounced soberly. "The blow was too high." He showed Mike. "Right between the eyebrows. A quarter of an inch either way and we would have had a dandy black eye, a quarter of an inch lower and a cracked bridge. You're very lucky, young lady. I doubt if there's even contusion. You'll have a discoloration, but I think that's the extent of injury." He turned to Molly. "Be sure to write up an injury report just in case, however. I can be mistaken. Now let's see the patient who did this."

They went off down the hall, Donovan and Mike and Molly, with Ruth trailing behind. Althea stayed with Kathy.

"You don't know how glad I am," Althea said shakily. "I was so afraid that bitch had broken your nose. When I came in and saw you lying on the floor, I wanted to get hold of her hair and pull it out, roots and all."

"She couldn't help herself," Kathy said in a small voice. She put her head in her hands, not daring to look at Althea. So this was how it was when one knew, without mental compromise and beyond argument, that one had fallen in love. If she looked at Althea, surely Althea would see in her eyes the strange, the fantastic, the unbelievable thing that had happened. I looked at him, I *smelled* him, she thought, and then I *knew*. She wondered when it had happened and why she hadn't become aware of it sooner. Maybe that's why she had been so angry so long; subconsciously she had known and had been fighting it because he was going to belong to Althea. He didn't know it, perhaps, but Althea was counting on it desperately, and she was Althea's friend. She could not now, even knowing what had taken place, change everything around and begin to be Althea's enemy, her rival. Everything was so strange; she would have to get used to herself, a new Kathy, and this awareness, this knowing. And hide it—God, yes, hide it so deeply that no one else would ever know.

They were coming back, Donovan talking paranoia technicalities with Mike, Molly looking benign and placid because the ward was now quiet and controlled and things as they should be, and Ruth following with her efficient, absorbed manner.

Donovan saw her. "Why don't you take the rest of the day off?" he suggested, thinking of shock. "Go to your room and try to sleep. Have you got some nembutals on the ward, Molly?"

He gave her the pills, but although she took them, she knew that she would not be able to sleep.

Soon after Kathy had been hurt Althea began to sense a strange indifference in her friend. She blamed it on Kathy's loneliness and her wanting to go home; she did not attempt to get to the bottom of it. She was too full of her own problems, making herself indispensable to Donovan yet maintaining a casual, just-friends relationship, carefully sidestepping Larry Denning's rank overtures. She liked Larry, but she wanted him to understand clearly that it was hands off as far as he was concerned. All she could do for Kathy was to point out repeatedly that Mike Stewart was a nice guy, and why didn't Kathy see how the wind blew, while Kathy made no response to this, merely seemed indifferent and uninterested.

Then the period on Hydro was finished and they were assigned separate wards for two days. The third day an emergency arose and the office sent them to Surgical Convalescent, so that they were back together again.

Althea said, "We make a good team, Kathy. Wonder how long we'll be on this ward."

Kathy had nothing much to say. She had lost eight pounds and gained circles under her eyes from not sleeping well. Elizabeth Leslie was concerned about her, but Lucretia and Margaret would only take notice when her chart began showing Mrs. Beck's demerit marks.

The two girls came to work in Surgical Convalescent the same day Millie and Ruth did, but they no longer did general hospital duty; they were specials with certain defined tasks. From this ward they would go to their last placements before graduation. It was the end of June, and in September they would receive their stripes and pins. They did not care whether Charlotte Range was a gossip, a liar and a troublemaker, because she was not supposed to be able to do anything to them or for them. Althea had been placed as special on the case of a woman named Sarah Smith, and Kathy had been given charge of the minor surgery and the little drugroom. But Althea's main concern was still Donovan. In the evenings, as they worked together, Althea and Donovan called each other by their first names. To Althea it was almost a declaration; it held possibilities beyond imagination. She dragged out the typing, fearful that the book would be finished before anything really significant took place. She was sure that Donovan felt something beyond appreciation and mere liking; he was innocent, in spite of his age and all his theoretical knowledge, and probably did not realize how he felt. She would have to make him seduce her, she thought.

But it was slow work. She took to wearing perfume and heels and once a black dress that had cost her forty dollars —not much for a seductive black, but a lot for the town outside Canterbury. He paid no more attention than when she wore a tweedy skirt and loose sweater. She might have become discouraged, but the next night he took her out to dinner, saying something about how little he was paying her and a hard-working girl deserved a dinner out occasionally. They went to a brightly lighted dining room in the YWCA building, where no one could be seductive and not even wine was served, let alone anything stronger. She did not let it bother her. After all, he did not know she was determined to have him. The idea must seem his. Intuition told her this, and she had great faith in her intuition. She could afford to wait, since she intended to be with him the rest of her life.

Faithfully she told everything to Kathy. Kathy had been

in on it from the beginning and she was entitled to know everything that took place. If Kathy painfully endured these confidences, she was doggedly determined that Althea would never know it to be a matter for endurance. She prayed wildly every night that for some reason, any reason, she would be taken off Surgical Convalescent, but she had no valid excuse and knew she would never dare go to Mrs. Beck without one. Mrs. Beck was too shrewd, too sharp, too much like a ferret. She would have no trouble smelling out the truth—a silly girl falling in love with a man who hardly knew she existed and who was already tagged by another girl. What a field day Mrs. Beck would have with something like that! Love! she would snort. What do you girls know about love? You just want to go to bed with some man. That isn't love!

And she would be right, of course. But it isn't that we just want to go to bed with him, Kathy thought. We want to iron his shirts and clean his kitchen and polish his shoes. And have kids, Mrs. Beck. Is that abnormal? We want to have kids and get them by sleeping with him in a nice, clean bed with white sheets and the covers out of the way. Is that so wrong?

I want to budget his money, Kathy thought, ready to cry because she hurt so inside. And serve coffee and cake when his colleagues come to talk about important things like new medications and research. I'd be so proud, so happy, because he's fine and good and decent. Then she would shake her head, plunged into desperation.

God, she prayed, don't let it show how I feel. Don't let it show . . .

CHAPTER 12

IN THE SMALL reception room with its square, oak table, three hard oak chairs and frayed rug, Jim Blayton sat in one chair, Mary Elsie in another, and the third was occupied by Ruth with a magazine in her lap and a bored expression on her face.

"How are you, honey?" Jim asked Mary Elsie.

"I told you," she replied politely. "I'm just fine."

"Oh, sure—I did ask that. About six times already, I guess." His laugh was embarrassed and his eyes kept straying back and forth between Mary Elsie and Ruth.

Mary Elsie looked very well. She had a becoming new hair-do, short with little curls wisping around her face. She wore the new dress he had brought, a pink organdy with black bows all the way around the hem of the skirt. Dressed as she was, she seemed about twelve instead of her actual age.

"I see you got your hair cut," he said lamely.

"You told me that, too," she murmured, touching her hair with one finger.

"Did I? Sure, sure."

A silence fell. Ruth turned a page with a sharp crackle and Jim looked at her, his face uncertain. "Lady," he said, swallowing audibly, "how's Mary Elsie been? I mean, she's lots better, ain't she?"

Ruth looked up, shrugging indifferently. "You wanta know anything, you'll hafta ask the doctor. I can't say a thing."

"Sure, sure, I remember now. I just forgot." He shuffled his feet.

Mary Elsie said thoughtfully, "Her name is Ruth. You can call her that if you like. Can't he, Ruth?"

"Sure, might as well," said Ruth, going back to her magazine.

The silence returned. Jim glanced at his watch and began to sweat. "You—they feed you good, Mary Elsie?"

"I told you," Mary Elsie said a little sharply. Didn't he remember anything they talked about? "It's wonderful. The food's just wonderful. Isn't it, Ruth?"

Ruth grunted but kept her eyes on her story.

"You sleeping good, honey? You—you got a good bed?"

"Oh, Jim, I told you. I've got my own room even. My very own room. My bed's got a green spread."

"That's good." Jim swallowed. "The—the girls sent their love. Said they're waiting for you to come home so they can play some more bridge."

Mary Elsie smiled. "Oh, Betty and Junie and Laura, huh? They're my friends, Ruth. We got a little foursome to play bridge once a week and have some refreshments. You know, pop and little sandwiches cut like hearts and spades and clubs and diamonds."

Warmth touched Jim's face. "They sure like Mary Elsie," he told Ruth, but looked at his wife. "They came over twice and cleaned up the house, Mary Elsie. Did a real nice job and wouldn't take a cent. Said you'd do the same for them if they ever needed it."

Mary Elsie's eyes become slightly cloudy. "Are you watering the violets, Jim? They're all right, aren't they?"

"Every three days just like you did—do. The pink one's got a lotta new flowers on it."

Her eyes cleared. "You look in the spoon drawer in the kitchen and you'll find some little tablets. Mash one of those in a cup of water and put a few drops in each pot. That'll feed them. You won't forget?"

"Of course I won't," he assured her earnestly. "Anyway,

86

you'll be coming home one of these days. You're lots better. I can tell."

The blue eyes regarded him roundly. "Sure, only I kinda like it here. But I like it there, too—with the girls and all."

Jim stared at her. "Say, you know that chair you wanted me to fix? Well, I did. I sanded it and repainted it. You know, that pretty pink color you like. It's just the same color as the ruffled bedspread you made. Sure is pretty. I put it in your bedroom right by the window."

There was another silence, a long one. Suddenly Jim said loudly, his voice ragged, "For God's sake, lady, can't I see my wife alone for five minutes?"

Astonished, Ruth looked up. She gazed at him fixedly for several seconds. "You oughta know we're not supposed to leave Hydro patients alone with visitors, Mr. Blayton. Didn't they tell you that in the office?"

"What's the matter? You think I'm gonna sneak her out that window?" Jim pointed to the one window. It held panes of glass impregnated with heavy steel mesh.

But Ruth held her gaze and finally he looked away. "Yeah," he said sheepishly. "They told me in the office. Only I thought—well, just five minutes couldn't do any harm, could it? It's kinda hard for me to kiss my wife in front of strangers, la—Ruth—but I'd sure like to. Kiss her, I mean. This is the first time they've let me visit her, you know."

He wanted so much to take Mary Elsie in his arms. But not as if they were on a stage with an audience to see how he did it.

"You—you married?" he asked, his eyes coming up.

Ruth looked at him another second, then she shrugged. "Oh, shoot, I hadda go to the john anyway." She stood up and dropped her magazine into the chair. At the door she looked back. "Don't let her go outa this room, Mr. Blayton. I'll be back in a few minutes."

The instant the door closed, he was across the room and down on his knees in front of Mary Elsie. "Honey," he said excitedly, slipping his arms around her waist, "I couldn't talk about it in front of that woman, but something wonderful has happened!"

She gazed at him thoughtfully, rubbed her mouth against her shoulder and let her hands rest passively on his arms.

"Mary Elsie, I've been to another doctor. He's a new one in town and some of the fellows in the mill got to telling me about him. And guess what? He says he thinks he can help us. You hear, Mary Elsie? He thinks he can fix me!"

"Fix you how, Jim?" she asked politely.

"Fix me, Mary Elsie, *fix me!* I gotta draw you a picture? This doc says I would have been all right if I coulda had more treatments at first. He says it's been more nerves than anything else. I was scared, see, and I been scared ever since. Just plain scared. Had everything scared right outa me. Then, with you getting sick and me knowing I was to blame, that really finished things. See what I mean?"

The blue eyes stared at him coldly, but he was too excited to notice. "The VD's gone, so we never have to worry about that again, and now if this doc can really fix me, why, don't you see, everything'll be like it was before, like right after we was married. In time, all of this—" he waved at the room—"will be like a bad dream. We'll forget it as fast as we can, won't we, honey?"

"Fix you how?" she said patiently as to a child.

"Well, he's giving me some hormone stuff. It's got a real fancy name, only I can't pronounce it. Shots, Mary Elsie. I go twice a week to get 'em at his office. Then I have to take some pills—anti-sterility vitamins, he calls 'em. Real expensive. When I get my shots, he makes me lay on a table under some kinda lamp for a while. He talks to me, too. I told him everything, honey. How it all happened—everything. About you, too. He's real nice. He says when you get ready to come home, I'll be a new man. Won't it be wonderful? Just think, you and me again. I can hardly breathe, thinking about it. God!"

His arms tightened around her waist. He pressed his face for a moment between her breasts, then lifted it. "Kiss me, honey," he said urgently. "Like you used to. When it was so good, you and me. You don't know how I've suffered. I've really suffered, Mary Elsie. Every day while you've been here I've died. Darling, put your arms around me and kiss me like you used to when we were so happy, like back there before all the trouble started. Kiss me—"

He pulled her closer, working himself between her knees, bringing her head down with his hands until his mouth was fastened over hers.

For a moment she endured him, then she twisted, pulling her knees up until she could plant her feet in his stomach. With a violent shove she sent him rolling. When he regained his equilibrium and turned his astonished face toward her, she had reached the protection of the chair back, standing, her eyes glaring.

"Sonofabitch!" she shrieked. "Keep away from me, you hear?"

He staggered to his feet, aghast. "Mary Elsie! Honey—"

"Keep away from me! You want to do it to me! Keep away!" Her voice was filled with hate.

"God's sake, don't talk that way. God's sake, Mary Elsie, I wasn't going to do anything. You mean *here*? Are you outa your mind? Oh, I didn't mean that. I didn't mean to say that —but honest to God, I wasn't even thinking such a thing! Mary Elsie, don't!" He held out his hands, his consternation making him clumsy.

She laughed wildly. "Honest to God I wasn't!" she mimicked. "Honest to God, you never think of anything else. Well, let me tell you something. I don't want you. I got something better. I don't want you, hear? Screw, screw—that's all you ever want! You want to get my clothes off as fast as you can. All right, I'll show you. I'll just take 'em off. Right this minute."

Her hands tore and ripped wantonly at the new dress. "Mary Elsie—stop that!" He came after her around the chair.

She screamed and darted the other way, her hands working without letup on her clothes. He made a lunge to catch her, but she outguessed him, coming back with a fresh scream. Soon it was a game, ripped garments dropping with each maneuver until she was naked, and still he had not caught her.

He stopped, his breath tortured in his lungs, his eyes looking at her body with bitter hunger. "My God, Mary Elsie, I'm your husband," he sobbed. "Doesn't that mean anything?"

Abruptly the door opened and Ruth stood there, taking in the tableau. "Well," she said flatly. "I see it happened. I was afraid it would. You ought to be ashamed of yourself, Mr. Blayton."

Dumfounded, he started to explain, but Mary Elsie placed her hands under her firm breasts and shook them at him, screaming, "He hurt me! He hurt me!" She began to cry, still shaking her breasts, and ran over to one of the chairs to straddle an armrest, where she worked herself back and forth slowly, the tears streaming down her small face.

"My God, you get outa here," Ruth said harshly, grabbing up a garment. "I can take care of this."

He was unable to move. He stood rooted while Ruth pinned Mary Elsie's arms behind her back by wrapping the garment around her swiftly and literally dragged her loose from the chair. Ruth was easily twice as large as Mary Elsie, yet for a few moments she had her hands full. She got Mary Elsie to the door and stopped long enough to say, "I got to get her back on the ward, then I'll come back and let you out. You sure messed up my day, Mr. Blayton!"

When she returned he had gathered up the torn clothes and straightened the chair. His face was numb, stricken. She took the pile of clothes.

"You sure oughtn't to of done it," she said, staring at him curiously. "I hadda tell the charge what happened on account of she'll go on like that now until we can get her into pack." Ruth tipped her head. "Hear that? It's your wife screaming. She'll keep that up until we do something. Once she gets started, she does it all the time."

"Let me out of here," he said hoarsely. "Goddam you— let me out!"

"Sure, sure. No call to get sore. It wasn't my fault, mister. I didn't set her off. In her condition, you oughta know better."

"I didn't do anything, goddam it. Let me out of here!"

"Okay, okay. Be sure to turn in your slip at the gate."

Jim Blayton drove home afterward like a crazy man. He went through red lights and stop signs without stopping and never braked once, even in traffic. He did not want to go back to his empty house, but he could think of nothing else to do. He couldn't sleep unless he was exhausted, and he hadn't been hungry since the day Mary Elsie left. He had done little jobs to keep himself occupied. The yard had never looked better. He had repainted the picket fence, replanted several spots in the lawn where he fancied he spotted crab grass getting a start, and trimmed and sprayed the two peach trees in the back yard. As he had told Mary Elsie, the girls had come over to clean up inside and had done a swell job, even washing windows and shaking out the draperies, but he could hardly wait until they were gone and the house was empty and quiet again. If he couldn't have Mary Elsie in it, he wanted it that way, empty and quiet.

He reached his house, left the car parked in the driveway and went down to the basement to lift the shotgun off the ledge. He had found the gun down there shortly after buying the house, supposing that some previous owner's kid had stolen it, perhaps, and hidden it up on the ledge until the time he could palm it off as his own. He did not know whether it could shoot or not and he had left it there, having no place upstairs to keep it, and seeing no reason to remove it from its hiding place.

Now he felt there might be a reason. He carried the gun up to the kitchen and placed it on the table. Stolidly he examined it. He would have to buy shells before he could really tell what it would do. He set about cleaning it with rags and some distillate he kept in a glass jar for the anthills around the ash pit. When he finished, he took the gun into the living room and stood it beside the television set, then sat down in the big chair and studied it. How did they go about using guns like this? he wondered. He could see it might be managed by placing the muzzle against his stomach and triggering it with a toe, but it would be clumsy and messy as hell. Maybe he could rig up something in the bathroom so that he could sit in the bathtub, close his eyes and pull on a string or wire. Then it could be aimed at his head. That would be quicker than shooting his guts out. Not that he was afraid; either way he had nothing to lose. He decided to get some shells and see what the gun could do.

By the end of the week he had found out that the gun would shoot very well. He kept it upstairs from then on, underneath the bed.

CHAPTER 13

MIKE STEPPED OFF the graveled path—the sound his shoes made on it irritated him—and walked across the grass. It was dusk, but there was no relief yet from the day's heat; he was sweating under his thin shirt. He felt angry and frustrated. He was in love with Kathy Hunter and didn't know how to tell her so—he of all people, the tough journalist who was never, or very seldom, at a loss for a word! He had never felt so voiceless, so incapable.

He felt he had so little to offer her—some money in the bank and a salt-box house in Maine which had once tempted him and so he had bought it before he could change his mind. The house stood empty; he hadn't seen it for a couple of years. It probably looked like hell now with no care. He couldn't really imagine any girl wanting to cope with frozen plumbing in a salt-box house in Maine.

Still, when he sat in his room looking out the window, he could think of nothing but Kathy, her face and her body, and the way he wanted to marry her, not just go to bed with her. But how to let her know?

His feet reached a break in the slope, a level stretch of shrubbery and trees and benches, and he stopped and turned to stare down at the buildings. Lights were on, hundreds of them, winking in the half gloom like yellow eyes.

He had seen and heard a lot in those buildings. He had seen coercion and subterfuge and marble-hard authority. He knew that some of the doctors were aged or alcoholic or both and that many of the supervisors were callous and indifferent. He also knew that there were doctors and nurses and attendants who were dedicated. He would never forget what he had learned. His sympathies lay first with the patients, then with the attendants who worked around the clock as custodians, teachers, nurses and father confessors. He assumed that they assimilated their training by observation, by pure blunder born of desperation. They gossiped furiously, he knew; belonged to cliques; probably experienced many moments of troubled regret over mistreatment of the patients; and he had seen how acutely uneasy they became when they were called in before Lucretia for any reason whatsoever. But they were Canterbury, as much so as the buildings, and unwittingly they had created the despotism of the supervisors by placing them collectively on the pedestal of job advantage and superior schooling.

He was glad he didn't have to describe Lucretia to the public. What a picture that would be! She was tall and angular and wore shapeless uniforms, clean but with no style. Her dull hair was pulled tightly back, making her face all sharp planes and angles. Only a terrible vanity would let a woman be so careless with her appearance. Her voice was always loud and harsh. He was sure he had never before heard a woman's voice so extraordinarily unpleasant. But then Lucretia was not a woman; she was authority personified and she wanted the world to know it, to know she held a position of great importance and responsibility. The thing that impressed him most of all was the way she managed the hospital's nursing service. She was a dictator, shrewd and waspish and arrogant. She could reduce anyone to a zero with ridicule and withering criticism. She could even disregard her own regulations without batting an eyelid, should they prove embarrassing or inconvenient. He tried to tell himself that she could be forgiven a lot because she was accountable for the work activity and behavior problems of a large group of employees, that she was responsible for the general welfare of a vast multitude of mentally ill and senile people, that she shouldered a tremendous and complex burden. Why, though, he asked himself, did she have to be so damned mean about it, so tart and shrewish?

But, at that, he liked her better than he liked Margaret, with her rubber soles and starched skirts. He wondered if any man had ever taken *her* to bed, but then shook his head. She would be too efficient, and efficiency did not exactly encourage male urges toward copulation. She was efficient and obsequious. It was obvious that she hated Lucretia, but hid her feelings behind a front of fawning animation. Lucretia had placed her in charge of the training program for the aides, and her first lecture always dwelt on certain patterns of behavior; before she was finished, every new class realized that she viewed masturbation as the cause of man's original downfall, after which they all became quite self-conscious about doodling on their notepads or crossing their legs. She always managed, too, to make them feel substandard, to impress upon them that they must work diligently to achieve the fine edge of rapport *she* had toward the patients and others. Mike watched her working hard to make everyone believe that she was warm and sincere and chiefly concerned with the welfare of Canterbury patients, but he believed that it was Lucretia's throne that really interested her.

People have faults, Mike told himself. They are products of certain environments and conditions and times and are born with shortcomings or equipped with values acceptable only to themselves. Lucretia, Margaret, Walter Sturgis, others—why should he judge and condemn them because they saw the system only in relation to themselves? Who was he to judge anyone? What had he accomplished in thirty-one years? How had he made the world better even in one fraction of a way?

Still, he would have a lot to forget. Keys, for instance, and the locked doors that went with them. Bits of steel or brass, scepters in miniature, rods of control, authority and dominion. Kings over a kingdom of derelicts and alcoholics, over schizophrenics and psychotics, over epileptics and morons. God, what a kingdom!

Locked doors, flushing toilets, hard oak chairs, Mike thought. The sitting and waiting, the selfishness, bigotry, intolerance and ambition. Was all this the inheritance of the children of men? He moved uneasily. Maybe he was making too much of everything, making a simple situation complex; maybe he did not actually know what it took to take care properly of insane people, would only know if he could divide himself into many parts, each to spend a lifetime working on different wards and finally, after many, many years, pool the information gained this way into a comprehensive whole. Even then he might not know enough.

It's because I'm lonely, he almost said aloud. I've found a girl and fallen in love with her, and she hardly knows I exist.

A sound penetrated his consciousness, coming from somewhere nearby. Frowning, he glanced around, his senses sharpened by a stillness that held only a light whisper of wind and several muted bird sleep calls. The sound had been human, he was sure. A patient? They were supposed to be back on their wards by suppertime, those who had ground paroles. Still, he could have sworn he had heard someone weeping.

Softly, he moved between the low bushes and around the tall ones, his eyes searching the shadows that were growing denser by the moment. He had almost decided he was mistaken when he saw the bench with the girl sitting on it. She heard him as he moved close and her crying stopped with a startled gasp. Then he recognized Kathy. There was a hesitation between them, a moment of adjustment Kathy's shoulders straightened, a little angrily because she had been caught crying. He sat down on the end of the bench. But he was still silent, and after a moment or so Kathy stirred uneasily.

"I guess any girl has a right to cry," she said, her voice a little defensive because his silence was making her talk. "Crying is natural for girls. They have to cry sometimes. But maybe you don't know about that. Maybe you think girls are just emotional and silly. What if they are?" She waited a second and asked it again. "Well? What if they are?"

Don't speak to me, she was thinking. Just sit there and don't talk. Who cares?

But he said something finally, very carefully, as though he had to feel it out, to edge up to what he wanted to say.

"Anyone has a right to cry—or not to cry. Even a man has that right. Maybe men would be better off if they cried more. It's not shameful to cry. It's only shameful to be ashamed of doing it."

They were both silent for a moment, she thinking about what he had said and he realizing that he had finally climbed over the barrier, that he was at least able to talk. He turned a little and put one arm up on the top bar of the bench. It brought his hand within inches of her shoulder. If he moved again he could touch her with his fingers. But it wouldn't be skin, soft, tender skin; it would be the material of her crisp uniform. He sat still, willing himself to make no move; she might be frightened and get up and leave.

"Do you smoke?" he asked.

"Sometimes."

"What were you crying about?" he asked abruptly, his voice rough because he wanted her so badly.

None of your business, snoop! she thought, then was a little ashamed. He probably thought he could help her by being sympathetic and asking questions. At that, maybe he could. He wasn't going to be around Canterbury much longer, so if she told him anything, whatever she said probably wouldn't go any farther than the bench they were sharing. On the other hand, what could she say? "I love a man but another girl saw him first"? Or "There are two girls who want to go to bed with the same man. What's the proper course of procedure—fight or run?"

Her breath caught in a little shudder and she began hunting for a tissue. She would blow her nose quickly, before he could offer her a clean white handkerchief. Men always have clean white handkerchiefs to offer weeping girls. But he let her use her tissue and made no move to give her his handkerchief. Perhaps he doesn't care whether I have a runny nose, Kathy thought, with another little catch. I'm just a hysterical female with imaginary troubles, neurotic, unstable, and he doesn't like me. But why should I care? I hardly know him. We don't know each other. Why doesn't he go away and leave me alone!

"What are you crying about?"

"If you must know, a man," she said bitterly.

Angrily she began to tell him the whole story, clinging to his presence, desperate for someone to listen to her own jealousy and misery. At first she spoke slowly and hesitantly, with embarrassment; then the words began to pour out by themselves, in a stream of emotion and intensity. Appalled at herself, she stopped, and they sat for a few moments in silence.

"I'm sorry," she said. "I shouldn't have told you any of this. You couldn't possibly understand. Go away, please go away."

She began to feel that she was making a fool of herself and it brought back the compulsion to talk, to get something out of her system.

"No, don't go away. I'm sorry, I can't stop being rude. It's because of the way I feel. I can't understand why it had to happen. You know, I didn't like him at first—I couldn't *stand* him. I thought he was no good, that he would hurt my friend—oh, I thought all kinds of bad things about him. Then that day on Hydro—you were there, remember? I don't know. I just looked at him—" Her voice hurried along nervously as she tried to explain something that she felt was extraordinary and undesirable but which she could not help, this falling in love with Donovan Macleod.

I was there, Mike thought. I saw it happen and didn't know it.

Kathy took a deep breath and inched toward Mike. She put a hand on his arm. "Crying's no good. That's what you've been thinking, isn't it? I know that, too. But what can I do? What should I do? Go away?" The face he could barely see was anxious, pleading with him not to give the wrong answers, to help.

"It's infatuation," he whispered from the pit of his pain, feeling her touch on his arm.

She drew back. "Oh, no," she said steadily, keeping her hand on him, waiting. "It's not infatuation. Why do you say that? You don't know how I feel."

"I suppose not," said Mike.

"So what would you do if you were me?"

"What would anyone do?" he said harshly.

95

She stared at him. "Why, fight, I guess," she said uncertainly.

"It's up to you," he said. Then, without saying goodbye, he got up and stomped angrily down the path away from her.

Was she going to do what Mike had suggested and not hesitate or falter? She did not realize that he had really suggested nothing, that her own mind had given birth to the idea.

CHAPTER 14

"WELL," LARRY DENNING SAID HAPPILY as he caught up with Althea. She was heading for Surgical Convalescent, hurrying as usual. "I hoped this would happen if I hung around long enough."

She looked up and smiled.

"Working hard?" he asked her.

"I'm still on Surgical Convalescent. I'll be there until Donovan assigns someone else to the Sarah Smith case. She's my patient, you know. Then I'll get an up ward and after that my ward management."

"And then you'll graduate and the whole thing will be over. Are you staying on?"

"Of course I am. I wouldn't think of leaving Canterbury." Leave Donovan? she was thinking, hoping her face did not show her thoughts.

He looked around. "Wonderful morning, isn't it? I wish we didn't have to go to work. How about it? Let's play hooky. I know a spot about twenty miles out of town. There are woods, and the creek makes a swimming pool. You'd like it, I think. We can stop at the cafeteria and pick up some sandwiches and some beer and have ourselves a ball. How about that?"

"Oh, Larry," she said, smiling. "And how many demerits would I get if I did that? It sounds wonderful, frankly—I would love it. But my patient is critical and I couldn't possibly take the day off."

"Now, look. There are a dozen affiliates I can name who know what to do for critical patients."

"But this one is special, part of my training. She's had digitalis poisoning and she has to be watched all the time. She's on the edge, you know. We think she's going to make it, and I certainly wouldn't want anything to happen now. One little slip . . ." She still smiled but she shook her head.

"You're a fine girl, Althea." He bent toward her as they walked along. "I want to tell you something that may surprise you." She looked up at him questioningly. "I want to marry you," he said softly. "I want to very much."

She was so startled she stopped walking and stood still. "Larry!" she said.

"I mean it. I've thought about it since I first saw you. It's very simple. I'm in love with you."

She put one hand up and pushed at the heavy, pale hair. "But—to say it so suddenly, just like that . . ." She took a deep breath.

"I've shocked you," he said contritely. "I'm sorry, I didn't mean to. No, that's not true. I did mean to. When a girl thinks she's in love with one man, it may take something drastic to make her realize that there's another man around. I meant to be drastic, Althea. There's not much time."

"Oh," she said faintly. "You—know?"

"Everybody does but Donovan," he said. "Your heart's out in plain view. He'd see it himself if he weren't so selfish and absorbed in himself and his work."

"You're wrong about that," she said quickly. "He's not selfish, not at all. I haven't expected him to fall in love with me right away."

"But you're working on it," he finished for her. "That's what I mean. That's what shows. Well, I'm doing the same thing. As I said, there isn't much time."

"What do you mean, not much time?"

"When you graduate, when you're ready to take your exams and perhaps leave the hospital, he's going to wake up, isn't he? He's going to have to decide whether to let you go or keep you. If the book's finished, it won't be that. It will be because he wants to keep you. So I'm getting my bid in now. You don't know me very well, really, but you'll discover I can be a pretty steady fellow. If you would tear yourself away a few times from your absorbing afterhours occupation with Donovan and go out with me instead, I think you'd find me interesting, too. I think we could have a very nice time together."

She shook her head. This was happening too fast; it hadn't begun to make sense to her, yet. According to Larry, everyone realized what she was trying to achieve with Donovan, and she was somewhat upset about that, but, to her surprise, she was rather pleased at Larry's declaration of love. It was always pleasant to know that a man was really interested in you, even if you were completely absorbed in another man. It was like buying a dress or a fur coat, something that flattered your figure and made you look special but which you did not really need; it made you feel luxurious and a little sinful. Maybe you'd take the coat or the dress back to the store the next day and get your money back, but you'd still feel that special, cat-purring way."

"I'm sure we'd have a nice time, Larry, but you'd feel cheated." And she added frankly, "Yes, I'm in love with Donovan. I've been in love with him for a long time. So you see we would just be two people working at cross-purposes and one or both of us would get hurt. A thing like that wouldn't make sense, would it?"

"It might make sense if you'd try it. People change, you know. Aren't you getting a little tired of not getting anywhere with Donovan? If I were a girl—God forbid!—and a girl with looks like yours, I wouldn't just sit back and wait."

I'd have too much pride, his tone implied, but she was not offended. "So? Well, what are you doing?" she asked.

"All right," he said a little wryly. "I deserved that. But I'm not sitting back any more, I warn you. I'm coming after you, and I won't admit that I'm beaten until you and Donovan are married."

Her shoulders lifted. She considered him for a moment as if she were puzzled about something in him she had not noticed before. "You really mean all this, don't you?"

"That I love you and want you to marry me?" His tongue touched his upper lip. "My God, you're not going to question it, are you?"

"No, I meant . . ." But she did not say what she had meant. She turned and started again for Surgical Convalescent and he fell into step beside her.

He looked at her, and then looked straight ahead. "What are you going to do, Althea, if you find out that Donovan doesn't intend getting interested in girls and marriage?" he asked as though the question had just occurred to him.

She was not surprised, having asked herself that question many times, always with a little dread. She did not know what she would do if after all this time Donovan was not interested in her and showed that he never would be. But she had no intention of letting anyone know that she was aware she might fail, that in the end nothing might come of her intense love and devotion. She made her shrug and her voice as casual as she could.

"He'll be interested," she said. "As you mentioned, I've been working on it." Then, as Larry stiffened, she realized that she had been cruel. "Just the way you are now," she added. She was glad they had almost reached her ward. The excitement and lift of Larry's proposal were fading and she was beginning to feel harassed and threatened. She realized that she had a slight headache and wondered, as she had a number of times during the summer heat, how she would look with her hair cut. She would certainly be cooler.

Now she was anxious to get away from Larry. She turned and put out her hand in a friendly way.

"Be a good boy and forget about me," she said, smiling for him. "Think of all the other girls who work out here. My friend Kathy, for instance. Have you noticed her? Or Barbara Larkin or Flo Cassidy or Lenore Hathaway?" She rattled off names, looking at him intently.

He waited until she ran down, then shook his head. He hadn't taken her hand, but it was because he couldn't trust himself to touch her, merely touch her, hand against hand like that. But he smiled back.

"Thanks, but it happens that I don't want Barbara and Flo and Lenore and Kathy."

"You could try," Althea said. "I'm just a girl, too. You might feel the same way about me if—"

"No," he said firmly. "No. Never. I love you. That's altogether different."

"But . . ." She wanted to say, You've been as promiscuous as hell. How do you really know? Only it would just keep the conversation going. She had better leave well enough alone. After all, none of this would mean a thing by tomorrow or the next day.

She started to take out her keys, but he was ahead of her, unlocking the ward door and holding it open for her. She felt the throb of her headache at the back of her neck and blinked as she made her way into the coolness of the ward. It felt a little strange just to go in and leave him standing on the step after all that had been said—and not said. She hesitated, turned to look up at him. How pale he was!

"I'm not going to kiss you," he said. "I'm not going to try. But someday I am going to marry you. Remember that when you're with Macleod, Althea. I don't care what you do, what either of you do. Someday you're going to be my wife."

He turned then and walked away, as casually as though he had been discussing the weather.

"Well!" she said, staring after him. Then she closed the door and locked it and stood inside for a moment. "How do you like that?" But it was not exactly a question; it was nothing that could be answered.

Presently she moved down the hall toward the ward station, ready to sign in and relieve the night special on Sarah Smith's case and begin her routine for the day. But she was a little absent-minded, even in speaking to Kathy and making the proper remarks to Charlotte and the others.

He had sounded so determined, she thought irrationally. She was a little shocked to think that she might have fallen in love with Larry if she had known him before she met

99

Donovan. She picked up her charts without really seeing them and went down to Sarah Smith's room.

Outside, Larry walked toward the male unit he was supposed to check. He did not believe that Donovan could ever really love a woman. He would go to bed with one, perhaps, and even get married, but it would not be a matter of the heart. He felt that he had been around Donovan long enough to know what he was like.

Suddenly he wanted to lash out physically at Donovan for letting Althea work so hard. Didn't the fool realize she was not made of iron, that she couldn't go on indefinitely like that?

"No," he said softly, savagely. Of course Donovan wasn't aware of her full-time job, the evening job, all her studies. He was only interested in his work and the books he wrote and the research that went into the books. He studied his patients, but he did not even look at the other people around him. If Donovan hurt him, if Donovan ever hurt her . . . He was surprised how vicious he could feel.

As he neared the ward, he met Walter Sturgis coming out of the office building, and he lifted a hand in salute. "Hot, isn't it?" said Walter, stopping to mop his face.

"That time of the year," Larry agreed. He found his cigarettes. "Smoke?"

"Thanks, I just threw one away. Say, what do you think of Stewart?"

"Can't say. I don't know him very well." Larry lit his cigarette and prepared to move on. Walter was always a little jumpy, nervous, always wanting an opinion from someone.

"Fine writer, fine," Walter said. "But no rapport, none whatsoever. And snoopy. I think he deliberately looks for trouble. A pattern there, I suppose. Aggression, perhaps, or transference."

He enjoyed using technical terms. He had been at Canterbury so long he was convinced he knew as much or more than many of the doctors.

Larry smiled a little. "You may be right," he said, then changed the subject with "Where are you heading?"

"Oh, that Lucretia—God, I wish she'd drop dead or something. No," he added hurriedly, "no, I didn't mean that. It's just that there's simply no pleasing her!" He sounded aggrieved and mopped his face again. "It's the new building, Rehabilitation. None of the elevator keys work right. As if I made them. Know what I mean? I've got to run all over the grounds looking for an electrician who knows something about elevator keys. It wouldn't hurt those patients to use the fire escapes once or twice, would it?"

"Six floors?"

"Hell, it might take some of the fight out of them. That's all they think about in that building. Set up like a deluxe hotel and what have you got? A bunch of women squabbling all day and all night."

And you want another and another, Larry thought, not fooled. You want people to say Canterbury was made important by its building program during the time Walter Sturgis was business manager.

"Well, I hope you find your electrician," he said, turning away. "What happened to the regular man?"

"On vacation, wouldn't you know?" He went off at a trot, mopping his face a third time, and Larry threw away his cigarette and went on, his thoughts going back to Althea.

Dreamily, in the few minutes he had left before he reached his ward, he closed his mind to everything but the way she looked and walked, and the sound of her voice. It made him feel as if he were soaring into the sky. A mental aphrodisiac, he thought, his imagination. But with one girl only. One.

In her office, Lucretia Terry sat staring at her desk. She was seldom idle, but she was shaking a little and she did not want it noticed, especially by Margaret. She was shaking because she had seen Walter Sturgis place his hand on Margaret's hip just before leaving on his errand, a small action but done covertly, and that was significant. It had been a year now since Walter had last talked about marrying her. She knew the score; it didn't take a year to learn that. She could have him fired, of course. She could even do it in such a way that he'd never get another job in state civil service. But everyone would know why she had done it and she'd have that to face in addition to losing him to another woman. Maybe it would be simpler and easier to fix Margaret's little red wagon. After all she had done for Margaret, after all she had done for both of them . . . She could not bear to look at Margaret. It was like having someone you trusted slash you across the back with a knife. You were too hurt to move, to stop shaking. In a moment, she thought, she might be able to manage a cigarette.

The Surgical Convalescent ward, where Millie was sent after Stationary, was almost luxurious. There were tiled floors, glass brick walls, the best quality monkscloth drapes, fluorescent lighting fixtures, tubbed plants. Each cubicle held six beds with a stand for each, and there were several private rooms, reserved for patients fresh from surgery. The ward had its own minor surgery and even a small drug room, while the station was special, with walnut and chrome and marble tops and well-padded chairs for the employees. Even the carts were different from those on other wards—stainless steel with large, rubber-tire wheels, so easy to manipulate when loaded with stacks of linen, basins of hot water, sacks of soiled bedding or full bedpans.

Millie realized that she should have no complaint. It was considered a privilege to work on Surgical Convalescent after having been broken in on untidy or terminal wards. Still, whenever she looked at Charlotte Range, the ward charge, she thought of her first wards almost with longing.

Charlotte was a heavy woman. Invariably she sat sprawled in her swivel chair with her fat legs apart and her wrinkled skirt barely touching her knees. It was rather peculiar that anyone who looked so untidy could be charge of a ward as nice as this one, Millie thought, noting the deep pockets in Charlotte's uniform, the edges almost black from her dipping constantly in and out for cigarettes and matchbooks or keys. Charlotte was corseted, too, but it was impossible to keep from noticing how her massive breasts hung almost to her belt. Millie did not like to think meanly of anyone, but she almost hated to look at Charlotte. There was something cruel about the little eyes and thin mouth. She was deeply grateful that Ruth was also working on the ward; at least she had someone she could turn to for counsel if the going got too rough.

When not busy with some task, the attendants were supposed to sit in the station behind the barrier of the desk, which was open waist-high to the ceiling but built in a circle with a small, swinging gate as an entry. Millie could scarcely endure this enforced inactivity because she realized that all Charlotte wanted was an audience for her malicious gossip, usually about other employees Millie did not know, or about the doctors and the affiliates. Millie was sure most of it could not possibly be true.

She acts as if the office don't dare fire her, Millie thought. Nobody's that important.

But Charlotte was important. She made out Millie's merit rating with barely enough points to let Millie keep her job, and the office let it pass. It was an unfair rating. She had worked hard and done exactly as she was told. All she had felt and thought about Charlotte she had kept to herself, not even confiding in Ruth, in case it might show on their faces that they had been talking about the charge. So the rating was simply not justified. If the office hadn't questioned it, that showed how much they thought of Charlotte.

No wonder she was so mean, Millie thought indignantly; she knew just where she stood.

On Surgical Convalescent, Kathy watched Althea go down the hall, with her charts under one arm. What was she going to do to take Donovan away from Althea? Or could she do it? She did not compare with Althea in looks, she would have to remember that. And that meant she would have to be very clever, very subtle about what she did. I'm not the same person, she thought unhappily. This is my friend, but it doesn't seem to matter today. Yesterday—I never could have believed yesterday that I would be planning something contemptible today. Then, last night . . .
Yes, last night had done the trick. Last night she had changed, turned over a page, stopped crying and feeling sorry for herself, grown up. Nothing mattered as much as fighting for her love, certainly not the friendship of a girl she scarcely knew. Before I came to Canterbury, I didn't even know her.
I love Donovan, she thought. I want him, I'm going after him. You take care of yourself, Althea. It isn't as though I'm after something that already belongs to you, because he doesn't; he's never said or done a thing to show he belongs to you. You've told me that yourself. But even if you hadn't, I'd still go ahead and try. Because I love him, too.
She took the drug-room charts and went slowly down the hall behind Althea.

Part Two

CHAPTER 15

THE FOURTH OF JULY dawned bright and hot and by nine o'clock the temperature was soaring in Lucretia Terry's office, despite the air conditioning. Lucretia was trying to go over the program for the day. A small municipal band from town would play, badly as usual. There would be games organized by charges and seconds-in-charge for some of the wards, and perhaps a little talent discovered among the patients would be encouraged to perform on the stage erected for the band. Afterward there would be a picnic, complete with soda pop in bottles and the charges working agitatedly to see that things went smoothly, that no fights were started and that all the bottles were accounted for. The hospital always provided some kind of entertainment on holidays for those patients able to enjoy it, but the charges hated holidays, and Lucretia, who had to make all the plans and see that they were carried out, hated them also.

Now Walter was adding to the confusion of the holiday morning with his own stupid, hysterical dithering about something of utter inconsequence. She wished he would hurry up and get out of her office.

"Are you going to the picnic?" she asked, stopping him in mid-sentence.

"Do you think I should?" he asked petulantly. "I'm letting both my clerks off, so I should be in the office part of the time. I get so many interruptions, I'll never catch up with my work."

You're just like a housewife, Lucretia thought, afraid you won't get your ironing finished and your dishes washed and dried and put away.

Of course she could get him to go and mix with the rest of the employees—you couldn't have too much help at these affairs. She could even force him to be her escort, since she intended to go, feeling that this was one duty she could not evade; the patients felt pleased and honored when the superintendent of Canterbury and the director of personnel came to their parties. But why bother? She believed that any emotion he had ever felt for her was now turned to hate. Why make it any worse? Why give him an excuse for more grumbling and another grudge?

From the pinnacle of her job, so much more important to the hospital than his, she looked down at him and despised what she saw, yet she suffered a little every time she caught a glimpse of what was going on between Margaret and him. She would even have taken him back, although she knew that she meant nothing to him any more. He had cared for her as long as he could use her, not one second longer.

All my life, she thought, looking down at her desk, all my life I've wanted to be just an ordinary sort of woman, attractive enough so that someone would love me for myself and not just because I could do him favors.

"Never mind," she said, "we'll get along without you." She paused. "By the way, what do you think of moving Edna Horne to Rehabilitation?"

Walter eyed her warily. Was she leading up to something? Didn't she have any pride?

"I don't think it'll do much for Edna," he said carefully after a moment's hesitation.

He used to be amazed that she could name and describe almost every patient in the institution, and lately her ability frightened and unnerved him. It seemed inhuman, almost devouring. At the moment he did not want to be inveigled into a discussion of Edna Horne because he was sure something unpleasant would come of it, either an unpleasant task for him to perform or an attempt on Lucretia's part to re-establish an intimacy that had long since become repugnant to him. Usually he could predict her efforts in this direction. They had taken on the nature of a war without weapons, a series of little skirmishes that left Lucretia pale and himself sweating.

Evidently she had no ulterior motive this time. "I suppose not, but she's doing well on Thorazine and her cousin is anxious to have her taken off that untidy ward."

The cousin would be Althea Horne, Walter remembered. A beauty, a real beauty!

"Althea graduates next month," Lucretia said, looking at her hands. "I'd like to have her stay on. I'm thinking of letting her take her ward management on Rehabilitation, the day shift, and if she does all right and wants it after graduation, I'm going to let her have it." Her eyes came up. "Then she can handle Edna's therapy personally."

She seemed to be waiting for something, but he nodded cautiously and muttered, "Mmmm—well, you know best."

Whoever was made supervisor of Rehabilitation, the newest building in the institution, would be getting the cream. Surely it was not the place for a young, inexperienced graduate, nor fair to older women who had been much longer with the hospital. And letting a young affiliate take her ward management in such a dangerous building might prove disastrous. But Walter knew better than to let his thoughts show. Lucretia could not bear to be criticized. All he wanted, desperately at the moment, was to get out, to meet Margaret on the other side of the gate, the town side. They had made their plans, convinced the day would be so confusing to everyone that they would never be missed. He waited, hoping breathlessly that he could get away without an argument.

She waited, too, hoping against hope. When she finally was sure nothing more was coming from him, she felt a sharp pain begin in her abdomen; it recurred whenever she though too much about all that had happened in the past year. As usual, she had to wait for it to let up before she could speak again. If only he would say, Lucretia, let's make it up, let's get together again. Or, Lucretia, what happened? Let's talk it over.

The pain left her. She felt the sweat on her face. "Well," she said, breathing a little more deeply, "that's it, then. I won't decide about Althea until later, but I will have Edna moved. I'm sure it will be a good move."

It was almost an ultimatum. He nodded and went out before she could call him back. He was giddy with relief by the time he reached the outside door, while Lucretia sat looking at her hands. Her hands were trembling.

I hate him! she thought. I hate his guts! It had taken him a year to shame her before the whole hospital. He would probably never know what he had managed to accomplish, but she knew it every moment of every day. Someday, she told herself, as God is my judge, someday I'll see he gets what's coming to him!

She had already made a few plans. She was positive he did not really care for Margaret. He was going to use Margaret as he had used her. He knew the way the wind was blowing and he was making his preparations in advance. Well, I know how to take care of that, she thought grimly, her mouth tight. You'll see, Walter, you sonofabitch!

In his own office, Donovan was getting ready to check his

wards. He never went to the institution affairs. He never had in the six years he had been in the institution. He was the chief of staff, not an attendant.

At the moment he was thinking of Madge. He had released her from Hydro and now she was in her cubicle, typing furiously. He knew what that meant. She would waste a ream of paper on something that made no sense, then she would place the mess before him proudly, as if she wanted him to see how complete her recovery was.

It's as if we were brothers, Donovan thought impatiently. An older and a younger brother. I'm the older and I have to approve of what she does. She can love her own sex, but from the male sex she has to have what men give each other—approval and understanding and comradeship. She's jealous of Althea, not because Althea is a woman but because Althea and I are so close to each other as friends.

He could not apply normal standards of conduct to her or put pressure on her in any way. She would simply revert to hysteria again. Unfortunately, he was in no mood to put up with her today. It was going to be hellishly hot and he had other problems to deal with.

What am I going to do about Althea? he wondered. Would she be embarrassed to know that from the very beginning of their association he had realized what she wanted from him? The story was so old to him that he usually never permitted it to go beyond the first stage, the "Look at me, sir, I could be had" phase. He was not abnormal in his feeling toward women; he just did not intend to become involved in any way that would interfere with his work. Someday he might marry; he didn't know. He was cold-blooded and ruthless about his private life. He believed that to take any time off from the demands of his work was selfish.

I've slipped, he thought angrily. I've let this thing go too far. He remembered Althea's approach, her voice saying breathlessly—and how he recognized that breathlessness!— "Dr. Macleod, I'm Althea Horne. May I ask you something?"

He remembered his shock when he had turned and seen her face. It was possibly the most beautiful face he had ever seen at Canterbury. But he had been cold and distant; he hadn't given her any leeway because of her beauty. He had even thought, as he usually did with the affiliates, By God, she'd like to bite me! Then she had said, "Do you know if there might be someone here on the staff who could use the services of a good typist?" She hadn't made a pitch, said could *you* use *me*, and she had added, earnestly and calmly, that she was a good stenographer and needed the money.

She couldn't have picked a better time, because Madge was having one of her hysterical attacks and was in pack on

Hydro, something that occurred regularly every five or six weeks. And the book was waiting; his publishers were writing polite little notes reminding him of his deadline.

So he let Althea come to his rooms and begin laboring with his writing, asking endless questions because it was so difficult to decipher, making coffee for both of them, working so late that he began to feel a faint alarm that the office might say something. She cheerfully accepted the pay he had first insisted upon and refused as cheerfully to accept more when he began to feel guilty about it. If there was one thing he did not like it was to have anyone make him feel guilty about something! So he took her out to dinner several times to make up for it. She wore a slinky dress and perfume and he could hardly keep his hands off her. What in hell is a girl like that doing in the nursing profession? he wondered. She ought to be an actress or a model. He felt betrayed and furious because he was being enmeshed in something that he should never have permitted to start.

Still, he could not do anything about it yet. In three weeks Althea would graduate and in three weeks the book should be finished. It was nearly done now. There were just some minor revisions to make. Soon he would let Althea go.

Or I'll catch myself letting her finish out the night in my bed, he told himself. Not that it didn't sound like a good idea, but she might take it seriously, and it wouldn't be like Larry Denning's numerous affairs. This girl meant business. It was perfectly clear what she wanted and what she intended to get.

Madge's door opened. "Look, Dr. Macleod," she chirped, holding up a stack of typing for his inspection. "I timed myself. Ninety words a minute and not a single mistake." She proudly placed the stack on a corner of his desk.

He had a glimpse of the top page, numerals and letters marching at random across the paper, line after line making no sense. He looked up thoughtfully. If he were very careful, perhaps in a week or so she would really be able to type again; she could put sense into her work.

"That's fine," he said, getting up and hunting for his keys. "Leave it right there and I'll look it over when I get back. Are you going to the picnic?"

She relaxed. He was pleased; he liked what she had done. "Oh, I wouldn't miss it for anything," she said, smiling. "I like the music and I get to see all my friends. Thanksgiving and Christmas we have our parties on the wards, but Fourth of July is always out on the lawn, just like in town or anywhere. Everybody'll be there."

"I won't be there," he said, smiling back pleasantly. "I'm checking wards as soon as I can get started." He did not explain that he was getting a late start because he had been up part of the night on Surgical Convalescent with a critical patient there. Often he explained things to Madge because his attention always pleased and flattered her, but this time he wanted to get away from her as quickly as possible; her look of humility and her desire to please sickened him. "I'll be seeing you," he said, waving his hand at her and going out.

Away from the building he sighed with relief, then his frown returned, and his irritability. Which was less trouble, a girl who stirred every sexual impulse in him or one who nauseated him when he looked at her? Perhaps the best solution would be to call in a typist from the main office and ease Althea politely out and let Madge throw her tantrum. The idea was worth considering. He found his keys and started across the lawn toward a nearby building.

CHAPTER 16

ALTHEA AND KATHY signed their names in the ward record book and talked idly for a few moments. There was a sensation of coolness from the air conditioning when they first came in, but they knew it would be temporary. Soon they would begin to sweat and feel sticky again.

Sitting all spread out as usual in her chair, her fat legs far apart, Charlotte Range stared at them. "You girls going to the picnic?" she wanted to know.

"I can't," Althea said quickly. "Sarah was bad again last night. Dr. Macleod called me early this morning and told me to watch her closely all day."

"I can't think of anything I'd rather do less. There's so little shade," Kathy said. Picnics made her homesick. Right now, the sound of the word alone made her feel pinched and lonesome. For their benefit she added, "It's my luck to always get the last chair right out in the sun or else have to stand."

Millie and Ruth said nothing. They were getting ready to special and already had a cart loaded with clean linen and basins of hot water. They had discussed the picnic once between themselves, agreeing that they would have enjoyed it but that since none of Surgical Convalescent patients were able to go, they could not go either. Charlotte, as charge and with enough help to leave behind on the ward, might have gone, but as Kathy had pointed out, there just wasn't enough shade. She was not going to sit for an hour or two holding a newspaper over her head while a bunch of nuts cavorted and made bigger fools of themselves than usual. She dug into her pocket for a cigarette.

"God, ain't it hot! You'd think we'd get a rain or something out of this weather." She lit the cigarette and frowned sharply at Althea and Kathy. "Yeah," she said, blowing smoke toward them. "By noon it'll be hot enough to cook what brains some of those patients got left. I wouldn't go over there if the office gave me an extra month's pay."

Althea, on the edge of rudeness, said, "The patients like it. They've been talking about it for weeks."

Kathy nodded. "They have so little to do. If we were patients . . ."

She and Althea looked at each other. We are still the same, Kathy thought. Nothing has changed. I thought it would have by now, but it hasn't.

"Well, you ain't patients," Charlotte said shortly. "And you ain't charges yet, either. The charges get all the grief on a holiday, believe me. They've got to herd all the patients over to where the picnic's held, then watch 'em like hawks. There ain't enough help to handle it if something starts, so they don't dare relax, not a minute. Last year, the bandstand collapsed and a couple of patients got hurt. Year before, there was a free-for-all. Some woman patient got to singing with the band and some of the other patients didn't like it, so they ganged up on her, come pretty near beating her to death with pop bottles. That was a headache, let me tell you."

"It must have been awful," Kathy said, but her eyes glinted. What excitement! she thought. Why didn't they gang up on one of these bossy, self-important charges?

"Oh, you must have had your hands full," Althea said. "Funny—they do that at football and baseball games and no one gives it a second thought."

Charlotte's skin mottled. Not all of the affiliates were hell to put up with, but these two had gone out of their way to needle her. With what she had to put up with from Ruth and Millie as well, she was just about ready to blow her stack. She smoked furiously for a second. "Well, let me tell you. Some of these patients, you don't dare turn your back on 'em. If you do, that's it—you've had it. They ain't got no conscience. They'd just as soon kick you to death as look at you."

They nodded and pulled back from the smoke. "We know," they said together and left the desk and went down the hall side by side.

Out of hearing, Althea snorted. "God, I'd hate to have her turn on me. She probably gouges out eyeballs."

"No, I don't think so. She's underhanded. She'd do some-

110

thing sneaky and really mean—like trying to ruin your reputation or get you fired."

"Not my reputation. No one can do that but me."

"Sure, but she'd try," said Kathy. "I don't intend to give her a chance to talk about me if I can help it."

"She'll talk anyway. Have you ever noticed how she phones other wards to give out with the gossip?"

"And that Ruth and Millie. They must be scared to death of her. They sort of creep around like they hate to get her started, she gives them such a bad time."

"They have to be careful. She makes out their merit ratings. It must be tough for some of these attendants when they have rotten charges."

Kathy nodded. "And the other way around too, I suppose. Isn't it awful to have to work for a living?" she laughed. "We never gossip, of course."

Althea grinned back. "Well, hardly ever." She stopped before the door of Six. "Be seeing you," she said and went in to relieve the night special on Sarah Smith's case.

Kathy went on down to the drug room. Once inside and out of sight, she leaned against the wall and put her hands over her face. What was she going to do? The days were dragging by and nothing was happening. She could think of no way to make things happen, no practical way to attract Donovan's attention away from Althea to herself. She knew how he disliked overeager affiliates, and if she did anything as simple as saying, "I can type, too—let me do your typing instead of Althea," he'd probably think she was losing her mind. Althea still faithfully reported everything that happened during her evening sessions in Donovan's rooms, and Kathy knew she should feel relief because there was so little for Althea to tell. Donovan was completely absorbed in his book and treated Althea as if she were his grandmother.

Sometimes Kathy wanted to go home, to run away from everything. These were the times when she loved Althea. Then in panic she would think, I can't go home. My mother would know something is wrong; she'd take one look at my face and know. And I'd have to tell her what's wrong, because when was I ever able to keep anything from her whenever we were together? I can't hurt her like that, letting her know what's happened to me inside. I'm sick inside.

Then she would see Donovan, perhaps very close. He would come into the drug room and ask her for some seconal or a sodium luminal shot for one of the old ladies in pain, and he would wait while she prepared it, talking casually but watching her hands as she worked until she became so nervous they began to shake as he looked at her. When he took the syringe on its bed of sterile, alcohol-soaked cotton and left the drug room, she would lean against the cabinet and shake all over. After these encounters, she would sometimes slip down to the employees' toilet and cry bitterly there. And at night she would lie sleepless, staring out her window, looking at the stars, but seeing his face as clearly as if she were staring at a photograph. He has a beautiful face, she would think, narrow and dark and masculine, but beautiful. His eyes are wise and kind and his brows sweep up at the ends. She wanted to touch his brows and smooth them with her finger tips. She could imagine him leaning over her, kissing her, and she would become faint with the excitement of this fantasy. Then Althea's face would come between them and she would wake up, realizing she had fallen asleep and had been dreaming. She would be wet with sweat, furious with herself because now she could not go to sleep again and must lie there until the robins started their racket outside and the faint, blue light began to announce dawn. She lived in a constant state of up-and-downness, one moment vowing to herself that nothing really mattered except finishing her course, taking her exams and getting a good job somewhere and forgetting Canterbury. The next moment she was sick and anxious, wondering desperately what she could do to supplant Althea, knowing she would die if she could not have Donovan; and almost in the same moment, swinging back, telling herself that Althea was her friend.

Now, in the drug room, with her hands over her face, she went through a moment of total depression. I can never compare with Althea, she thought. I'm not the glamour type. I can work, that's what I can do. I'm the working type. Angrily, Kathy walked out of the drug room and next door into Minor Surgery to prepare items for sterilization.

Down in Six, Althea discussed Sarah Smith with Pauline Mayberry, who was happy to be going off to bed after a rugged night.

"I thought sure as the devil she was a goner," Pauline said, taking off her cap tiredly and dropping two white bobby pins into a pocket. "About two o'clock she had a sinking spell. For about thirty minutes I thought, Well, this is it. I never closed my eyes the whole night."

They looked at Sarah. It was not for them to question why this cadaverous-looking psychopath should be kept alive as long as possible. Their duty was to follow orders.

"Wonder what's the trouble. She's been getting better."

"Come off it, kid. She's an old woman. Aren't you surprised she's lasted this long?"

"She's only fifty-seven," Althea replied. But when she said

it aloud, it did sound old; it sounded ancient. Would she ever reach such an age? Not like this, she hoped fervently. She bent over the chart on the nightstand. "No changes?"

"Only one—no bed bath today. Just turn her over every hour as usual and dress the bed sores."

Althea nodded. "Okay. Dr. Macleod was here last night, wasn't he?" She was formal in front of Pauline—Dr. Macleod, not Donovan, because this was not Kathy; this was merely another student, one she knew from classes and from this particular assignment.

"Yeah—at ten after two." Pauline's mouth opened in an enormous yawn. "He stayed until after the crisis. Said he might be late coming in today, so watch Sarah closely and get plenty of liquid down her."

Althea nodded again, knowing this already. Donovan had called her at seven, sounding tired and impatient, having been up most of the night but concerned about Sarah and the heat and what the day might bring. Concerned about Sarah Smith, Althea thought, but not about me. He still doesn't know I exist. I'm a machine, a digit. For a moment she almost hated him for being so unobservant, so uncaring. Then she was filled with swift, deep love. She did not care, just so she could be near him; she would forgive him anything if there might be the faintest chance that someday he would turn to her and really see her and want her as a woman. She had learned to be patient—she had had to learn that in her disturbed life. She remembered much more of her childhood than she had ever told, the terrified waiting while Aunt Nodie committed her vicious acts against Edna, and then the sob-shaking, patient resignation until Edna could come and hold her in her lap and they would sit in a dark, protective corner underneath the stairs, hoping Aunt Nodie would forget for a while and not come searching them out to begin it all over again. Sometimes when she remembered (not that she wanted to) she would get terrible headaches, almost migraines. She did not tell anyone about those, either. She endured them, took aspirin and Phenobarbs cadged from the drug room, and wondered if she should cut her hair. She was working too hard but refused to acknowledge it, even to herself.

Her feet dragging, Pauline left, going down to the desk to sign out, and Althea went to work. She got out a clean muslin surgical gown, put it on, tying the top strings, then gave Sarah an enema, using exactly two cups of warm water and one teaspoon of olive oil, and measuring the amount that came back into the bedpan. Gently and competently she washed Sarah's hands, face and teeth, then her vaginal tract. She brushed her hair, carefully dressed the decubiti ulcers and changed Sarah's gown and the bed linen, keeping Sarah well covered during the procedure. She had just enough time left to clean the night stand and check supplies before Sarah's TPR, after which would come the lunch tray. She had finished the TPR when Charlotte opened the door and put her head in.

"She doing all right?" She nodded toward the bed.

"Yes."

"Well, come on down to the desk. You're wanted on the phone."

She did not offer to stay with Sarah but was gone before Althea could protest. Althea thought about it and shrugged. Sarah was sleeping, her pulse reading had been good, her temp two points below normal. Her respiration was shallow, but that was usual because she was an old woman and had been sick a long time. And it might be Donovan calling. Without stopping to think that she might be doing something he would disapprove of highly, she stepped out into the hall, leaving the door open an inch or so, and rushed down to the desk. She was certain that it would be all right to leave Sarah alone for a few seconds.

Kathy had returned to the drug room and emerged just in time to see Althea walking quickly down the hall. Impulsively, she stepped down to Six and went in. Althea knows better than this, she thought, leaving a critical patient alone! Her first instinct was to stay and protect Althea.

She moved to the bed and stared down at the twitching eyelids, the colorless lips mouthing faint, unintelligible sounds, and strange, unbidden thoughts began to mill in her mind. She was hypnotized by them, scarcely conscious of actually thinking them, almost as though there were two separate people in the room. She had been cleaning shelves in the drug room and had dropped a purodigin bottle, still containing two tablets, into her pocket to return to the clinic for a refill. The fingers of one hand felt and twisted at the bottle as she remembered that purodigin had been removed from Sarah's list of medications; she had been given so much digitalis in the past that it had become toxic. If Sarah were given purodigin now, how would she react? The thought was so extraordinary that she did not realize it was her own speculation.

But she could not stop herself from examining the idea further. If two pills—the ones in the bottle in her pocket, for instance—were placed on Sarah's tongue, they would slip down and into her stomach and dissolve. The reaction would surely be mild because Sarah had been off the medication so long, but still alarming to anyone not knowing what had caused it. Althea would become frightened and notify Donovan immediately. In turn, he would discover that Sarah had been left alone during the very time the reaction was setting in. Every piece of the supposition dovetailed in Kathy's mind, even the idea of Althea losing prestige and trust and respect. Prestige, trust, respect were the only qualities so far that Donovan Macleod seemed willing to recognize.

Mesmerized, beginning to shake, she unscrewed the cap from the bottle, extracted the tiny tablets and placed them between the gray lips of the sleeping Sarah. Then for a second she was still as her stomach turned in sick protest. *No!* she screamed silently and bent over the bed, poking a finger frantically between Sarah's gums. They clamped together like a vise. She pulled her finger loose with difficulty and grabbed a towel from the nightstand in an effort to pry the gums apart but gave up as soon as she saw she would have to hurt Sarah to get her mouth open. Now her imagination filled the room with sounds; she would have to get out, someone was coming, someone would catch her. She whirled fearfully. She didn't dare be caught in Six or even be seen leaving it. The medicine was gone by now; she would have to let it take its natural course.

Get out, get away, she told herself. But fold the towel first, don't let anything look as though someone had been in with Sarah, look around, look carefully, you can spare one second for that. Now, out into the hall, don't look around, don't act as though you were frightened, as if anything's wrong. Just go across the hall and five steps to the drug room. Quietly but quickly. And don't look around, no one's coming, no one saw you. There's the drug-room door, push it open, go in—now you can stop, fall on the floor if you want to—you're safe!

CHAPTER 17

ALTHEA CAME DOWN the hall, hurrying, her uniform swinging crisply around her knees. The call had been from Elizabeth Leslie to ask her if she would care to take her ward management on Rehabilitation and to think it over quickly, as Miss Terry would want to know definitely by the end of the week. She implied that there was really no question of thinking it over since it was the best placement in the institution, in a new building with picked patients. More than pleased, a little frightened, too, because of the responsibility it would entail, Althea nodded and said yes, to be sure, in all the right places, then went back to Six in a bemused glow. If Terry gave her ward management of that building, it meant she wanted her to consider staying on permanently after graduation. There was a place for her in Canterbury. A place near Donovan!

Looking poised and competent, she hesitated briefly outside Six to adjust her cap, then pushed open the door and went in.

A few feet away, Kathy crouched against the wall. Feeling suffocated inside the drug room, she had come out, wanting no part of what was to happen yet unable to remove herself completely from the scene. Motionless, she watched the hall and waited. She wanted to rush down to Six and force the clock to turn backward, long enough for her to come out of this with two purodigin tablets still in her pocket. But all she could do was to put her fist to her mouth and a knuckle between her teeth, biting until the blood oozed but feeling neither the biting nor the blood, until Althea came down the hall and entered Six. Then there were a few moments of suspense.

God, God, don't let anything be wrong! God forgive me, she whispered frantically, like a child. It was all wrong. She didn't want Althea to get into trouble, she didn't want anything to happen to Althea . . .

The light flashed over Six and the emergency bell rang shrilly. Suddenly Althea stood in the doorway, beckoning frantically to Charlotte. Charlotte stood up and bent over her desk to see better. Then she moved out of the desk circle and back toward Althea, waddling but swift about it. They entered Six and she came out in a moment or two and went back to the desk.

Now there was confusion, but swift and silent. Uniforms swished and rubber-soled shoes slapped in half-running spurts. Her arms loaded, Ruth darted into Six and out again. Millie came jogging like a coolie, pushing the emergency cart with its drugs, instruments, bottles filled with serum and glucose and rubber tubing to park it near Six. The door opened and shut, opened and shut. Ruth returned with an intravenous feeding stand, went into Six, and did not come out.

Donovan made his appearance, walking faster than he usually did, his stethoscope out and ready for use. Kathy shrank at the sight. I'm dreaming this, she thought wildly. In a minute the alarm will go off and I'll wake up and be in my room, hunting for the clock. I must be dreaming it. God, let me be dreaming it. Around her terror she tried to trail a stubborn, clinging belief that there simply could not have been enough reaction to warrant so much activity in Six. She began to realize that if she stayed where she was, she would be seen. She knew she should go down to Six and pretend to be as curious and concerned as anyone normally would and make some exclamation of horror or shock, depending on what was taking place. It would seem peculiar for her to be caught not being curious. With great difficulty she pushed herself away from the wall. The door to the linen room was closer than the drugroom door. Stumbling, she got there and went through, then leaned limply against it, waiting.

When the excitement began, Ruth and Millie were in the stool room at the other end of the ward. They were washing bedpans with a mixture of hot water, green soap and methyl salicylate, which took away obnoxious odors and left a peculiar peppermint smell of its own. They were not supposed to use the methyl salicylate—it was actually to be used as a liniment—but Charlotte had sanctioned its use by ordering large quantities of it from the supply department and cautioning them to be discreet in the amounts put into scrub water. They knew that this was one thing they could do without being hauled over the coals by Charlotte; they were also taking advantage of this time away from her prying domination to chat. Ruth was telling about Mary Elsie Blayton, knowing that Millie still felt a sense of guilt about Mary Elsie.

Millie was fascinated. "Are they going to keep her on Hydro all the time?"

"They still had her when I left. Molly said—that's the charge—they were trying everything they could and she hoped to God the office wouldn't forget and just leave Mary Elsie there. Shock, pack, tubs—nothing works for that kid, believe me. She'll be real good for several days, then she starts tearing up her clothes and running naked all over the ward."

"I know," Millie said uncomfortably. "I saw her. Who is her doctor now?"

"Well, Andreatta is, but he can't do nothing now. How could he on Hydro? He did all his doing before the office sent her over there, believe me. Her husband came to see her one Sunday afternoon and if that wasn't something!"

Over the door the emergency light came on. Startled, the two women looked up at it.

"I'll tell you about it later," Ruth said, already drying her arms and hands and starting to push open the door. Millie was right behind her.

They swung down the hall to the desk. Charlotte was standing inside the circle, looking at the phone, but not touching it. "Six," she snapped, glancing up. "On the QT. Get everything ready for Dr. Macleod. He'll be here in a minute. And one of you stay there—you, Ruth. Don't leave that nurse alone after you get everything set up." She chose Ruth because she was experienced, knew what to do, almost

117

as much as any nurse would know. When they scurried away, she was looking at the phone again, her expression strange.

On the QT. Be quiet. Don't alarm the patients, don't stir them up, they get frightened, cantankerous, they want to know what's going on. Millie and Ruth moved quietly but swiftly and competently. "What's happened?" they whispered to each other, but they did not stop long enough to guess at answers.

It was a full ten minutes before Donovan arrived on the ward and twelve before Mrs. Beck made her appearance. In Room Six, Donovan stared at the contorted face on the pillow, then made a quick examination which told him that in all probability Sarah had been dead most of the ten minutes. He wondered why he hadn't been called immediately when he might have still been able to do something. Crossly he pulled the sheet over her face. Then he turned and looked at Althea, standing white and frozen at the foot of the bed. She had told him, without preliminaries or excuses, that she had been absent from the room using the ward telephone when it started.

"Do you know why this woman died?" he asked sharply.

Ruth was standing on the other side of the bed, so Althea did not dare call him Donovan. He looked so strange, so frightening, she could scarcely breathe. "No, Dr. Macleod," she whispered.

"Well, I'll tell you. And I want you to listen, I want you to listen very carefully, Miss Horne." The way he said her name, formally, was like a slap. "This patient choked to death. Is that clear? She choked on her own saliva. Where were you when that happened?"

"I told you," she said through stiff lips. "I told you—"

"Yes. I know. You were using the telephone. You—" He looked furious, outraged. He was a stranger; she had never seen him before. "You left a critical patient unattended, Miss Horne. Do you know what I'm trying to say? You left her and she *died!*"

She was filled with horror. "I barely stepped out of the room—"

There was a sound at the door, Charlotte pushing it open. "Do you need me, Dr. Macleod?" She looked at Althea with an odd expression. When he shook his head, she beckoned to Ruth and they withdrew together.

Then Althea moved. She put her hands together and took a step. "Please!" she said. "I didn't mean to do anything wrong." She had never seen anyone look so angry as he did at this moment. "Please . . ." she said faintly.

He crossed his arms over his chest. "You didn't mean to

o anything wrong. You're sorry, no doubt. Will that bring his woman back to life? Answer me. Will it?"

In a second she would faint, she knew she would. She shook her head and the room rocked. "Please . . ."

"Please, please! Is that all you can say!" He stood over her, looking as though nothing would have pleased him more than to strike her with his fists. "You let this woman die. Do you understand that?"

But she could only shake her head at him foolishly, like a doll with a broken neck. She could not believe they had been so close and that he could change so fast, from mild affection to blind anger. He was hating her with his eyes, despising her, seeing nothing in her but evil.

"All right," he said furiously. "You will not come back to any of my classes. I will have you transferred to Dr. Denning. From now on, you will get your assignments from him. Is that clear?"

She began to cry, a soundless crying, the tears spilling, but nothing else showing in her face; it looked queer and frozen. "Donovan," she whispered, staring at him, too numb to lift her hands or move.

"For God's sake, control yourself!" he exclaimed harshly and jerked back toward the bed to keep from looking at her face.

Then Mrs. Beck came in with a quick but thoroughly aware glance at Althea before she stepped to the bed. "Too bad," she said with delicate scorn. "These girls always get caught, don't they?"

Althea remembered the time she saw Mrs. Beck deliberately mutilate a patient's letter from an only son abroad in order to help herself to the foreign stamp for her stamp collection, and the way afterward the patient had cried over the desecration because the letter meant so much to her. She did not care what Mrs. Beck said or implied. She lifted a hand jerkily toward Donovan, but Mrs. Beck saw the stiff gesture and stepped in front of it.

"I'll take care of everything," she said smoothly to Donovan. "What was the cause of death, Doctor?"

He saw the little byplay and looked at her angrily. She wasn't any better than Althea. "I'll put it on my report later," he said and abruptly left the room.

Mrs. Beck flushed and glanced maliciously at Althea as she picked up his stethoscope and prepared to follow him. "Come to the office as soon as you can. Miss Terry will want a full explanation and it had better be good." No lies, no evasions, her look said. What were you doing when Sarah kicked the bucket? Why weren't you at her side, digging the slime out of her throat? Mrs. Beck was young

and pretty and eager to humiliate a younger, prettier woma
in order to take away the sting of Dr. Macleod's curtnes
Composed now, she trotted in his wake.

Stiffly Althea went around the bed to the window. In
moment or so, Ruth and Millie pushed a surgical cart int
the room. She was looking out the window and they eye
her back curiously as they set to work. She could hear th
sounds they made preparing the body, washing it, stuffin
all openings with cotton, crossing the hands over the ches
wrapping them with cotton and tying them together wit
cord. She knew the exact second they forced Sarah's leg
straight and tied them as they had the wrists. The final, heav
rustling was the sacklike shroud being pulled firmly ove
Sarah's naked body.

Millie observed the way Althea's shoulders were pulle
together. "You don't have to stay," she offered kindly. "We'
take care of everything." It wasn't in her province to offe
this, but the girl looked so miserable that she was touchec
"No call for you to feel bad. Sarah was ready to die any
time."

"Good thing when it happens with some of these ol
women," Ruth added. "What have they got to live for, any
how? No one wants to be bothered with 'em—nobody care:
They don't know enough themselves to care about any
thing."

Mille looked down at Sarah. "Well, now, you never know,
she hedged. "Sarah was ready to die, but whether it's
good thing or not, I don't know. Take Sarah here. She wasn
so old, not much older'n me. What if they'd found a cur
for her trouble? Why, she would have had lots of good year
left. Don't you know? I buried my mother and my husban
and there ain't a day passes I don't wish they could hav
gotten strong and well again and able to do everything the
used to do 'fore they got sick. I just don't think it's right t
have to die, you know? Maybe someday these here scien
tists'll find a way we can live forever steada making all ther
bombs. Wouldn't that be something?"

"That's up to the Lord, not scientists," Ruth said sharply
"Wait until you start getting up mornings, feeling like I do
That'll be the day, Millie. You'll want to turn over in bec
and never get up again. I'm telling you. I still say, what di
Sarah have to live for—you call that living?" She poked th
sack with a finger. "Say, we better hurry this up."

Millie glanced quickly at the rigid figure in the window
Althea had made no response to any of their conversation
She shook her head warningly at Ruth. "Right. Let's get
move on. We still got to clean this unit."

"What did you do with the string?" Ruth asked.

120

"In my pocket—no, the other one."

They finished quickly, slid the bag from the bed to the cart, stripped the bed hastily, stuffing linens and blankets into a laundry sack which they balanced composedly on Sarah's middle section, and pushed the cart silently out of the room, intensely relieved to be done with an unpleasant task.

Althea listened to the gentle hiss of the rubber tires moving down the hall. In a few moments, Ruth and Millie would ride downstairs with it to a waiting, closed cab, then return to the ward and take up where they had left off with their ward duties. The cab driver and his assistant would be responsible for Sarah for several miles, then a mortician would have the job. Eventually there would be flowers, probably carnations and lilies and white roses, and organ music. A few mourners would sit in their special section, holding soft, cambric handkerchiefs which they would not need, while a man with his collar on backward would read from a book. But it would be nothing that Sarah could enjoy. People would mourn her dead, Althea thought numbly, when they had not once come to mourn her alive.

No one will really cry over Sarah but me, she thought, and I will cry because she has destroyed my life today. An hour ago we were both breathing. Now we are dead, dead, dead . . . The word went into her head like a hot needle; she felt that her head was going to split from the heat. There was pain on the back of her neck that was crawling and squeezing like something alive. It suffocated her, made her struggle for breath. She put her hands to her head and pressed. In a moment, she panted, in a moment it's going to break open. For a second she forgot everything but the angry, hot pain and the light. Then it all began to subside and she could breathe again, she could think, she could tell herself what to do. She had to go over to the office. She would be humiliated and scorned there—Terry, Beck and Range, Rich and Leslie—all of them waiting, their heads nodding, their mouths moving, their words spouting at her in the inevitable clinical discussion of her transgression.

Only Donovan would not be there. Why should he be? He was through, he had washed his hands of her, he could eliminate her from his scheme of things because he had not cared in the first place, he had not cared . . .

No one to help her, no one to tell the truth, such as it was. I had to answer the telephone; it was Miss Leslie calling. You don't let Miss Leslie wait; she's almost as important to this institution as Miss Terry. Why didn't Mrs. Range stay with Sarah—why didn't she? She's ward charge. I was only gone from the room three or four minutes—I swear to

God it was only that long! Only three or four minutes—while an old woman *died!*

Blindly she stumbled out of Six and down the hall away from the desk. She passed the open doorway of the linen room without seeing Kathy standing inside. White, her eyes bitter-bright, she moved on, and when she reached the utility closet she turned and went inside.

CHAPTER 18

Now I MUST DO SOMETHING, Kathy thought. I can't stay in here forever, I've got to find out what's going on.

She stepped out of her hiding place, reached the utility closet and hesitated a second, then leaned her head against the door and listened. She heard sounds clearly, someone vomiting spasmodically and then making little gasping sounds afterward. She put her hand out and opened the door, then held it open with the heel of one shoe. She saw Althea bent over the utility sink. Her own mouth was so dry she could hardly speak.

"What's the matter?" she whispered. "Are you sick?"
"Yes."

Is that all you have to say about it? something screamed inside Kathy, just—yes, you're sick? Tell me what's happened! She tried to clear her throat, unsuccessfully.

"Can I . . . do anything?"
"No."

"Some Kalpec—aspirin? Let me get you something," Kathy begged in a dry whisper. She moved in a little farther, still holding the door open with her shoe. "Isn't there anything I can do?"

Althea lifted her head from the sink and wiped her mouth with a wad of tissue. "She's dead."

Kathy shook her head. "Dead?" she said in a small, stunned voice. "Dead?" she repeated faintly, her voice beginning to rise. She stared at Althea, trying to understand something incredible and unbelievable. "I . . . heard all that . . . noise but I thought—"

She was almost afraid to say anything more with the fright beating up from her stomach. She would give herself away, say the wrong thing. She wanted to run out, quickly, to get away from Althea and from the sickening smell in the closet, but she couldn't move, she couldn't let go of the door or move her foot.

Althea looked at Kathy but did not really see her. "Dead," she said, her voice bitter and dull and angry as though Sarah had died deliberately to spite her.

"I . . . thought she was getting better." Kathy clung to this inanity, a safe remark in which to hide. "She was getting better . . ."

Althea did not answer this. She saw Kathy; she knew she was speaking; but it meant nothing. When she spoke, she was really talking to herself, listening to herself. "When I told Donovan I'd stepped out of the room for a few moments, he looked at me and I could see it in his face. I killed Sarah. I killed her because I wasn't there when she needed me. His eyes cut me to pieces. He—he hated me!"

Kathy felt far away, disembodied, suspended in horror. "What do you mean?" she quavered. "Why did you tell him you left the room? Did you have to tell him?" Why did you make a fool of yourself, do the very thing I had hoped you would do!

"Mrs. Range would have told him. Wasn't it better to come from me than from her? You know how she twists things. When I told him, I didn't feel I had done anything awful. I could have gone to the toilet, couldn't I?"

"He shouldn't blame you. She was old. She was ready to die."

"Yes. It could have happened any time. But not then, the one time I was out of the room."

It could have happened any time! thought Kathy. It wasn't because of two little pink pills. They hadn't been responsible. The relief sweeping over Kathy was almost as frightening as the dismay had been.

"You see. It could have happened any time," she repeated. "So why should you blame yourself? Why should he blame you? Did you tell him that?"

"Tell him? Do you think a nurse ever tells a doctor anything when he's all *doctor*?"

"Maybe he just doesn't understand. Maybe if you tried to explain—"

"I did explain. All he understands is that I was assigned to special Sarah Smith, that she was critical, that I left her alone for five minutes or less and came back to find her dying. I can't explain that even to myself. I had just checked her pulse and respiration and I thought she was asleep. Then Range stuck her head in and told me to come down to the desk—which I did. When I got back—maybe it was four minutes, not five—there was Sarah, already cyanotic—her mouth wide open, her throat rattling—"

"Stop it, stop it!" Kathy shouted. "You're getting hysterical. You should have told Donovan about Range calling you down to the desk. You should have told him. Why didn't you?"

"I did, but it was worse than no excuse at all. He looked at me, and then he said things—"

"She was ready to die. You know she was. He knows it. Stop acting like this. It doesn't make sense. You're too intelligent!"

"Intelligent? He doesn't think so. After all these weeks we've worked together on that damned book of his you know what he did? He *fired* me. I'm finished. I can't even stay in his class. I'll be under Dr. Denning's supervision from now on until graduation. Dr. Denning, Kathy—after all these weeks!"

She gasped and turned to be sick again in the sink. Kathy held herself rigid as saliva poured into her own mouth. What would Althea think if she vomited too? But the sour odor and the sounds Althea made were almost more than she could stand. She tried wrapping her arms tightly across her middle and swallowing repeatedly.

"He'd have to do that," she said raggedly for what comfort it could give. "He's part of a hierarchy, the medical hierarchy. He couldn't let you get away with anything. You know, do something on your own without his say-so." She thought, Why am I doing this? Why do I want to comfort her? Isn't this exactly what I hoped for? But not Sarah. Not that—only, I didn't do that, thank God. I'm not responsible. She was ready to die any time. It couldn't have been the pills.

"I wasn't doing something on my own." Althea's voice was muffled by the sink.

"I mean like answering the telephone as though you had every right to do that. If we all made our own decisions, there wouldn't be any discipline."

She was ready to die any time. It went over and over in Kathy's mind; she clung to it foolishly. Abruptly she realized that Althea was not listening. Althea had lifted her head from the sink, had turned and was backed up against the wall, staring intently at Kathy.

Out of Kathy's words, Althea had caught one phrase. How had Kathy known about the telephone call? Her head was aching again, pounding with pain, in fact, but through the pain she tried to recall what had been said; nothing about a telephone call, she was sure, nothing. I said Range called me down to the desk, that's all I said. How does Kathy know? Where was she?

Kathy stared back, suddenly afraid. What had she said to make Althea look like that? Something about Sarah? There was a new expression on Althea's face. Along with the shock and bitterness and pain, now there were fury and hate.

"Why don't you go over to the canteen and get some

coffee?" She meant, why don't you get off the ward and stop looking at me like that until I can figure out what's really wrong, what I said or did just now? Kathy did not recognize her own voice, it had become so high and thin. "I'll tell Range you've gone so you won't have to explain to her."

Althea turned and deliberately, slowly, moistened some tissue and cleaned her face. She dropped the tissue into the sink, turned on the water full force until the tissue disintegrated and slipped down the drain, then turned off the water. "I have to go to the office," she said, stepping past Kathy as though she were not there. "Range knows."

Kathy opened the door wide and watched Althea move away. Her back was stiff; her feet made spaced, even steps. It was like nothing Kathy had ever seen. I said something, Kathy thought, I gave myself away, I made her suspicious. But what does she know? What could she know? There has to be a witness. Sarah could have died any time, I have to remember that, I must never forget it. Never, never forget that Sarah was ready to die. Never!

In a little while she was able to follow, although she waited long enough to make sure Althea had left the ward. When she got near the desk, she hurried, hoping she could get by without having to stop and talk, but Charlotte seemed to be waiting for her.

"My God, slow down. What's your hurry? You leaving the ward, too?"

Kathy brought her feet to an unwilling halt. "I've got to go to the clinic."

Charlotte smiled without humor. "You nurses are always in one hell of a hurry when it doesn't mean anything. Now if I was going to tell you about some man, something spicy, you'd probably break your neck to hear what it was. Didja hear what happened on the ward just a little bit ago?"

I won't stand here and listen to her talk about Althea, Kathy thought rebelliously, looking white and wretched. "Yes," she said coldly.

"Dr. Macleod sure wasn't happy about it, no sir. He came down here afterward, made out his papers at the desk. He looked sick, let me tell you. Won't look so good on his record, one of his nurses letting a patient die like that."

"The woman was sick. She could have died any time. She was ready to die." Kathy stared furiously at Charlotte. You slob! she thought.

"Yeah?" Looking sly and pleased, Charlotte lit a cigarette, let it dangle from a corner of her mouth. "You think that was it? Well, let me tell you something. I saw what he wrote, what Dr. Macleod wrote on that death certificate. Would you like to know what he put down there?"

"No."

"Well, I'm going to tell you anyway. You and that Horne being such good friends, you won't care. Dr. Macleod put one word on that piece of paper. Asphyxia." Charlotte sat back and waited for this announcement to take effect.

For a shocked, dumfounded instant, Kathy dropped her guard. "Did you say asphyxia?" she whispered, reaching for the support of the desk.

"I told you I saw him put it down, didn't I? Then I asked him what he meant and he said it was because of saliva or some other foreign substance filling the trachea."

The room, the building rocked around Kathy. No! No! something screamed inside her. She shook her head stupidly. "She couldn't have—she couldn't have died that way!" Something was terribly wrong here. Sarah was supposed to have been ready to die.

"You mean Sarah couldn't have choked to death on her own spit? Oh, but she did, my dear. That's exactly what she did. And all because Miss Althea Highass Horne wasn't there to turn her over and slap the spit out of her windpipe and let some air in." Charlotte looked almost gleeful.

"When you called Althea out of the room, you should have taken her place," Kathy said accusingly. "Then none of this would have happened."

"Don't tell me my business!" Charlotte shouted. "I knew what to do and I did it. That Althea needed a lesson, so I saw to it that she got one. Next time, she'll know better than to run all over a ward and leave a critical patient. You affiliates, you're all alike. You never turn your hands to a little honest work if you can get out of it."

"That's not true," Kathy said faintly. "We work hard. We worked before we came here and we've worked since we came."

"Oh, God, how many times I've heard that. I suppose next you'll say you're *so sorry* for these poor patients. You don't mind a bit cleaning up one of these old women who's shit herself from her neck to her ankles and who'll pee all over you if she gets a chance. Sure, you girls are so Christian! You wouldn't slap the hell out of a patient if she tore your uniform to bits, would you? Oh, no, of course not."

"You're changing the subject," Kathy said thinly. "Althea didn't want to leave Sarah. She knew the regulations. But you're in charge here. You called her away from Sarah. Why didn't you stay a few moments with Sarah? Why? And prevented this terrible thing?"

Charlotte glared. "You make me sick. Because that isn't my job. I'm not supposed to wait on these patients. They get waited on enough. You see anybody running to wait on me? Making me feel filthy rich, like I had servants? God!" She pointed a fat finger at Kathy. "You listen to me. It's the attendants who do the work out here, not you affiliates. I know what your kind does. By God, you affiliates are always chasing doctors and crawling off into the bushes with 'em. Don't bother to deny it because I know, I've got eyes, I see what's going on. Now, tell me again, where are you going?"

"I am going to the clinic." Kathy gripped the desk as the sickness inside grew and spread.

"Get the hell on with it, then, and let me tell you something which you can be thinking over on your way. You do too much damned running around in the hall. From now on, see to it that you stay where you belong, the drug room or Minor Surgery. If you need errands done, there are people working here who should be earning their pay checks instead of sitting on their fat asses while you girls neglect your assignments. Understand?"

Kathy focused her eyes with difficulty. "No. Any more than I can understand why you didn't tell Dr. Macleod that you left no one with Sarah while Althea answered the phone. Don't you realize what you've done?" She was whispering now because it had become such an effort to talk at all.

Charlotte stood up. She seemed vast, towering. Her face came at Kathy. "You trying to make trouble for me?" she said furiously. "Can you prove I didn't send somebody into Sarah's room, somebody no one saw? You got witnesses to prove I didn't do that?"

Kathy stood her ground, petrified and silent.

"You just try telling anything on me over in the office. I'll make you out the worst liar this institution ever saw. What's more, they'll believe me in the office. I've worked out here too long to not know how to protect myself."

"I don't—"

"I've made people lose their jobs out here. I can do it. I know exactly how to go about it. Every trick. You get smart and see what I can do."

"I know—I know what you can do. Everyone knows." From some unknown source, Kathy found strength for this, although her voice was scarcely audible. "Everyone knows what you can do. You've demonstrated often enough. You've done plenty of things. But this is the worst."

"Next you'll try to say I didn't call Macleod right away, that I waited, maybe five, six minutes." Charlotte twisted her head, her face so close to Kathy that Kathy could feel a fine spray of saliva.

Kathy was suddenly horrified. You said it, you said it, you wouldn't have said that unless it were true! "You let Sarah die, didn't you? You said Althea needed a lesson and you saw to it she got one. That's what you meant. You did your share, too. What did Althea ever do to you? Sarah wasn't dead when you went back to her room. She could have been saved. Is that it, Mrs. Range, is it?"

Charlotte began to shake. She was so angry her eyes looked like polished stones. Her lips were pulled into a snarl and her shoulders pushed up so high that her neck was gone, sunk between the humps of her shoulders. Her voice became high and shrill, almost a scream.

"What do you mean, I let Sarah die? Tell that over at the office, you bitch, tell it and see what happens! Do your goddam worst. But you better make it big, you better make it big, because when I finish telling what I'll tell, you'll wish you'd never seen this institution! Now, get out of here and don't come back. Get out! Get out!"

Her anger reached across the desk. It was all she could do to keep from hitting out at Kathy.

"Get out!" she screamed. "Get off this ward!"

Kathy closed her mouth. She pushed herself away from the desk with wrenching effort. She moved away from the sight of Charlotte's purple face and glaring eyes and turned down the aisle leading between beds toward the ward door. She wanted only to get out of Surgical Convalescent, to leave the ward. Each step became a strange, fumbling adventure as she made her way between the beds and the nightstands. She put one foot down carefully, picked one up carefully. The way seemed endless, the obstacles unbelievable. It's like sleepwalking, she thought, stumbling and plodding along. After an eternity of this desperate battle, she reached the door and again came the methodical concentration, the careful, forced movements as she took out her key, got it into the keyhole, unlocked and opened the door. She passed through with obstinate perseverance, pulled the door shut and relocked it, replacing the key in her pocket.

Now it was done. She was off the ward, outside. There were two steps to negotiate and she would be down on the path; she could walk away from the building. Away from Charlotte. Away from Sarah Smith.

In the security of the stool room where they had returned to finish cleaning bedpans, Ruth and Millie looked at each other.

"Listen to 'em," Ruth said. "They're really chewing each other out."

"That poor little nurse ain't got a chance."

"Well, she's giving it right back. Wouldn't surprise me none if she knew what she was talking about."

"You mean Mrs. Range shoulda called sooner?"

"Why not? Come to think of it, Millie, why didn't she?"

"Sure," Millie said, thinking about it. "You know, I think she did everything else first. Was she using that telephone when she called us?"

"You're right, you must be right. She got everything going first, then she called the doctor. That gave her five minutes anyway. When we went to the desk, she was looking at the phone, not using it."

Millie hated to think anyone could do such a wicked thing. She began to shake her head, slowly but obstinately. "We shouldn't say anything, Ruthie. She probably knew Sarah was past help, don't you think?"

Ruth looked sternly at Millie, paused to let suds drip from her hands. "Millie, there ain't anybody past help until they're completely dead. Finished. Not breathing."

They both became silent, thinking about it as they stacked pans, still almost too hot to handle, in orderly arrangement on a cart. Millie was terribly confused. Here again was something not to be ignored. So many things happened—she sighed, remembering them all. In the first place, you couldn't tell on everybody when you didn't know how to go about it, and in the second, did you have any right to tell? The jumbled trail her mind went back over always led to Harry. Did a woman who had killed her husband have any right to judge others or tell about their misdeeds? At times she wanted desperately to confide in Ruth, to tell her the whole thing, but when the words reached her tongue, she couldn't go on; there was something too precious in thinking about Harry, not his death, but what had gone before, and that she could not share with anyone, not even to relieve her own conscience. My goodness, she thought, if I was to tell everything I've seen done out here, nobody would believe me. They'd think I was crazy for sure.

"You think somebody oughta tell Dr. Macleod about her not calling in time?" she asked with a quick glance at Ruth.

"I don't know," Ruth said thoughtfully. "Somebody oughta, I suppose. No telling what kind of trouble she'll try to make for that nurse."

"And the other one. She's getting the blame. Didya notice her face? She looked like she was about ready to cut her own throat."

Ruth looked uncomfortable for a second, then shrugged, "Oh, she'll get over it, I guess. Her pride's been hurt, that's all." She reached into the cabinet and began handing rolls of toilet tissue to Millie to be stacked on the cart for the nightstands.

"I guess you're right," said Millie. "She'll get over it, just like everybody else."

CHAPTER 19

ON THE FIFTH OF JULY, Kathy was transferred to a male up-patient ward for one week and Althea was sent to Dr. Denning's office for a consultation. In spite of what had happened on the Fourth, the office did not intend to discipline her too severely, feeling perhaps that Dr. Macleod had already done enough. Also on the fifth, Charlotte Range decided to vent her anger on Ruth.

As usual, Charlotte was dispensing gossip and wanted Ruth to stand still and listen politely. She had caught Ruth off guard at the desk, hunting for diet tabs, and now Ruth stood shifting restlessly from foot to foot, obviously anxious to get on with her work.

"Like I said, that Horne leaves Sarah and comes down here to the station, so what could I do about it? I have to stay here at my desk. Did she think I was going to baby-sit with Sarah while she floated around in the hall? Not on your life. I'm the charge. I'm not supposed to do those damn affiliates' work."

What's she trying to tell me? Ruth thought, looking at the sour, self-righteous face. She don't know Millie and me heard it all, her fight with that other nurse. She waited in silence.

Charlotte's lips pulled straight, showing sharp, narrow teeth. "The affiliates know the rules. And they know what's liable to happen to critical patients. Horne used my phone and went back to Six and then signaled to me and when I got down there, she says, please, call Dr. Macleod. Her face is white, mind you, but her voice is smooth. Like not a thing was really wrong, when I could see for myself Sarah wasn't going to make it unless . . ." Charlotte looked odd, then shook her head. "Giving me orders like that. I been watching that tart ever since Macleod sent her over to special Sarah."

A sound made both of them jump. It was Millie plodding softly up to the desk. "Sorry," she said, her eyes curious. What was going on now? "What you want me to do next, Mrs. Range?"

"You finished putting the laundry away?"

"Yes."

"Then you can take bedpans around."

This was a task she ordinarily shared with Ruth. She hesitated a second, wondering why Ruth was being excluded, then moved off, her crepe soles soundless on the tile floor.

Charlotte shifted her eyes to watch until she was out of

130

hearing. "How long was she listening in, do you suppose?" she remarked thinly. "Sneaky sonofabitch. Someday I'm gonna bounce her goddam ass right off this ward."

Such remarks were customary from Charlotte, so Ruth did not say anything, although, like Millie, she was now thinking about the bedpans. Why was she still standing here when there was ward work waiting to be done? She stared at Charlotte with a little touch of apprehension.

Charlotte was silent a moment. One fat hand fell on the desk and began fiddling with a pencil. "Like I was saying," she said as though there had been no interruption, "here was Horne giving me orders, only she didn't really mean *please*. See what I mean? Well, I called Macleod, all right. But I waited a bit. Not long, you understand, but long enough to scare hell outa Horne. She's had a good scare coming ever since she landed on this ward, and I figured that was as good a time as any to see she got it. I wanted her to find out she stinks same as everybody else. Maybe worse."

Ruth did not say anything. She already knew the story and all she could say would be something Charlotte would resent. Silence was the safe, the only course. But her silence made Charlotte furious. She lit a cigarette, her hands shaking.

"God!" she said, hooding her eyes. "Is this ever going to be a day. The office is sending us six patients from Surgery and we have to transfer two to Untidy. I tell you, I've been going around this morning like a cockroach in a bowl of chili."

Ruth knew this too and began to speculate on the reason she was being held at the desk. Errand, perhaps? She took a tentative step and was stopped by a sharp stare. Here it comes, Ruth thought. I've done something she doesn't like, so she's going to lower the boom. Maybe it's because she knows I think she was a louse about yesterday.

"You don't talk very much, Ruth," Charlotte said. "What's the trouble? Don't you have anything to talk about?"

Ruth let a cautious shrug lift her shoulders. "Sure, I talk sometimes. But not when I'm working, on account of I can't do both."

Was that a safe remark to make? She waited tensely.

"Maybe you think I didn't do right yesterday, not calling Macleod right way, huh? Maybe you think I should have busted my ass getting back to the phone when nothing could have saved Sarah, not even Jesus Christ himself. Maybe you don't know she died of asphyxia."

Anger surged up in Ruth. She forgot for a second to be careful. "But you didn't know that either when you didn't call the doctor right off."

131

Instantly she stopped and tried to suck back in the words. But it was too late.

"So!" Charlotte said, coloring to the roots of her mud-colored hair. "You can talk. And when you open your mouth, you certainly put both feet right in. By God, I hope you never tell that around anywhere. If you ever do, and it gets back to me, you'll be in all kinds of trouble. You have no idea just how much trouble you'll be in." She jerked open one of the desk drawers and took out a folder. It was already clipped together at the edges, showing that whatever she had planned to do with it had been thought of in advance. Her voice was thin again. "You are to take this folder to Miss Terry. She is expecting you because I have already called and told her you were on your way."

She looked at Ruth confidently, so certain was she that Ruth would leave the ward immediately and go directly to the office, without even looking at the contents of the folder. She settled back in the swivel chair and dug for another cigarette, thinking with satisfaction of the shock coming to Ruth. She was not afraid that Ruth would talk, either. After all the years Ruth had worked in Canterbury, she would know by now how little it would mean to the office if she tattled on a charge. Sometimes, a thing like that had a hell of a way of being a boomerang. She hooded her eyes again and watched Ruth pick up the folder, watched the speculative expression come into Ruth's face, the little tinge of alarm and apprehension. Ruth turned finally and walked away without a word. Yes, by God, Charlotte thought coldly, these old-time employees could stand a lesson now and then as well as some of the affiliates. She glanced over the rampart of the desk, noted Millie busy with the cart and bedpans, snuffed out her cigarette and settled comfortably back for a light nap. All in good time, she thought drowsily. Now that Ruth was out of the way, Millie would be next.

Ruth was uneasy, but she did exactly as Charlotte had anticipated; she left the ward and walked quickly over to the office and into Lucretia's office. They were waiting for her, Lucretia behind the piled-high ash tray and Margaret standing respectfully behind Lucretia's chair. When she looked at their cold faces, she understood instantly. Charlotte hadn't been decent enough to prepare her in advance, but she was bumping her off Surgical Convalescent! And the only way she could have managed it was to say that her work had been unsatisfactory. She knotted her hands behind her back, feeling the clammy stickiness in the palms, and abruptly hated Charlotte with an appalling savagery. And she hated herself, too, because she was frightened and knew it must be showing. She watched sickly while Lucretia broke open the folder and read the report stapled to Ruth's file inside.

"Well, why did you do it?" Lucretia asked crisply.

"I don't understand."

"Don't give me that. You know very well this is about Aggie Leemaster."

"Aggie Leemaster?" Ruth repeated and had to think a second before she could even remember who Aggie Leemaster was. Then it came and her fury soared. To think Charlotte would use *that* as her reason. "Aggie is not a bed patient, Miss Terry," she said, her voice shaking. "I didn't know Mrs. Range wanted her to use a bedpan all the time. During the day I thought—"

"What you thought is immaterial. It's what you did. You are not supposed to take authority into your own hands. Mrs. Range is the charge on Surgical Convalescent."

"Mrs. Range didn't tell me—"

"She says she did. She says she told you any number of times."

Ruth managed to shake her head. "She told me once—once—that Aggie Leemaster was to use a bedpan at night because she made so much noise when she went to the stool room, flushing the toilet and cleaning and everything, but she didn't say a thing about daytime. Aggie's up and around and does all kinds of ward work. Mrs. Range makes her help with the beds and the laundry bags and—"

"Spare me. I am well acquainted with Mrs. Range's ward procedures. I am also well aware of the way most of you attendants feel toward your charges. Let me tell you something, Ruth. Mrs. Range is completely justified in her action with regard to Aggie. Aggie has a cleanliness phobia. She wastes hot water, soap, even toilet tissue, cleaning places which offend her sensibilities. Mrs. Range is responsible for the amount of supplies used on her ward and has to curtail the activity of patients like Aggie."

The toilets do get dirty, Ruth thought. Would you sit on somebody else's BM or somebody's urine? "Yes, ma'am," she said. "But she didn't tell me, Miss Terry. If she had, I certainly wouldn't have gone against her."

Lucretia ignored the faint protest. "You are not a charge yet, Ruth. You work under Mrs. Range and you are expected to obey her order."

What order, for God's sake, what order? "I didn't know Mrs. Range wanted Aggie to use a bedpan during the day. She never told me that," Ruth insisted, her voice still faint but stubborn. Let them fire her, she thought sullenly. At least all her property was clear, all paid for and no tax bills not taken care of; she could get by if she had to. Nicely, in fact; she worked now only because she didn't dare stay home, didn't dare let herself get lonely. She might do what Mille had tried that time right after her husband died. She looked at Lucretia and Margaret and hated them, hated all the people who had authority over others, the big people over the little people who didn't count except to do all the dirty work and take the insults and be hounded by credit associations and pay taxes all their lives for poor paving and crowded schools with no decent recreation in a town—only beer joints and more beer joints. Yes, God, yes, she hated big people. They made wars which the little people paid for and which didn't solve a thing, only made rich people richer and killed off men like Bill Ellison—two years of laughing with him and going to bed with him, and now all she had to show for it was a bunch of silly medals. Why should she like people or take orders from somebody like Charlotte Range, who had just the same as killed Sarah Smith?

Margaret looked at Ruth's face and smoothed the front of her crisp uniform. "Surgical Convalescent needs the very best help Canterbury can find."

"I done my best. Look at my record. Never been late, never took a day off when I didn't have it coming, never."

"You're not trying to understand," Margaret said smoothly. "There is more to nursing than just being on time. Employees must exercise tact, sympathy, understanding. This is especially true of Surgical Convalescent. The patients there should not be able to sense something is wrong with the personnel."

"A personality conflict," Lucretia said. "Which is what this amounts to. Naturally, we can't have that going on."

"Personality conflict? I don't conflict with anybody. I'm good to the patients and I do my work. And I keep my mouth shut."

"There is conflict between you and Mrs. Range and it disturbs the patients," Lucretia said firmly.

"I'm good to the patients. It isn't me upsetting them. It's Mrs. Range. She upsets them. She upsets everybody."

Lucretia and Margaret exchanged glances. "You see? We were right," Margaret said, while Lucretia agreed. "That sort of attitude explains why we are making a change," she said to Ruth.

Ruth's shoulders stiffened. Here it came. Well, let it. Just so they stopped playing cat-and-mouse with her. They didn't believe her because they didn't want to. No one could be as smart as Terry and not know about Charlotte Range—no one. She hunched herself together, waiting for the blow to fall. "You are not to consider that you are being rewarded in any sense of the word, Ruth, but we have decided to make you charge on one of the wards in Rehabilitation," said Miss Terry.

"What did you say?" Ruth stammered.

Lucretia said smoothly, "We find it poor policy to force ward charges to use attendants they have developed an animosity toward, so we must take you off Mrs. Range's ward. As a corrective measure, Ruth. Please understand that. But we do not intend to fire you. Quite the contrary. We need you. You have been here a long time and are experienced. We can't afford to lose experienced employees."

Ruth was too dumfounded to speak. She could scarcely breathe. They were making her a charge! Of all the crazy . . .

Lucretia's expression was speculative. "Pull yourself together," she advised dryly. "Did you think we were going to cut your throat? As I said, we need you. All the placements on Rehabilitation have been made with the exception of two, both on night duty. We want you to take Ward Five on the night shift."

"Night shift?" Ruth whispered, thinking she couldn't have heard right. If they started her as a charge anywhere in the institution, the shift they gave her would be forever that, until she quit, retired or died. "Night shift?" she repeated foolishly.

"Anything wrong with that?" Lucretia asked, her voice turning cold.

The light behind Ruth's eyes was sudden and red. Why, the bags, the dirty, conniving bags! What a corner they had maneuvered her into, scaring her to death first, then shocking her speechless and finally exposing their joker. That explained their smug cat looks. Her thoughts milled furiously as she realized how neatly she had been trapped. And they would expect her to be grateful! Thank you, Miss Terry, thank you, Miss Rich, thank you both for not kicking me out on my ass but instead letting me finish out my miserable, no-count life in this great, wonderful institution. What if I do earn less than a sonofabitchin dollar an hour? At the most I could only get thirty-five cents for baby sitting and fifty cents for ironing. Thank you both even if you are stupid enough to believe everything Charlotte Range wants to tell you. Is anything wrong with a night shift? God, no, I don't sleep well enough anyway. Now I can stay up around the clock and think what to say when I get kidded about being kicked up the ladder.

"When you first started working at Canterbury, you were on night duty," Lucretia said, watching Ruth closely. "And you've done periods of night duty since. I can't recall that you ever complained." There was a note of warning in her voice.

Margaret snorted. This was ridiculous, putting on the soft pedal for an ignorant, maladjusted employee. "If you don't want the ward, just say no, Ruth. Someone else will be glad to get it and you—you could retire, possibly. I checked. Your retirement comes to sixty-five dollars a month now."

Ruth swallowed the sour saliva filling her mouth. Damn you! Can you live on sixty-five a month? I don't mind the nights; it's just that you weren't decent enough to ask me about it, to let me have a little say-so for the sixteen years I've given your goddam hospital. You've got to make me charge in such a roundabout way I'm almost ashamed to take it. Big as this place is, I know there must be some ward I could fit on and still have day duty. But no. Mrs. Range says I don't follow orders and you believe her when she's the worst sonofabitch liar God ever was ashamed of letting live. I've been faithful and loyal and you kick my ass for it and then give me a pillow to sit on. Sure, you want experienced employees on that new building. It's going to be a dangerous building, tricky as hell. Why don't you put Range over there and give me her ward? What harm would it have done to leave Range out of this altogether and just tell me I could have Ward Five and did I *mind* working nights? You think maybe I'd brag around I got *pull* in the office? If I did, what harm would it do?

She wiped the sweat from her hands on the back of her uniform. Damn them, she'd take it; she wasn't going to let them shove her out. When she left Canterbury, it would be because she had quit!

"Sixty-five isn't very much," she said through stiff lips. "And I'm not—not complaining. I'll take the ward. Thank you." But it was bitter to say.

Margaret's mouth spread a little. It was almost a smile. "That's the spirit. You see, everyone has to make changes as they go through life, Ruth. It keeps us from feeling we are completely indispensable. We know you will like Rehabilitation. It's a splendid building."

Indispensable? Me? Ruth thought. But not you with your high-tone education and your fat job and the way you look at a person like they didn't have clothes on. Ruth averted her eyes from Margaret's florid face.

Lucretia said briskly, now that it was settled, "I'm glad you are not complaining. When employees start complaining, about their work or their patients, they soon leave Canterbury. There is no place here for whiners and fault-finders."

"No, ma'am. Of course not."

"You need not go back on duty today. Tomorrow night,

you will take charge of Five in Rehabilitation. The change will be on the schedule when it comes out next week."

"Yes, ma'am. Tomorrow night. Ward Five."

Walking woodenly, Ruth left their presence and knew she had left her dignity there, too. They would always believe that Charlotte had been a little right about her. She had backed down; she had not stayed with her convictions. The job was more important than truth. Well, she'd give them their job someday, but on her terms, not theirs, not because they let her go but because she quit first. For some obscure reason it had to be that way.

Ruth went from the office straight to her house. In the small kitchen she stood looking out the window. Outside the air was hot and bright and beautiful, and the rose hedge separating her back yard from the alley was so heavy with bloom in all stages that it looked artificial.

At the moment she was too angry to notice it, too disturbed by what had happened. She had been reasonably content on Surgical Convalescent; she had done her work well. Maybe she did have only an eighth-grade education; hadn't she finished it out in Canterbury? And she watched what she said and where, she never took home a thing which did not belong to her, she never took time off—never late—never once late in a little better than sixteen years. What more could an institution ask of any employee? Then their gall, making her charge right after they finished letting her know she was cheap and expendable, turning her from a human creature into a shoddy piece of merchandise!

She began to shake with suppressed fury. If she didn't do something quickly, something rough and physically harsh, she would pull open the second drawer on the right side of the cabinet, snatch out a knife and slash it across her throat. It would not be hard to do. She felt her hand moving toward the drawer, her foot sliding a step; she could almost feel the blood spurting in great leaps across the spotless counter. It would serve those bitches right if she did it and they found her. But they wouldn't care. They'd say she was crazy. They wouldn't remember her two seconds after she was buried. Suddenly she jerked open the kitchen door and darted outside, grabbing up something from among the tools stacked neatly beside the steps. Moments later, leaves, twigs, stems and blossoms were flying in every direction as she slashed and tore at the hedge. Her hair began to string around her face, her breath came in gasps, but she did not stop until the once beautiful barricade was a jagged, twisted collection of stumps and piles of debris.

Dripping with sweat, she dragged herself erect, glanced once at the mess and went silently back to the house. She placed the clippers beside the other tools, entered the kitchen and shut the door with a stabbing clack. Breathing heavily, she leaned against the door. I'm all alone, she thought wildly. Nobody cares about me—nobody. I could drop dead and nobody'd know—except Millie, maybe. She's sorry for me because she ain't got sense enough not to be sorry. She probably thinks I'm queer because I've lived alone so long, but she don't care. One friend, one friend in all my life. What have I lived for?

She pushed herself away from the door and stumbled into the bedroom, pulling the shade against the lovely, bright sunshine, and lay down across the bed. She stared at the ceiling where a narrow shaft of light from the edge of the shade wove an intricate pattern. She began to cry.

Shortly before, Lucretia had watched her stumble blindly out of the office. When the door closed, she turned to Margaret. "That goddamned Range! If she doesn't stop doing this to me, I'm going to boot her out of this institution."

Margaret forced herself to be tactful. "Range does pose problems. On the other hand—"

"On the other hand what?"

"She certainly knows ward procedures. And she's devoted to her husband."

"She ought to be devoted to him. He's the only reason I put up with her. If I fire her, he'll quit and he's been a good employee. It isn't his fault he's tubercular."

Maybe it isn't her fault she's so troublesome, Margaret thought waspishly. We all have our problems. Her problem was right there in the room, but there was nothing she could do about it. She couldn't take over the throne until there was an abdication. She wished Walter would come up with something sensible instead of wanting to fool around all the time. When she thought of fooling around, she looked a little warm and complacent and well fed.

"Charlotte loves her husband," she said primly.

"Because she can dominate him," Lucretia said shortly. "That's her trouble. She has to dominate everyone around her or else there's hell to pay. I'm warning you, Margaret. I made you head of the aide-training program, and it's up to you. You talk turkey to that woman, otherwise I'll get rid of her in spite of him. And don't put it off."

She wasn't being nasty because she hated Margaret; she hated her, of course, but she had too much pride to let Margaret know what she felt. She just wanted it understood that Charlotte was not important to Canterbury, important enough to cause so much unpleasantness. If the office covered up for her too much, others might begin to expect the same concessions.

Margaret could feel heat in her face and knew she was coloring. She stepped quickly behind Lucretia's chair to hide her blush on the pretext of dropping something into the wastebasket. There was venom in her eyes as she looked at the back of Lucretia's head. She would bide her time, she thought furiously. She was twenty years younger than Lucretia and could afford to wait.

"One other matter," Lucretia said. "I want Edna Horne transferred to Rehabilitation. This is—" she looked at her desk calendar—"the fifth. See that it's done by the eighth."

"But I thought . . ." Margaret came around to where she could see Lucretia's face. "You mean you're still going to let Althea Horne do her ward management there?"

"Why not?"

"But she—I thought . . ." She couldn't very well mention the word "discipline." That lay in Lucretia's province and at her discretion. But she was thinking it very plainly. Put a girl on that building who is unreliable? It was nonsense, sheer folly. She said the next thing that came into her mind. "Isn't Edna too unstable to be on Rehabilitation? She is certainly highly unpredictable."

It was like waving something in front of a bull. Lucretia sat back in her chair where she could really stare at Margaret and did so for several seconds while Margaret began to fidget. Hold everything, something told Lucretia. Take it easy. Don't let her know what you're thinking; it'll give her an advantage over you that you'll never be able to regain. It took an effort to hold back what she wanted to say. She wanted so much to slash at Margaret, to whip her verbally and then crush her with a final, unanswerable statement, "You're fired," but a sharp edge of common sense prevented her from making this kind of a fool of herself. Margaret's as good an assistant as you can get at the moment, and what would the hospital say? That you got rid of her because she took Walter away from you and is trying to get your job as well? She swiveled back to her desk.

"When I want your opinion, Margaret," she said in a very remote voice, "I'll ask for it. You will take care of having Edna transferred immediately. Today, Margaret. If it seems that I am singling Edna out for special favors, you will remember that I still have the final authority in such matters in this hospital. And I would appreciate it very much if you do not discuss this transfer with anyone. You understand?"

Something in that carefully controlled tone said, Watch your step, I'm on to you. Margaret nodded without saying anything and walked stiffly out of the office and to her own desk, where she sat for fifteen minutes, doing nothing until she could stop shaking. *Bitch, bitch!* Someday my turn'll come!

After a time she was able to start filling in the forms necessary for Edna's transfer to Rehabilitation.

CHAPTER 20

MIKE WAS ALWAYS waiting for Kathy in between her assignments, but she thought that they met completely by accident. And each time, drawn to him almost against her will, she found herself telling him more and more of her troubles. She desperately needed somebody to confide in, and Mike had already proved himself a sympathetic listener. To her he was no more than that—a strange young man who came and went at mysterious intervals in a quiet, almost clandestine way without accounting for his presence, or absence, to anyone. She could not see, so great was her blind love for Donovan and her horror at what she had done, that the expression in Mike's eyes was more than sympathetic.

She had not told him of her part in Sarah's death. She had just spoken of the consequences and said that she was to blame. Now, five minutes later, they were quarreling.

"Stop putting words in my mouth I did not say," he told her indignantly.

"You said—you said—"

"All right. Just what did I say?"

Then she stopped and thought about it. "Didn't you—didn't you tell me to fight for what I wanted?" she asked in a small voice.

"No. You thought that yourself. I couldn't tell you anything. I could hardly talk because I hurt too damn much."

"You hurt?"

"Yes," he said grimly. "If you weren't so wrapped up in this infatuation of yours, you'd start using your head. What do you think I'm still in this pesthole for?"

She shook her head. "I don't know."

"How much time have you got?"

She looked at her wrist. "Not very much. Is this a long story?"

"No longer than yours." He took a deep breath. "I happen to be in love with you and I want to do something about it." He spoke so calmly that he might have been talking about the weather.

She thought she hadn't heard him correctly. "What did you say?" she stammered.

"I said I love you." He lost a little of his calmness. It was all he could do to keep his hands away from her.

Through the great misery of her guilty conscience, she felt shock and a little exasperation. She had told him how she felt about Donovan and then babbled out something about getting Althea in trouble, and he had tossed this at her! "Are you trying to say that what I told you about my feeling for Donovan, that's infatuation, but what you feel for me isn't? You know what the real thing is, you're really in love with me?"

"Now, wait a minute, wait a minute. Let me tell you something. I've been around. I've had girls, all kinds, thin ones, fat ones, nice ones, not-so-nice ones. This isn't infatuation, believe me." He was almost glaring at her with angry sincerity. If the situation had not been so nearly tragic, she might have smiled.

She looked at him, really looked at him. His eyes were not the color of cold steel as she had believed. They were warm and alive, a pleasant gray-blue. Behind their intensity was something that suddenly disturbed her terribly. Why, she wondered, was everything so complicated? Why did this man have to come into her life at a time when she was frantically trying to think of some way to solve the problems she already had?

"You shouldn't have done it," she said foolishly, then knew she was being foolish. You can't turn love on and off like water. If he would just go away, get out of her path and let her go on to work. She had her own problems; she didn't want the burden of his.

He guessed what she was thinking and shrugged. "It's not that simple. You ought to know that. I fell in love with you and there it is. I've known it for a long time. Sure, you told me you were in love with Macleod. You were crying like a silly little kid and I felt so bad that I couldn't say anything at all. Well, now I can. I don't care what you've done to this friend of yours. Whatever it is, she'll get over it probably. And I'm going to say what I think. I think you're not in love with this guy. You're kidding yourself. How many boy friends have you had in this hospital?" He watched her. "I thought so. You haven't had any so far. You aren't meeting any men, right? Just a few and they aren't too attractive. So all of a sudden you fall for Macleod because he's older, a dedicated man. I know how his type makes the rest of us look, like something out of the stone age."

"You don't know anything about it," she spat out with sudden anger. "You don't know how I feel at all. You're guessing. Well, it's all wrong. Now I have to go. I'll be late."

"Please." He put out a hand to keep her from walking away. "Don't go. I'm sorry."

When he smiled, he was amazingly nice. She was confused and curious in spite of her anger.

"Well, you should know better than to tell a girl she's not in love when she knows how she feels."

"Look—can I see you tonight when you get off duty?" His hand touched her arm lightly. "Let me have this one evening to explain myself."

She hesitated, looking at her watch again and thinking that it could hardly do any good. He saw the hesitation. His fingers pressed a little harder.

"There's a little café a couple of blocks outside the grounds," he said, making himself sound as casual as he could.

She remembered her lonely room and the bitter prowling and thinking she did in it lately. Anything would be better than that. Anyway, she just couldn't keep standing there with his hand on her arm. She would be late. "All right," she said, pulling away and walking on without looking back, sure that Mike was watching as she went.

There was hardly anyone in the Italian restaurant he took her to that night. They sat in a booth and a stout, elderly man with a sweeping handlebar mustache brought them menus.

"What would you like to drink?"

"Whatever you like."

"Martinis, dry," he ordered from the stout man, and then looked at Kathy. "How did it go today?"

"I didn't like it," she said.

"What would you like to eat?"

"Anything. I'm not very hungry."

"How about the specialty?"

He was frowning at his menu. She laid hers aside. "Have you been here before?"

"Yes. It's all family, from the old gentleman there down to nine great-grandchildren. He and his son own the restaurant. His three grandsons are professional men—one a dentist, the other two lawyers. His one granddaughter is a nun and all the great-grandchildren are of school age."

Kathy stared over the edge of her glass. "Where and when did you learn all this?"

He got out cigarettes, offered her one, took one himself and lit them. "One night. I was lonely and went for a walk. When I passed this place, they were having a party, somebody playing an accordion and kids running in and out. They were celebrating the old man's wedding anniversary.

142

I came in and got invited to stay." He lowered his voice. "Mama weighs about two hundred pounds, I would guess. About five feet high and hair like snow. But they were all treating her as if she were Cleopatra and Helen of Troy combined. I drank homemade wine and ate salami and cheese and hard rolls right along with everybody else—even tried to sing their Italian songs—and felt right at home." He looked at her glass. "Another drink."

"This one's fine."

"I like that dress."

"Oh." She glanced down. "It seems so funny to be wearing a dress. I want to keep feeling for my cap, to see if it's on straight."

He looked at her hair, wanting to put his fingers in its thick brown softness. The old man came to look at their glasses. He remembered Mike and smiled behind his handlebars. "You want to order now? We have eels tonight and eggplant fixed with tomatoes. Very good."

"And some *panino*—you know, with the poppy seed? And some of your Chianti." The man nodded and went off.

"What's *panino?*"

"*Panino* is homemade bread, real crusty, and the Chianti is the old man's own wine. He told me one of his friends living in California sends him the grapes." He scowled at her. "Or would you rather have something else?"

"Sounds fine. I'd like to try it, I think." She wasn't sure at all, but what did it matter? She would probably never come back to this place again. She tapped ashes off her cigarette into a big, square ash tray. "How much longer are you going to be here? In the hospital, I mean?"

"Until I get somewhere with you," he said, watching her. "I've finished what I was hired to do here, so now I'm on my own, more or less. It's a perfect setup for me in a way. No work, no obligations to confuse me. What's to keep me from seeing you every night?"

She sat up in alarm. "Now, look. You can't plan that."

"Why not?"

"You know very well why not."

The old man pushed a cart up to the booth. They were silent as he filled plates from a covered tureen and poured wine into big mugs. He put the bread between them on a tray and a saucer near the tray with at least half a pound of butter on it. The bread was long and black with seeds. The eggplant was in its own bowl, and there was a plate holding sliced cucumbers and little green peppers. Then he lit a candle in a bottle and went away, after indicating that they were to eat all they wanted.

Mike looked at her in the twinkle from the candle. "He

wants to take care of you. He just looked at you and he knew you don't eat enough."

"I used to eat like a pig. My mother's a wonderful cook. It's just here lately that I haven't been hungry."

He broke the bread and handed her a piece. "Tonight we will have none of that guilt complex, please," he said grimly. "We will talk about me with relationship to you. Well, I own a house. It's not much. But it's paid for. Two stories, stone fireplace, covered cellar at the back for vegetables. There's a nice view, particularly at the north side. A cove and a beach and a piece of rotted wharf. We could fix that. The wharf. I mean, we could keep a boat. The house is white. Outside. I haven't furnished it, just a desk and some cartons of books." He hesitated. "I want you to decide what kind of furniture you want."

"Oh, Mike, really."

"Wait—let me finish. I have this house. I have a reasonable income. You wouldn't have to work. I wouldn't want you to work. I want us to have a family. You won't be bored—I promise that. We could get some dogs. My nearest neighbor sells beagles. His wife, by the way, works out by the day, so that would take care of any housekeeping problems. Weekends, we could go in to Bangor and take in a movie. We'll get a boat, too, something you and I can handle." He took a deep breath. "Marry me, Kathy. Right away. You don't have to stay on at Canterbury, you know."

Now she knew he must be out of his mind. Besides, what right had she to any man's love after what she had done?

"I've got to finish my course," she said through stiff lips. "I owe that much right to my parents. Another thing—I should have told you right away—I'm going to help Donovan finish his book." She flinched at the look of shock in his eyes but forced herself to tell him how she had taken her lunch period and gone to see Donovan in Althea's behalf. "After you said what you did—about *not* telling me what to do. Remember?"

She stared at Mike, hoping he could understand how important this was, that she had gone to Donovan to set something right. "But he wouldn't let me say anything about her. Instead, he asked me to help him. He said there was only a week's work left and then he'd be through with the book." Her eyes were almost frightened as she stared. "What could I do? He did all the talking—he shut me up when I tried to tell him things. I just couldn't—well, I simply couldn't handle it."

His expression was strange, as if he were studying her and finding something he hadn't noticed before. "You mean you're going to muscle in on this Althea's territory now that

144

you've got a chance? After all that talk this morning about your guilty conscience?"

"I tried," she said shakily. "You've got to believe me. I tried to tell Donovan all about it—but every time I got started, he shut me up. He said he made his own decisions and that confessions—that was the word he used—were for cheap magazines, and that he wasn't interested in my confession, he was only interested in getting his book done."

"My God!"

"Mike! I did. I told him Althea hadn't done any wrong and he came right back by saying that he would decide what Althea had or had not done and that I must never forget I was on probation as long as I worked in a hospital. I was not a free moral agent. I could not make decisions or offer advice to supervisors and doctors or even criticize them."

He shook his head. "This Althea loves him," he said, his voice thick. "You told me she's crazy about him. If you take her job, she'll hate you. She'll think you deliberately pulled something. What kind of friendship is that?"

"I told you. I told you—I tried to make everything right, but he wouldn't let me."

"You don't have to do his goddamned typing!"

"He wouldn't listen to me! You've got to believe me! He said—he said—one week. One week and it'll be done. Don't you understand?"

"More than you know. One week for you to work on him just the way this Althea tried to do."

She looked down. "I can't help it," she whispered. "I love him. Is it so wrong for me to have this little bit of time to see what I can do? It isn't as if I had planned it to happen this way."

"Maybe not, but you're sure not going against it, are you?" He saw that she was crying. Suddenly he reached across the food and seized her hands. "Kathy, don't do it. Don't be that kind of girl. I don't know what you did to start all this—and I don't want you to tell me, either. I just want this much clear. I love you and whatever you've done won't make any difference about that. I might hate what you did, but I'll always love you. Always. Now, listen to me. Listen. You can't do this to your friend."

Her head lifted. "But—if you love me like that, can't you understand how I feel about him?" she asked pitifully.

After a moment, he released her hands and sat back. "Yes," he said tiredly. "I suppose so. I'll do anything I can to get you in my way, and what you've done is your way. But I know that you couldn't be happy with a love you've had to tramp over a friend's heart to get."

She put her elbows on the table and her head in her hands. "It happens all the time."

"Don't do it, Kathy," he said. "Don't come between them. Let Althea find out for herself that Macleod's really finished with her. You stay out of it until the thing's completely over."

Through her hands she muttered, "I have to start tomorrow night. I promised."

He fought his rage, his feeling of impotence, his inability to handle the moment. He hunted desperately for something worthwhile to say but could think of nothing but clichés. Abruptly he got up and came around to her side, hemming her in. "Kathy, listen to me. I love you. Come away with me. We'll get married right away. Later you can go to some other hospital and finish your training if you still want to. Please, Kathy." He had the sudden feeling that he must save her from some great danger, although he could not explain the feeling to himself.

She did not answer. He pushed her hands aside and took her chin in his hands turning her face to him. "I love you and I don't care what you've done," he added quietly.

She began to shake. "You don't want a girl who's in love with somebody else."

"I want you anytime, all the time."

"Oh, Mike, don't torment me!" The tears ran down her cheeks.

His heart turned over with pity. "Darling, I'm just trying to help." He bent his head and kissed her. When he straightened, the tears were still running in two lines down her face. "All right," he said softly. "We won't talk about it any more tonight. Eat your dinner."

But neither of them could eat. The old man came, gave them a troubled glance, cleared the table and then brought strong black coffee and a bowl of grapes. "From California," he said, his mustache quivering. "From my friend in California."

"It's nice to have friends in California," Mike said.

"Yes," said the old man, looking more distressed and going off.

"Mike, why don't you go away? There's no point in everybody's getting hurt, is there?"

He picked a grape from the cluster, examined it closely. "I'm afraid that point has already been reached and passed. No, I think I'll hang around. There may be some pieces left over. I'd like to be here to pick them up. Here, drink your coffee while it's hot."

She drank obediently. The tears had stopped, but her face was sad and lost. "You shouldn't have to pick things up—ever."

"That's all right. I'm a good picker-upper. Been doing it all my life. From information to colds at the wrong time of the year."

He was trying to cheer her up now. She was grateful enough to manage a pale smile. "Were you poor when you were little, Mike?"

"Moderately. And ornery. From about seven to ten I got in with a bad crowd. We swiped everything we could, from fruit off the neighbors' trees to candy in the corner grocery store. Then at ten I fell in love for the first time, so I had to behave myself."

"Why?"

"She was the principal's daughter. Naturally, her father watched us like a hawk. But it didn't last too long. I recovered when she had a party and wasn't allowed to invite me because my clothes were shabby."

To her surprise, Kathy felt indignation. "How mean!"

"No, not at all. The old man was just being practical."

"For ten-year-olds?"

"Well, it might have gone on until we were sixteen or so. Then he might have had trouble prying us apart. Anyway, I got over it. Driven by what I thought was a broken heart, I went to work."

"Work?"

"A paper route. That lasted until the night I lost all my collection money. Coming across a vacant lot, I was waylaid by a bunch of kids all bigger than I was. In five minutes they had the money and I never did recognize them in the dark."

"What did you do then?"

"They let me work it out," he said lightly. "They gave me a job wrapping the newspapers they mailed out to subscribers." He finished his coffee. "And that's why I became a reporter. I stayed there long enough to get printer's ink on my hands and jeans and in my system."

Unconsciously she began to relax. "Have you always been a reporter?"

"Well, I did my hitch in the Air Force. I signed up for it because I thought I would get to fly a plane. However, I'd wake up every morning with my eyes gummed shut and my eyeballs as red as a dozen hangovers in a row and nothing the doctors did seemed to help. I finally figured it out for myself. It was sleeping with a window open over my head that did it, but by that time I was running around in coveralls with a grease gun in my hands and nobody seemed to care. I'd have made a lousy pilot probably." He saw that she did not look quite so tense and unhappy. He put his face close to hers. "What kind of a little kid were you?"

She put her head back against the leather covering of the seat. "I—isn't that queer?" she said. "For a second everything was just as blank . . ." She glanced around. "As blank as those napkins. You were trotting around with a grease gun and I was trotting after you, I guess."

"Were you?"

The old man came up with another dish. "Cheese," he said. "Goat's-milk cheese. From a friend in Colorado."

"Nice to have friends in Colorado," Mike agreed.

The old man went away and they sniffed the cheese. It was white and fragrant. They each sampled a piece.

"Come on, let's get out of here before he brings us another meal. He's worried about us long enough."

He went over to pay the bill, and Kathy, thinking about him, waited at the door. She was wishing now that they hadn't had this date because it would only add another problem to all the rest. Somehow, she must make him understand that nothing had been changed; she still intended to have her week with Donovan. Mike couldn't shame her any more than she already was ashamed.

When they went out the door together they walked slowly away in the darkness while she thought of ways to tell him that he absolutely must leave her alone. All he could think of, with the soft, fragrant darkness around them, was that they could have been lovers if it weren't for her obsession.

CHAPTER 21

ALTHEA WALKED FURTIVELY past Donovan's office door in the Surgical Building. She wondered whether he was inside or not. She entered Larry's office and stood with the door open, looking around her. Larry was at the window and she didn't see him right away. When he spoke, she started a little.

"You can shut the door," he said, watching her from the window. She did and moved forward hesitantly. "Sit down, Althea," he said pleasantly. There was no reproof in his voice, none of the coldness that she had expected to humiliate her. Nor was his voice sly and insinuating, or gloating. He was just kind in an ordinary way, in the way he would probably be to any student in a jam.

She sat down with relief in one of the two chairs in his room and he came around his desk and sat down in the other. He took out his cigarettes, lit two and handed her one. She accepted hers gratefully and for a moment they smoked companionably.

Finally he said, looking at her, "I won't say I'm glad this happened. You know I am."

She looked down at her cigarette. It would be pointless to ask him if he were glad Sarah Smith had died. She knew what he meant, and it had nothing to do with Sarah. She wished she had the courage to tell him that nothing had changed, that she could not stop thinking about Donovan and wanting him.

"How would you like to follow me around the hospital for a week?" When she looked up, he was playing with a pencil. "The office is still going to give you ward management on Rehabilitation. That will be your last two weeks before graduation. In the meantime, there is this week. I would like to take you around to the different wards and explain their procedures. No two are really alike, you know."

Ward management on Rehabilitation! They still wanted her there! She felt the beginning of a little headache. As she reached over to crush her cigarette in the tray on the desk, she felt the throb in the back of her head increasing with the slight motion. She looked up at Larry.

"Why are you so kind," she asked abruptly, "when you know what I've done?"

"What did you do?"

"They think . . ." She hesitated. "I left this patient," she said slowly, "and she died."

"So? She might have died with you there."

"She choked to death."

Larry put his finger tips together. "It's not unusual. Cardiacs do sometimes choke to death."

"But Donovan—Dr. Macleod—"

"Made a federal case out of it. I know." Larry nodded at her. "That's his way. I'm glad you found out in time. All the more reason for you not to let it ride you." He plainly meant, All the more reason for you to forget him.

At least he was not being personal and talking about marriage again. Perhaps he did not care any longer, she thought; perhaps what she had done had cured him. She felt very tired suddenly, too tired to let it bother her. How could she go on living now? she wondered. She was exhausted with her grief and with her attempts to hide it, to keep it decently to herself. She was also irritated at Larry. This was supposed to be an official interview. She felt, strangely, that she could have almost enjoyed his anger, but not this kindness, this tolerance. It wasn't proper. She deserved punishment. She wouldn't have minded being whipped if physical pain could take away the pain of knowing that whatever had been about to flower between herself and Donovan was now dead.

Larry observed her closely. For a moment he wished that

his profession did not help him to know what was going on in her mind. Somehow, it wasn't decent; it withheld from her the status of an individual with the right to think freely. Then he was glad he could know, because he loved her so deeply. She needed help now; she was as bereaved as any widow, more so because her love had never been consummated. He wasn't thinking of himself and his own needs especially. She would reject them more than ever for a while. But the way her eyes clouded over worried him, made him realize how much she was alone and how difficult it would be for her to turn to anyone for relief. At this moment she was probably feeling resentful toward him and she would turn against him first, because he was there. He would have to be very casual about what he did, he told himself grimly, and hope that what he really wanted to do would go unnoticed.

"We'll trot around this morning," he said as though he had a blueprint of a plan for her laid on his desk. "This afternoon, you will rest and do things to yourself, wash your hair or fix your nails or whatever you do when you have an afternoon off. And tonight we're going out, you and me. Wear your prettiest dress. Something glamorous—because I'll find a place in this damn town outside the gate where it's all right to wear a glamorous dress."

Her breath caught. She was afraid for a second she would cry. "I can't—I mean, will it be all right with the office?" she asked raggedly.

"It will be all right. It's an order from Dr. Denning." He smiled at her and she could breathe again. "We'll find a place where we can get a Martini before dinner and some brandy afterwards. We'll relax and forget our troubles and maybe we'll drive out into the country. We'll turn on the radio. And we won't talk shop." He tried to make his face as serious as possible. "Even Dr. Denning gets tired of talking shop."

She stared at him, her eyes wide. "Then maybe I can sleep," she said without thinking.

"If you can't, I'll see that you get something to help you." But one pill at a time, he thought, one every day, just one. She could save them, of course, and take them all at one time later. But if she really needed something to help her sleep, she might not think of that; she might not remember that it was a trick some patients used to attempt suicide.

He put the pencil in one pocket, his cigarettes in another and got up from his chair. "All right, Miss Horne, are you ready?" he said in his best professional manner.

She stood and smoothed her uniform, straightened her cap. "It isn't very simple, is it?" she said, not looking at him.

"It will be what we let it be," he replied gravely. He knew

what the hospital thought of him. Donovan thought he was some kind of a male tramp, the office felt he had the makings of a good doctor, the affiliates wanted him to take them out to motels, and Herrington thought him rather young and immature. But at this moment he was sure he knew the remedy for Althea, and when the time came, the right time, the right place, he would let her know it.

"You take things too seriously," he added gently.

"Yes, I suppose so," she murmured and went out with him into the hall.

When they passed Donovan's door she very carefully did not look at it.

Donovan was as disturbed as Lucretia this same morning. From his office window he had seen Althea approach the building and had remembered that Larry was taking over where he had left off. It was what he had planned and expected, certainly nothing to feel upset about. The girl had proved she wasn't too good after all. She was not reliable, she had been negligent, she needed disciplining. As chief of staff, he could not afford to be lenient or overlook her weaknesses just because she was beautiful.

He left the window and moved about restlessly, glancing at his files, lighting a cigarette to take several deep drags and then crushing it out and almost at once lighting another. When the sound of Larry's outside door opening and closing came to him, he was still for a few moments, his head bent to listen. He heard a murmur of words but nothing distinguishable because of the deadening effect of Madge's cubicle between the two offices. He felt a swift impulse to join the discussion but restrained himself. It would hardly be proper now for him to interfere in whatever Larry decided to do. Still, merely thinking about Larry filled him with uneasiness. Larry was conscientious where patients were concerned, but he was vigorously amorous. Donovan felt that the affiliates had never been safe around Larry. But why should he care now what happened to Althea? The matter of Althea Horne was no longer under his control. A girl who looked like that ought to be able to take care of herself. With her looks, he presumed, she must have had plenty of experience.

But somehow he could not be entirely disinterested. They were more than just doctor and nurse; she had helped him with his book; they had become friends. They called each other by their first names; there had been a casual but pleasant relationship between them. He remembered her difficulty in spelling many of the medical terms in his notes until he realized his crimped writing was partly to blame; but she had had no trouble at all in making wonderful coffee in his percolator. She had simply taken out the inside, soaked the pot for a time with some solution of her own making, then rinsed it thoroughly and boiled the coffee directly, letting it settle well before she poured it. It had tasted exactly like the coffee his father used to make on camping trips—strong and delicious. And the many nights they had worked late, slaving actually, she had always come up with something, sweet rolls or special cookies, cadged—she said with a little smile—right from the best cook in the institution. That, of course, would be the head dietitian for Hydro. So the girl had made friends, she was not antisocial. In fact she seemed to love her work, everything she did. Why, then, had he got so angry over the death of one patient? Why, yesterday, had he felt that he never wanted to see her again?

He had spent the rest of the day and most of the night trying to rationalize his feelings. She was just a student. He had known her less than six months, yet long enough to evaluate her thoroughly. She was competent, loyal, honest. She had to be honest, or else she would have lied yesterday when she saw that she was in trouble. But she hadn't quibbled or tried to evade her responsibility. She hadn't even tried to take advantage of their friendship. She had simply looked at him . . . As if I were cutting her heart out, he thought, almost angry with himself for thinking it.

He heard sounds outside his office and listened intently. They were leaving now. He heard the outside door close and steps going by his door and then the ward door being opened and closed. He moved hastily to the window and watched them walk away. She's almost as tall as Larry, he thought, remembering that she was as tall as he himself was and, with heels, an edge taller.

He went back to his desk and sat down. Hell, he thought. Why don't I face it? I know what's wrong. He had known from the very beginning of their relationship. And yesterday, just yesterday, before he started his tour of the wards, and before he was called to Surgical Convalescent because of Sarah, he had seriously thought about what he could do to ease himself out of a situation that might become both embarrassing and enslaving, certainly undesirable. Now the thing had happened—through no fault of his—and he was out of it, well out of it.

So why should I sit here and feel that I've behaved badly? he asked himself angrily. She's just a nurse, an affiliate. I haven't ruined her reputation. I won't do as much to her as Denning will if he gets a chance. Is it because I *want* to take her to bed? Instantly he had a vision of taking her into his bedroom and undressing her, filling himself with the sight of her body, letting his hands know her also. He was stunned at the swift way the picture seized him and the way it held him immovable until it came to a conclusion like that of a pornographic movie. He was shocked that he had so little mental control.

Someone knocked on the door. He rubbed his face against a sleeve and the sweat on his hands off on his trousers before he tried to speak. "Come in," he said, turning his head.

It was Kathy standing in the doorway. She had come to confess. It was something she had to do and had known she would have to do it since her talk with Mike. The charge on the ward where she was working had given her an early lunch period, and she had come directly to Surgery and Donovan's office. When she opened the door, she could go no farther, but stood looking at him, wondering frantically how she was going to get it out, the most shameful thing she had ever done. It would be easier to cut open her stomach and pull out her entrails than to tell Donovan she had killed Sarah Smith. Would he have her sent to jail? Committed as a patient? What would he do? She couldn't say, "I did it because I love you!" He would think she was crazy, overemotional, unstable, unbalanced, paranoiac—all the handy words of the profession went through her mind as she saw him applying them to her. What could she say? How could she start saying it?

"Well, don't just stand there," he barked. A standard opening wedge for doctors, teachers and parents, she thought. Don't just stand there. If you've done something you shouldn't, come in and get it off your chest.

But he was not thinking that she looked guilty of anything, or that she looked anything at all particularly. All he knew of her was that this girl was a close friend of Althea's, that Althea had often talked about her.

"Come in," he said a little more gently. Whatever she wanted to say, she was obviously frightened, and that made him feel calmer and more at ease, more relaxed. A frightened nurse was something he could cope with. He had often noticed Kathy. Plainly she liked her work and liked the patients. "I've been thinking about you," he said, which was not true but gave him an excuse for what he intended to say later.

He must already *know*, she thought in panic, and was lost. Mesmerized, she crept to the chair he pushed out for her, sank down and waited. She was too frightened to notice how pale he looked and the nervous way he kept wiping his hands.

"Well," he said pleasantly, "did you have a nice Fourth?"

She was so astonished she could scarcely think. A nice

Fourth? What did that have to do with Sarah Smith's death? She stared at him. Then she realized that whatever it was he had on his mind, it had nothing to do with Sarah. He did *not* know about Sarah; he was not going to help her a bit in her confession; and now she was filled with a terrible sense of desolation because she was so alone with her sin and did not know how to go about telling it. Why don't I just say, I love you? she wondered helplessly. I love you, I love you. What would he say in return?

CHAPTER 22

IT HAD BEEN A STRANGE, terrible and surprising week for Kathy, a long week since that hot, humid Fourth of July when her world had been rudely turned upside down. She had done things which she had never imagined herself capable of, and now she seemed to herself a monster, unfit to associate with normal, decent people, yet unable to admit her guilt to anyone.

For the worst thing about her crime, it seemed to her, was that it had succeeded in getting her what she had wanted. She had her own ward to supervise, however difficult it was to work there in her present state of mind. And—much to her surprise—Donovan Macleod had been friendly and receptive. Now, replacing Althea, she was doing his typing at night, finishing the book which had made her so jealous. She could hardly claim, it was true, that Donovan was passionately interested in her. But he seemed to like her, and when she was with him he put aside his habitual sternness.

It was just what Kathy had wanted, just what she had envied, but it gave her no pleasure. The memory of her crime sapped her strength and confidence, and the first day on the male ward to which she had been newly assigned—thanks to her new friendship with Macleod—became a nightmare.

She entered the ward to find one charge, two attendants and a huge roomful of men. They were young to middle-aged, one hundred and fifty of them, seated in rows of hard oak chairs. Never had she seen such apathy, she thought, such listless indifference. Some of them rocked slowly and ponderously. Others were immobile, like lifesize carvings. A few stared back at her while others gazed out nearby windows, and a certain number were pushing heavy weights wrapped in pieces of blanket around the floors. This task obviously was designed to keep these patients busy; the floor was already highly polished, and the pushers leaned as much as they pushed.

The charge was a slender man. Pretty, Kathy thought. "Make yourself at home," he told her, not getting up from his desk chair. "Pete Mahoney said you'd be here this morning." He introduced her to the attendants sitting near the desk. Then he took off his glasses, placed them in a shirt pocket, lifted his feet to a comfortable position on the top of the desk and immediately drifted off into a half-conscious doze.

Of the two attendants, the man remained sprawled lumpishly in his seat. The woman rose to pull another chair into their little circle. "Sit down," she said loudly but not unkindly. "There's nothing to do until breakfast and that won't be for—" she looked at her wrist—"forty minutes. Sit down, sit down."

The man stared at Kathy lasciviously.

"Don't pay him any mind," the woman said, amused by the sudden flow of color into Kathy's face. "He's always like that, 'n' don't make any difference whether it's somebody like you or somebody eighty years old and wide as a barn door. We'll go down to the clothes room in a minute and make ourselves some coffee."

"Our own, by God," the man said. "None of this hospital rotgut for us. Eats your guts clear through, by God."

"I'll tell you about the ward while we're waiting," the woman said. "You won't mind working here once you get the hang of things. There ain't a thing to do, really."

Kathy listened, her eyes glazing in an effort to understand. It was more or less a matter of translation. If she took their words and omitted all the "my Gods" and "by Gods," it made sense. The men slept in dormitories which were kept locked at night. Once each hour, the night shift checked the dormitories, making sure everything was in order. They looked at the beds with flashlights and poked or pulled at covers if something did not seem just right. The patient whose bed was found soiled was in for a bad time.

The smell inside the locked dormitories was terrible, a combination of urine, fecal gas, sweat and bad breath. Nearly as bad were the combined sounds of groaning, whispering, singing and cursing. Some of the men tried to get into bed with other men. A few succeeded; others crawled hastily back to their own beds, followed by hoarse shouts of anger.

The men were allowed no private possessions, no rings, watches, billfolds, photographs, clothing, the woman told Kathy. "They fight over that kinda stuff," she said. "My God, you should see the squabbling they can do over a piece of soap, a little piece of soap."

"What happens to their things?"

"They're wrapped, labeled 'n' sent to be stored. When they

leave they can have it all back. That is, if they're walking."

"What do you mean?"

The woman sniffed. "What do you think?"

The charge opened one eye. "She means most of 'em go out in a box, in which case their relatives get their stuff." He closed his eye and returned to his nap.

He's been listening, Kathy thought; he's heard every word. The woman went on with her account. Twice a week each man was given a sack of coarse-cut tobacco and a package of cigarette papers, and a few were allowed plugs of chew. These men carried empty gallon fruit tins which they guarded carefully, because if they were caught spitting on the floor, punishment was swift and sure. Magazines came in regularly from people outside the hospital, but the attendants checked these for their own benefit before giving them to the patients, since for the most part they would be shredded wastefully, used as packing under lumpy mattresses or stuffed into pants legs, for some unknown reason, or even down the toilets.

Hour after hour the men sat in the hard chairs. They shuffled to the toilets and back to the chairs. They drifted to the desk and waited patiently for a light from the matches they were not permitted to carry. When the charge looked up, they held out corn-cob pipes or hand-rolled cigarettes dripping tobacco at both ends. Sometimes an epileptic would have a convulsion, often hurting himself when he fell during the initial stage and creating mild excitement among the attendants, all of which the patients watched pleasurably until the attack subsided. Often there would be quarrels between patients resulting in flailing fists and obscene remarks, although not much of this was permitted to happen on a well-managed ward, the woman said; a good charge could smell out the quarrels almost before they started. And of course there was a certain amount of teasing on the part of the attendants. A person can't work on these wards and not have a little fun, or he'd go crazy himself, the woman said. Like that little old man there—see him? Well, he's been out here so long he don't remember nothing about living anywhere else. He does ward work, empties trash barrels and carries out laundry. Sometimes we lock him out instead of in, see? While he isn't looking, maybe digging down inside a trash barrel. We lock the door and when he tries to open it to get back in on the ward, he can't; he sees us inside but he can't get the door open. He cries. My God, he cries like a baby. When he starts banging his head against the door, we let him in. My God, you'd think we was letting him into the finest place in the world. We never been able to figure out why he acts that way.

What makes you act your way? Kathy thought, but did not

ask aloud. What right did she have to question others when they did something she felt was cruel or inhuman? Wasn't she a greater sinner?

The patients had their own dining room, opened only for the meals which they looked forward to eagerly, not because they were so hungry but because it gave them something to do. When the meal gong rang and the lines began to form, the stronger men pushed and shoved ahead, leaving the feeble and lame and blind for the attendants to guide in. For recreation small groups were taken for strolls on the grounds, but this happened rarely since there were so many men and only four caretakers. However, the men were accustomed to waiting; they were always waiting for something.

Infrequently, the occupational-therapy department of the hospital sent over a film to be shown on the ward. When this happened, the men scurried around, pulling the shades on the long, barred windows, finding blankets for those without shades, placing the oak chairs in audience position, then settling, forgetting temporarily the hardness of the chairs. The excitement of these times permeated the ward for hours afterward, although the films were ancient and the sound track either dubbed in or indistinct from hard use.

When visitors came, the torpor lifted. "For me?—for me?" the men would cry, and those who could would rush to the heavy ward door, all trying at once to see out a six-by-twelve window into the reception hall beyond. There was always a kind of desperate anxiety in most of their faces. They clutched small possessions, a rubber band, a sliver of soap wrapped in toilet tissue, a ragged magazine, a banana skin, some shreds of tobacco. These trifles gave them a feeling of independence and inner security. The trifle became a treasure representing the impenetrable fortress of the spirit. Yet these men were vegetables, Kathy thought, they are vegetables now. Was it possible that they had been born sweet, lovable babies, that they were once earnest little boys, taking mechanical toys apart to discover the toys' magic? Had they ever looked around them and asked questions about the universe no one could answer? She could scarcely visualize them as anything but these lumpish men, when actually they were all sons and some of them were brothers, husbands and fathers. What if one of them had once belonged to me? she thought with horror. It was such a painful thought that for a moment she forgot her own terrible situation.

Every morning for the rest of that week, Kathy went on duty feeling as if she were getting ready to do battle. The first thing she did on the ward was to look around uneasily at the men coming out from their night of confinement, most of them just as dull and tired as they had been before they went to bed the night before. Then she unlocked the door to the closet reserved for the use of the employees on the ward, hung her cape on a hook, put a box of matches in one pocket, and composed her face. When she emerged, she felt she was reasonably well prepared to sit near the desk where she would be listening to waves of gossip punctuated by "my Gods" and "by Gods." She heard about supervisors who were not RNs but had come up the hard way, and about affiliates going to be RNs slipping down the easy way. No one was excluded from these exchanges, not the office force or the medical staff or other attendants or the dietary workers. Even the charge's wife was brought into the conversation when he was momentarily absent.

"No wonder the goddam sucker's so tired he's gotta nap all the time. She has to go to these joints, see? You know, beer joints. And he tags along."

"Then he spends all his time dragging her out from under the tables, by God."

"Or else she sneaks outside with some other guy and he has to be looking under all the bushes."

"All I gotta say he's a goddam fool, putting up with all that whoring around. She ain't that good-looking."

The woman looked at the man. "How you know what she looks like? You seen her without any clothes?"

"By God, I don't hafta. She wears them sleazy nylon things you can see right through."

Kathy gritted her teeth. I won't say anything, she thought, I won't, I won't! They're just baiting me, trying to make me lose my temper. She did not know how safe they felt around her. They were sure she had troubles, and though they could never trap her into discussing what bothered her, still, whatever it was made her reliable. Having her own problems, she wasn't going to bother or be bothered with theirs. When they became aggravated and slapped patients, or rifled their pockets in disgust and dumped what they found into the trash barrels, they did not worry about Kathy. She wasn't going to run to the office. Not even when they broke into the cartons of cigarettes brought some patient by a friend or relative and sold the same cigarettes to the patient instead of giving them to him. They teased her because the ward routine was so humdrum to them.

But they were also patient with her. The woman showed her how to herd the patients into the dining room at mealtimes. Kathy moved between the small tables and was glad the food looked good and plentiful. She had heard about institutions where the dietary departments were disgraceful; at least these patients were well fed. She noticed that there were fruit and rolls, meat and vegetables, and always milk and dessert, along with strong black coffee. She stood by the patients who shook most violently and watched to see that they got the food into their mouths. She nudged the vacant-eyed who just sat and stared.

"Eat," she said. When they shifted the stare to another spot, she lifted a spoon and fed them.

"Don't let them think you'll do that all the time," the woman cautioned from a corner of her mouth. "My God, they know what they're doing. When they get hungry enough, they'll eat."

"But they're so thin. Maybe they'd eat more if someone helped them."

"You feed 'em and they'll let you and not eat any more, either. God, see what I mean? Lookit that!"

A patient had grabbed up a spoon and was forcibly feeding one of the vacant-eyed men, but instead of doing it gently and carefully as Kathy had, he was cramming food into the other's mouth so that it oozed everywhere. Impatiently, he discarded the spoon and began using his hand, shoving and mashing food against tongue and teeth until his victim rose in choking rebellion.

The woman said disgustedly, "He saw you do it, so he wants to try. I tell you, leave 'em alone. They'll make out all right."

Kathy looked at the two men, her stomach turning. "What if they don't?"

"They'll get transferred to an untidy ward, so why should we worry? There's a hundred and fifty patients on this ward, and us four employees, and the charge don't count, so that makes three of us. We ain't got time to take care of everything, believe me."

Feeling sick, Kathy turned away. Why should we worry if it's just another step downward? Why indeed? Shove them along, push them further into decay, tease them, take away their treasures, their identity. She felt something touch her skirt and looked down.

"Here," said a man, offering her an orange. He had an idiotic expression and looked to be eighteen or nineteen.

"Thank you." She dropped the orange into a pocket and took out a stick of gum to give in exchange. She stared at the blank eyes and the saliva bubbling over the boy's lower lip. Why, he wasn't a man yet, he wasn't anywhere near a man yet. She wondered what he could understand. Had he ever driven a car or lived in a nice house with a patio and a garden and some flower beds? Had he ever been told by his mother that he could help himself to what was in the refrigerator (all but the roast; that was for tomorrow's dinner)? Or to get home from the show by eleven-thirty or else he would hear from his father? She placed the gum in his outstretched hand and for a moment was blind with tears. Where was his mother? she thought foolishly. Why didn't his mother come and take him home?

Kathy didn't mind Shave Day too much; it came only once a week and the men seemed to appreciate the smooth feel on their faces afterward. The only real arguments were about who was first in line or whose turn was next.

But Bath Day! Whoever invented such a hellish procedure? Twice a week, Tuesday and Friday, the men lined up in naked rows and herded into the shower room for scalp-to-toe scrubbings.

She stood with the man and woman at the door of the clothes room first. Inside, two patients assembled clean overalls, shirts and socks into neat rolls, each tagged with a name. It made Kathy feel a little peculiar to realize these patients knew the name and clothing size of every other patient on the ward. It would have taken her six months to learn all that, she was sure.

When the bundles were ready, the dormitory doors were unlocked. Immediately, a wave of naked men poured out, some clutching at themselves in an agony of embarrassed modesty, the others making the most of the moment with obscene manipulations. A few carried some treasure they had managed to conceal the night before, a shirt stiff with an accumulation of sweat and spilled food, a pair of overalls crammed with bits of paper, a lone sock. One old man had pencil stubs and an apple core clamped against the sparse gray mat of hair on his concave chest. He protested with hoarse cries as these were confiscated.

As Kathy watched, the woman stood outside and slapped or punched the men into the shower room. The man posted himself at the other door and pulled or jerked them out. When a patient began the cycle, he was dry; he stank and itched and always cursed loudly as he received his slap or punch from the woman. He emerged, dripping with suds and water, shaking with a nervous chill and still cursing. He was inspected by the man, and if his hair, his hands or his genitals were not clean, he was started on the cycle again.

Kathy could scarcely tell who swore the loudest, the men or the two attendants. Helpless, completely confused, she stared. She was surrounded by patients standing over small pools of water as they shook themselves into clean shirts and overalls. They looked, noisily, usually for lost items—a sock, a shoe, a comb. Kathy jumped as a voice came around her elbow.

"Lady, you see a little green comb? Well, a red one, then?

No? Well, dadgum it, you got a match to light this here pipe? I sure fooled 'em, kept this here pipe right with me when I took m' bath. Sure don't wanta lose this pipe on account I got it broke in just right. Here, put your nose down close. Smell that? Rubber bands. I find 'em on the floor sometimes. Yessir, nothing makes a pipe smell better'n rubber bands less'n it's a good, big wad of hair. I always say there ain't nothin' like rubber bands or a big wad of hair."

The man came up to them. "My God, Chester, what you smoking, for crissake? Not rubber bands again! Jesus Christ, you ol' sonofabitch, you know better'n that!" His nose working like a rabbit's, the man confiscated the pipe and sent it clattering into the trash barrel.

Sadly the old man trotted off, remembering belatedly to fasten the fly on his overalls. Kathy gazed after him. He must be an awful liar, she thought moodily. He probably got a new pipe every day or so, immediately forgetting the previous one. But what would she have done or said, she wondered, had she been in his place and the ward all her life, every dreary moment of it? Would she have been able to keep track of anything beyond something to hold in the hands like a pipe? The months and seasons and years, for instance, the other existence that held a mother or sister, perhaps a wife and children, the time before the headaches began and everything got confusing and frightening and finally the job was gone, the job which kept a man decent, because who would hire a man who couldn't keep his wits about him? After that, a man wasn't a man any longer; he was just a vegetable.

A young man in white unlocked the ward door and sauntered in. "Donations," he said cheerily when he reached the desk.

The woman grunted, the man swore, the charge sat up in alarm. "Godamighty, what for now?" he demanded while Kathy stared questioningly.

"Come off it, you know what happened. This is for Pete. Everybody's gonna donate to help pay for his lawyer. We gotta help him outa his jam."

From the side of her mouth the woman told Kathy, "Pete Mahoney. Our supervisor, you know. Driving too fast. Hit somebody with his car."

"Aw, they can't do nothing to Pete," the boy boasted. "He's a supervisor"—as if that placed Pete on a special pinnacle beyond the law. "Anyway, it was accidental."

"Paper said it was manslaughter," the charge snorted.

"You didn't read that very good. The paper don't dare say too much. That editor gets a cut from Herrington, don't you know? Yes-sir, that editor gets *something*. That editor—whatsisname—Tabor? He don't ever say anything too bad about the hospital."

"Yeah, I heard you the first time. He don't *dare* on account he might get his tit caught in a wringer."

"So that manslaughter means it was accidental. He couldn't help himself, see?"

"I don't know, I wasn't there," the charge said sourly. "Offhand, I'd call it a killing, just plain killing. The damn fool was driving seventy-five miles an hour."

The young man looked at them all disgustedly. "Look. You want me to put it down that you wouldn't donate on account you think your supervisor *killed* somebody? You want that, huh?"

It was exactly what Kathy was thinking. No matter how guilty she felt herself, it wasn't right to give from what little she had to help another killer go free. "I won't donate to anything like that."

To her surprise the charge was agreeable. "By God, you don't have to. I wouldn't, either, if I could get away with it. But Pete Mahoney makes out my rating. If I don't ante, I'm liable to find myself third or fourth on a drag ward. Even worse, on a bed-patient ward. God, I'm getting too old for that, wrestling around all day cleaning up messes and making beds."

"I'll give," the woman said reluctantly. "But it ain't because I want to. I need every cent of my pay check. What if it was *me* hit somebody with *my* car? You think Pete would help me? God, no! He'd be the first one to tell on me, and look righteous and proper while he done his duty. That's exactly what he'd do."

Moodily the man surveyed the room beyond the desk. "Godddam, if it ain't one thing, sure as hell it's another. Just the other day they put the bite on me for flowers for somebody's grandmother I never even heard worked out here. Well, I sure as hell ain't gonna give more'n five bucks to stay second on this stinking ward, by God. Not for a stinking stool pigeon like Pete Mahoney!"

The patients stared at the little group around the desk. One old man picked up his spitting can, cradled it under one arm and shuffled to the desk.

"Kin I have some paper? Wanna write m' folks."

"You ain't got no folks," the man said crossly. "God, you never did have no folks. They found you inna alley behind a whorehouse right after you was hatched, you ol' bastard."

The other spit in his can and raised rheumy eyes. " 'N' a pencil. Envelope, too."

"Get away from this desk before I kick your stinking ass clear across the room." But the man said it mildly, not really meaning it. He rummaged in a desk drawer, pulled out tablet, pencil and envelope. Then from his own pocket he added a slightly flattened candy bar to the collection and shoved it all into the old man's free hand. "Now don't come near this desk again on this shift, you hear?"

The old man snuffled vigorously, clutched his loot and plodded back to his chair. He placed the can between his feet, the rest in his lap. Concentrating carefully, he unwrapped the candy and broke the bar into small pieces, passing them to those men nearest him. Suddenly, he discovered he had given them all away; there was nothing left for himself. Swallowing repeatedly, he stared at his lap, then lifted the candy wrapper and licked the paper. Finally he dropped it into his can and began his letter. At the desk, the young fellow making his pitch for the supervisor's benefit stuffed the contributions into his box and left the ward, whistling cheerfully for mission accomplished.

Kathy remembered the candy bar as she listened to the shouts and curses and slaps. A boy of seventeen passed her, his head down, his mouth sullen. Kathy turned her head to watch him. His case card stated that he had killed his father. He was thirteen when it happened and vaguely remembered that he had stolen fifty cents from his mother's purse and sneaked off to a show, returning home with the good smell of chocolate candy on his hands to find his father waiting, strap in hand. From there, his memory was hazy, a dim recollection of the strap going up and down, then his father knocking him down and stamping on him. He also thought his mother stood in the bedroom door, screaming or crying, but from that point the picture was obscure. Someone got off the floor, but whether it was his father or himself, the boy could not say. Yes, he had been told he was taller and a little heavier than his father when it all happened, but he couldn't tell anyone what his father looked like. Blond, dark, heavyset—he did not know. The sight of blood sent him into screaming frenzies and no one ever came to see him. He usually sat very quietly, his eyes staring with an expression faintly like horror at his large hands spread flatly on his knees.

Kathy swallowed a lump in her throat as her eyes followed him. Then she looked at Chester, trotting sadly off down the hall, still mumbling and shaking his head. Leave that poor little Chester alone, she thought wildly. What difference does it make if he smokes rubber bands in his pipe? Outside this hospital, people put up with all kinds of smells. Let Chester have his rubber bands, let him have them, it's all he'll ever have!

The boy came back, almost bumped into her. He slouched

like any teen-ager. She wondered why his mother hadn't kept him home instead of letting Canterbury have him. Perhaps her grief and shock had been too great to let her protest the decision of a court which believed it was doing the best for all concerned and providing the proper care for a boy who could kill his own father.

Chester, too. What if he was small and harmless and could live on a dull, weekly routine of food, bed, roof, two baths and rubber bands for his pipe? Obviously no one wanted to be bothered with him in the outside world. Maybe he peeked in the neighbors' windows.

What's the matter with you, Kathy? You think it's time for the kingdom of God for these people? Maybe Chester's relatives have their own problems. Maybe Chester hasn't got any relatives. And that boy needs care which he'll get in Canterbury—that is, if he gets a little, just a little, of something he probably didn't get when he was growing up—sympathy, love, understanding, anything you want to call it. Just see to it that he gets it now from people like you —caretakers! And don't question, don't judge, until you earn the right.

I killed a patient, Kathy thought, shuddering. She bent to pick up a small green comb her shoe had carelessly kicked. She thought that she was going to be sick. She took the comb and went to sit near the desk. Her head ached with pity. Her face filled with it; it flooded her eyes. They live out their days always waiting, she thought, and she could not help them because she was waiting, too. For what? Compromise? She had done that when she stopped trying to straighten out matters about Sarah's death. Forgetfulness? As if she could forget. Full of self-scorn, she bent her head and listened to the sounds of men with nothing to do but sit all day, day after day, endlessly waiting for God knows what. Inside, she felt as if she were crying, not only for the patients, but also because Althea was not her friend any more and because the thought of Mike Stewart made her feel that she was unkind and most of all because she had killed a patient and the knowledge was always there, in the background of her thoughts.

Tonight I'll see Donovan, she said to herself, turning to this thought almost greedily because it might help her stop thinking about other things. Tonight and tomorrow night and the next and then it will be over; there won't be any reason for me to go to his apartment again. So what will happen then? Will he care or will he be just as glad the book's finished, to? Mike—she saw him every day somewhere on the grounds. He trapped her, after a fashion, either going or coming from her ward, but she refused to date him as long as she could help Donovan. She didn't see Althea at all, hadn't seen her since the Fourth of July, the day of Sarah's death. But on the fifteenth they would meet, because they had both been assigned to Rehabilitation for ward management, Althea on day duty and she on night, so they would cross paths twice every twenty-four hours; they would have to speak, because as supervisors the building would be their responsibility, and the one going off duty would give to the one coming on duty a full account of all the activity during her shift.

Why has she avoided me? Kathy wondered, her mind going helplessly back to the day of Sarah Smith's death. Has she guessed something? She certainly acted suspicious that day. I think she must have guessed. Or did I say something to give myself away? She supposed she would always wonder that. She missed Althea dreadfully. Their friendship had been deep and complete with feminine understanding. It happens only two or three times in a lifetime, Kathy thought sadly, that a girl finds a real friend in another girl. The rest are just acquaintances. We call them friends but they aren't, really, and I had a real friend, and what did I do? When she got to this point in her thinking, her mind would become blank, as though deliberately trying to slide over the picture without seeing it clearly, and then she would be back at the beginning again.

She asked herself whether she should request ward management somewhere else. But that would look strange, wouldn't it? She would have to give the office a good reason for her request, and what could she say? But perhaps they were already wondering why she and Althea were no longer close and what had happened. Well, it was odd. You just don't have a friend one day and then the next day no friend, without a reason, without something serious having happened between you. Only that was the most peculiar part. She and Althea had never had any words at all since the Fourth. Althea hadn't come to her and said, "Hey, kid, what's the matter around here?" Nor had she gone to Althea and said that if they weren't speaking, she would like to know why. They just did not see each other. Althea no longer knocked on her door to borrow a pair of nylons, or had time for a cup of coffee at the cafeteria, or told her some story they could both laugh over.

She doesn't come to me because she's been so terribly hurt and humiliated, Kathy thought. It's for me to go to her. Ordinarily it would be, but I can't, I simply can't. I can't knock on her door and say, "Althea, I'm so sorry things have gone wrong for you," because she would look at me and know *why* they went wrong. Anyway, it's too late. I might have been able to do it that same day or the next, but here it's the ninth, so I've waited too long. It would be like sending codolences to the bereaved a year or two after the bereavement, or calling somebody up and telling him you can't come to his party after the party's over.

She had hope occasionally that Althea would believe she had kept away from her because she was afraid the office might now view their friendship with disapproval. She would rather Althea believed that, believed that she was a disloyal snob, than that she know the facts. But it was only a faint hope. Deep inside, she knew Althea would never believe that. She and Althea had been too close; they had laughed at the same things, made fun of the same things, been concerned together over too many aspects of Canterbury. No, just as with Donovan, she had waited too long. She was sure if she confessed to him now, he would think she was trying to save Althea—from a young girl's imaginary "fate worse than death," probably. He wouldn't believe her. And, besides, no mental hospital was going to dig up an unimportant female patient already buried to find out what her lungs contained. Hospitals and chiefs of staff did not fool around with the dead and buried unless someone outside cared, and who had cared about Sarah? Nobody, Kathy thought.

CHAPTER 23

LATE ON THE TWELFTH OF JULY, Larry drove his car deep into an unused lane behind Surgery, put on the brake and turned off the ignition and lights. The place was fragrant with rich, matted grass and dark with shadows, cool after the day's heat. Through the branches of nearby trees, the lights of Surgery gleamed, but they were too high to send down any illumination. The spot was fully concealed. Larry glanced up at the windows, then turned to Althea. "I've got a blanket in the back seat," he said to her. "Let's put it on the lawn and sit there for a while."

She withdrew a little from him. "Don't be silly."

"I'm not. Just practical. It's cooler outside the car." He listened to the soft sounds of the night as he watched her, and thought how desperate and confused he had become.

"Why did we come here?"

"Well, we've had dinner somewhere every night while I've tried to talk to you. We've seen every show in town. We've visited every beer joint that wasn't too dark. I hate dark joints! Think what bad liquor they can serve and how dirty the glasses can be, and nobody notices. Then that place again last night . . ."

They had driven out to his favorite spot where he had taken her the first night, and again he had talked, trying to help her. He wouldn't go back there again. It hadn't meant a thing to her, the high point overlooking the lake and the tall sycamore they had parked under. As far as she was concerned, they might have parked on Main Street, watching the evening traffic.

"You can't get over him, can you?" he asked suddenly. "It's still there, isn't it? I can feel it in you. All these discussions haven't helped. Why don't you try to do something about it? You can't go on tormenting yourself like this. Don't you know it will lead to trouble?"

"I know."

She thought momentarily of poor Larry. He had been so generous, had really tried to help her. She didn't deserve such kindness, because she couldn't give anything in return. He knew how she felt about Donovan.

"You've been so good to me, Larry. I don't know how I can ever repay you."

She hunched herself over her knees as if her stomach were hurting her. What a wonderful person Larry was, really, and how little people knew him. He was young and impulsive and loved life and everybody thought he was amoral and promiscuous. Unhappy as she was, she couldn't think about him without feeling gentle impulses to smooth his hair with her hand. He has really tried to help me, really tried; he's hardly had a moment to himself lately because of me.

"I haven't done anything I didn't want to do," he said.

"That's what I mean. You've been good to me."

"I haven't done a thing I didn't want to do," he repeated.

"I know."

"What's that you're wearing?" He touched a strand of hair waving loosely at the side of her face.

"What?"

"What do I smell?"

"Oh. That's Emeraude. Coty. Do you like it? It's only cologne."

He did not answer. He had to be careful when they were close. After a moment he said, "I'm used to soap and water, plain soap."

"I'm sorry. I won't use it again." But she was thinking, A girl has to do something. She can't feel rejected every waking moment, and even a little cologne sprayed in her hair helps her to feel human for a little while.

Suddenly he put his hands on her shoulders and twisted her toward him. "You're a fool!" he said harshly. "Look at me! You know how much I love you, don't you? I know, you have problems already. You don't need another one. But maybe another one would make you forget the first batch."

As if it were possible! She pulled back from him. His hands tightened and brought her closer. "You need my help as a doctor, a psychiatrist, and I've failed you, haven't I?"

"Don't say that. Don't blame yourself."

His face was only a few inches away. "Althea, maybe I've failed as a doctor, but as a man I can succeed. Let me show you what I mean. I can make you forget Donovan. I swear it."

"Don't Larry," she murmured. "You're just making it harder for yourself."

He released her, got out of the car and reached for the blanket, shutting the door after him and coming around to her side.

"Get out," he said fiercely.

When she made no move, he opened the door, put his free arm around her and lifted her out, setting her roughly on her feet. Breathing heavily, he said, "We're going to settle this now, Althea. I've got no choice. I've got to help you the only way I can now."

He spread the blanket but did not touch her. He said, "I've done a lot of things I'm not especially proud of. I've had lots of fun, avoided responsibility, broken some hearts —so I was told—and even thought mine was cracked once or twice."

She folded her arms across her breasts, aware of the intensity in his voice.

"I've never taken advantage of my position," he went on. "I do what I can. I'm not the best psychiatrist, but I'm not the worst, either. I mean I really try to help these patients out here." He paused for a moment. "What I'm trying to say, Althea, is that I'm not like Macleod, nothing like him. I'm not going to pretend that I am. He's totally dedicated to his job; it comes first. But I like women—fun."

He waited to see if she understood. When she remained silent, he said quietly, "I don't save my money. It goes as easily as it comes. You see? I'm not much compared with Macleod. But I love you, Althea. And not just because you're a beautiful woman. Remember what I told you once? Someday I'm going to marry you? I love you the way you think you love him, only I hope you don't. Can you understand what I'm trying to say?"

"I . . . am trying to," she said faintly.

"It's like this. I never thought it could happen this way after all the women I've had, but it has. That's why I'm going to try to show you're only infatuated with Macleod. It's not love, it never was love. If I can make you see that, then

168

you'll get over him, he'll never be able to hurt you Althea, will you marry me?"

He waited tensely. In the darkness, her face was her mouth soft and lost.

"Larry," she whispered, reaching up to touch his face with the tips of her fingers. "How nice you are, how sweet. But I can't. I can't, Larry. It wouldn't work."

Her touch set him on fire. "All right," he said savagely. "Then I'll have to show you it will. I want you. I have to have you. Do you understand? When I saw you in the clinic this morning with Andreatta—"

"I don't encourage Dr. Andreatta," she said. "He pats all the girls. Everyone knows what he's like. Why, his reputation is even worse than—" She stopped abruptly.

"Thanks, I'm entitled to mine," he said angrily. "Andreatta is married and has four or five children. And he wasn't patting your behind. He was rubbing against you with everything he had and he had everything, believe me."

"That's a narrow space between the sterilizers," she said reasonably. "I moved as soon as I felt what he was trying to do."

"If he ever so much as touches you again, I'll kill him!"

"I could have slapped him," she said gently. "And then he would have reported me for misconduct or for lack of co-operation in performance of duties, or something like that. You doctors have quite an advantage, you know."

"Don't talk that way," he said roughly. "I'm a man who wants a certain woman and wants her badly enough to put up with session after session of Donovan Macleod. Marry me tonight, Althea. We could find a justice of the peace somewhere. I love you. I could make you forget him. You'd be happy."

She shook her head, and he breathed in the perfume of her hair. "Larry, Larry," she said, sighing. "Don't ask me. Don't—"

"All right. Then I'll have to do this my way." Urgently he pulled her toward the blanket, his hands moving over her uncontrollably, pulling the net loose and letting her hair tumble around her shoulders.

"Larry—don't!"

His hands went through the hair, forcing her face to his. His mouth came to her irresistibly. For a second she was suffocated by the kiss, then she began to struggle. He lifted his head. "I can't think any more," he muttered. "I just see the way you walk, your eyes, your mouth. That stuff in your hair—God, that sweet smell. And your neck. I think of your neck, your soft, white neck. Your breasts."

"Please!" she whispered, suddenly frightened.

169

"Please what?" His hands began to tear at her clothing. "Please what? I told you what I had to do. Tell me again you can't forget that bastard. Tell me!"

Her hands fought back. To save herself, she said brutally, "I think about him all the time. It's like a cancer, it won't heal, it won't stop hurting. It just grows and grows and grows. You know I'd get over it if I could. I hate myself for the way I feel about him, honestly. Larry, I hate myself. But I think about him all the time! Do you hear me, Larry? Do you hear?"

He ripped her blouse loose and tore it from her shoulders. His fingers found the zipper of her skirt, and when it wouldn't work he tore the skirt open.

"Larry! My God, stop!" Her hands beat at him ineffectually. "Didn't you hear me? Didn't you? I love him, I love him! Didn't you hear me say that? Stop it, Larry! You must be crazy!"

He dragged her down on the blanket, his hands going over her with hot violence.

"Shut up," he said. "Shut up."

"Larry! Larry, my God, stop! Stop! Larry, listen to me. I'm a virgin. Don't do this, can't you hear me? My God, Larry!"

"Put your arms around my neck. I told you what I had to do."

"Larry, I'm telling the truth. This will be rape, don't you understand? I'll have you arrested!"

"I don't care, my darling. Kiss me."

"Larry, I think about Donovan all the time."

"Don't say his name! Don't say it again! Put your arms around my neck. Althea, Althea—like this. Listen, darling, I can make you forget him. I know how. Darling, listen. I'm going to prove it. I can help you—I *will* help you."

His mouth covered hers. She was drowning again in his kiss. She pulled her face away. "Don't!" she sobbed. "Don't do this. It's no good, Larry. It will never be any good. I'll hate you and then you'll hate me."

His mouth found hers again, and again she pulled her lips away. "Don't kiss me. I get confused. Stop, Larry—please!"

"Darling, darling!" he moaned. "Your hair—that smell is driving me mad! On your hair, your neck—" His mouth slid from her chin down to her breast.

"Larry—stop! Please!" She said it faintly, hopelessly.

His body came over hers, hard and furious. His hands covered her breasts; his mouth went back to her lips.

"Larry! Larry!" She beat at his shoulders. She tried to push his weight aside while her sobs filled her throat.

He twisted, forcing her legs apart with his knees. "Stop fighting!" he panted. "It won't hurt then. Raise your hips."

But she was too frightened to co-operate and he could wait no longer. He thrust himself down into her secret sweetness. She gave a wild cry of pain and thought she would faint. His fury and need and heat were so great he could not stop his violence until he reached the first, terrible, joyous expulsion, his outcry high and sharp. Immediately he began again, his hands stroking and caressing her flesh, his hips becoming gentle and controlled, erasing the pain he had had to inflict, showing her finally the mounting ecstasy they might have together. Afterward, she lay in his arms, her sobbing reduced to an occasional deep intake of breath, while he felt and explored her with a tender, possessive hand, following every curve and smooth hollow and contour of breast and flesh, his mouth against her throat and then against her hair.

"I love you," he whispered.

"We'll hate each other," she moaned. "We won't be able to look at each other."

"Be quiet," he murmured. "You talk too much. Be quiet and just feel. Listen to my heart and feel what I do."

She moved a little under his hand, unconsciously molding herself against him. "I'll leave Canterbury. I'll go away. I will, Larry." She stopped as his lips touched her breast. When he raised his head, her hands came at him urgently.

He laughed joyously. "What did I tell you? You'll forget him. I promise, my darling. And I'll never hurt you again, never. So gently, so gently . . ." His mouth came seeking. "Tomorrow," he whispered, "we'll get married. But tonight —tonight we'll know each other, we'll have each other. This is our marriage. This time you will give to me—you must meet me more than halfway. Give, darling. Give . . . give . . ."

She could not help herself. Her hands reached to touch, to explore, to know what he was like in his strength and hardness. Her mouth nibbled at him softly; she made little sounds of pleasure. She moved convulsively under his tender, expert guidance, meeting him thrust for thrust, rising with him to an exultant peak of delirium.

Dear God! she thought. What are we doing? Then she did not think at all, lost in the great and terrible sacrament of their oneness while the night closed in on them, silently and tenderly.

CHAPTER 24

DONOVAN STOPPED HIS CAR in front of Nurses' Residence. Sitting beside him, Kathy said, "Thank you for bringing me home. All of two blocks from your apartment down to here, if you measured it city-wise. I could have walked."

"Too dark. This is one of those really black nights. Even the stars are hiding."

Kathy looked out of the car window. "So they are. It's cloudy." She listened. "And so quiet. Did you notice? I think it must be getting ready to storm."

"It may be—it's hot enough." In a moment he would be wanting her to get out and go inside, but for the present he was content to sit and relax. Thank God the book was done, he thought. No more nervous girls to worry about. Still, he felt a little contritely, he was grateful to Kathy, as he had been to Althea.

For the past few days he had tried not to think about Althea, but he could not stop himself. He knew it was ridiculous to keep remembering things about her, but he would find himself recalling her walk, the way she placed her long, beautiful legs and the little unconscious swagger in her hips. And her hair, so smooth and thick in the bun she wore. How long would it be, hanging down over her shoulders or spread out on a pillow? he would wonder. Then he would catch himself. You're Donovan Macleod, he would tell himself, chief of staff of Canterbury State Hospital. You mustn't let yourself get involved with these nurses.

Kathy turned back. "I could have walked," she repeated. "What could happen in two blocks on hospital ground?"

"Nothing, I suppose. But you might have tripped on something and fallen. A broken hip or ankle would be inconvenient, right now especially. In a little more than two weeks you'll be ready for that stripe on your cap. Are you looking forward to it?"

She shrugged, knowing she would never dare tell him what she really felt, and gave him the answer he anticipated. "Of course. The whole class is. We'll be getting real salaries for a change." And we'll go away, most of us, she thought, but you won't care.

She accepted one of his cigarettes and bent down for a light. For a second she saw his hand, steady and strong, and had a wild impulse to seize it with both of hers and pull it to her breast. Then the cigarette was lit and the light out and she sat back, catching her breath.

"Yes, I suppose so," he replied a little absently, thinking again about his book. "You've been assigned to Rehabilitation on the fifteenth, did you know?"

"Yes, Miss Leslie told me." She hadn't learned to inhale yet, but she dragged deeply on her cigarette. "Night shift," she added.

"You'll like it. Nice new building and small wards. Never more than thirty patients to a ward. I think you and Althea will do well together."

"Althea?"

"Yes. She's getting the day shift for her ward management." He knew that the two girls were friends, Kathy having come to him the day after the Fourth to tell him that he was wrong about Althea. She had tried to tell him, that is; he hadn't let that go very far. But after that one time, she hadn't mentioned Althea again, although she had worked for him seven evenings in a row. In the darkness he was frowning, but Kathy could not see his face, only a light blur where it should be and the glowing tip of his cigarette making an arc occasionally up to his mouth and down to the steering wheel where his hand rested. "You've been splendid, helping me," he went on, "but I imagine you're as thankful as I am that it's finished."

"Oh?" She hadn't realized he felt that way about the book. But then, why not? After all, this was his fifth or sixth book, she had heard. Well, she thought, she might as well be thankful that it was over; he had never once looked at her as if he recognized that she was young and female and interesting. She might as well try to forget all her impossible dreams and get ready for the ordeal of facing Althea for two weeks. From the fifteenth to the end of the month, she told herself, we'll see each other going off duty and coming on. It made her frantic. Why hadn't Leslie let her know Althea was getting the other shift? Could it be because she suspected something? But that was foolish because what was there to suspect? No one knew anything, no one except herself. Even Mike did not know, and Althea could only suspect.

But I know, Kathy thought broodingly, watching Donovan's cigarette as it glowed. And Althea must suspect something because she's been so distant and hostile since the Fourth. She hadn't approached Kathy in all that time and Kathy could not go to her. She could not stop remembering. It was like one of those things you read in newspapers, when some fellow who's been steady and reliable all his life, holding down a good job and earning the respect of his friends and neighbors, suddenly walks by a counter in a store and steals something and cannot explain afterward why he did it. We all make excuses for bad conduct, she thought, like the shopper who accepts too much change from the clerk and says, "Oh, well, they charge too much anyway," when she knows very well that the clerk will have to make up the loss from her own paycheck. I keep making excuses to myself for not doing the right thing about this, and it's Althea who's paying. No wonder I can't be happy. No wonder!

"Yes, I certainly have appreciated your help," Donovan repeated. His cigarette was almost finished and he was beginning to get a little impatient.

"I haven't minded. It kept me from thinking too much about that male ward I was on." She brought her wrist close to her face and peered at the luminous dial of her watch. "Goodness, it's late, much later than I realized. What will people think!"

It was just an expression and she said it without thinking, but her cheeks grew hot. She was grateful that the streetlight did not penetrate into the car through the heavy shadows thrown by the trees near the curb. Donovan started to move and she touched his arm, a timid touch, dropping her hand away afterward. "Don't get out. I'm perfectly capable of opening the door and walking inside unescorted. I didn't thank you for the coffee we had, but I will now. Thank you. It was very good coffee."

"Even if you did have to make it."

"Well, it was your percolator and your can of coffee. Now I must go. Thanks again for the ride."

"I'll be watching for you in three days."

"Three days?"

"The fifteenth. When you start on Rehabilitation."

"Of course. I forgot. Good night."

She started to get out, then hesitated as another car pulled to the curb in front and turned off its lights. Donovan moved slightly and she said sheepishly, "It's not that I'm doing something I shouldn't be doing, but it's just so awfully late. May I sit here until they're gone?"

"Of course." Donovan leaned forward and stared at the other car. "It's Dr. Denning's car. He won't notice us. He's probably bringing one of his girl friends home. You sit here until he's gone."

They waited in silence until a girl stepped from the car ahead. She was only a dim figure beside the open car door until the shadows from the trees shifted suddenly, and then for a full second or more she was clearly revealed in the light from the street lamp. Kathy and Donovan both saw her as she tried to fix her clothes. Her blouse was torn and her skirt ripped and she was desperately buttoning and tucking and smoothing and brushing. A man got out of the car on the other side and came around to stand beside her, reaching and taking her into his arms, stopping the furtive movements, the shamed attempts at concealment. The two people merged in a long embrace, the man's mouth pressed deeply against the girl's. Then the shadows moved again and the girl turned her head and saw Donovan's car. It seemed to Kathy that time had stopped altogether, that it would never start again, while the girl stared over the man's shoulder. Then she pulled loose from the man and fled toward the house, her hair and torn skirt streaming back from her body. The man turned to look at Donovan's car and teetered on the balls of his feet as though he contemplated either following the girl or coming over to talk to Donovan. Then he got into his own car and drove off.

Kathy and Donovan sat frozen. She was too shocked to turn her head and look at him. She could still see the torn clothes, the exposed breast, a thigh gleaming white through the ripped skirt, the face so beautiful even in the bizarre light. And the man coming at her, possessing her with his embrace.

"That was Althea!" Donovan whispered.

Then she realized that her shock was nothing compared to his, that his stillness was gone and that he was shivering. Her breath caught in a strangling lump in her throat. She knew she would have to say or do something or scream. "I've got to go," she gasped.

"That was Althea!" he said again. He sounded stupid and numb and perplexed, as though he couldn't believe what he had just seen. He started to shake his head back and forth, like an automatic toy—she loves me, she loves me not, it was Althea, it was not Althea. "Did you see her?"

"Good night!" Kathy said wildly, and then she was gone from the car and going toward the building exactly as Althea had gone, her hair and skirt whipping behind her. There was a brief flash of light when she reached the door and a faint protest of hinges, then the door shut and darkness hid the spot.

Donovan gripped the steering wheel savagely, ready to yank it from the car. He was caught in a maze of emotions, recognizing something he had been concealing from himself for many weeks. It made him want to pound his fists against the windshield of the car, to break it and destroy his hands on the shards of glass. He wanted to hurt himself in some terrible, physical way because there was a bitter, unrelievable fury in him and he could satisfy it only through the girl who had been in Larry Denning's arms.

He made a wrenching effort to control himself. God, he thought, if ever a man needed help, I do.

He was shaking now too hard to trust himself to drive. He tried to light a cigarette and couldn't. Finally, he gave up and submitted to the shaking because there was nothing else to do. Saliva surged into his mouth and he jerked at the door handle. He managed to get the door open in time and he retched onto the ground. He fumbled for a handkerchief. Abruptly he almost hated Althea because she managed to upset him so violently. He should have had sense enough to take a woman occasionally and none of this would have happened. Maybe it was all for the best that it had, he told himself. There wouldn't be any more hidden emotional conflicts. It was out in the open; he could hold it figuratively in his two hands and study it with the same intensity he studied the problems of his patients, and resolve it as he did theirs. He would not get involved or hurt that way.

Eventually he stopped shaking and lit a cigarette. Then he started the car and drove back to his rooms.

Inside Residence, Kathy saw Althea waiting in the dimly lit hall, but it was too late to retreat.

"You saw us, didn't you? What did it look like—when I got out of Larry's car?" Althea was still holding the torn blouse over her breast, still pulling the skirt together.

Kathy stared desperately at her ashen face, then with hopeless longing at the stairs beyond.

"Donovan never speaks to me any more. When he sees me, he turns and goes in the opposite direction. As if he's afraid of something. What did he say when I—could he see my clothes?" Her voice was high and thin.

Kathy shook her head helplessly. "He—didn't—"

"He didn't say anything? He didn't see me?"

"I meant—"

"Did *you* see me? If you saw me, then he must have. Tell me."

"I don't know."

"Why are you lying about it?"

"I don't know what he saw, or how much," Kathy said, her heart surging.

"What did you see? He must have seen as much."

"I don't know!"

"You're lying to me. Why? You know he saw me. How could he help not seeing me? Does he ever talk about me at all? Does he ever tell you anything?"

"No—no! He never mentions you, never."

"Didn't he say anything just now, anything at all? Wasn't he shocked? You know, this is the first time, Kathy. I can prove it. See—blood. This is the first time for me, Kathy. Donovan doesn't know that. He may think—don't you see, I have to know what he said. Kathy, tell me, what did he say?"

"Nothing," Kathy stammered. "Nothing!"

Althea came toward Kathy slowly. Her eyes were staring and set. "You're lying! He must have said something, some little thing."

Kathy stepped back. "No," she whispered. "No, believe me."

Althea was silent for a moment, studying Kathy's face. Kathy reached out a hand. "Althea," she whispered, "what's happened to us? Why can't we talk any more? You haven't spoken to me for over a week. Where have you been all this time? What's wrong?"

Althea took another step. "What's wrong?" The hand holding the blouse went up to push at the tumbled hair, and the blouse fell apart. In the dim light her breast was the color of old porcelain. "You ask *me* what's wrong when all the time I feel that you should be telling me, not asking. What is it, Kathy? What do you have to tell me?"

Kathy stepped backward and came up against one of the hall chairs. Her hands reached down and back, grabbing for support. "Oh, Althea, what have I done!"

"It's that woman, isn't it, Kathy? You think I killed her, just as Donovan does. So you're ashamed to be my friend, or afraid. You think the office will care, they won't approve of our friendship because I killed a patient. That's why you've changed so."

"But I haven't changed—it's you." Kathy couldn't go on pretending something that wasn't true. She had changed; they both had.

"Then it's Donovan. You know how much I love him, yet you stepped right into my shoes. Didn't you think I'd find out? Well, why did you do it? Are you in love with him, too? That would explain a lot of things, Kathy. That's why you keep your door locked all the time now and why you're always hiding from me. All this time you could have been helping me.

"You could have helped me," she repeated. "I needed you, Kathy, I needed you. Maybe this wouldn't have happened tonight if you had helped me in time. I had to turn to somebody. I *had* to—don't you understand? And there wasn't anyone but Larry. He understood, he was kind, he was everything you might have been if you had only wanted to be. So tonight—well, you know what we were doing. Down on a blanket, a blanket out of the car of the notorious Dr. Denning! I did with him what I should have been doing with Donovan, what I might have been doing if—how dare you two sit in judgment on me. How dare you!"

"Oh," Kathy gasped, "but we weren't, we weren't!"

"You will! Tomorrow—or the next day. Give yourself time to think it all over and it will come. You'll judge me! And I know what Donovan will say—I'm not only a murderer but a whore as well!"

Kathy moved backward, behind the chair, until her shoulders touched the wall. She was not aware of it, but tears were running down her face. "No, Althea, we won't say that. Why should we say that? What business is it of ours? We haven't any *right!*"

Althea acted as though Kathy had not spoken. In the dim light her face was full of rage and frustration and shame. "How dare he think that!" she almost screamed, moving closer to Kathy. "Sitting in judgment on me, damn his soul! And you—what are you hiding from me, Kathy? What did you have to do with all this? Someday, damn you, you'll tell me. I'll make you tell me!"

She let go of her clothing, clenched her fists and raised them directly over Kathy's frozen figure. "Someday I'll make you tell me. If you've done one thing to take Donovan away from me, I'll kill you!" Panting, she stood swaying a moment with her fists in the air, then turned and ran furiously to the stairs and up them.

Kathy sagged against the wall, shaking so hard she could not move. She was filled with horror. Everything came back to her, from the moment Donovan's hands had glided over her face, testing for broken bones, to the moment when she placed the fatal pills between Sarah's thin lips. Was this what love did to people? Did it make brutes and liars out of them? First you were a kid and boys fixed your bike or bought you sodas or took you to the prom, then suddenly you were catapulted into a new world and you fought to get what you were so sure you had to have. Was that love? What kind of love? Not something your father read about when he picked up the Bible in the days before TV and read a scripture at the supper table after everyone was finished. Certainly not the kind your parents had felt for each other and for you, giving up and doing without where they felt your welfare was concerned, and sticking with each other in spite of the little irritations and quarrels, growing old and bald and losing teeth and knowing that in the end they wouldn't have much to show for all the years, just a sense of loss when one should happen to die before the other.

Oh, Kathy thought, how could I do it! How could I? I had everything in the world, love, real love, and an example to follow, and Althea had nothing, nothing, nothing. Althea had crazy people tormenting each other and killing each other. Slowly she slid down the wall in a heap on the floor and cradled her head in her arms, sobbing heavily now for what she had done to her friend. So much had been given to her and she had given nothing in return.

CHAPTER 25

BY THE FOURTEENTH the story of Althea and Larry was all over the institution. Althea caught Elizabeth Leslie in her office before the older woman set out on her round of ward inspections.

"You've got to help me," she said abruptly and without any preliminaries. "I've been placed on Rehabilitation."

"I know. Sit down and let's talk about it."

Althea ignored the invitation. "Why did Terry do it?"

"It's the pick of the ward-management assignments. Don't you realize you've been given preference over all the other girls?"

"I don't want it! I don't care what it is, I just don't want it!"

"You don't want Rehabilitation?"

"I don't want it. I won't take it! You've got to help me!" Althea said wildly. She was trembling like a leaf.

Elizabeth pushed back her chair. Her face was apprehensive. "Of course I'll help you, but first I must know what this is all about. What in the world's the matter with Rehabilitation? Why don't you want it?"

"I just . . . don't want it."

"Is that what you expect me to tell Lucretia? What kind of a reason is that?"

Althea tried desperately to control herself. "First, I can't understand why I was given preference. You know my record, what happened and all—I mean about that patient who died." Elizabeth nodded and Althea gulped a deep breath. "Have you heard the other, about me and . . ." She couldn't go on.

"Dr. Denning?" Elizabeth finished quietly.

"So you did hear."

Elizabeth shrugged but kept her face from expressing too much. "I couldn't help myself," she said frankly. "It's all over the hospital."

Althea hunched her shoulders together. "Okay. Then why am I being given preference? Why haven't I been expelled?"

Elizabeth thought about it. "In the first place it has to be proved. Are you, or Dr. Denning, going to trot over to Lucretia and brag about it? Unless you do, Lucretia is going to treat the story as so much gossip. Secondly, this hospital doesn't expel students the way a general medical hospital would. Lucretia, Dr. Herrington, the supervisors—we all regard you girls somewhat the way we do the patients. You are training to be nurses and if your value outweighs any social problems, then the social problems must be secondary. Further, if your actions are neurotic in origin, you need help, so why drive you away from the very place where you can get competent care?"

There was a brief silence. "You mean that Terry thinks I may be a nymphomaniac? You know that's not so. I'm not sexually unbalanced. She can't be serious!"

"Have you forgotten your cousin Edna?"

"Of course not, but those aren't Edna's problems and they're not mine."

"You are an intelligent, lovely girl," Elizabeth said gently. "You could be popular, have friends, love, marriage. I am assuming the story about you and Denning is true because you haven't denied it. So I will ask you, why are you behaving this way? Are you in love with him and he won't marry you, perhaps?"

Althea looked at her with wonder. "I come in here to get help and you start lecturing me."

Elizabeth felt a twinge of mothering pity. "We can make him marry you, Althea. The hospital will see to it if that's the trouble."

"I can marry him any time, any time," Althea said softly.

"Then for God's sake do!" Elizabeth exploded. "Make the affair legal. For your own safety."

Something stopped her, something in the proud, stiff face. Her hands moved involuntarily. "What is it?" she whispered. "What are you trying to tell me?"

"How can I marry someone I don't love? When I love someone else? How?"

"Althea!"

"Isn't it funny? Isn't it the funniest thing you ever heard? A girl sleeps with one man because she loves another man?" Her stiff face twisted a little. "I actually let Larry push me down on a blanket because I had this crazy feeling that if I didn't resist too hard, maybe I'd get over the other, maybe I'd fall for Larry, only it didn't change me a bit. Now I'm just a slut and I still love the other man. I think of him more than ever."

"It's Dr. Macleod, isn't it? I thought, 'way back there—" Elizabeth stopped.

"Yes."

Elizabeth could hardly bear to look at the white, sharp pain in Althea's face. In a minute she would cry, she thought, old as she was.

"I found out that Donovan's going to be ward doctor for Rehabilitation until next month and the office is putting Kathy Hunter on night duty for her ward management. I'll be caught between them, don't you see?"

"What has Kathy to do with this?"

"I don't know, I don't know!" Althea's voice rose. "I just don't want to be near them!"

"If you went to Lucretia, told her the truth—"

"Oh, God! And have everyone know? So far I haven't let even Donovan know how I feel. I couldn't bear to have him realize what a fool I am. I couldn't stand his pity!"

"That is not important!" Elizabeth said sharply.

Althea looked at her wildly. "It is to me. You know how it would get told. Rich would do it—she's the one. You know how she tells things, how clever she is. Soon it would be not just that I slept with Larry Denning, but that I did it because I love Donovan Macleod. Then all the doctors would start getting fresh, calling me a party girl, a pushover. The other supervisors would look and watch and wait—waiting for me to take on other men."

Elizabeth was appalled. "Stop it! Stop that kind of thinking! Are you out of your mind?"

"You said to tell the truth, didn't you? Well, the truth is that I'm in love with Donovan. That's the truth, the simple truth. I might have gone to bed with Donovan—I say might —but I killed a sniveling, drooling patient. It isn't important that she was dying, that she was beyond hope; it doesn't matter that thousands of people are killing or getting killed all the time. They use cars and wars and selfishness, and that's quite all right, that's legal. But me—little old me—I step out of this patient's room for five minutes and she chokes to death on her own spit, and all the rest of my life I have to pay for those five minutes, I have to be punished."

"Althea! No! We all know it was an accident!"

Elizabeth's protest went unheeded. Althea put her hands on the desk and leaned forward. "Do you still want me to talk to Terry? You know what she'll say. Excuses. I'm using excuses as crutches to help me do what I want to do. A behavior pattern. I like to sleep with men, so why do I bother to explain or protest or apologize? It's perfectly clear what I want to do."

"My dear, she's no fool. Give her a chance to understand."

"Miss Leslie," Althea said in a dead voice, "you know perfectly well that all I can ever do—unless I kill myself and God knows how hard I tried at first—is to keep my mouth shut and let everyone believe I *am* a tramp. Just a very few out here—a very few—have the decency to want to believe something good about each other."

"It was an accident," Elizabeth reiterated as though somehow by insisting this, sense would come to both of them "An accident. It's entered that way in the hospital records. I know, Althea, because I entered it myself."

Althea straightened. "Donovan doesn't think so. He called it wicked carelessness and lack of responsibility. And he is all that counts." Tears began to spill down her face. Like a small child, she added foolishly, "I wish I had never seen this place. I wish to God I never had."

Elizabeth rigidly kept control of herself. She wanted to cry with Althea. "My dear, why don't you go away? In an-

181

other hospital perhaps you'll be able to forget, find happiness again. If it's a question of funds, I have some bonds that I'll never need in my lifetime and I certainly can't take them with me. They're yours if you want them." Then to save Althea's pride, she added quickly, "You'll be able to pay them back someday, I'm sure."

"Oh, Miss Leslie!" Althea was silent a long moment; then she began to sob, her shoulders shaking, but her face blind and frozen. When she could get her breath, she shook her head. "I can't even do that. It's like the times I tried to kill myself. I'd hear his voice or see his face and it would stop me. Finally I knew it just couldn't be, I couldn't do it. I'd rather—suffer thinking about him than be dead and not able to remember." Her voice thickened. "You see, when Larry and I were together, there were a few moments, just a few, at the height, I suppose, when it was Donovan. As if unconsciously I put Donovan in Larry's place. When I was a little girl, growing up, dreaming—you know how little girls dream—there is a prince or a movie star and it's very wonderful but sweet and innocent with kisses mixed in it but nothing else yet? In all my dreaming I never once knew a man could mean so much to a woman. How can that happen? How can a man—his body, his physical contact—mean so much to a woman? Well, that's how it happened. It was Donovan, not Larry, until afterward."

Elizabeth nodded. "I know. I used to dream, too," she whispered.

"Afterward, it was Larry, really Larry. And this terrible headache." Althea touched her face with one hand. Suddenly she looked exhausted, her face almost gray. "How did it get around so fast? I mean, *we* didn't talk about it." She was remembering Donovan sitting in his car, that terrible moment of shame and humiliation, and later the encounter with Kathy. Surely, neither of them would—

"Nothing is secret out here. There are dozens of ways. A maintenance man saw you or a supervisor taking a short cut from one building to another or another couple doing the same thing but far away enough so that you didn't hear them."

Althea put both hands up and pressed her finger tips against her temples. "I suppose so," she said dully.

"All right. I'll talk to Lucretia. But what can I say?" Already she was planning a campaign. She would help Althea if she had to become the most proficient liar in the institution.

Althea dropped her hands and shook her head. "No. I guess we'd better leave it alone."

"Well, I'm not very good at manufacturing stories, but I'll do my best," Elizabeth said grimly.

"No. You'd end up telling everything and then you'd feel terrible because you'd think you had betrayed me. I should have known that before I came in here, but I was so desperate I felt I had to do something. I guess if I got myself into this mess, I can get myself out." She found a handkerchief and dabbed at her streaked face. "So I'll—I'll take the assignment. Maybe I can think of something on my own later. You are so kind," she added forlornly. "The kindest person I've ever met except for the woman who gave me a home when my mother died." She turned her head and began to cry again, softly and hopelessly.

"My poor dear!" Elizabeth said despairingly and then was silent because she could offer nothing else.

Almost as though she were alone, Althea said, "I'll take Rehabilitation. I'll go there, hating it, hating her, wanting to put my hands around her throat and choke the life out of her body. I'll think about it until I can feel her throat right between my two hands."

Horrified, Elizabeth gasped. "But why? Why should you feel that way about Kathy?" For it was obviously Kathy that Althea was talking about.

Althea looked at Elizabeth, her eyes cloudy. "I don't know," she said. She glanced down at her hands and curved them. "I don't know," she repeated and walked quietly out of the office.

Outside she stood still for a moment. Her headache had returned and she couldn't think of anything but the pain and how it spread from her eyes up and across the top of her head and down to the back of her neck like a cap that was too tight. Through the stupefying effect of the headache she gazed down at her twitching hands and tried to spread them flat. Finally she gave up and thrust them into her pockets just as they were. Better to concentrate on one thing at a time. Carefully, with stiff steps, she walked slowly away from Elizabeth's office.

CHAPTER 26

WITH RUTH transferred to Rehabilitation, Millie was left alone with Charlotte's temper and spitefulness. Occasionally she caught a gleam of hostility and suspicion in Charlotte's eyes, as if she were preparing some trap for her and gloating in anticipation over what was to come. Millie disliked her more than anyone she had ever known, and she knew that her friendship for poor Ruth was going to spark a storm of anger between Charlotte and herself some day.

Many times Millie stood at silent attention when Miss Leslie or Mrs. Beck made supervisory ward checks and had to listen in sheer astonishment to Charlotte's out-and-out lies or the sly half truths which were worse. A lie could be tracked down to its source, but the other always left room for doubt. Charlotte was always taking naps, bedding herself comfortably with blankets and pillows in a small utility room and timing the naps carefully between the supervisory checks.

"I never worry about Leslie. You can set your watch by her. She's too much of a lady to sneak up on a ward to catch somebody doing something they shouldn't. But that Beck, or Terry and Rich, they try it all the time. What they wouldn't do if they caught a charge taking a nap! Don't you let 'em catch me, you hear?"

How sharp she had been about it—don't you let anyone catch me if you know what's good for *you!* But in spite of what she expected, she did not return the favor, as Millie discovered when she got her first merit rating on that ward. Loyalty to Charlotte was an investment without value. She had given Millie as low a rating as she could possibly give and still let Millie keep her job.

Millie thought about protesting but remembered what she had heard about those making complaints to the office and finally decided to leave well enough alone. She reasoned that Charlotte was one of those people who had to be a big toad in a little puddle to be happy, so she might as well conform. She wanted to do her work well, she wanted to keep her job; if it meant putting up with Charlotte, she could do that too. She submitted to tyranny and domination; she accepted caustic criticisms and accusations. She learned to turn her head when Charlotte was unkind to patients. She did not watch when the blankets and pillows were gathered together for the nap. She even closed her ears to Charlotte's outrageous lies. What else could she do but take it when Charlotte sprawled untidily in the desk chair and used some unwholesome tidbit gleaned from the hospital grapevine with the malicious and deliberate intention of hurting someone? She needed her job too much to take sides in something that wasn't any of her business.

The blowup came because Charlotte wanted it, not Millie. The two women were sitting at the desk. Charlotte was talking and Millie was sorting file cards. She was half asleep with a headache and had not been listening too well until she happened to glance up and saw the sharp, warning expression in Charlotte's eyes.

"Huh?" Millie said through the pain in her forehead.

"I thought you wasn't listening. I said, all that time she

was trotting after Macleod like a bitch in heat. It was disgusting, absolutely disgusting."

"Yeah?" Millie didn't have the faintest idea what she was talking about but she tried to seem intelligent and alert.

"Yeah. Then he turned right around and took on that fat, homely little nurse. Jumped from the frying pan into the fire, if you ask me."

"The fat one?"

"God, where you been? The fat one, the one named Hunter. Homely as a mud fence. Nasty little bitch! I'll bet Macleod has to marry her before he's through with that book of his, I'll bet five bucks."

Millie made a desperate effort. "I sort of see her in my mind. She was short—"

"Short and fat. Chunky in build. Altogether different from that Horne. God, there's two nurses I'd never say a good word for," Charlotte said viciously.

The headache lifted enough for Millie to recall the morning Sarah Smith had died. She had been the only one who had seen Kathy go into Sarah's room and come out almost immediately and then step into the linen room, almost as though she were hiding. This action on Kathy's part meant nothing to Millie because the affiliates took orders from the ward doctors and their counselors, not from the charges; they did not always adhere to the ward routines followed by the attendants. But now she remembered that after Sarah's body was on its way to the mortician, she had been sent to the linen room for something and had passed Kathy coming out, and at this moment it came to her as clear as day how peculiar the little nurse had looked, her eyes glazed, sort of, not really seeing anything. She had thought, when it happened, that the girl had seen Sarah's body going down the hall and was suffering from shock; lots of folks couldn't stand the sight of death. So she hadn't seen any point in mentioning it to Charlotte then and could see none now. However, the girl was not chunky, not in the least. She grunted noncommittally and kept silent.

Charlotte glared at her. She was accustomed to Millie's withdrawals and had been waiting for the proper time to do something about her. She teetered gently in her chair.

"Yeah," she said. "First it was Horne and Macleod. Now it's Hunter and Macleod. Been that way practically since Sarah died. Wonder if the little bitch figures on marrying him."

Her look made Millie uneasy. She decided she had better show a little enthusiasm for this conversation. "You never know," she said, trying to sound philosophical. "Them's the kind usually falls hardest, the kind that don't ever plan on marrying."

"Dr. Donovan Macleod? You crazy? He wouldn't have to

get married to get what he wants, not him. Why, there isn't a nurse in this institution he couldn't have just by crooking his little finger. Don't know what he's got, but they all want it, so it must be good."

Millie found a file in her pocket and began working on her nails. "Hunter," she said thoughtfully. "Can't remember her being so fat." She examined one hand absorbedly.

"Short and fat," Charlotte said crisply. "I can see Macleod taking that Horne to bed, but not that fat little Hunter." Charlotte's eyes brightened at the picture. "Funny about him. Having time for his writing and women, too. He's one of them kind thinks we're here to wait on these slobby patients."

Millie looked at her hand but she saw the open ward, the beds in their cubicles. "I'm cold—I'm cold," a voice cried somewhere, and she realized with a start that she had been hearing the cry for some time but had not acknowledged what her ears were trying to tell her. Unaccountably she thought of Harry and her mother and made a slight, startled movement, half rising.

"Leave her alone," Charlotte said sharply. "It's that goddam Newton. She's probably pissed again, so let her lay in it. Next time she'll call for a bed pan, I'll bet." Her glance in the direction of Georgia Newton's bed was vindictive.

Both women listened until Georgia became quiet, and then Charlotte nodded righteously. She had known that Georgia, with her broken hip, would eventually give up. Millie permitted no expression of any kind to cross her face.

Charlotte returned to her subject with relish. "The day Sarah died, I had a feeling something was going on, something funny. Did you?"

Millie looked straight at Charlotte. "No, can't say that I did," she lied calmly.

"Well, something happened," Charlotte insisted. "I missed it because I was all wrapped up in thinking about buying me a house." She looked regretful that she had missed whatever it was.

Millie speculated briefly on the way Charlotte kept harping on the little nurse being fat and chunky. She probably hated her guts because of the quarrel they had that morning after Sarah's death. Sure, that was it, that was what bothered Charlotte. It would probably bother her until she could do something mean and nasty about it, Millie thought. "I thought you already had a house," she said, hoping to get the subject changed.

Charlotte looked a little vexed. "We just rent," she admitted unwillingly. "Been there ten years. My old man likes it, but I'm sick of it. Nobody speaks to nobody on that block. Even the dogs are mean, snapping and barking all the time. I've taken all of that I want, believe me."

Millie wasn't fooled. There was good reason for nobody to speak to Charlotte, she thought, looking at her nails.

But now that it had been mentioned, Charlotte couldn't leave it alone. "I want a house kinda out in the country a ways. My old man needs—" She stopped, then went on, not bothering to explain what her old man needed. "Got one picked out if I can ever find out who owns it. About ten miles outside town. Nice, all clean and painted, even a telephone wire running into the house. We drive out past it on our day off and it's always empty, but somebody's taking good care of it. Nice and quiet out there. Smells good, not like where we live now. We get smoke right from the flour mills."

Millie looked at Charlotte in surprise. Why, she sounded almost like anybody else when she talked like this, Millie thought. She wondered why Charlotte couldn't be like that all the time. Charlotte caught her look and said crossly, "How'd I ever get to talking about that? Started with tramps and switched to houses. Been thinking about that place so much I kinda forgot my business here. Being a charge sure ain't easy. You gotta keep your mind on your job every minute."

Her expression dared Millie to argue this, but Millie had gone back to the safe contemplation of her hands.

Charlotte returned to her recollection of how she had been taken to task by Kathy. Her face set in lines of pure dislike. "Like I said, that Horne's a tramp, but I still thought she'd get Macleod. Fat one's a tramp, too, only she don't show it on account of she puts on that little-girl act."

Fat one's a tramp, Millie thought. You'll tell it so often you'll get to believing it yourself, and pretty soon you'll have everybody believing it when the little thing's not fat at all and most likely not the other. She forgot and shook her head a little and Charlotte caught the slight motion.

She said sharply, "I said tramp, both of them. I'll bet you anything you like that Horne and Macleod were going to bed together all those nights she went to his rooms. Typing! I heard. Yeah, I'll bet. Him typing on her machine, more likely. If you and me was to act like that, we'd get kicked outa Canterbury."

After a moment of uncertainty, Millie said, "Maybe they was planning on getting married. Lots of people don't wait. Soon's the man asks the girl and they're engaged, they start in—"

"Having themselves a piece every time they turn around? You know as well as me Macleod's never been engaged to anybody. If he was, the whole hospital'd know about it."

"But maybe she thought they were. Engaged, I mean. And he thought—"

"Maybe he thought she was good for a lay and she was," Charlotte said with authority. "Why would he bother to get engaged when he could have it for free?"

"That Horne seemed like such a nice girl," Millie said absently. "I worked with her on another ward once and my friend, Ruth, worked with her on Hydro. Don't recall too much except she was sure nice to get along with. Nice to the patients, too." Abruptly she came to her senses and stopped, appalled, raising her face to look at Charlotte.

Charlotte's eyes were narrow slits. "So you worked with her before. How come you never mentioned it? I suppose you don't think she's a tramp, huh?"

"I don't know about that. I just meant—"

"You meant you don't like to hear me call her a tramp. That's what you meant, isn't it?"

" 'Course not. I just said—"

"You just said right to my face that she was nice to the patients. You said that on account of you don't think I am. Isn't that what you meant?"

"Goodness, no! I didn't mean a thing personal. I was just—"

"Personal, huh? Nothing personal in you telling me right to my face I ain't nice to the patients?"

"No, no, I was just wondering about that Horne, about what you said, her going all the way with Dr. Macleod. It don't seem hardly likely—"

"Hardly likely she would? You think I'm lying?"

Millie began to sweat. "Mrs. Range," she said, "did it sound like I said that? What I meant—"

"I know what you meant. I know exactly what you meant. You haven't been fooling me for one minute with all that smug, quiet look on your face. Believe me, you haven't fooled me once. From the very first day you came to work on this ward, I had you all figured out. Let me tell you something. I don't like the way you do your work or anything about you. You hear that, Mrs. Higgins?"

Millie turned white. "No, no!" she said faintly. "I never lied to you, never. Not about my work. If I didn't know something, I just kept still and watched to see how you did it so I could learn how myself. But I never lied. I never said I could do something when I really couldn't. You're putting words in my mouth I never said." Oh, it hurt, it hurt, to be told she hadn't done her work right when she had tried so hard!

"Two days ago when I was sick and off duty and you

were charge in my place, what did you do?" Charlotte hissed.

"Do? I—what in the world do you mean?"

"You just listen and I'll tell you. You upset my whole schedule. Just because I wasn't here and couldn't see what you were up to, you thought you could run the ward to suit yourself. But I found out what you did because I have ways of finding out things, Mrs. Higgins."

Mrs. Higgins, Millie thought crazily. She's really teed off when she keeps on calling me that! "But when you're gone I'm supposed to do things the way that's easiest for me. Miss Leslie told me so. She told me to take full charge and do whatever I felt was proper. I never changed things except maybe I cleaned the desk here the first thing when I came on because there was so much work to do and I had to do most of it myself. That's all I did that was different, cleaning this here place right where we're sitting and only on account of I wasn't sure I'd have time before the next shift. Why, I wouldn't dream of upsetting your schedule. I couldn't begin to improve on it. Anyway, Miss Leslie knew what I did that day. She didn't say anything about it being wrong."

Millie couldn't believe she had heard Charlotte right. Such a little thing to make anybody so mad.

"I don't give a goddam what Leslie told you! This is my ward and nobody changes things around here but me— nobody!"

"I—I wasn't trying to change things," Millie began, then stopped, realizing every word she said was wasted effort. How could she put it so Charlotte would understand just a little of what she was trying to say? "I haven't changed anything, but I've tried to do my work right," she said, so earnestly that she stammered. "You know, the way you've wanted me to do things. I know I ain't very smart, but nobody else ever told me right to my face I wasn't doing what I should."

Charlotte said cuttingly, "You wasn't trying to change things, oh, no! You've done nothing else since the office sent you here. You don't appreciate a nice ward, Mrs. Higgins. You'll sure miss it when you get slapped back on an untidy ward or a bed ward."

A bed ward? My God, what's this! Millie thought, staring.

Charlotte leaned forward and pointed a finger. "Another thing. You go to lunch with Ruth Ellison. She wasn't off this ward one day when you two were seen at the cafeteria, thick as thieves. Thick a. thieves, Mrs. Higgins."

"What?" Millie asked incredulously.

"Thick as thieves. What were you talking about that was so goddam important? Both you women kept looking around as if you were afraid somebody might see or hear you. I know

189

how you acted because I got friends and they tell me things."

Stool pigeons, other gossips like yourself, hanging around the cesspool to enjoy the smell! Millie looked dizzily at Charlotte. "What in the world are you driving at?"

"I'm telling you. Ruth Ellison. You and her eating together in the employees' cafeteria the very next day after she was taken off this ward. That's what I'm driving at."

At last Millie understood the drift of the conversation. It had all been leading up to this.

"She's my neighbor, my friend!" she said a little wildly. "We was talking about how to make it easier for her to get to work, her being on nights now and me still on days. She's got no car and I have. We was taking the bus in the daytime to come to work and go home, but at night it's different. A woman's got no business waiting all alone on a dark corner for a bus. So I wanted Ruth to use my car. No reason for her not to. It's just been sitting in the garage with the tires rotting away. That's exactly what Ruth and I was talking about."

Suddenly she stopped talking. She was so angry, so terribly angry, that the room jumped and her heart almost stopped beating. It was all she could do to keep from stretching out her hand and slapping that fat, sneering face until it popped wide open. She knew if she did, there wouldn't be any blood, just slime pouring out. She waited a second until she could breathe again. "What are you trying to do, get me off this ward like you did my friend Ruth?" She pulled her mouth back and showed her teeth the way Charlotte was doing. After all, what did it matter what she said or did? This was it, the end of the careful manipulation of words. She had never hated anyone as she did Charlotte right now.

Charlotte's expression was triumphant. She saw the hate in Millie's flushed face. "Hah!" she said.

"You ain't very pretty when you blow through your nose like that," Millie observed tightly. "You look just like a nasty, warty toad." Having been glared at, she could now in turn enjoy the red mottling Charlotte's face. "Ruth Ellison is my dearest friend. I'll eat with her whenever I damn well please and just what are you going to do about it?"

"You—you called me a toad!" Charlotte choked.

"There you go, lying and putting words in my mouth. I did not call you a toad. I said you looked like one."

"You—you—you'll go to the office for this!" Saliva flew from Charlotte's spluttering lips. "I'll see you get fired, you bitch, if its the last thing I ever do. I'll see you get fired!" She was almost incoherent with fury.

"Well! You think it's any worse to be called a toad than a

bitch? I don't think you can get me fired. You don't own this hospital. You work out here same as me. Anyway, right now I'm thinking you've already been to the office about me. You've already done that, haven't you? When are they taking me off the ward? Whenever you ask them to, huh?"

Charlotte was too angry to try to tower over Millie as she had over Ruth. It was all she could do to keep her words in the proper sequence. "Let me tell you something," she grated. "Let me tell you something. You're just a cheap, goddam attendant while I'm an aide. The office has put money into my training and believe me, they're not gonna waste it, not for some fat old woman like you, when they can get fifty others just like you to take your place. As for me having already gone to the office, you are so right, so goddam right. I certainly ought to know when I want somebody who can do the work right on this ward insteada somebody who can't, like you. Get that through your head, Mrs. Higgins!"

"That's not what's eating you," said Millie. "You never stir up a tempest till your own storm shutters are up, do you? Sure, I can see myself trying to stand up to you in front of Terry and the rest, you lying like hell and me trying to tell the truth. I know they'll take your word before mine. I sure know that. I know my house ain't paid for, too. If I lose my job I probably won't find another very easy at my age, so I'll probably lose my house as well."

Millie thought about her cats as she stared into Charlotte's furious face; with the house gone, what would she do about the cats? She went on resolutely. "But if I lose everything I got, you ain't gonna tell me who I can or cannot eat with. Ruth needs me. She needs me for a friend and I need her. Just you remember that. And something else. When you're telling all those lies you're thinking up right this minute about me, you better be careful, because I'll be remembering all those naps you've been taking on the job and all those patients you've slapped and how you let 'em lay in their pee until they're so scalded their backsides are as raw as liver, and I'll remember how you use the ward telephone to call around making trouble for somebody." She halted to suck in a deep, ragged breath. "No matter what you say or do," she almost shouted, "you can't tell me who to eat with, you hear? I was looking for a job when I got this one and I can sure as hell look for another. There's only one thing I'm sorry about. I'm sorry if I didn't run the ward right because I sure tried. Maybe I did all right at that because nobody would ever suit you unless they was willing to polish your big, fat behind until they could see their face in it. So there! Now I'm getting my things and going home, and you can either take these keys and let me out or I'll let myself out and drop the keys outside the door. And you don't need to call the office on account of I'll call them when I get home. Because that's where I'm going. Home!"

After it was over, she was fiercely glad she hadn't crawled on her knees, making a spectacle of herself to apologize so Charlotte could tell it all over the hospital, because she wasn't going to eat humble pie for anybody like Charlotte, not in a million years. When she got home, she cleaned the whole house, gave Georgie a bath, much to his chagrin, and then let him know she was sorry by feeding him and Jennifer and the kittens the steak she had planned for her own supper. It seemed as though she just wasn't hungry even after all that work.

To her surprise, the next day the office called her and curtly ordered her to report in. She finally decided there was no point in not going because they owed her a little salary which she could use in a dozen ways. Then she was really astonished because they didn't even reprimand her. Miss Terry made a few dry remarks about her getting "sick" and leaving without permission, and asked her if she would care to try nights again. When she gulped and swallowed and managed to nod, they told her she was being placed on Rehabilitation and she would have charge of Ward Six. She was too dumfounded this time to gulp. All she could think was that she never would understand the why and how of things in Canterbury.

CHAPTER 27

WHEN MOLLY DISCOVERED what was wrong with Mary Elsie, for once in her life she lost her temper. "Goddam that man!" she raged to the crowd around her desk. "Look what he's done. The office will probably take me off Hydro and I've been here sixteen years."

She regarded the matter almost as a personal insult and went around all morning goddamning everything and everybody she could think of, while the O.B. sent over by the office made his examination and confirmed the report she had not dared hold back. However, the office did not blame her for Mary Elsie's condition, since she had been prompt in notifying them of Jim's behavior during his one and only visit.

The office sent Jim a note, requesting him to put in an immediate appearance. When he came, Lucretia Terry tersely told him that Dr. Herrington wished him to remove his wife from Canterbury. If he wished, he could take her to a private sanitarium. He had violated hospital ethics by his conduct, and Dr. Herrington had personally signed the release permitting Mary Elsie to leave the institution.

Jim was dumfounded. He protested vehemently. He even became angry before he hustled Mary Elsie into the battered convertible and drove her away from the hospital. Neither Lucretia nor Margaret believed him. Elizabeth was the only one who felt sorry for him.

"Wouldn't he like to make us believe nothing happened," Margaret said indignantly, her color high.

"After he has to go through the courts again to have her recommitted, he'll watch his step. All the fool had to do was to get a parole and take her home for a few days where he could use something to keep her from getting pregnant," Lucretia said grimly.

"But she wasn't ready for parole," Elizabeth said.

"She wasn't ready for copulation, either. We didn't ask him to do it, did we? He was warned by Dr. Andreatta how to conduct himself. It's on Andreatta's report here."

"She's his wife." But Elizabeth agreed on this point. Mary Elsie was not yet ready to resume the duties of wifehood. Still, it was tough for her husband. "Those poor people—what kind of a child will they have?" she asked. It would probably be perfectly normal, but at the moment she could only visualize a congenital idiot.

"In a way, I'm not too sorry it happened," Lucretia said thoughtfully. "It will be interesting to see what happens now."

"I think it's shameful," Margaret said with an unusual spurt of courage.

Elizabeth looked at Lucretia. "You think pregnancy might restore Mary Elsie to a more normal pattern?"

"It's happened, you know."

"Conceived in a mental institution?" Margaret sniffed. *You fools!* her eyes said. She took herself off to her own desk.

"There goes a pornographic mind," Lucretia said. "She sees the act, not the consequences."

"She should get married. She's turning into an old maid."

"What's that got to do with it? We're old maids, too, aren't we?"

Are we? Elizabeth thought, looking at Lucretia with pity.

Jim was in a daze as he took Mary Elsie home. On the way he told himself over and over that those women in the office had lied, that Mary Elsie simply could not be pregnant. She was okay when she went into the hospital for treatment, and he had not done a thing that day he visited her on Hydro. These facts went around in his mind until his head felt that it would split from the pressure. A man had to plant something in a woman before she could have a baby, and he hadn't planted anything in Mary Elsie for a damn long time. So Mary Elsie could not be pregnant. It was simply impossible.

Yet that Terry had told him Mary Elsie had menstruated once, right after being received, and then no more. The hospital had ignored the first miss because the shock and the ice-pack therapy often upset the female patients' cycles; but after his visit and the attendant's report on his behavior, the charge on Hydro had requested a gynecologic report on Mary Elsie and her condition was discovered. No use trying to go against that, he thought; the doctors knew what they were doing.

Mary Elsie sat quietly by Jim's side. She was quite content at the moment, as long as he didn't talk and bother her with questions. She was feeling much better now.

It must have been all the pills and the shock treatment that straightened her out, she thought, because now she was feeling good again. It was wonderful to be so alive and gay inside. She could even think better. One little place in her memory was blank, but she was not going to let that bother her, not when she felt so good, so alive and happy. All that vomiting—lots of girls vomited right after shock, she remembered. They were the ones who managed to sneak a little breakfast when they were only supposed to have black coffee and dry toast. But with the help of certain friends, there had been ways to get around that, and who cared afterward even if the attendants did go around goddamning everybody on account of all the extra work it made, giving baths and cleaning up puke? All but mine, Mary Elsie thought smugly. I always got to the toilet in time.

She wondered vaguely why she was going home. Didn't they like her any more at the hospital? She had learned to leave her clothes alone and not play with herself, at least when anyone was around, because of what was sure to happen. First those tubs, putting her into a canvas sling thing which let her down into warm water with only her head out through a strapped-down cover. That was boring although she discovered she could turn herself any direction. She hated the packs. God, they were terrible—those sheets right out of the cooler, all crusted with ice. After they strapped her so flat and tight she couldn't wiggle a finger, she always got warm, of course—hot, in fact—but sometimes they got too busy to repack her every three hours and then she couldn't hold herself but went right there in the sheets.

Did that make everybody sore! Then came the shock. And dozens and dozens of pills. Sometimes she wouldn't swallow them, just stored them in her cheek until she could spit them out somewhere. Once she managed to save eleven pills and took them all at one time just for spite. God, they made her sick! But she was better now, she knew she was, so why was she being sent home? Was it because of that times she dug a hole in one of her arms just to see the pretty red blood spurt everywhere? What excitement that made, Molly screaming for help while she sat on Mary Elsie on the floor and tried to stop the squirting. They didn't even take her to Surgery. The doctor came and sewed her up right on the ward. That was the time they put her into a strait jacket, then slapped her flat in bed and stretched a canvas tub cover over her and the bed. They were going to be absolutely sure she couldn't get loose. She sweated so hard she almost dehydrated herself. She knew, because she heard Molly say so. So now she had to go home. She shook her head, wondering about it.

The convertible was almost there. She began to recognize the neighborhood. She guessed none of her friends knew she was coming, because the street seemed deserted. She mentioned this to Jim, but he only grunted. He had hardly spoken two words all the way. She observed him closely, quite pleased in some obscure way that he was sitting beside her and that in a moment or so they would reach their little house. She could scarcely wait to put on one of her pretty aprons and see how her violets were doing.

"How are they?" she asked, and when he gave her a puzzled glance she added, "My violets."

He came out of his deep silence to tell her that her friend, Junie, had taken all the potted plants over to her house because she was afraid he would forget to water them. As far as he knew, the plants were fine. He hadn't seen any of the girls since last Sunday.

Mary Elsie murmured how nice it was to have friends like that. In her mind she tried to count how many plants Junie would have in her house which belonged in Mary Elsie's house, but gave up finally. Counting was still confusing. The car turned into the Blayton driveway and she forgot the plants as she stared at the neat house. Suddenly there were tears in her eyes and she was completely rational for a moment. Home, hers and Jim's.

Jim carried her things inside while she darted around like a bird, opening windows and examining drawers and shelves with intense interest. She marveled at the way he had kept things clean, the floors shining with wax, not a speck of dust or lint anywhere.

He watched her with the strange silence around him like a piece of wearing apparel. That Terry had told him a baby might be the best thing that could happen to Mary Elsie, that it might restore her sanity. She had also told him that to get Mary Elsie back into Canterbury he would have to go through the courts again. The goddam stupid bitch! Trying to make him admit he'd had intercourse with Mary Elsie that one visit! He recalled the tedious hours he had spent cleaning the shotgun, then taking it out behind the flour mills to test it, and then his shame and self-scorn because he could not bring himself to use it the way he had planned. After all he had endured, the honest-to-God tears he had cried—something a man should never do—here was his wife. Pregnant. Carrying a baby inside her body, not put there by him. Not his, by God!

Still, she did seem better. She moved about as she had in the old days when their marriage was new and wonderful and they could hardly leave each other alone five minutes. And she liked him again; she kept looking at him with little secret glances. He thought about testing her by coming up quietly behind her, slipping his arms around her waist and pressing his mouth against the back of her neck where the curls lay thick and damp. Would she turn and put her arms around him, squealing the way she used to do? He could not bring himself to experiment. If she were not better and his touch set her off, what in God's name would he do?

For several days he was very careful. She slept in the bedroom, he on the hard sofa in the living room. He kept out of sight when she undressed or did anything intimate. He used some of his accumulated sick leave to stay home from the mill, and he never left her alone once; he just stayed out of the way and thought constantly of her pregnancy. His face was pale and feverish from thinking about it, but he could not bring himself to ask questions. Besides, he was so sure she would not tell him anything sensible.

Then, quite by accident, he found out what he wanted to know. One night she served a casserole for dinner that he would have sworn was chicken but which turned out to be liver.

"Mmmm—good," he said, really liking the dish.

She bubbled happily. "We had it once a week in the hospital. Every Wednesday. Sure fools you, doesn't it? I bet you thought it was veal or something. Well, it's liver. One of the girls told me how they fixed it."

He ate two helpings. "You can make this any time. Uh—they good to you in the hospital?"

196

"Sure," she replied vaguely. "They were swell. But I'm glad to be home. I was getting tired of all those treatments and everything. All that throwing up I did—gosh, it was awful." She was happy to tell him about it.

"Uh—how come you threw up all the time?"

"Shock. It made lots of the girls throw up. We weren't supposed to eat anything before treatment but coffee and toast, but some of the girls who weren't gonna get treatment would sneak us sweet rolls and cereal and stuff. They were sure nice to me."

"Who did you like best—that Molly?"

"Oh, she was the charge"—as though that took care of *her*. She didn't count; it was the girls who counted. "There were several I liked—you know, not best. I liked them all. My best friends live on this block." Her voice was mildly reproving.

"Sure, I forgot. But there. In the hospital, I mean. Which girl did you like best?"

"Oh, I don't know. I can't remember all their names. There was one, her name was Cerilla. Isn't that a pretty name? And another, I never did hear what her real name was. We all called her Butterball because she was so fat. But cute, you know, real cute. And that Madge was there for a while. Ugh."

How stupid can I get? Jim thought, watching her. It takes a man to get a woman pregnant, and all Mary Elsie talks about are the women. What about the doctors? She never once mentions them. That Andreatta, for instance. He almost laughed, thinking about it. The idea seemed so fantastic—that little pipsqueak of a doctor and Mary Elsie! But he couldn't let it go; he worried at it like a dog with a bone. Why didn't Mary Elsie ever talk about Andreatta? Had she forgotten him already? His eyes followed her as she went into the bathroom, partly shut the door and turned on the water in the shower. He was still on the couch, filling his cigarette lighter with fluid, when she came out, still damp, with only the bath towel wrapped around her body.

"We couldn't do this in the hospital," she said, elated at being able to take a shower without the watchful supervision of an attendant. "We weren't supposed to ever run around the ward without our clothes on."

She pulled the towel loose and rubbed at her wet curls. Jim sat perfectly still on the couch, his face beginning to gleam with sweat.

"Dr. Andreatta tell you girls that you weren't supposed to run around naked?" he said hoarsely.

He saw the cloud begin to gather, its edges creeping faintly over her features. Her eyes filled with strangeness. "Dr. Andreatta?" she repeated softly, the texture of her words steeped in wonder as though the name had somehow blanked out until this moment of remembering.

It came in waves, he thought in sick horror, the disintegration making its way slowly across her face and into her eyes. Her breath became shallow, coming into her throat with a little moaning sound as she said the name again. She rubbed her hair in slow motions with one hand, the towel trailing down against her thigh, swinging gently, while the other hand crept to one breast, cupping it tenderly. She spread her feet slightly apart. She looked at Jim but he was sure she did not see him.

"He came to see me almost every night," she whispered. "He didn't want me to wear any clothes at all when he came, only I wasn't ever supposed to tell anybody. He said he wouldn't come back if I did. You don't blame me for not telling, do you? I wanted him to come back. It's hard to keep secrets, but I kept that one, all right. I never told anybody."

Jim stared at her. He could not move. His face had congested with blood, but all strength had left his feet and legs. For one second he thought he would throw himself at Mary Elsie and bear her down to the floor and stamp the life out of every inch of her contaminated, impregnated body.

Mary Elsie sat down on the floor, still rubbing her hair, one hand still cupping a breast, her legs crossed Indian style. Her eyes were candid and contemplative. Sounding almost normal, she said, "Come down here, Jim. You haven't done a thing since I got home. Don't you want to any more? Come on, let's do it before I get dressed."

She tossed the towel aside and held out her hands. "Hurry, sweetie pie," she coaxed, her eyes teasing, her mouth sweet, her hips beginning to move sensuously. "Hurry, hurry, get your clothes off. Hurry up. Come on, come on. What's the matter? Don't you love me any more? Hurry, Jim."

He could not leave the couch; he could not move. His throat made noises and a flood of tears began to run from his eyes. He had to sit and watch Mary Elsie do things he had never before seen her or any woman do, little movements and acts only an expert teacher could have taught her. He wanted to say, Don't do that, honey, please don't do that, please, but the words stuck behind his teeth. This is my wife, my wife, he thought with a sort of helpless horror. Who did this to my wife? Why didn't they take care of her? She's sick, sick! Then he thought, I'll kill the sonofabitch. I'll kill him!

Jim Blayton walked slowly down Marett Street and crossed over to Sycamore, stopping in the shadows near the ornate façade of the Elks lodge. He had read something in the evening paper which had brought him here, and he waited patiently until a crowd began to trickle out from the building. Then he straightened himself alertly, throwing away his cigarette, and watched carefully to make sure he did not miss the person he had come to see. When the main speaker for the affair inside came through the doors, chatting casually with several people as he adjusted his hat, Jim's breath made a low, harsh sound in his throat.

The goodbyes said, the man walked briskly down the avenue. Jim followed him, not too closely, until the business section dropped behind and elderly sycamores made their appearance along the edge of the sidewalk. Then he stepped up, swiftly and softly, choosing the next heavy shadow in which to stretch out an imperative hand.

"Hey there."

More than a little startled, Dr. Andreatta whirled. "Who? Who?"

"It's me. Jim Blayton."

Dr. Andreatta peered intently at the shape looming over him in the darkness, then remembered the name of Blayton and went limp with relief. This was someone he knew, not a robber. He laughed a little shakily.

"Ah, yes, the young man who wept in his car. How are you, Mr. Blayton? Pardon how I shake, but you—you gave me a fright, no?"

"You don't say so? Sorry. I would have spoken some time back but didn't figure it to be the right time, yet. Read in the paper how you were giving a talk at the Elks tonight."

Jim could almost feel the doctor begin to beam. "You read that, eh? Yes, I had a most in'resting subject. It was called Phenomena of Dual Identities. It fascinates me. Were you there to hear about it, Mr. Blayton?"

"No, I don't belong to the Elks, Doctor. Besides, I don't like to leave my wife alone too long. She's home with me now, you know."

"Ah, yes. I read the report. How wonderful for you that you are to be parents. It will do much for her, I believe. It will possibly provide a cure, no?" He said it warmly, feeling truly happy for the Blaytons.

"That's what they tell me. All them people, that Miss Terry and some of the doctors. I sure hope they're right, because I don't want Mary Elsie to have to go back to the hospital. She's being real good this time, although if she wasn't, I'd still keep her home—if I could. A man can put up with most anything when he feels about his wife like I do about Mary Elsie, Doctor."

"Good, good. All is very good, young man. I am glad we met so that you could tell me this good news." He lifted his hat courteously and would have walked on, but Jim stepped quickly in his path.

"Not so fast, Dr. Andreatta," he said softly.

"What?" The doctor strained his gaze up at the hulking figure.

"Not so fast. I want to ask some questions, Doctor."

"Questions? At this time of night? Forgive me, Mr. Blayton, but I am very weary. Are they questions that cannot wait until a more suitable time to be answered?"

"Oh, they could wait, all right. But I can't, Doctor. I'll do you this much of a favor and make it brief and to the point. What is a man supposed to do when he discovers his wife is pregnant—but not by him?"

"How—how you say that?"

"I said, here's a man. He's married. His wife is knocked up—going to have a baby. But he didn't do it, he didn't knock her up. What's he supposed to do about it?"

"I—this is confusing. I do not understand."

"What's the trouble, Doctor? Didn't you hear me?"

"Ah—you mean a certain man has a wife and she has become impregnated by another man? Is this what you mean?"

"Exactly what I mean, Doctor. Mary Elsie, for example. We both know she's pregnant, she's going to have a baby. But not mine, Doctor, not my baby. I didn't do it."

Dr. Andreatta was suddenly aware of the ominous quality in Jim's voice. He stepped back nervously, his eyes darting back and forth, seeking a way of escape from the other in the dark, tree-lined street.

"Come now," he remonstrated, making his voice as light as he could. "It is all in the records, no? You visited your wife and you . . . did things, instead of waiting until she was well enough to return to the home. The attendant on duty swore to this. It is your child, of course."

"It is *not* my child, Doctor. What you don't know would fill a goddam good-sized book. In the first place I haven't been able to do anything for a long time. In the second, I'm sterile. I didn't do anything that time to Mary Elsie whether the whole goddam, sonofabitchen hospital believes me or not, but if I had, it still wouldn't have counted. I can get statements from three different doctors to prove that. Real doctors, not quack psychiatrists. I think you know whose baby Mary Elsie is going to have, don't you, Doctor?"

"I—I don't know what this is you are talking about," the doctor stammered.

"You don't say." Jim's voice was heavy with sarcasm. He put out his big hands and grabbed up the doctor's coat front. "You don't say! You know something, Doctor? I'm waiting.

Just waiting. They told me that having a baby would be the best thing in the world for my wife. And she is better, I can see she is. Maybe it will really work, her having a baby. But if it doesn't—if it doesn't, I'll take that man who's responsible for knocking her up and I'll beat him to a pulp. You know why? Because I think nothing could be lower than a sonofabitch who'd do such a skunking thing to a sick woman like that, like Mary Elsie is. Why, a man who'll do that, he'll do it to anything, maybe even a bitch dog. That kind of a man ain't fit to live, is he? He ain't a man, he's some kinda animal. Ain't he, Dr. Andreatta? Ain't he?" He shook Dr. Andreatta, holding him off the ground.

Even in the dark, the sweat could be seen gleaming on Dr. Andreatta's face. "Please! How can you prove this? This is most undignified to a man of my position! I know nothing of your wife's condition except what I have studied in the records."

"Of course not, Doctor, you don't know a thing. What's the matter? I didn't accuse *you* of anything, did I? I just wanted to ask some questions. What are you shaking for? Huh? Answer me. What's scaring you?"

"I—I warn you, sir. If you do not put me down this very moment I shall call for assistance. You are trying to disgrace me with these stupid questions! Or blackmail me, perhaps! I'll call the police!"

Jim's laugh was cold. "Stupid? Don't see how you figure it's stupid for a man to want to know who's the daddy of his wife's baby. Go ahead, Doctor, call the cops. They might be real interested to know my wife says that you are the daddy of her kid, Doctor."

The doctor picked ineffectually at the hands holding his coat. "Oh, my goodness!" he squealed shrilly. "Your wife says that? Your wife is a very sick woman, Mr. Blayton. Her word would never be accepted for truth. I think you know how it would be, sir. You do not frighten me!"

"Goddam you!" Jim said softly. "If you weren't such a little squirt, I'd beat the goddam shit right outa your guts, only I know if I ever get started, I'll wind up killing you. Then there would be nobody to look out for Mary Elsie. I sure as hell couldn't do that, sitting in a penitentiary someplace. Listen to me, you sonofabitch! If this doesn't work with Mary Elsie, you better get yourself outa this town. You hear me? You better get outa this town, because if you don't—" He broke off, shaking the doctor the way a dog would shake a scrap of cloth between his teeth. Then he released him so violently that the doctor went sprawling backward and fell to the ground.

"Just keep in mind what I said," he told the small man

with deadly intensity, after which he turned and walked rapidly back the way he had come.

Goddam sonofabitch! he thought. Just let something go wrong with Mary Elsie and I'll kill the dirty bastard!

CHAPTER 28

KATHY MET MIKE FOR LUNCH in the employees' cafeteria, agreeing to the date after the three phone calls on his part. He was there at one of the tables for two at a window by the time she could get away from her ward and walk over. He stood up when he saw her come in and beckoned.

"Here, use my book," he offered. "It's still practically full."

"Thanks, but I'm not in the least hungry. Just coffee for me."

"That's no way to keep up your strength," he scolded, but went for the coffee, bringing back a potful, cups and saucers and a plate of coffee cake as well. When he had everything arranged to his satisfaction he leaned back and looked at her. "What have you been doing to yourself? You look terrible." He scowled angrily. He hadn't seen her since their dinner at the Italian restaurant outside the hospital grounds, and she looked unwell.

She was a little startled. "Well, thanks!"

He took his fork and separated slices of the cake, then looked up again. The scowl was gone and had been replaced by something rather pathetic, a contrite little-boy look. "What I meant is that you're beautiful but you've got a morning-after-the-night-before look. It doesn't suit you."

She sipped coffee and toyed with the cake. "It can't be that kind of a look, because I went to bed early last night," she said, frowning. Why had she made this date, after she had promised herself she wouldn't see him again if she could help it?

"Donovan's book finished?"

"Yes."

"Well, thank God for small favors. Now we can go to dinner and a show."

"No."

"No? That's a strong word coming from anyone your size."

"Is it?"

"And I want to know why."

She lifted her head. "Mike," she said earnestly, "you've got to understand that I have a job. I can't run around like a kid still in high school." And above all, listen to you make love, she was thinking. "Tomorrow night I'll be starting my ward management, night duty, so I'll have to get all the rest I can."

"What an excuse. Don't tell me you're afraid to go out with me, Kathy."

"Why should I be afraid?"

"You can answer that better than I can."

She shook her head. "I don't want to hurt you," she began.

"You've said that before. What's happened since I saw you last? Macleod got around to making love to you?" He spoke as though he were talking about something very unpleasant, like smallpox or bubonic plague.

"Mike!" she said sharply.

"All right, so I shock you. Well, that's what I'm hoping, you know, that if I shock you enough it won't happen." His eyes were speculative. "Something's happened to give you that burned-out look."

"You're not very nice today."

"Knowing how I feel, if you were in my place, would you be nice?"

"I wish you wouldn't talk that way." She was pale. "It makes me feel so much more—so guilty."

"More than you did before?"

"Well, yes."

"I don't know why. It isn't your fault I fell in love with you. My complaint is, you're not giving me a break."

"I can't, Mike, I can't," she whispered.

"You could." He stirred his coffee aimlessly. "But you can't see the forest for the trees."

"Is that the way it seems?"

He put down the spoon. "Tell me one thing, Kathy. As honestly as you can. If things had been different, how would you have felt about me? I mean if Macleod hadn't been in the way?"

She looked up quickly and then down again. "That's not fair."

He reached over the table and took one of her hands. "Just this once and I'll never ask it again. But honestly, Kathy. What would it have been like for me?"

She was quiet for a moment, her hand tense under his. Then she shrugged. "I suppose you know that I like you. I don't know very much about you, but it doesn't seem to matter too much. I feel that I've known you a long time."

"Yes?"

"Isn't that enough?"

"No. You haven't gotten around him yet."

Her face looked stubborn. "That's as far as I can go. If I went any farther, you'd get a wrong impression."

He was very still for a few seconds. "That's all I wanted to know," he said quietly. Surprisingly, he looked quite pleased.

Kathy disengaged her hand nervously. She pushed her cup back and looked at her watch. "Don't go yet," he said. "This ward-management business. How long does it last?"

"The rest of the month."

"And then graduation?"

"And state-board exams."

"And then you're finished. What will you do afterward?"

"Get a job."

"Here?"

"I—I don't know, Mike. It depends." She looked depressed for a second. "I haven't thought that far, really."

"But you did, once. You told me you owed it to your parents to finish your course. I suppose you meant paying them back something, didn't you?"

"Oh, that. Yes, I want to do that—I *will* do that." She was decisive enough about it, but the shadows under her eyes deepened.

"Kathy," he said impulsively, "once you tried to tell me what you did that was so awful, remember? And I wouldn't let you. Maybe I should let you go ahead. Would it help to get it off your chest?"

"Oh, Mike!" Abruptly she looked confused, uncertain. "Mike, why don't you go away?"

"Why?"

"Because . . ." Her expression turned to helpless exasperation. "Why won't you understand anything? Yes, I could have told you something once, but I can't now. I don't know— maybe this isn't rational, maybe other people go through the same thing, but I waited too long." Her shoulders lifted. "Am I making sense?"

"Oh, yes. You passed the point of return. I knew that the other night, really. But I think I could help you do something about it if you would just give me a chance. That's why you want me to go away, isn't it? I keep reminding you of something you should be doing. It isn't that you're so afraid I'll make love to you."

"It's both," she admitted tiredly.

"All right. I'm sorry about that, but it isn't something I have much control over. I'm not going away, Kathy, not until I am absolutely certain I don't have a chance. Maybe you'll tell me about this thing you've got on your conscience, maybe you won't. It doesn't matter either way. As I told you before, I don't care what it is. It won't change the way I feel toward you."

"I remember you said that, but you just don't know . . ."

She didn't finish, but pushed her chair back determinedly and stood. "I've got to get back. Just because it's my last day on the ward doesn't give me the right to be late."

"I'll walk over with you."

"All right."

She walked swiftly when they left the cafeteria. Mike was sure it was because she wanted to get away from him. Stubbornly he matched his steps to hers. To reach her building from the cafeteria, they had to pass behind the huge geriatrics building. There was shade here from the building itself and it was a little cooler, although the day was spitefully hot with a promise of a storm ahead. He put a hand on her arm and held her back. "Slow down. You're almost running."

"I'll be late."

"So you said. Haven't you ever been late before?"

"Yes."

He stopped and pulled her around. "Look, Kathy, you don't need to be afraid of me. I'm the guy who loves you, remember?"

Why did he keep on being so personal, she wondered. Didn't he sense how frightened and resentful she was? She had a strong impulse to tell him everything, right from the very beginning. Then he would leave her alone. He would look at her in horror and walk away. But she couldn't bring the words to her lips.

Suddenly she was sobbing. His face filling with consternation, he put his arms around her, and she felt relief welling up, the desire to enjoy this sanctuary. The need was there to have his arms pull tighter and tighter. She could not hold back the sigh that shuddered up around the sob; she could not stop the feeling that as long as she stood in the circle of his arms, she was safe and sheltered. Then he kissed her, quite naturally, as though all his life had been directed toward the action and there was no reason he should not satisfy the impulse. He had kissed her once before, in the Italian restaurant, but this was something else again. The next moment her arms were around his neck.

He let his hands slide up to her hair. "My God!" he whispered. "My God!"

Then he was holding her head and kissing her cheeks and chin and throat.

"Don't go," he muttered. "Don't go back to work."

She began to struggle. She wanted to stay, to be kissed, to kiss back, to let his strong, experienced hands feel their tender way over her body, but the realization had come, like a sharp knife, that as long as she could believe her love for Donovan was deep and great and honest enough to be the cause of what she had done, she could keep on living. Without that belief, she was lost. She opened her eyes and saw Mike's face. Her shock and confusion turned to terror.

"Mike!" she said sharply.

When he lifted his head, she had her chance, breaking away as she had been taught to do from the clutch of an overeager patient. She ran desperately down the road. She heard him cry out, but she did not look back. She kept on running, the ground going by under her feet like a twisting, brown ribbon. After a while she had to slow down to catch her breath, and then she knew he had not followed. She took a quick glance behind her and saw that he was standing in the same spot, his hands in his pockets, his head down. His dejected appearance made her feel as if she had done nothing well or right in all her life, as if she had done nothing but ruin everything she came in contact with. Yet she was not an impulsive or headstrong person ordinarily. Or a malicious one. She had never really disliked a single human being, with the exception, perhaps, of Charlotte Range. It all seemed so unfair!

Sadly, she turned and made her way toward the ward, sure only of her duty.

CHAPTER 29

"YOU'RE A FOOL, LUCRETIA," said Elizabeth Leslie. "I'll say it right to your face. You're a fool, putting Edna in that building. She'll kill somebody!"

Lucretia shrugged. She would take almost anything from Elizabeth because never once had Elizabeth aspired to her job or tried to knife her in the back.

"Thanks," she replied dryly. "Did you think I came back to work tonight just to hear that? I've been hearing it every day since I did it."

"Why are you working tonight?"

"Well, since it is my office, Elizabeth, I can't see that it's any of your business." She shoved drawers shut with a bang and shuffled papers on top of the desk. "But I'll tell you. Occasionally there are a few things I'd like to do without Margaret Rich looking over my shoulder."

Elizabeth looked. "Those are your assignments," she said flatly. "That's another thing. Why are you letting those two affiliates have Rehabilitation? They don't know how to manage a building like that."

"How else are they going to learn?"

"But not there. It's too dangerous, Lucretia."

"Dangerous, dangerous! Is that the only word you know?"

"It's enough at the moment. Put experienced women on the

building and give those girls untidy wards like the other affiliates."

Lucretia sat back and lit a cigarette. "Althea Horne and Katherine Hunter made the highest grades in their whole class. I'd like to keep those girls. If I put them on untidy wards, they'll leave as soon as they graduate and they won't come back. If they take their ward management on Rehabilitation, they may like it well enough to consider staying on after they finish their state exams. I don't think I need to tell you how badly we need good supervisors, do I?" She squinted at Elizabeth.

"You haven't been listening in on the grapevine. Althea and Kathy hate each other. So you put them working together. What will you get? Trouble, trouble, trouble."

"Elizabeth, you are certainly in a rut tonight. Don't I do anything to please you?" Lucretia's look was sly.

"All right, so it isn't any of my business. There's one thing, Lucretia. You can't fire me, because I'm here on borrowed time already. I can retire this very minute if I want to, so I'll speak my piece. You're making a terrible mistake about this whole thing. You're putting Edna Horne in that building to please Althea, you're turning the building over to girls who haven't had the experience to handle it properly. And right now you'd like to back down but you won't because you think you might lose face if you did! So what, what if you did? Wouldn't that be better than having to face something even worse?"

"What?"

"A dozen things could go wrong. I don't have to tell you what they could be."

"Oh, stop worrying. I'm not going to leave Kathy and Althea out on a limb. I'll be checking constantly." She put out her cigarette and looked up again at Elizabeth. "In my usual fashion," she added, her face beginning to take on an annoyed expression. She wished Elizabeth would get the hell out and leave her alone. She felt bad enough without having to argue with someone she liked too much to get harsh with, the only person in the institution whom she could really trust.

Elizabeth was silent a moment, then she sighed. "Lucretia, what difference does it make about Margaret—and others? Do you think they'll criticize you if you decide to countermand an order you've given? If they do, it just shows how stupid they are. It takes a smart person to know when she's made a mistake and a smarter one to do something about it. I called you a fool, but you're not, Lucretia."

"God's sake!" Lucretia erupted. "You want me to admit to anything in front of that pornographic weasel Margaret when

207

you know how I feel about her? I can't do it, Elizabeth. I simply can't. She'd never stop crowing."

"Well, fire her, then."

"I can't do that, either."

"Why?"

"Now who's stupid?"

They looked at each other. Lucretia looked away. "What can happen in fifteen days, Elizabeth? What can possibly happen?"

"I don't have to tell you. You're head of this nursing service. You know all the answers."

Lucretia shook her head angrily and lit another cigarette. "You're an alarmist. I'm not going to let anything happen any more than I'm going to let Margaret get my job. She's taken everything from me she's going to get."

"That's beside the point. That's something else again. This other is something you might regret all the rest of your life."

"Oh, stop it, for heaven's sake," Lucretia said testily. "We're friends, Elizabeth, but by God, you can't tell me what to do. For the last time, can't you understand I have to decide things for myself? That's how I got where I am. I can make decisions—good ones! Now suppose you clear out and let me do my work. You've got me so nervous now I'm spilling ink all over the damn desk." To prove her point, she shook her pen vigorously and spattered ink freely on the floor.

She pretended to write until Elizabeth left, and then she sat very still, looking at her papers without really seeing them. Why couldn't Elizabeth understand about Margaret and Walter? And about her, about the Benzedrine she took to see her through the day and the Seconal at night to help her sleep. Now the pain never quite let up; it was there in the pit of her stomach like a deep heartbeat, and while the specialist she had gone to see in Dover had assured her that the mass in her uterus was benign, she did not believe him.

Once it had been interesting and stimulating to control the hundreds of strings she had to manipulate. Lately it took sheer tenacity and grit. But with Margaret waiting to take over, she wasn't going to give up until she dropped in her tracks. She made mistakes and had to work alone at night to hide them, juggling records, doing anything to keep Margaret from finding out about the mistakes. At times she could tell herself that nothing would have gone wrong had she been able to get married when she first planned to. She would have been in a home of her own by now, relaxed and taken care of. So Walter, then, was to blame for everything. But Margaret had done her share, too.

And now I'm going to die, Lucretia thought bitterly, because I can't bear to quit this damn job and go to a decent hospital and have myself taken care of properly, knowing that when it's all over I'll be just a has-been on the shelf, no damn good to anybody, including myself. If there were anyone here to take my place but Margaret—Elizabeth can't; she's too old. There isn't anyone but Margaret!

All right. So I stay and suffer. Big deal, Lucretia told herself grimly, lighting still another cigarette—a great big deal! I cut for it myself when I didn't chop Walter down to size.

In Dr. Herrington's office the next morning, Lucretia was delivering herself of a few choice opinions. She had gone there to consult with him on a decision she had made which she was not sure would be honored by him. Much to her surprise he had instantly concurred, having other matters on his mind, which he mentioned cautiously, feeling certain she would be angry. She was.

"We've worked together in this hospital for twenty-three years and you have the gall to suggest I won't back down on something because of hurt pride. When did I ever not put the interests of the patients first?"

"Now, I didn't say that, Lucretia, I didn't say that. I merely asked if it's wise to put patients in the new center just to save face or to please the supervisors?"

"In this case you're talking about Edna Horne, of course," she said coldly. "Who told you about it?"

He cleared his throat noisily. "Look, my dear, I may not be trotting all over the place, but I do keep in touch, you know."

"No, I didn't." She glared at him. "I didn't know you had time, along with entertaining all the state legislative body and any other politicians who come poking a big nose into our affairs to find out why we're spending so much or what we're doing with what we don't spend. I know who told you. It was Walter, wasn't it? It had to be either him or Margaret Rich."

"Well, if you go ahead with what you're planning, you don't have to be concerned with Margaret, do you?"

She nodded. "I thought so. It was Margaret. Well, let me tell you something, Jubal. I have seven years to go before retirement. I don't intend to have my decisions questioned."

He stirred uncomfortably. He hadn't quarreled with Lucretia for years because she always got the best of him in an argument. "Now, haven't I always told you that you know best about your own department? If you say this patient is safe, is capable of being rehabilitated, I'll take your word for it. After all this time, you certainly ought to know what you're doing."

"All right," Lucretia said, but she wasn't mollified. She

209

seethed inside because Margaret had gone over her head. How preposterous! Did she think that Jubal wouldn't reveal his source of information? Now, more than ever, she was determined to do something about Margaret. "I *do* know," she declared firmly.

She marched to the door, her back stiff and uncompromising. But when she glanced back with her hand on the doorknob, she caught a strange look in his face. It was pity, and instantly she was humiliated and furious.

"If I don't know, if it proves to be a mistake, what difference will it make?" she asked savagely.

It could make a difference in many ways, Herrington thought, but in her frame of mind nothing would be gained by pointing that out. "Your question," he replied noncommittally.

"Only to me, Jubal, only to me," she answered herself and went out.

He shook his head. He hoped she was right, because she suffered more from her own mistakes than anyone else, merely from the fact that she could make them. He supposed he should be firmer with her, more decisive himself, but he did hate arguments. If something went wrong, he could manage, especially if it was something the public might hear about. The hospital always got good editorials in the town's lone newspaper. That was the way a lot of things were handled, favor for favor, in more ways than one, so he wasn't going to start worrying about Lucretia and her problems now. It was too damn hot. He took out his handkerchief and mopped vigorously, then went to the cooler and had a drink. If the heat didn't break soon, along with a full moon on its way, the hospital would get higher than a kite. He never told anyone, but he had noticed for many years that a full moon played hell with ward routines, especially in the hot weather. Maybe that had something to do with Lucretia's foul temper. He shook his head, thinking about her.

Outside the building, on her way back to her own office, Lucretia could hardly see where she was going. Fifty-seven, she was thinking bitterly. I am fifty-seven and what have I got to show for it? A job's that's been a torment to hold and a disposition everyone hates, not even a home to look forward to when I retire, a love affair that couldn't even get me pregnant. All I've got inside is a growth that will eventually kill me. And a woman I tried to help who turned around and knifed me.

She stumbled and shuddered. Now this thing of Edna Horne! All of them, picking on her about it! As though she were planning something diabolical, something fiendish.

When had she not put the interest of the hospital first? Even her deep, hot desire for Walter had been kept secondary. Only now it was not desire; it was hate, dreadful and consuming. She stumbled again. Was she letting the hate come first? Was it blinding her, making her judgment unwise, unsure? Was she making a mistake putting Edna on Rehabilitation? She wanted suddenly to crawl off somewhere and cry her eyes out, cry until she was blind. But wouldn't that look fine! A tall, middle-aged bag of bones like Lucretia Terry crying like a ten-year-old. After all the years and getting to the top, making more money than a lot of men ever make, you don't crawl off and cry. You put on a front and stare everybody down and get a little madder than the rest of the staff because it's dog eat dog and no favors given, even with love. It's Competition, not the Golden Rule, that decides the regulations.

She remembered an argument she had had with Elizabeth over some new custodial practices in use in an English institution, and her own irate answer to Elizabeth's assertions.

"If I did all the things you advocate, Elizabeth, this place would go to pot. Apply the rules of Christianity! Generosity, kind and tender affections, expressions of love! These are insane people. They can't respond in a normal manner because they aren't normal. They can be handled only certain ways. Your rules don't apply to them!"

"You haven't tried them," Elizabeth replied.

"We don't need different rules, we need money."

"Money. Of course. We spend it all for wars and pleasures or for covering up centuries of mistakes. We must have our cars, television sets, cosmetics, atom bombs, for everything under the sun but a comprehensive program of welfare. Poor Grandpa goes around peeking in somebody's bedroom window, so he gets stuck in a place like Canterbury, behind a locked door, to vegetate and die. And what about the spastic babies, the epileptics, the idiots? They can't be kept at home; they *bother* somebody. Somebody has to worry about them and train them and watch over them. It's too much fuss and bother, so turn them over to people who can be *paid* for taking care of them, people who'll lock them in and watch over them, all for a pay check!"

She had nodded. She never could make Elizabeth back down from a stand once she had taken it. And she had said, "In the abstract, Elizabeth, in the abstract you're right. But I didn't create the system. It's like saying there should be a law against gluttony or cheating or gossiping. Anyone would benefit by not gossiping or overeating. But how would such a law be enforced? Answer that if you can—and you can't because those are defects or predilections and a law against them couldn't be enforced. I do my job and what else can I do? Buck the tide? How far would I get? How far?"

And Elizabeth had shrugged. "You would have tried," she had said and walked away.

What would happen if she went to Elizabeth now and told her she was getting ready to die? Elizabeth would be kind, she would be full of pity, she would try to help. She was gentle, understanding.

I'll stop taking Benzedrine, she thought, before I really make a fool out of myself. It isn't a mistake to put Edna in that building. I *know* what I'm doing!

In Walter's office, Margaret sat on the corner of his desk. He sat in the desk chair and let one hand slide experimentally up and down her leg, going a little higher with each slide until he reached the seam in her panties.

"Don't." She giggled.

He smiled at her. "How about it? I've got a quilt in my utility closet. We'll be safe. Nobody ever goes in there."

Her lips were moist. But her eyes were speculative. "First, tell me something. When's it to be?"

"When's what to be?"

"Look, Walter. You know what I mean."

He pretended to tease her. "Haven't the faintest idea," he said, shaking his head solemnly and letting his hand go as high as it could, all the way, and letting it stay there.

She threw her head back and wiggled her hips. "All right. I can play that way. I'm going—"

"Now, look."

She leaned forward and pressed her legs together. "Okay, stop kidding."

He squeezed with his hand. "Have it your own way," he said, sighing and rolling his eyes. "Any time you say."

"Thanksgiving," she decided instantly. "I have an aunt who's going to leave me her money when she dies. Not much but we could get a car or something. We'll get married there because it will please her."

"Nothing formal," he protested, alarmed.

"Of course not. At our ages? Don't be silly."

He relaxed, squeezed again with his hand. "Swell. Tell me again. How did you work it about Terry?"

She wiggled again, so excited she couldn't speak for a second. "Oh, I just told Herrington," she said finally. "I told him what she was doing, all the mistakes in her records and how she was having dangerous patients transferred to buildings where they don't belong. He's no fool. I could tell by the way he talked. He knows it's time to get rid of her.

She's outlived her job. Don't worry, he'll do something about her."

"Good." He stood up and pushed himself between her legs. Suddenly she began arching and contorting. She broke away and ran toward the utility closet, unbuttoning her uniform as she went. "Hurry, hurry!" she panted.

He was right behind her, but he did not start to undress until he had reached the closet door. He had always been a careful man. He did not unzip his trousers until his hand was on the doorknob. After the door was shut and they were safe in the darkness of the closet, he did not care that she whispered she was going to tell Lucretia they were engaged. It was definite; they were to be married on Thanksgiving Day. After all, hadn't she said Jubal would do something about Lucretia, and wouldn't that make her the next head of nursing personnel for Canterbury? Right now there was this business to take care of, damned good business, not those skinny bones of Lucretia's but comfortable, well-padded hips, a good fit, good business! He took care of it several times.

Part Three

CHAPTER 30

IT IS VERY RARE for an attendant in a mental hospital to be given charge of a ward without first receiving specialized training; he must become an aide, a registered nurse, or spend long years working in mental institutions before he is promoted. A nurse several months in such a place, however, is almost always given management of a ward before his or her course is finished. Even so, nurses not yet wearing their stripes are seldom made supervisors in buildings closely packed with violent, dangerous patients.

The Rehabilitation Center of Canterbury where Kathy Hunter and Althea Horne were sent as day and night supervisors was a huge, T-shaped building four stories high. Each wing held a ward ending in a steel mesh-enclosed porch. The center portion of the T was office space on the first floor, therapy, surgery and kitchen space on the others. In the basement were laundry facilities, heating and air-conditioning plants, and storage rooms. The building was a self-contained city teeming with activity.

Each ward had a central hall or corridor lined with bedrooms, stool, shower and utility rooms, a large living area called the day hall, an individual dining room serviced by its own kitchen, and a small office tucked away in a corner with a clear view through enormous, safety-plate-glass windows of the whole day hall as well as the long corridor between bedrooms. At the corridor's far end was the porch, and just inside from it was an opening out onto a fire-exit landing and stairs going down to the ground floor.

Between the two wards of a floor was a long room which served as a reception hall for both wards as well as the entrance and exit to them; it opened into another room which led to the elevators, therapy rooms and the kitchen. There were two sets of elevators, one for patients and employees, the other a freight elevator going down to the loading dock across the back of the building and to the basement. In front of the building were lawns, walks and shrubbery, all overlooked by row upon row of steel mesh-impregnated windows.

The day halls contained heavy, tubular-steel frame couches and heavier golden oak chairs and tables. The heavier the furniture, the more difficult for a patient to pick it up and swing it at another patient or at an employee. There were some homey touches: large stacks of magazines and boxed jigsaw puzzles and a few lightweight plastic containers of plants. Such things as cleaning implements and polishers were tightly locked away, and even linens and extra sweaters were behind locked doors. In the dining rooms every dish, pan, knife, fork and spoon was counted religiously before and after use.

When not busy with ward activity or dispensing medication, the ward charge and her assistants remained in the office. In this little island of security she recorded the events of her shift in a large desk ledger used by all three shifts. She filled out forms, studied charts and medical orders; she made calls to supervisors and doctors, wrote transfers, and in general assumed responsibility for the care and well-being of twenty to thirty patients, as well as the work and safety of the employees on her shift. Quite frequently she still had time to fix her nails, crochet, knit or even read the latest true-confessions magazine, knowing that in cases of extreme emergency, down in the main office on the first floor a supervisor was ready to bring help in an instant.

Most of the patients on Rehabilitation were roughly classified under the term "psychopathic." They came from homes which would not tolerate them any longer, from gangs in large cities, from slum districts, from wealthy neighborhoods. They often knew the right course of action but seldom took it. They seemed to enjoy any excitement they could create, even when it was destructive to themselves. Their ages ranged from thirteen to thirty-five or forty, and most of them were physically strong. Outside the institution they had indulged in sexual promiscuity and perversions, in lying and stealing, in arson and robbery, and in the uncontrolled use of drugs and alcohol. They were cold-blooded, self-centered, and had no capacity for remorse. When they were committed to Canterbury and assigned to Rehabilitation, along with the rest of the patients on the wards—the schizophrenics, accident trauma victims and syphilitics—they were regarded as detention patients.

Each charge walked carefully among the patients on her ward. She was quick to note the small deviation which could mean that the patients were forming a gang, were planning to knock somebody on the head, grab the keys and make an escape. She had to watch the lone patient going off into a catatonic trance from which he might emerge like a screaming, furious banshee to leap on some unsuspecting employee's back during an unguarded moment. It was a byword at Canterbury that there was never a dull moment on Rehabilitation. However, the patient continuously out of contact with reality was usually not sent there. It was assumed that an out-of-contact patient could not tell the difference between nice wards or untidy ones. In spite of the steel mesh and the locked doors, Rehabilitation was the latest in modern institutional décor, shining and clean and not yet saturated with the musty odor of the living dead. And because Rehabilitation was considered a place for the potentially curable, Lucretia Terry's decision to transfer Edna Horne there was as precedent-shattering as the placements of Kathy and Althea. Edna was considered to be the most dangerous patient ever sent to Rehabilitation, and supervisors and therapists and ward charges throughout the hospital gathered to talk about it.

Only Ruth Ellison and Millie Higgins were unaffected by the furor. They settled in as charges on their respective wards, and after the strangeness of the first night they acted as though they had been in the building for years. In spite of the way they had received their placements, and although they were in a potentially dangerous building, they were pleased that they were charges. For eight hours every night they were managers. They had an office of their own, and there was no one to look over their shoulders except a fully accredited supervisor. If they were careful, did their work properly and had no trouble on their wards, they would probably remain where they were until they retired.

On night duty, they worked alone. Before they came on, the afternoon shift had bedded down the patients and locked the doors; the office reasoned that one employee to a ward was sufficient for the ten-to-six stretch. Since there were only two wards to a floor, the two charges were required to check their wards together, once an hour. Otherwise, they remained in their separate offices, doing what they called their paper work. Twice during the night, the supervisor from the office on the main floor made a complete circuit of the building, checking each ward with its charge, hearing complaints if there were any, and making a point of examining any patient who was receiving special medication or who had been unusually disturbed during the day. The supervisor always read everything: the desk ledger, the doctor's reports, the medical sheets, the histories of new transfers, the case cards on old ones, and the notes left for one shift by another or by a supervisor to the charge.

Actually the night was the best shift on Rehabilitation. There were no meals to supervise, and no ward cleaning, because the ward had to be quiet. The night charges cleaned their offices in order to stay awake and gave medication occasionally. To fill up the rest of they time they brought knitting and crocheting and mending from home, wrote letters, clipped recipes, worked jigsaw puzzles and took carefully timed naps.

Ruth, having been with the hospital so long, adapted herself to her new freedom and responsibility swiftly and easily, and helped Millie to do the same. On the night of the fifteenth, Millie shuttled back and forth between her office and Ruth's a number of times to get advice, but the next night she was calm and relaxed and she began to enjoy her ward and to appreciate the dignity and importance of being a charge. When she came on duty, the afternoon charge seemed delighted to see her and immediately turned over the keys, the ledger and the medications. They checked the ward together, looking through the little door windows at each patient. They counted the narcotics and discussed new medical orders. Then the afternoon charge and her assistants gathered up their belongings, and Millie unlocked the ward door to let them out into the connecting hall, unlocked the hall door to lead them to the elevator and finally unlocked the elevator itself. If the attendant on duty on the main floor was temporarily absent, Millie would have to ride down with the afternoon shift and unlock the main door too. It gave her a sense of deep responsibility to have so much authority.

The first thing she did after everyone had left was to sit at her desk and gaze around her. This was her home for eight hours—her throne, her kingdom. It came to her with awe that she was almost like a mother to the patients. She must be careful, very careful, to take care of them properly. She looked through the windows of the offices and observed the day hall, clean and shining, the floors spotless, freshly waxed every day, the furniture gleaming with polish. The attractive draperies at the huge rows of windows looked as if they had just been hung. Even the stainless-steel cabinets in the office and the modern pink refrigerator looked new and unused. Just outside one office window was a long table piled high with magazines. There was a piano on this ward, too. It was an ancient upright and was always kept locked, but it gave a certain distinction to the rooms, and on top of the piano in its exact center sat a plastic pot holding a large bunch of gaily colored paper flowers.

Through an archway, Millie could see part of the dining room with its small tables, four chairs pushed up to each one. On each table was a paper cup containing more paper flowers.

When Ruth came in to show her how to make her first check on the patients, Millie commented on the cleanness. "Ain't it nice? After putting up with that Range, this'll be just like heaven. Hardly a thing to do all night long. I keep pinching m'self to make sure I ain't asleep."

"Nice? Too nice if you ask me. What do these patients do all day long?"

"Huh?"

"Well, what do they do? If it was you or me, we'd go crazy without something to do, wouldn't we?"

"But—they're already crazy," Millie said, frowning. "Maybe they can't do anything. I mean like housework or office work or anything like that. That's why they're here."

Ruth sniffed. "These are mostly psychopaths. They can do anything they've a mind to. Mostly they want sex and good times and liquor. They need to be kept busy on account of when they got nothing to do, they get meaner'n hell. They oughta be put to work, every single one of 'em. I got one on my ward that's been down in restraint two weeks. According to her chart, she's had over two hundred shock treatments. Over two hundred! Thinka that!"

"God," Millie said reverently. "Wonder she ain't dead."

"She's nineteen. Only nineteen."

"How come she's in here?"

"Killed her baby. It was one day old and she smothered it with a pillow in some cheap rooming house and left it there for the landlady to find. Landlady didn't even know she was gonna have a baby. She wasn't married."

"No wonder she's crazy."

"Girl like that, I think they oughta lock up the fella who did it, don't you?"

"Yeah, only sometimes it's mor'n one fella. Sometimes the girl don't even know who——" She shook her head.

"It's the girl who always pays," Ruth said with conviction.

"Yeah. I got one on this ward. Just read her chart. Poor kid. Out in a car with a bunch of teen-agers and they had a wreck. Everybody killed but her. Her folks are rich, I guess. They did everything, all kinda surgery, but nothing worked. She can walk and that's all. The afternoon charge said to be sure to check her bed on account of she wets all night long. The charge says nobody comes to see her. Ain't nobody

218

been to see her for three years, not even her own mother. She's a hopeless idiot from having her head mashed. She's harmless—got no strength at all. They only keep her in Rehabilitation because her folks are so rich."

Ruth thought about it. "But look, if she makes a lotta noise, you'll have to do something or she'll wake up your whole ward. You don't wanta let that happen."

Millie was silent a moment. "I won't," she said finally. "I already got it figured out what I'll do."

"What?"

"Why, she's harmless, ain't she?"

"Yeah, I suppose so."

"Well, I'll just go back there and act like her mother oughta be acting. She probably cries 'cause somewhere inside her jumbled-up brains she remembers a little about that wreck and she's scared. She needs somebody to pet her and make her feel she's going to be taken care of. Shucks," Millie said comfortably, "she's only seventeen now and her chart says she weighs less'n a hundred pounds. You think I'm scared of that?"

Ruth looked uneasy. "Well, you be careful. Remember, we're supposed to check these rooms together. Don't go taking any foolish chances. I'd hate to come over to your ward and find you stamped to death in a dark corner."

Millie laughed. "My goodness, that's the last thing I'll let happen. Don't worry, I'll take care of myself. Just been thinking. Kids like candy. You s'pose if I brought some of that hard stuff—you know, like Christmas candy—I could carry a few pieces in my pocket and give it to this kid when she starts her crying? Would that upset her stomach the next day so the morning shift would find out?"

"God, no." Ruth stared at Millie, her eyes soft. "You are a sucker for little things, ain't you? Kittens, kids, name it and that's it. Well, come on, let's check this ward. I'd like to see this kid you're talking about."

"Okay." Millie picked up her flashlight and stepped out of the office behind Ruth, turning to pull the door shut and lock it. "Okay," she said again, whispering now, and they swung together across the day hall and started down the dark corridor to check the rooms.

CHAPTER 31

ONE NIGHT, SHORTLY AFTER Kathy and Althea had been assigned to Rehabilitation, Jim Blayton stood waiting in the shadows of Canterbury's stone archway at the entrance to the hospital grounds. The night was dark and his dark form blended into the shadows. He had parked his car a block away in the driveway of an empty house and had walked back carrying a shotgun close to his side. It was the fourth night he had waited, the fourth night since Mary Elsie's death. Yesterday she had been buried in the town cemetery.

He tried not to think about her dying so suddenly, but he could think of nothing else. A tubal pregnancy, the doctor had said, explaining that the fetus had not clung to the inner wall of the uterus where it belonged but had remained instead in the narrow confines of one ovarian tube. When the fetus became large enough, it simply burst its bonds, and before anyone knew what was happening Mary Elsie was dead. The night he heard her begin to scream he ran into the bedroom to find her writhing and contorting in the first convulsion. When she was finally quiet the doctor pulled her body straight and covered her face with the sheet. Jim stepped out to sit in the dark living room, unaware that he was dripping with sweat and shaking violently. The doctor mixed him something in a glass, made him drink it, and even waited with him until the mortician came to take Mary Elsie away. But from then on Jim was alone. When the girls came over, cleaned the house, cooked and baked, it meant nothing to him. Mary Elsie's mother and father came for the funeral, and that meant nothing, too. Finally he was alone again, the house quiet and dark because he could not bear to raise the shades. The only thing he was really conscious of was the brutal urge to take himself and the shotgun and to wait in the shadows of the archway. It was what he had to do.

Eventually the waiting came to an end.

It was a humid hot night with sheet lightning making occasional flashes low on the horizon behind the hospital buildings. Jim saw a little man step off one of the town buses serving the institution route. Patiently, he held himself quiet. He could afford to be patient for a few seconds more. When the little man was near enough, he stepped from the shadows and into the glare of a nearby streetlight.

Too late the man saw what was in store for him. He was not completely unprepared; he had carried a razor-sharp scalpel in his coat pocket for some time. He managed to get it out and use it for one slash which cut Jim's arm open from shoulder to elbow before the butt of the shotgun came down across his head with such force that his skull was split into four sections.

Jim did not run from the scene. He turned, tucked the shotgun under his injured arm, and, using his other hand to pinch together the gushing flesh, walked without haste back to his car. He placed the gun on the floor but had some difficulty getting his shirt off. When he had it off, he wadded it as best he could around the wound, somehow got the car started and drove to the police station. While a nurse scurried around to get the first transfusion started and before he was given a blacking-out hypo, he told what he had done, grimly claiming that he had been attacked and was only defending himself.

Dr. Andreatta did not actually die for some time. He was unconscious from the time the ambulance reached his side until he stopped breathing, but because he had been found with his billfold intact, his clothing in good condition and the scalpel still clutched tightly in one hand, the Medical Examiner decided to hold an inquest and put out a plea for witnesses.

The news hit the town and the hospital like wildfire. Public opinion was divided. The town's newspaper was in favor of murder, having found an elderly woman living near the gate who didn't sleep well and had seen Jim Blayton stalking down the street carrying something that looked like a club. Why was he walking around with the gun? the editorials asked. Why would Dr. Andreatta attack *anyone*? And why attack a man twice as large as himself? For that matter, why was an inquest being held when murder was admitted? Was there bribery involved, or could it be possible that the Medical Examiner was looking for a little free publicity before he had Jim Blayton bound over for a criminal trial? The paper was determined to keep its good standing with the hospital.

The Medical Examiner—a man who had once worked for Canterbury and had been fired because he was caught giving small bottles of fine bourbon to an old alcoholic patient who turned out to be a distant relative—set the inquest for the day after Dr. Andreatta's body started on its way back to Portugal. By then, excitement was so high that he shifted the meeting from the small, dark basement of the county courthouse to the auditorium of the city hall, although it cost him fifty dollars—which he paid out of his own pocket. The District Attorney, a close friend of the Medical Examiner's, shook his head but contributed ten dollars.

"Open-and-shut case," he commented tersely. "Hope you know what you're doing, Bud."

"I was looking for a job when they gave me this one, Riley," Bud said. "You know as well as I do there was some good reason for all this. No man's going out and wait in a dark corner to kill another man without robbing him unless he has a reason. I think it's up to us to find the reason."

"Hell, won't make any difference. You get six men to decide it's justifiable, I still gotta have him up for trial. He's guilty. You know he is."

Bud looked hard at Riley. "I've known you a long time,

right? All right. We've done some things together we might not like to brag about. We've been friends a long time. You know I never worked on a hunch when there wasn't something to it in the end. I still say this Jim didn't commit murder. It was justifiable homicide. I don't give a goddam if all the newspapers in the state ride my back about it. I'm going to have this inquest and I'll try to find some witnesses to back up my hunch."

Riley whistled. "Boy, you sure cut yourself a piece of material this time. One witness so far—one. And what does she say? Look, why don't you drop things before you get us both in dutch? You're going to look mighty silly at this hearing with six of your friends trying to help you out and nothing to go on."

"I'm not going to use my friends," Bud said flatly. "I'm not that much of a fool."

"It won't work. You have to have witnesses, something to go on."

"Will you stand by me?"

Riley looked uncomfortable. "Well," he hedged, shrugging. "To a point. If you can find reasonable evidence and your jury goes along with you, I'll probably drop the whole thing unless—"

"Unless the hospital screams its head off?"

"Something like that."

"Who are you for—the common people or this big nuthouse and the local newsboys?"

"Look, I didn't set this up. I'm for the innocent and against the guilty."

"Okay, that's all I wanted to hear. If I can prove Jim was actually defending *something*, will you go along in spite of what the hospital and that two-bit newspaper of ours does?"

Riley began to sweat. "I can't promise anything, Bud. You know I can't." He stared imploringly at his friend.

Bud was not impressed. "Well, we all need our jobs," he commented dryly. "Thanks for the ten bucks," he added and went off to round up his jury.

As he told Riley, he did not go to his friends, but cleverly selected men who did not have to worry about jobs or fear adverse criticism from the newspaper. There was a druggist who was independently wealthy, a retired school principal, and the head of an insurance agency who he had heard was planning to leave the town soon to live in Florida. He also called in two elderly former employees of the hospital, now carrying on a trash-hauling service. They were the only trash haulers in the town. The last man was the town's retired postmaster. So Bud finally had his little panel, all of them elderly, all of them independent. But also they were all honest men and would not be influenced by his hunches. They would have to be convinced of the facts by reliable witnesses. And where were these witnesses? So far, one old woman who would testify against Jim.

Nervously, the Examiner set to work. He could not go to the paper and ask for aid in finding favorable witnesses, but he could let it know what he had done and what he hoped to accomplish. As he expected, the paper gave him excellent, if biased, coverage.

Here was Dr. Miguel Andreatta, a fine doctor, badly needed by Canterbury, with a wife and family in his native country waiting for him to finish his training and return to them whole and sound, stricken in a moment of brutality. Did Mr. Medical Examiner really think he would find witnesses to justify this crime? And what was the District Attorney doing, sitting on his hands? Let Jim Blayton languish in jail where he now sat. Let him come to criminal trial where he belonged and receive the state's full reward for his act, the hottest seat of all. That would be *justice*, the paper said.

Back from a trip to the state capital, Jubal Herrington called his editor friend.

"Keep us out of this," he said.

"That's a big order. You're already in it."

"Don't I know that! What I meant is that it has to be something personal between those men and I don't want it to be anything that happened here on the grounds. I suppose you know by now that Andreatta was Blayton's wife's doctor?"

"We know all that, but we haven't mentioned it."

"Good. And don't. It has nothing to do with the killing, I'm sure."

The editor wasn't so sure, but he was eager to please. "Okay on that. But what if it comes out at the inquest?"

"Inquest, inquest!" Jubal muttered. "How did that damned M.E. get away with that?"

"Blayton swears he was defending himself, and the Medical Examiner believes him. Blayton got cut, you know. Took seventeen stitches and six clamps to close the wound."

"I know, I know." Who attacked whom? Jubal wondered, but kept his doubt to himself. Just because Andreatta had been Mrs. Blayton's doctor did not necessarily mean anything. He hoped to God they wouldn't stress that the woman had recently died and that she had been dismissed as a patient prior to that under questionable circumstances. Anyone with an inventive imagination could create any number of situations with such material. He was beginning to wish he had

223

stayed in the state capital or even taken a vacation, say a hunting-and-fishing trip in Colorado or Idaho.

"Well, do what you can," he told his friend unhappily. "Only keep us out of it if possible. We're going to miss Andreatta. He was a good man."

In the long room between Wards Five and Six on Rehabilitation, Ruth and Millie sat at a table with a jigsaw puzzle between them. They had discussed the killing until Millie was sick of the subject. It was an argument now, not a discussion. With all the newspaper's articles, all the gossip seething in the town and through the hospital, she and Ruth had not missed the Medical Examiner's urgent plea for any or all witnesses to come forward and take the stand. That was what she wanted to do—in fact, she felt she had no right *not* to.

Ruth forbade her to do it. First she said, "What if you do tell what you saw? They probably won't believe you."

"Why not? I ain't carrying a grudge of any kind."

"What good will it do? Tell me that. What good will it do?"

"Well, it could show why he did it. He hadda do it, Ruthie. We woulda done it if we'd been in his place."

Ruth shook her head. "There's no excuse for murder," she said flatly and offered her final argument. "You'll get canned, sure as hell. Then what'll you do?"

"Why should I get canned?"

"My God, use your head. You think they'd keep you on out here if you tell something nasty about the hospital?"

Millie looked unhappy. "I shoulda done it right after it happened. I shoulda told Miss Terry the very next day."

"You should keep your mouth shut if you wanta stay working and paying your bills."

"But it's not right not to help him out when maybe—"

"Millie, I've told you and told you. You can't change things out here. We're just attendants, we don't count. Now forget the whole thing. You didn't see the killing and that's all they want. They want eyewitnesses, not something that happened weeks ago."

The jigsaw puzzle was nearly complete. Ruth's side was finished. Millie had a handful of pieces and was fumbling them. "Can't find that little piece anywhere. Oughta look like a duck. See—that corner there's where the bill goes."

Ruth reached to turn something over. "Here, right under your nose. If it'd been a snake, it would have bit you."

"Now, how about that? Right under my nose alla time. Why couldn't I see it?"

"You just ain't concentrating."

Millie sighed. "Suppose not. I can't stop thinking about

224

that inquest. You saw in the paper where it's to be held day after tomorrow?"

"Yeah, I saw."

"You think—" Millie stopped.

"No, I don't," Ruth said shortly. She was tired of the subject. "I think you oughta keep your job, that's what I think." She was very fond of Millie, as fond as she could be of another woman, and because she had no relatives she had done something that, if Millie outlived her, Millie would appreciate some day. But right now if she heard Andreatta's name spoken once more she would scream, she was sure she would scream. She looked at her watch. "Hey, it's almost time for the supervisor. Let's step on it, huh?"

"Okay." Millie pushed her chair back from the table. She and Ruth separated and she returned to her own office, where she opened the desk ledger to the day's entries, set the desk chair just so, and got ready for Kathy Hunter to come in to check the ward. She liked Miss Hunter, liked her very much. Miss Hunter was sweet and pleasant and shrewd, too. She wasn't going to let anything happen that oughtn't to happen, not her! But she wasn't a snoop, either. She was nice—real nice. And she had stood up to Charlotte Range, Millie remembered. She had told Range off that time. It was something worthwhile remembering—it really was. Range had sure been wrong about Miss Hunter. She wasn't fat, she wasn't chunky; she was just a cute, nice girl.

"What if I was to tell her about it?" Millie said aloud with sudden inspiration. Then she shook her head. No, no, it would never do. Miss Hunter would be sure to do things the correct way and send her to the office and that would finish everything. They'd never let her take a step inside the city auditorium the day of the inquest. No, if she was going to do anything, she would have to do it on her own, without telling anyone. I'll wait, Millie thought. There's still tomorrow and tomorrow night to make up my mind. Might as well wait till the last minute. That won't do no harm.

CHAPTER 32

LARRY DENNING walked rapidly down the path behind Surgery and stepped into a sheltered spot where the grass was deep and matted and the cinnamon odor of the oleanders clung heavily.

He tried to think about something other than Althea, deliberately making himself recall the recent, shocking death of Miguel Andreatta. He had disliked Andreatta to the point of contempt, but he could not condone his murder. And yet, if the town's Medical Examiner wanted to make a fool of himself by holding an inquest—for that matter, if he could find six men who would agree that it had been justifiable homicide—what difference would it make? Patients would still be committed to Canterbury because Canterbury was a state institution, and Jubal would not be replaced by another superintendent because a qualified man would be difficult to find. Although there was Donovan Macleod . . .

When Donovan came into his thoughts, Larry frowned. Undoubtedly Donovan could handle Jubal's job, but would he be willing to give up his self-centered existence and learn the necessary tact and diplomacy? Was he the kind of man who could unbend enough to ask favors at the right time and in the right place? Would he sanction some of the things the staff doctors did in the name of medical research and go all out to cover up for them when there was any danger of lawsuits and unfavorable publicity? Hysterectomies, for example, when the authorized permission for the operation was doubtful, or the casual appendectomies some staff residents did for practice, or the spinal tapping which was too casually prepared and performed far too often?

Larry shook his head. He was sure Donovan would never consider accepting Jubal's job. He could not be bothered, he would say. His own job was even more important than Jubal's.

He stood in deep shadows and smoked through two cigarettes before she came walking toward him. She walked slowly, almost reluctantly. As soon as he could, he drew her into his arms and breathed out her name in an anxious sigh. "What took you so long?"

She gazed up at him somberly for a second. "I didn't want to come." She turned her mouth away so that his lips touched her cheek and slid down to her throat.

He lifted his face. "What's the matter? Is anything wrong?"

"Anything wrong? Is anything ever right?"

"Don't talk like that," he said roughly. "Don't say things like that."

"Why not? It's true."

"It's only true if we let it be true."

With a great effort he kept his hunger for her under control. "Do you know what I have in my pocket?"

Her shoulders moved in a slight shrug. "Now we play guessing games."

"Don't you like guessing games?"

"All right. Something to keep me from getting pregnant?"

He put his face against her hair. "You don't like me very much right now, do you?"

She sensed what he wanted, but she was too tired to answer. Her head had ached all day, and every problem of Rehabilitation had seemed magnified beyond all reason. Now she must go through this with Larry. For a short time she had pretended and dreamed and said to herself that some miracle would come along to change things. She had done this until the night Larry brought her back to Nurses' Residence with her clothing torn. Since that night she had stopped pretending and dreaming and hoping. All she had now was a frantic urge to torture herself, as if with her misery she could scour her mind clean of every dream and hope. She did not blame Larry for what had happened. She did not dislike him now for what he did. She gave in because she was too tired to quarrel or argue. It was easier to be agreeable.

"Okay," she sighed. "What do you have in your pocket?"

"A marriage license."

"Oh?"

"And two certificates."

"Certificates?"

"To go with the marriage license. To prove that your blood and mine is pretty good stuff. There's a law in this state, you know."

"But we didn't—"

"What's a little fraud between lovers?" He stared down into her upturned face. "That means we don't have to wait. We can be married anytime. After all, it isn't exactly fraud. I know my blood is all right and I'm pretty sure about yours. And who's to say I didn't test us? I've got one of those things hanging on the wall, frame and all, that says I have the right to sign all kinds of certificates and records. Remember?"

"Yes."

"I've had this license for two days. How about it? I know a minister in town. He's retired, but he's still legal and he doesn't object to performing ceremonies at odd hours."

How did you get acquainted with a retired minister? she wondered dully. Have you tried this before? But all she said was "What a mind you have, Larry," and shook her head.

He was suddenly savage. "What's the matter, don't you like my mind? You like Donovan's better?" His arms tightened until she could scarcely breathe.

"You're hurting me."

"I know," he said angrily. "I'm always hurting you. But what are you doing to me? It's been every night now and

227

you still aren't getting over him. I don't think you're trying. You meet me here, you let me sneak you up to my room, we go out in my car—none of it means a damn thing to you!"

"I've never deceived you," she said. "You should have guessed what it would be like. I never once tried to make you believe things would be different."

"My God, how much can a man stand! You need help and I've tried to do something about it. You promised you'd try to forget Donovan. Instead, I believe you're actually worse."

"You're hurting me!" she whispered.

He buried his face in her hair. "Darling, darling, I don't mean to! I can't help saying these things. I love you so, when I think of the way you still feel about that bastard I just go wild."

"Poor Larry," she said softly. "You've tried to help me, you've really tried. But you shouldn't. Because inside I'm a tramp!"

"God, what a thing to say!"

"It's true. I'm cheap and common. I've got no excuse for what I've done."

"Which means you've let me have my way because you didn't care enough to resist."

"Am I supposed to be overjoyed because you raped me?"

He was so hurt that his voice quivered. "Couldn't you at least admit that I gave you a little pleasure? What we've done together is holy to me!" he said. "Every moment of it. I happen to love you. Remember? I love you completely. I want to make a home for you, protect you, give you my children, my seed."

"I'm sorry." She shook her head. "These headaches—I just can't think, sometimes." She steadied herself. "Seed? That sounds so old-fashioned. Like planting a garden. A garden full of kids." She laughed a little hysterically. "I'm not very good dirt. I'd probably come up all weeds."

His arms tightened again. "Darling, let's go away from here," he said urgently. "No, don't turn your head away. We could make a whole new life. It would be wonderful. I'd make it wonderful for you. You'd forget all this, the hospital, him—Donovan—all the grief. Believe me, you would, because I wouldn't let you remember any of it, not one goddamned thing. I love you so. Let me try to make things better for both of us. Darling, listen to me." He put his face against hers and felt her shiver.

"I wish I could, I wish I could, Larry," she whispered. "But it wouldn't work out right, I know it wouldn't. Maybe I'm not normal. Maybe there's something wrong with me. There must be when I keep on wanting him so—so terribly much. All the time. I think about him every second I'm awake."

"Then why did you give in so easily?"

"I don't know. Maybe it was because I hoped it would change me. I still hope it will. Instead, all it does is make me want him more and you—not at all." She turned her face and put her cheek against his. "Dear, dear Larry, I have to tell you this. I have to be honest. Yes, I could marry you and things might go along all right for a while. But eventually Donovan would come between us and you'd hate yourself because you hadn't succeeded in making me forget him, and you'd hate me as well. What would we do then?"

"I'll take that chance. God, just let me try!"

"You're not trying to understand."

"More than you think," he retorted grimly. "I'm your doctor, remember? You believe a one-sided love couldn't be successful because it wouldn't be deep and strong enough. You just don't know how wrong you are. You could never hurt me so much that I wouldn't want to be married to you." He put his lips against her temple for a second. "I've got some money," he muttered. "Enough to get us away from here and to live on until I get another job. How about it, darling, will you come?"

"I would ruin your life."

"Bull!" he said rudely, then was silent. He decided to try another approach. "All right," he said, his voice more authoritative. "Let's forget me for a moment and think about you. For your benefit we ought to clean up our affair. I'm serious, Althea. It's absolutely necessary."

"Even you call it an affair," she said piteously.

"That's what the hospital is calling it. They're all calling you my woman." He was being deliberately cruel, wanting to jolt her into alertness.

"You've had other women," she said tiredly. "Probably for their first time, too. Why should I be special—even if you did rape me?"

"I'm not excusing myself," he replied stiffly. "But rape's a peculiar word. If I had women for their first time, it was because they were willing. I gave them what we both wanted. I love you. If you feel I raped you, all the more reason for us to be married."

"You did—and you didn't," she had to admit, filled with shame as she remembered her unwilling yet hot, deep pleasure, that first night.

"I was your first teacher and you were a wonderful pupil," he whispered against her face. "I want to be your teacher for the rest of our lives, your only teacher."

She pulled back. "Let me go," she said as the heat of his body came through her clothes.

"Something terrible is going to happen," he said quietly. "You don't realize what's building up inside you."

"Just because I'm willing to go to bed with you but won't marry you, you think I'm becoming a neurotic?" There was scorn in her voice.

"Well?"

"All right. I'm neurotic. Is that it?" He was silent. Suddenly she flared at him. "Well, why don't you say it? I'm getting as crazy as my poor cousin Edna. All twisted inside, that's me. But what a good lay I am, what a swell lay!"

"Darling, darling . . ." He pulled her close, held her shaking body tight. "Not yet, darling. But it could happen and we mustn't let it. Don't you understand? We can't let it happen."

She shook her head, her shoulders rigid against his hands. "You don't know everything, Larry. I never met a doctor yet who didn't think he had all the answers. Every one!"

"You little fool!" he said between his teeth. "I know what I see. You're withdrawn, you're tied up in knots. I could give you the names of a hundred patients who show exactly the same symptoms. I'm going to tell you something and I hope it gets through. I hope it scares the hell out of you. You are trying to become two personalities!"

"So now I'm a schiz! Thanks!" She twisted away. "Okay, I might as well tell you. I thought I wanted to change, but I don't, really. I want to think about Donovan. I want to be eaten up with thinking about him. If it's the only way I can reach him, I'll do it that way. Even when we make love! I won't see you or feel you, Larry. It will be Donovan."

"Darling . . ."

"Why don't you leave me alone!" she panted. "I love Donovan, do you hear? I love him, I love him, I love him!"

"Please, please."

She began to shake hard. "Now I'm on that damned building and he's the ward doctor, so I meet him every day. I can't avoid him. So I look at him. Sometimes we touch each other. Accidentally, of course. He hands me something, his hand touches mine. It's like a nightmare, I'm in it and I can't get out, I can't wake up!"

His anger disappeared. He was filled with helpless grief. She was like a child, a little child alone and terribly lost, and he ached to help her. Quickly he drew her back into the shelter of his arms. "Don't," he said brokenly. "I'm sorry, darling. I didn't mean to scold you. Don't cry. As much as I love you and want you, if I could give you Donovan, I would. I mean it."

Her teeth began to chatter. "Larry, help me. I'm so unhappy and I keep thinking the most dreadful things, all mixed around and jumbled, things I mustn't think about. Help me. What can I do to stop hurting so?"

His embrace was secure and tender and gentle with compassion, but his face was heavy with a terrible sadness.

"Larry, Larry, if she hadn't died—if that old woman hadn't died, I might have married Donovan."

It was dark but he knew from the sound of her voice that her eyes were too bright and her color high. "Don't think about it, darling," he soothed. "It doesn't help."

"Larry, I'm not bad inside, am I? Like everybody thinks? Tell me I'm not, Larry."

His body ached to possess her. He would have taken her then, but he knew it would not help her; it would only help himself. "No, no, darling. You've never been bad, never once."

"I'm so tired," she whispered. "I hope I wake up soon from this dream—I really hope so. You just don't know how tired I am. I feel as if I haven't slept for weeks, not for weeks."

"The dream will go away," he promised, holding her carefully. "You'll wake up soon and not be tired at all, my darling."

"You think it will?" She gave a deep, shuddering sigh and nestled her head against his neck.

He laid his cheek against her hair and closed his eyes.

"Let's go get my car and take a drive," he said softly. "I'll put the top down and we'll let the wind blow in our faces and we won't talk. Okay?"

"All right."

"And when we come back, I'll give you a pill to help you sleep."

"They don't always work."

"I'll give you two." *And watch you take them, so I'll know you're not saving them.*

"Donovan gave me a prescription today," she said.

"Donovan?"

"Oh, he has to talk to me. He can't get out of it now, you know. He asked me if something was wrong because I couldn't see what he had written on a patient's chart, and I said I had a headache because I wasn't sleeping well, so he wrote out a prescription for Seconal."

"Where is it?" Larry asked tightly. "Have you had it filled?"

She looked up. "It's right here in my pocket. I haven't had a chance to get to the drug room yet, but I will tomorrow."

"Let me see it."

Perplexed, she found the slip of paper and handed it to

231

him. Without a word, he tore it into little pieces and let them flutter to the ground.

"Larry! Why did you do that?"

"I'll give you any sleeping medicine you need," he said harshly. "Don't ever forget that, understand?" Then he took her arm and turned her in the direction of the parking compound where his car stood. "I'm your doctor, Althea, not Donovan," he added grimly.

As they walked slowly toward the car, he realized that he must do something he had put off too long already. It was time to have it out with Donovan.

"I think I'm getting your headache," he muttered.

"Well, you ought to get something for tearing up my prescription," she said. But she pressed his arm against her side and tried to match her step to his longer one. "Let's drive over to Bayport and get some beer. Maybe that'll take care of our heads."

He stopped and turned. "This first," he said, and bent to kiss her.

CHAPTER 33

THE NEXT MORNING, Larry went into the small room between his office and Donovan's and looked soberly at Madge, who was sitting behind her typewriter busily pecking away.

"How are you this morning, honey?"

He always called her honey. It wasn't very proper for a doctor to call a patient honey, but she was sure he didn't mean anything; he was just being nice. But she didn't really care for it—it was a little fresh. She guessed shrewdly that he was trying to help her remember that she was a girl. Well, not exactly a girl any more—a woman.

"Just fine, thank you, Dr. Denning," she said. She always fluttered when a doctor addressed her. This morning she felt more fluttery than usual because Dr. Macleod was not throwing her typing into the wastebasket. As hard as she snooped, she couldn't find where he was putting it, but it certainly wasn't going into the trash. She could only believe that he was taking it to his rooms and that therefore it was usable.

"How about a nice long coffee break?" he asked, just as though she were a real steno in some big office. Well, she did appreciate that. When she glanced up, he nodded. "Give me an hour," he said.

Suddenly she realized something. Why, he was her favorite after all; she liked him best of the two doctors. He wasn't only a doctor; he was her friend. She bent to take her purse out of the bottom desk drawer.

"Now, now, you don't need that just to go the canteen." He placed a dollar bill unobtrusively near the typewriter.

"A girl always powders her nose before she leaves the office," she said, not looking at the money.

"Sure, honey, I forgot." He glanced away. When he looked back, the bill was gone, her purse was in her lap and her compact was out. When she left, he walked into Donovan's office.

"We share offices and typist, but you're as hard to catch as last year's train," he said.

Donovan looked up. Larry always had clever remarks to make, he thought. College-sophomore stuff. It irritated him. "Sorry," he said coolly. He looked tired. The muscles around his eyes were tight with strain.

Larry noted the look as he hunted for cigarettes, coming up with a crumpled empty container, tossing it into the wastebasket and finding an unopened pack in another pocket. The little ritual finished of getting it open, a cigarette out and lit, he said, "If I didn't know any better, I'd say you've been avoiding me lately."

A flood of antagonism swept over Donovan. He remembered the night he had seen Larry and Althea revealed as lovers; remembered, too, the stories now circulating about them.

"Really?" he said stiffly. "Just say we haven't been seeing much of each other."

"All right. We'll put it that way." Larry took another pull on his cigarette and studied Donovan. "I sent Madge out for coffee. It's time we had a talk."

"If you like. Sit down," Donovan said, and indicated a chair. "What do you want to talk about?" He was sure he knew what was coming. A confession. Probably the fool had gotten Althea pregnant and wanted something done about it. But why come to him? "Is this important? I was just getting ready to go over to Hydro," he said coldly.

"It's very important," Larry said, "or I wouldn't be here."

After fidgeting a moment, Donovan sat back and put his finger tips together. "All right. What is it?"

"I think you know. I want you to let Althea go."

Donovan did not understand him. "What?"

Larry repeated himself distinctly, his voice level. "I want you to let Althea go. Get out of her hair. Or whatever you would call it."

"What in God's name are you talking about?"

Larry's expression was contemptuous. "Now, look. You may be tops as a professional man, but otherwise you can be a hell of a liar just like the rest of us. You know as well as I do that Althea's crazy about you and always has been."

Donovan was so surprised that he began to stammer. Of course he had suspected it in the beginning, but after the night he had seen her with Larry, the matter had been finished as far as he was concerned. "I—I don't mean a thing to her!" he said.

Larry was silent for a moment. Then, pleasantly, as though asking the time or when the next train left, he said, "Did it occur to you ever what a filthy sonofabitch you are?"

A roar filled Donovan's ears. "If what I've seen and heard about you and the lady in question is true, perhaps the word is more appropriate to you."

For a second he thought Larry was going to strike him. Then Larry lowered his fist and swallowed. When he spoke his voice was thick with anger. "Don't you care to hear the truth? What's the matter? Does it bother you?"

"You must be insane," Donovan said between his teeth.

"Sure, sure." Suddenly he hated Donovan; he hated him with a fury that was almost beyond speech. He wanted to strike him, to beat him down with his fists and stamp on him, anything to degrade and hurt him as Althea had been degraded and hurt. His anger was so great that he was sick with it, with the desire to express it in violence. "Doctor!" he said. "How long have you been in love with this girl? How long? And why didn't you tell her so while she was still—according to your standards, your code of conduct—clean and decent, uncontaminated? Fit to receive the embraces of a man like you? Before I took her!"

Donovan tried unsuccessfully to push his chair back. "You must be insane!" he repeated. "What do you mean, I love her? I never heard anything so—so— My God, what is this? Where did you get such a fantastic idea!"

"The great Dr. Macleod! Of course it's fantastic! You wouldn't be caught dead falling for a blonde with swinging hips. When you get hot for a woman, you call it a physical necessity and let it go at that. The holy one! The upholder of ethics and morality! The great Dr. Macleod!"

"For God's sake, get control of yourself. What the hell is this all about?"

"You bastard, you've ranted on often enough about your sanctimonious standards, but do you know what you've actually done? You've forced Althea to give herself to me as a —a sort of punishment. She's so much in love with you, all you had to do to save her was to give a little in return. But no, you have more important things to do than let yourself be in love with a woman. No, you wouldn't dare be decent to her. You might get involved some way. So you bottled it up, put a good, tight cork on your emotions so they wouldn't get

234

embarrassing, and then you pulled the dirty, stinking trick of humiliating her before the whole hospital."

"If you're referring to the time I had to make an example of her because she fell down on an assignment, I had no other choice," Donovan said angrily. "And in the frame of mind you're in, I'm not going to attempt to make you understand how I feel about the students and their duties."

"Spare me. I already know. As it happens, I'm well acquainted with your sentiments about Canterbury's patients, and believe it or not, I feel the same way. The patients come first. But that doesn't excuse you."

"What are you getting at now, for God's sake?"

"You mistreated Althea, you punished her. She didn't do something wrong deliberately, but you crushed her. You made her feel she didn't count at all."

Donovan raised a hand and passed it over his face. "What is that supposed to mean? She was responsible for this woman's care, wasn't she?"

"Yes," Larry said softly. "But she's important, too, just as important as any patient."

"When she left her patient, the woman died."

"How do you know she wouldn't have died anyway?"

"She choked to death."

"Many seniles choke to death. Convulsions, occlusions—"

"The woman died because she had been left alone. She was unattended. She would not have died if Althea had been there to turn her over and clean out her mouth," Donovan said harshly.

"But you can't prove that, can you? Can you? The woman might have died anyway?"

There was a moment's silence. "Yes," Donovan grudgingly admitted.

"All right. That's what I'm getting at. Here is a death that's almost certain to happen within a few weeks and the cause is definitely unproved. And here's a girl who's wildly in love with you. Yet you were willing to brand her for the rest of her life."

"Am I supposed to overlook a nurse's carelessness just because she's developed a juvenile crush?"

"The woman is dead, Macleod, and the girl is alive. Can't you see that? I've got books in my office that tell about patients choking to death with a corps of nurses and doctors at hand, administering everything from oxygen to direct heart-muscle injections. Do they get hell because they couldn't save the patient? But here's this nurse, she's got a good record, a wonderful record up to that point, and you go out of your way to condemn her. Every hospital she ever works in will know about it, because it's right there on her record."

"That's my job, by God! It's not necessary to call me a monster because I want to make sure the regulations in this hospital are enforced."

"This girl loves you," Larry said bitterly. "Doesn't that mean anything?"

He lifted his hands from the desk and crossed his arms over his chest. "You know something? You've kept your emotions in sterile cotton so long I'm not really sure you've got any left. I don't think you're normal, Macleod."

"Keep your concern for yourself," Donovan said grimly. "And as for Althea, I think you've taken care of that problem."

But Larry did not become angry this time. He looked at Donovan as though he were gazing at something dead that needed burying. "I wish I could say that I had," he said stonily. "Because I'm crazy in love with her. I don't just want to go to bed with her, I want to be with her all the time. You can't understand that, of course. But I'm so much in love with her I'm even willing to make an ass of myself and come crawling to you for help when I'd much rather beat the pulp right out of your self-important hide."

"Well!" Donovan said shakily. "Now we're getting to the real point of this unpleasant conversation. This isn't one of your usual shallow affairs, and you need a whipping boy, and someone to get you out of trouble."

"Goddam you!" Larry looked at him with hatred. "Althea's not pregnant," he said thickly. "If she were, there wouldn't be any problem. She'd marry me and I'd take her away from here so fast there wouldn't even be any dust to show where we went. You fool, you goddamned fool!"

Donovan's face turned gray, his eyes glittered. "Look, Denning, I think this has gone far enough!"

"You look! You think I like confessing to you? Now I'm going to tell you something. I loved Althea right from the very beginning of this whole affair. I deliberately took her. It wasn't her fault. I took advantage of her. I had an idea—a hope—that it would help her get over you!" he went on ruthlessly. "So you know what happens? We do it—God, every time I get her someplace where we can. But here's the thing you've got to get through your thick head. It isn't me, it's you!"

"Please! Don't tell me this."

"Why not? Does it make you sick? You could have had her. Just think, that beautiful body, all ripe, ready, waiting for the first lesson—a virgin, Macleod. She was a virgin!"

He looked at the sweat forming on Donovan's face. "A virgin, Macleod, and I got there first."

"All right, all right. So she was a virgin and you got there first. What am I supposed to do—give you my blessing?"

"Just listen, listen until I'm through. The night I took her, you saw us. You sat in your car like an avenging angel. Ever since, she's been almost fanatical about letting me have my way, like those religious perverts who maim themselves to prove their faith." Larry saw Donovan close his eyes. "I'm not trying to shock you with a lurid story, but how can either of us help her if only one of us knows what's going on?"

Donovan tried to turn away, tried to stop listening, thinking with shock that he wasn't going to be able to keep from making a fool of himself.

"See this?" Larry demanded harshly. "It's a marriage license. I've carried it around ever since that night because I want to marry her and I don't even give a damn that she's not in love with me. I want to take care of her all the rest of my life. But it's no good. Every time we make love—my kind—I know." He stopped, unable to go on.

He swallowed audibly and lit another cigarette. He felt dizzy and nauseated. "So," he said finally, "there it is."

"I didn't realize," Donovan said.

Larry looked at him steadily. Would he realize now? Would he change? He had been an important man at Canterbury a long time. Was it possible for a big wheel, an important man, to admit he could make mistakes?

Donovan turned and straightened himself. His eyes met Larry's stare. "What can I do?"

There was another long silence. Larry said, his voice thin, "I don't know. But whatever it is, do it soon."

"All right," Donovan said.

Larry nodded once, then left the office and walked out to the building, down one of the paths to a corner and up another to a bench on a little rise. He sat down and looked at the grass. He wished he had not talked to Donovan and he wished, violently, that Althea would come walking up to the bench and hold out her hands and say, meaning it, "I love you, Larry."

In his office, Donovan pushed the desk chair up to the desk, checked his pockets to make sure he had his pen and cigarettes, then stepped to the window and stood a moment, looking out. For once he did not see himself as infallible, completely competent and knowledgeable. He did not want to be alone any more; he wanted companionship, a woman to love and keep, one woman, the woman he had humiliated and hurt and driven to the edge of deep trouble. Was it a flaw?

He did not know or care. What if she was secondhand, used? Somehow it made her more precious, although he could not say why.

But he was a man of habit, of years of habits, of living alone and liking it or thinking he did, of rejecting ties and bonds and refusing to be subject to the will of others. He could not go this minute to Althea and set matters right; it would take a little time. It would take an hour or two, a day, perhaps several days. He gazed out the window and realized that he was shy, that his conceit was veneer. Now he knew why he had always disliked the affiliates: in spite of all his training he did not know how to be at ease with them, or else he had forgotten how. Chief of staff, a big man, he thought, wondering how he could have escaped analyzing himself when he could analyze others so easily. I had to be a big man, he told himself, almost humbly, because I didn't know how to be small.

Althea, he thought, tears coming into his eyes. How could I have been so blind!

CHAPTER 34

THAT SAME MORNING, Kathy stood politely by the desk in the supervisor's office and watched Althea sign her initials in the desk ledger, showing that Althea had checked it thoroughly, accepted what was written and was now ready to take over as supervisor for the day.

The two girls never said anything of a personal nature to each other. They discussed various wards and patients, new medications ordered either by Donovan or Lucretia, and any changes in regulations. When they separated they did not say goodbye to each other, they did not smile.

Kathy took off her cap and net and put them away in her locker. She had not worn a cape because no one wore anything more than was absolutely necessary in the July heat. She felt in her pocket for her pen and at her belt for the safety clip sewn into the fabric on which she carried keys while on duty. Then she turned to go, so tired she could scarcely see. Silently but politely, Althea left the desk and stepped ahead to unlock doors. In a few moments, Kathy was outside Rehabilitation, ready to take the long walk to Nurses' Residence and her room.

She supposed it would be smarter to stop at the cafeteria and eat something, if only coffee and toast, but all she could think of was the delight of tumbling into her bed. She knew that there was no reason for her to feel so exhausted. The night had been completely uneventful. There had been no complaints from any ward, no trouble. She was probably not yet adjusted to working at night and trying to sleep during the day. Her room was cool enough and on the quiet side of the building, but she had so far only been able to doze off for short periods and was awake more than she slept. As she stumbled along, her eyes half open, she thought about the new item of gossip circulating about the hospital, Dr. Andreatta's death. It had somehow reduced some of the unpleasantness between herself and Althea as they met every day at change of shift. That wouldn't last; it would be over when the inquest was held in two days, but she appreciated even a temporary respite. She didn't resent Althea's coldness as much as she hated her own continual feeling of guilt and shame, the constant impulse to get everything out of her system by telling Althea what she had done and begging her forgiveness.

When she was a short distance from Residence, she glanced up and stiffened. Mike was sitting on the top step, waiting for her. She had been finding him there every morning since the night they had had dinner together. To her surprise she liked him better every day, but she reasoned that it would be wrong to let him know this since it could never lead to anything deeper.

"Hello," she said.

"Hello, yourself," he returned a little gloomily.

She went up and sat down beside him. They were silent a moment, looking off across the lawn together.

"What kind of a night did you have?" he said finally.

She shrugged. "About the same. Very quiet. Everybody was good."

"Everybody slept?"

"Yes."

"That's more than I can say for myself." He waited for her to ask why. He wanted to tell her that the moment it became quiet and dark, he began to want her so strongly that he couldn't sleep. He sighed, not much of a sound, and looked at her. "You had any breakfast?"

She shook her head. "Too tired to stop," she admitted. "I'm sitting here and going to sleep without even trying. One of these mornings I'll fall asleep while I'm walking and wake up flat on the ground."

"You'll bump that cute little nose if you do," he said, studying it. "You shouldn't work all night and not eat anything when you come off duty."

"I suppose you're right. I'd probably sleep better if I had some food in my stomach."

"Don't you sleep either?"

He jumped at her so gloatingly with the question that she blushed. "I'm just not used to daytime sleeping yet."

"Sure, sure." But he did not press her about it. She looked so tired and sleepy that he only wanted to put his arms around her and cradle her.

"Let me put you to bed," he said abruptly.

"Mike!" Then she laughed. "You say the funniest things sometimes."

"I know. Get a kick out of 'em myself." He pulled off the stem of a tall weed growing against the steps and began to tie it in knots. He could almost see her narrow bed. It must be just like the one in his room, he supposed, hardly wide enough to turn over in but very clean, with coarse, unpressed sheets. He wondered if the same patient-help made her bed as did his. He wanted terribly to go to bed with her; the bed's width wouldn't make a bit of difference once they got there. "Kathy," he said, not looking at her, "will you marry me?"

She had been waiting for the question. He asked it every time they saw each other. Why did he keep on asking when she always said no? she wondered. Maybe he thought he could wear her down until she gave in. She shook her head.

"Not today?"

"I'm sorry, Mike."

"Tomorrow?"

"Mike . . ."

"I'll wait."

"Please." She turned to him and put one hand on his arm. "Why don't you go home, Mike? This isn't good for you, nothing to do but wander around all day long. Aren't you bored?"

He covered her hand with his. "Nope. I've got a lot to do."

"What?"

"Oh, make plans."

She pulled her hand away. "That," she said impatiently.

"Besides, I haven't got any home."

"But . . ." Her eyes were bewildered. "You told me you had a house."

"I do. But it's not a home. Not until you make it one. Savvy?"

For a moment she was silent. "Mike, how many times do I have to tell you—"

"A few hundred more, maybe. Until you either marry that dope you think you're in love with or somebody else. Has he asked you yet?"

"How can he?" she asked unhappily. "I never see him any more."

"You would if he wanted to see you."

She stiffened. "That wasn't nice. You're cruel."

"No, just fighting for what I want, and as long as you

think there's a chance with him, you're not going to be nice to me, are you?"

"I suppose not."

"Then we're even."

"You're impossible!"

"In love." She bent her head away from him and he leaned over. "Terribly in love, Kathy," he whispered. "You mean everything in the world to me. I don't think I want to live if I can't have you. Look at me."

When she did, his eyes were so sad she felt like crying. "Don't scold me for hanging on," he went on. "I can't leave until I know absolutely that I might as well give up." He came a little closer and put his lips against her cheek, very gently. "Has Donovan ever kissed you?"

"Mike," she said, "I ought to tell you something."

"All right."

"Donovan's in love with Althea. He won't ever kiss me."

"I wish I could believe that." His stare was speculative. "How do you know? What makes you think so?"

She turned her eyes away and looked down at her hands. "I saw—something. One night. I was with him—Donovan, I mean—when this happened. What I saw. Then I knew." Her voice was low. She couldn't tell him about that night she and Donovan had witnessed Althea getting out of Larry Denning's car, her clothes torn; it would be gossip, and she had done enough harm to Althea already.

"You saw something? Are you trying to tell me the great Macleod has finally fallen in love with someone? How did I ever miss it?" He saw how pale she had become. "I see," he said after a moment. "He's finally come to his senses and taken a dive for Althea, is that it? And I missed it because of all the excitement over this other thing, this crazy murder."

He reached for her hands. "I'm not going to be a hypocrite and say I'm sorry, Kathy. Because I'm not. Now I've got a chance. Maybe it's not too big yet, but I'll wait. Very impatiently, of course, but I'll manage. You couldn't drive me away with an army now, Kathy."

"Althea may not—be in love with Donovan any more."

"So? Well, who's going to lose sleep over that? Serves him right. He let her stew long enough, didn't he?"

Kathy closed her eyes. "He may really suffer," she whispered.

"I hope he does," Mike said reverently, remembering all his own suffering.

"No. You don't understand him, Mike. He can't help being what he is."

"That applies to all of us. But what kind of people would we be if we didn't try sometimes?"

"If he's in love now with Althea—and she's finally in love with Larry Denning—he'll be miserable, Mike."

"And you're in love with him and I'm in love with you and where do we get off this merry-go-round?"

She acted as though she hadn't heard him. "He'll be so miserable. And it's all been my fault." She was so tired that she felt she could go to sleep sitting there on the step, if it weren't for the hodgepodge of thoughts in her mind. "Miserable," she echoed herself. "And I'm to blame."

"Kathy, is Althea in love with Larry?"

"I don't know." Kathy opened her eyes and looked at him. "I don't know. But she might be."

"You're hoping she is," he accused.

"Yes."

There was a long silence. Abruptly he said, his voice gentle, "Why don't you go to bed? You're sitting there half asleep now."

"All right." She got to her feet obediently and stumbled toward the door. He opened it for her.

"Have dinner with me tonight," he said. "Before you go to work. We'll eat at Ruggiero's. Okay?"

She hesitated. "I don't believe so, Mike. There are some things I have to do."

"Tomorrow night?"

"Can I tell you tomorrow?"

He looked down at her with an odd expression. "Clear up until suppertime, sweetheart." Before she guessed his intention, he bent over and kissed her tenderly. "Good night."

"Oh, Mike," she said helplessly. How could she make a fuss about the little things he did when he was so sweet? She shook her head at him and went inside, but all the way upstairs her mouth felt the soft pleasure of his in a vaguely disturbing way. I shouldn't let him do it, she thought sleepily; he's too nice to be encouraged if it can't mean anything. But he knows, surely he knows. I've made it plain enough.

She could hardly wait to get into bed, shedding her clothes the instant she had closed her bedroom door and locked it, stumbling to the sink in the corner to wash her hands and teeth, thinking as she did every morning how funny it was to be doing these bedtime rituals when the sun was just getting a good start on the day. Then she couldn't bear to wash her face. She had to lie down, and in a second or two she was stretched across her bed, not even bothering to put on her pajamas. Hazily she thought, There's something I have to do, and then she was asleep, her face turned to the wall. She always went to sleep like this, quickly, but it never lasted. Soon she would wake up and be miserable until sleep returned again, and it would continue that way most of the day. But now she slept, looking sweet and innocent and untouched.

CHAPTER 35

MIKE WATCHED KATHY go upstairs and out of sight. He was strongly tempted to follow her, although he had no excuse to —his own room was in another wing of the building. Ordinarily the house mother sat in a rocker near a window in the downstairs hall. Her name was Mrs. Robinson and she pretended to knit or read while she kept a vigilant eye on everyone coming in and going out. At the moment, her chair was empty; there was no one to see him should he choose the wrong stairs, the wrong floor, the wrong door. But he remembered how glazed with fatigue Kathy's eyes had been and he shook his head.

He decided to walk over and see if Jubal Herrington was in his office. The news about Andreatta's death intrigued him. With his knowledge of reporting and editing, he was convinced that the real story hadn't been told in the local newspaper. Why was the town's Medical Examiner holding an inquest if it was murder? And why was the District Attorney silent? The town resents the hospital, he decided, but the paper is on Jubal's side. That editor is going to send young Blayton to his death if possible. And why not? Blayton killed Andreatta; it was a cut-and-dried affair with an unsolicited confession of guilt. Blayton had even turned over to the police the weapon he had used.

Still, there was the inquest to be held. Why, why, why? What had determined the Examiner's course of action? Would Jubal know? Would he tell if he did? Mike decided there could be no harm in going after the answers. He found Jubal in his office and Jubal seemed glad to see him.

"Hello, Mike," he said warmly, getting up from his desk to shake hands and then pushing forward a chair. "Sit down, sit down. How've you been?"

"Fine," Mike said. "I suppose you've been wondering why I keep hanging around."

Jubal put his finger tips together and made a little tent of his hands. "No, not at all," he lied smoothly. "You're welcome to stay as long as you care to. It's the least I can offer for good service rendered, you know. Are you being treated all right?"

"Fine," Mike said again. "Just fine." He lit a cigarette and looked through the smoke at Jubal. He was not deceived. Everybody including Jubal Herrington wanted to know why he had come back to Canterbury and what he was doing. Kathy was the only one who knew.

Jubal cleared his throat, took the cigar he was chewing on and looked at it closely, then relit it. "Everyone needs a little vacation now and then," he said. "Even fellows like you." But why here, of all places? his tone asked. What a place to spend a vacation!

"I've appreciated this one," Mike said, hiding his amusement. "You've never pinned me down once about it. Matter of fact, I had a little personal trouble and needed to be alone for a while to think things out."

"So that was it. Must confess I did wonder." He shifted his cigar. "Well, we all have our troubles."

"You mean it isn't restricted to a few here and there?"

"If I said that, it would be the understatement of all time." Mike looked innocent. "Of course. You're referring to that affair of your Dr. Andreatta and Jim Blayton, I suppose."

Jubal began to look a little harassed. "Not my Dr. Andreatta," he said stiffly. "His residency was almost completed. I won't say he hasn't been missed, however. You know how short of competent help we are here."

"I well remember all those figures on it you gave me," Mike agreed, tapping ashes into the tray on the corner of the desk. "Blayton, Blayton," he said thoughtfully. In a moment it came. The time Larry Denning had taken him to Female Receiving and he had watched a girl being committed to the institution. A young girl with beautiful hair and doll-like features. Mary Elsie Blayton, Larry had said. "Blayton," he repeated. "Isn't this fellow's wife a patient out here?"

Jubal harrumphed loudly and put his cigar down. "Was," he said briefly.

"Was?" Mike said quietly. He had sensed that he was about to learn something.

"She's dead," Jubal said noncommittally after a moment's pause.

"Dead?" Mike stared. "What happened to her?"

"A tubal pregnancy." It was clear from his tone of voice that Jubal was unwilling to discuss the matter.

"Pregnant? How in the hell could that happen if she was a patient out here?" Mike asked bluntly.

"Her husband came to visit one Sunday afternoon and they were left alone long enough for it to happen." Obviously the subject was very distasteful to Jubal.

"But why did it kill her?" Mike pressed. "Other women

get pregnant and have fine, healthy kids without too much trouble."

"I told you. It was a tubal pregnancy. When such pregnancies aren't caught in time, they rupture, causing peritonitis."

"Oh." There was another silence. "But I thought you doctors knew how to take care of things like that. I mean, aren't there ways to operate for such a condition? Surely you don't let all the women die who have—what did you call it?—tubal pregnancies."

"She wasn't here when it happened."

"Where was she?"

"In her home, I suppose."

"She got pregnant here in the hospital and you let her go home? Was she well—mentally well, I mean?"

"Of course not. Of course she wasn't well. She was as unstable as they come." Jubal was thoroughly annoyed.

"Ah," Mike said softly. "Her husband got her out and took her home when she became pregnant."

Jubal looked as if he wished the subject were buried under twenty feet of solid rock. "I wish I could say that was the way it happened."

"What does that mean?"

"It means we requested him to take her home."

Mike could not hide his astonishment. "You requested it? But if she wasn't cured—" He sat back and gazed at Jubal.

Jubal shuffled papers aggressively on his desk. "All right," he said crossly. "I suppose you won't leave me alone until you've heard the whole story. Blayton visited his wife one afternoon and they had intercourse while the attendant was absent from the room. The attendant came back in time to find out what they had been doing. When we discovered Mrs. Blayton was pregnant, we made her leave the hospital. We have to have a few rules, Mike. If we permitted that sort of thing to happen whenever some husband wanted it to happen, we wouldn't have a hospital very long. We'd have a hatchery."

"Naturally," Mike said, thinking about it. "But in this instance, if the girl wasn't all right mentally, shouldn't she have been kept here regardless? What if the Blaytons did break a rule? Would it be the first time you've had a pregnant woman in Canterbury?"

"Lord, no. We get many of them. Some women become unstable only when they're pregnant, so they have institutional care. But this matter of the Blaytons, it was so—so revolting."

Revolting? To a man who saw more revolting things in a

day than most people witness during a lifetime? It didn't make sense to Mike.

"So you made Blayton take his wife home and then it turned out to be the kind of a pregnancy that kills a woman unless it's discovered in time. Right?"

Jubel sighed. "Yes," he admitted begrudgingly.

"Well," Mike said. "That could explain why Blayton killed Andreatta."

"Impossible. Andreatta wasn't a gynecologist. Even Blayton wouldn't be that stupid."

"Then why kill Andreatta at all?"

"Who knows? Unless—"

"Unless what?"

"You ask too many questions," Jubal said tersely.

Mike stared at Jubal. "What was Andreatta to Blayton's wife?"

"I didn't say he was anything."

"You almost did. What was he?"

"All right, goddam it! He was her psychiatrist!" He stared back at Mike. "Does that satisfy your inquisitive little soul?"

"Not quite," Mike said calmly. "Was there anything between Andreatta and this woman? Was he helping her or making her worse, or was there some hanky-panky going on?"

"My God!" Jubal said, getting out his handkerchief to mop his neck. "What are you trying to imply? Don't let anyone hear you ask questions like those. You can't do it to me, Mike. You just can't. We'd be ruined if you ever talked that way around certain people." He stopped to get his breath and suddenly looked old and haggard. "Andreatta was a good doctor. He knew his field thoroughly. If he hadn't helped Mrs. Blayton, it was because she either couldn't be helped or because he hadn't had long enough time. After all, we can go only so far with some of these patients. At best it's a long, slow, involved process. Mental illness isn't like a contagious disease or a head cold or an organic deterioration or even something like cancer. It's much more—more complicated."

"I know. You told me all that the other time I was here. But that's beside the point. Blayton had a reason for killing Andreatta. He didn't just suddenly go crazy. He wasn't after money. He didn't want to steal a car. Right?"

"Who knows what really happened? According to his story, he was waiting there at the gate and Andreatta attacked him. Now, that's not a likely story, Mike. Why would Andreatta do such a thing? I say that Blayton was hard up. He'd just buried his wife and he needed money. He knew the

246

doctors all have to use that gate, so he planned to rob one of them and it happened to be Andreatta."

"According to your local newspaper, which very unwillingly admitted it, Andreatta had not been robbed."

"Of course not. Blayton was scared off before he had a chance to finish what he had started to do."

"You make it sound very pat."

"It has to be the truth," Jubal insisted, sweating freely. "Otherwise it's the most senseless thing that ever happened."

"Not senseless." Mike shook his head. "But you don't have the answer. I'm sure of it. Yesterday afternoon I needed a little exercise, so I walked over to Blayton's neighborhood and looked at his house. Nice little place, well cared for. Doesn't look like the home of a man who wastes his money and goes after some other man's money. I'd say if Blayton needed money, he's the kind who would go to a bank and borrow it, using his home for collateral."

"Why did he have a gun, then? Why was he carrying that shotgun?"

"All right, why was he? A shotgun isn't the kind of weapon that holdup men use."

"Perhaps Blayton was after me. Remember, I was the one who signed his wife's release. Perhaps he was on his way to get me and Andreatta happened to intercept him, so he became the victim instead."

"Are you trying to tell me that Blayton intended to find you and shoot you? How would he know where to find you?"

"The whole hospital knows I have a private residence out here and that I live alone. I have a housekeeper, but she only comes in by the day. It would have been very simple for Blayton to sneak up at that time of night and shoot me through one of the windows of my house."

"I'd buy that," Mike said, "if the police hadn't made the statement that the gun wasn't loaded."

They looked at each other appraisingly for a long moment. Then Jubal grabbed up what was left of his cigar, studied it, then mashed it down into the tray. "I suppose you're going to the inquest?"

"Wouldn't miss it for anything."

"No—no, of course not. People like such things. A big show. And free."

"Yes." Mike got to his feet and gazed down at Jubal without expression. "People will even pay for them, sometimes," he said politely. "That's why they buy newspapers, even a small-town local that's obviously presenting biased news. Will I see you at the inquest?"

"Why should I go? I'm not on trial."

No, Mike thought, but Canterbury might well be before it's over. "It will be interesting to hear why Blayton claims self-defense and why the Medical Examiner seems to feel it was justifiable homicide," he murmured.

You'll be there, he thought. You'll be afraid you'll miss something important if you aren't there.

"It won't be justifiable homicide unless they find some witnesses who can testify to that fact!" Jubal retorted grimly.

"All the more reason to be there. I can hardly see this Examiner making an ass of himself by holding an inquest when he has nothing to go on. He's probably got something he's going to surprise everyone with."

Jubal had been glad to see Mike a few moments earlier. Now he was just as glad to watch Mike leave. He could have enjoyed a little sympathy about the affair, but if Mike wasn't going to show a proper understanding and some respect for the monumental problems of the institution, he would have to pack his bags and take himself off. You do favors for some people and they turn around and kick you, Jubal thought. He wondered how soon he would be able to hint to Mike that his bed was needed by someone else. With a faint twinge of guilt, he remembered Mike's articles which had helped so much to make the hospital's fund-raising campaign successful. No, he thought, he wouldn't do the hinting. He would have Walter do it. Satisfied with this solution, he lit another cigar and let his thoughts dwell on Blayton and the inquest being held in two days. He had asked Mike why he should attend; but he had not said he was not going to be there. Of course he planned to be present! He intended to see that the truth came out, and the truth was that Blayton had deliberately killed a man who was valuable to Canterbury. A man with five children.

Thinking of children brought Mary Elsie to his mind. He looked at the ash tray that held Mike's cigarette stub and frowned. It had sounded as though Mike were criticizing him for putting the girl out of the hospital before the full extent of her condition was known. Surely Mike realized that after Mary Elsie left Canterbury, it was up to her husband to find a doctor and place Mary Elsie immediately in his care. We can't direct these matters for people, he thought resentfully; we can't be responsible for everything. And we have to have rules. Rules are absolutely essential. Without them what would we have? Chaos!

His cigar was out again. He looked at it as if it had betrayed him. He was thinking how he would handle it if something were said at the inquest about Mary Elsie, her condition and her untimely death, and the fact that she had been dismissed from Canterbury, however good the reason, without more investigation than had been made. And Andreatta being her doctor . . .

Jubal decided to forego the cigar entirely. Suddenly it tasted and smelled like a mixture of glue and wrapping paper. I'm smoking too much, he thought. Entirely too much.

CHAPTER 36

ON THIS SAME MORNING, in her office, Lucretia was arguing with Elizabeth about the inquest. Elizabeth was convinced that Lucretia should not attend; that it would look peculiar if she were there.

Lucretia looked tired, her color almost gray. Every day it was becoming more difficult for her to appear poised and controlled. She raged inside at being criticized by Elizabeth, because she knew that she was not deceiving her old friend. "It would look peculiar if I stayed away," she said shortly. "And if I send Margaret, who's just dying to represent Nursing Personnel, I'd never really know what went on."

Elizabeth shook her head emphatically, like a puppet being jerked by strings. For some time she had been observing Lucretia's bad color and lapses into silence.

"Let Jubal go alone. He's the one to represent the hospital, not you."

Lucretia snorted. "And let him put both feet into his mouth the first time he got needled into talking?"

"He's very diplomatic, Lucretia. He knows exactly how to handle any situation. If you go, you won't be able to keep from telling the truth. And besides, it will be a terrible strain on you."

Lucretia stared at Elizabeth, wondering how much she knew or had guessed. She had worked so many years on cancer wards, she could probably detect the telltale symptoms at first glance. Lucretia hoped no accusations would be made which she would have to deny in order to keep her secret intact. She was certain that the moment anyone, even Elizabeth, knew the truth, her authority would be ended.

"What's wrong with the truth?" she demanded tersely.

"I'm a firm believer in it myself, but do you want the whole town to know that Andreatta was Mary Elsie's doctor while she was a patient in Canterbury and that she died shortly after she left here? Are you willing to tell everyone just why she was thrown out of here? How do you think it's going to sound when you have to admit she wasn't ready to go home and that if she had been kept in the institution she might not have died?"

"Frankly, I have no intention of being that truthful. Because I don't think it has a thing to do with Andreatta's murder."

"Really, Lucretia! You're not going to tell me you think it was an accident?"

"Of course not. And it wasn't self-defense on Blayton's part. I think Blayton killed Andreatta deliberately."

"Why?"

"God knows. I don't. But I know this much. Andreatta had the soul of a mouse. He wouldn't have attacked anything that didn't wear skirts, certainly not a man Blayton's size."

"So you did know about him," Elizabeth murmured.

"Andreatta?" Lucretia's expression was stony. "I'm not even admitting to myself what he was. If I don't put it into words, then I won't let it slip where it might prove embarrassing."

"He was cheap and common, perhaps perverted, and we have no business letting Jim Blayton die because of it," Elizabeth said.

"He was Latin and hotter then hell, so how can we judge? He didn't recognize our standards."

"The standards of all decent people anywhere?"

"Our standards."

"You're hard, Lucretia, and it makes you blind. Why did Andreatta carry a scalpel in his pocket?"

"I'm not a wizard, Elizabeth. He may have forgotten to put it back into a sterilizer. I don't know all the answers any more than you do. I don't even know that his conduct toward Mary Elsie was probably not—was not what it should have been. I am going to presume—and say if questioned —that Blayton killed for retaliation and that he singled out Andreatta because he was acquainted with him, otherwise it might have been me or Jubal. In other words, I believe Blayton committed this murder in reprisal because we sent his wife home and she died. But I do not intend revealing that had we kept her we would have discovered her pregnancy was not normal and would have resorted to surgery. I will not reveal this because her husband should have placed her in the care of one of the doctors in town as soon as he got her home. God knows why he didn't. Perhaps he intended calling someone in and just waited too long. I don't know. At any rate, I am going to the inquest and if I am called upon to testify, I shall do so and recommend that Jim Blayton be bound over for the jury trial he deserves."

Elizabeth looked at Lucretia's cold face. No wonder she

had lost Walter. What man could face that analytical harshness day after day? How sad that Lucretia could not see what she had done to herself. "You've heard about Margaret?" she said involuntarily, then bit her lip. It was a tactless question; she should have known better than to ask it.

Lucretia's expression did not change. "You mean her engagement to Walter? Yes, I've heard."

Elizabeth started to put out her hand, then pulled it back. Lucretia did not appreciate sympathy. She scorned it, always had. Her pride would not let her acknowledge how much she needed it. "I don't think anything will come of it," she said hesitantly. "If I know Walter—"

"If I know Margaret, the engagement will stand like the rock of Gibraltar," Lucretia interrupted, her voice bleak. "Walter has finally been hooked."

There was a moment's silence. Elizabeth fought to keep tears out of her eyes. For more than twenty years she had worked beside Lucretia, a long time for friendship to form and set and become stable and enduring. Now she wanted to cry for the humiliation and pain that Lucretia was working so desperately to keep hidden. My friend, Elizabeth thought, and I can't help her; she won't let anyone help her. But she needs help now. Blessed saints, what a dreadful thing too much pride can be!

Lucretia looked into Elizabeth's eyes. Damn her! she thought; does she think I care any longer what Walter does? I couldn't care less! "They are going to be married Thanksgiving Day," she said almost viciously. "Margaret's been telling it all over the hospital. I already have a gift for them."

She did not say what the gift was, because it would mean telling Elizabeth what Jubal had told her about Margaret; and that was when she had told Jubal what she intended to do about Margaret, and he had agreed.

"Well," Elizabeth said faintly, "that's more than I can say." She was wondering rather foolishly what kind of gift Lucretia would see fit to give her former lover and his bride.

"Won't they be surprised?" Lucretia said. When Elizabeth did not reply, she answered herself. "Indeed they will. They'll be the two most surprised people you ever saw."

"Well," Elizabeth said again.

"All right, now," Lucretia said rudely. "Why don't you run along? I've got a lot of work to do and I'll never get it done by talking."

There was another silence. The color around Elizabeth's eyes deepened. Suddenly she walked around the desk and, before Lucretia could guess her intention, bent her head and let her mouth rest gently for a second on the hair drawn so unattractively back into the tight bun. Then she turned and walked unsteadily to the door. Before she went out, she looked back at Lucretia sitting still and deathlike, her face like a mask.

"Damn them!" Elizabeth said softly but distinctly. "Damn, damn, damn them!" When she pulled the door shut and was out in the hall, she walked blindly away, her face wet with tears.

Kathy slept two hours and woke slowly. She had been dreaming, a strange, involved dream about herself and Donovan and her home which made no sense while she was dreaming it nor as she began to waken.

For a little while she lay still, her face turned to the window. Then she got up slowly, slipped into her bathrobe and padded down the hall to the bathroom. When she came back she looked with distaste at the wrinkled, damp sheet on the bed, but she knew that if she didn't get at least two more hours of sleep, she would have a miserable time trying to stay awake when she went on duty that night.

She remade the bed, using the top sheet on the bottom and stuffing the damp one into her laundry bag. Then she dusted the bed liberally with talcum powder and lay down again. Instantly, the dream came back at her like flashes on the wall from a home movie projector. She started with the beginning, going up the walk between the two hedges her father kept neatly trimmed, reaching the porch and the swing and Donovan, and then both of them going into the house. When they got to the top of the stairs, she moved, stirring the powder and wrinkling her nose as its fragrance drifted up lazily in little puffs. She turned over and lay on her stomach, her hands gripping the corner bedpost. He is suffering, she thought incoherently. I know he is; he must be. She wanted to get up and go to something hard—the door—and beat her head against it. Instead, she tightened her grip until her knuckles were white and cords stood out along her arms.

I live my life in a series of flashbacks, she thought. I do something today and remember something I did yesterday and something I wanted to do the day before that and none of it's any good. Why can't I make up my mind? Why can't I? Why doesn't something happen? Something—anything.

By the time she fell asleep again, she had reached a decision.

An hour before it was time for her to go on duty, she went to Donovan's apartment. She was fresh from a shower, her hair still damp and curling softly around her face, but she had no make-up on. She had not eaten dinner. When he answered her ring, she said, without stopping to think how it would sound, "Well, I guess I'm lucky. I didn't know whether you'd be here."

"Come in," he said, a little startled. "I was just getting ready to leave." He did not add that he was planning to meet Althea as she came off duty.

"This won't take long," Kathy said awkwardly, following him into the cluttered living room, letting her eyes explore the place where she had worked a whole week of evenings to help him finish his book. How like a man, she thought helplessly. The mess isn't important; it's what he does that counts.

"Cigarette?" he said, picking up the box from the coffee table.

She shook her head and watched him take one and light it, his hands competent, wasting no motions. How I love his hands, she thought.

"How about a drink, then?" When she shook her head a second time, he added, smiling, "You really shouldn't, of course. You're on your way to work, aren't you?"

She could see that he was a little impatient, that he wanted to be on his way. She wished he wouldn't rush her. She didn't dare get nervous now; it had been so easy coming to his door with what she had to say firmly in her mind.

"I haven't got much time," she said, beginning to feel harassed.

He looked at his watch. "Fifty-five minutes," he said and she was lost.

"Fifty-five minutes?" she stammered.

"Yes."

Maybe she'd better come back another time. "There's something I've tried to tell you for a long time, but every time I get around to it, I never can get it out."

"Oh?"

She looked away from his face. "Yes," she said. "I—I don't know whether I can tell it now."

He began to recall other times she had made similar remarks. He vaguely remembered that they had had something to do with Althea and he frowned. Kathy and Althea were friends and Kathy had shown this compunction to protect or defend her friend. But Althea did not need protection any longer. Would it be wise to let Kathy start on some long, rambling story that was no longer important? He looked at his watch again.

"Tell you what," he said casually. "I'm on my way to Rehabilitation, so why don't you tell me on the way?"

"Oh, but I can't do that!" she exclaimed, dismayed. "I want to tell you right now."

"And I want you to tell me on the way over. Especially if it's a long story."

"It isn't that. It's—well, I just can't tell it like that. It's all I can do to talk about it anyway." Her voice went up a little.

He was silent a moment. "Have you tried to tell me this story before?"

"Yes," she admitted reluctantly. "A number of times."

"Confessions," he said and sighed.

"I've got to get this thing out of my system," Kathy said. "I don't care whether it's good for me or not."

"Self-pity?" He said it a little crisply.

"No," she said stubbornly. "Justice."

"Dramatic, too." He sighed. "Look, Kathy. I have a date with a beautiful blonde. Would you cheat me out of my date by insisting on being dramatic and overpowering with this confession of yours? Are you sure it won't keep until, say, tomorrow?"

She had never heard him sound so undignified, so much the way Mike or even Larry Denning talked. It made her realize that what she had suspected was true: Donovan was in love with Althea and knew it at last. But didn't he know that Althea was not in love with him any longer?

"You're meeting Althea?" she blurted out stupidly, her face turning pale. When he looked at her as though her impudence had finally gone too far, she added thinly, "But you can't. You can't do that. You'll get hurt!"

"Hurt?"

"She doesn't love you any longer."

"What did you say?"

"She doesn't love you. She loves Larry—Larry Denning!"

He felt his face growing stiff. He tried to laugh. "You're insane!" he said.

"I wish I were, but it's true," she whispered.

"Why did you say it? Why did you tell me?"

"I don't know."

"You had a reason. You must have had a reason."

"I can't bear for you to get hurt."

"What business is it of yours whether I get hurt or not?"

"I love you." It was out; she could not take it back. She put a hand over her mouth and swayed, her eyes closed.

He was silent, staring at her, his face bitter and cruel. He could not doubt what she had said, and if it were true, he had almost made a terrible fool of himself. He was so violently angry that he wanted to slap her or beat her, and then he thought of his talk with Larry and his anger turned in that direction. He was so filled with it that he could not move. "Love!" he spat, like a curse. "What do you know about love!"

I've hurt you, I've hurt you, she thought incoherently. I should have kept my mouth shut and let you find out for yourself. Then maybe you would have come to me. Now you'll always hate me!

She turned and ran toward his bedroom. In the doorway she hesitated and said, "Please, I do love you. I'll show you."

His anger became fury. What did she think she was doing? He forced himself to move after her. She had taken off her clothes rapidly and now she was standing by the bed, her eyes enormous, her breath shallow. Dumfounded, he stared at the small, golden-skinned figure.

"What in God's name!" he said, then the fury swung to passion, his face flaming with it. When he reached her, his arms pulled her so tight that her breath went out in a violent rush.

"What are you doing!" he said thickly.

She did not have time to answer. The instant he touched her, he flung her brutally on the bed, then tore at his clothing, finally plunging down on her, forcing her legs apart and thrusting himself between them. She did not whimper once in the moments which followed, although she thought again and again that she would faint with the pain. She gave herself freely, forcing her body to submit to his hunger, until at last he lay exhausted, his face pillowed on her breasts. Gradually he became aware of her sobbing, so repressed that her whole body quivered as if she had a chill. Then he knew what he had done, the shocking, incredible thing he had done. From the moment it had begun, it was Althea whom he had tossed onto the bed, Althea whom he had violated.

He became completely still, feeling the small, ravished body under his, the still-hot blood everywhere, the convulsive, bewildered, frantic sobbing.

When he lifted himself away, she got up quickly and staggered to the bathroom. She made herself a soap suppository, hoping desperately that she would not become pregnant, although she was almost certain that the blood would wash away the sperm. Then she took a shower, shaking as the water mixed with blood and ran pink down her legs. She was heavy with shame, miserable with it. Why hadn't this been beautiful, something to remember all her life as the most wonderful experience she had ever known, instead of the agony between her legs, the feeling that she had made a terrible, terrible mistake? Wasn't this exactly what she had wanted to do, to make amends, to take away his hurt? Instead it had been horrible, revolting.

When she came out, he was dressed and back in the living room. "You can't go yet," he said, running his hands frenziedly through his hair. "You'll have to marry me." She had been a virgin; he had raped her. At the moment he could not remember Althea. Her face was only a blur in his thoughts.

"No," she said.

"Why did you do it!" he raged. Why did you let me make a monster of myself! he was thinking. "I couldn't stop myself. It wasn't you—hell, how can I explain it?"

Don't try, she cried silently, picking up her purse. Please don't try. I made you do it. I was wrong again, but I didn't know. The sobbing began again, but she held it in.

"You've got to marry me." He was almost shouting.

"No." She did not look at him. "No, it wouldn't be right. You don't love me." She was suddenly very still for a second. "And I don't love you," she said with a horrified expression, turning and running from the apartment.

"Kathy, come back! We've got to talk about this. Come back!"

But she ran on without looking back.

CHAPTER 37

ALTHEA SAT AT THE DESK in the supervisor's office and waited for Kathy to come so that she could go off duty. She had one of her headaches, a throb of pain that blinded her every time it pulsed. She supposed she ought to see someone about them, but she couldn't bring herself to go to a doctor in town. She had heard that the town did not have any decent medical men, and she certainly would not let any Canterbury doctor know how she felt. She was sure she would be told the headaches were of psychosomatic origin, and she did not intend having that tidbit added to her reputation.

She heard a key turning in the outside lock and stood up, gathering her things together, her pen and Kleenex and notebook. When Kathy came through the second door, she was ready to leave, save for the formality of checking and signing the ledger. "Hello," she said coldly, thankful, however, that Kathy had come and that she could soon go.

"Hello," Kathy said, her voice barely audible. She was pale and her eyes looked smudged, as if she had been crying. She did not look directly at Althea.

Althea didn't care. Her animosity toward Kathy was no longer an active emotion. "Nothing happened today," she said tiredly through the pulsing pain. "The building was fairly quiet. Edna's upset, but no more so than usual, considering she's having her period. Forty patients went for a walk this afternoon and one, Geraldine Merton, was sent to Hydro. She swallowed a comb."

"A comb?"

"A small one about two inches long. She got upset because she wasn't allowed to go on the walk. Dr. Macleod came and prescribed ipecac. She got rid of the comb before she went to Hydro. She's in pack."

"And Edna?"

"Broody. I wanted to get an order for her door to be locked at night, but Terry said no, we weren't locking doors as long as we were giving tranquilizers."

The latest orders. Kathy nodded. She was not really thinking about Edna or Geraldine, but only about herself and Althea and what she had done just a short time ago. She had told Donovan that he was no longer loved by Althea, and then she had tried with her body to atone for his loss. And she had been shamed and abused, and Donovan was humiliated and furious. The worst of it was that now she knew she did not love him; it had been a foolish sacrifice, a degrading one, because there had been no value in it. She had to face the terrible truth: everything she had done, including causing Sarah Smith's death, had been pointless and futile.

She signed the ledger, writing her name neatly because that was her habit, and looked up at Althea, who, she could see, was waiting anxiously to leave. Suddenly Kathy wondered why she had thought that Althea no longer loved Donovan. What had made her believe that? Was it something she had wanted to believe, part of the pattern of mistakenness she had followed so consistently?

She stood up next to Althea. It had suddenly become very important to her to know just how Althea did feel. She could not let Althea leave until she knew.

"Wait," she said. "Do you mind if we talk a minute?"

Althea stared in surprise. What could Kathy want to talk about? They had already discussed the building and its problems of the day. There was nothing else they could discuss. They were not friends; they hated each other. "Make it just a minute. I have a terrific headache," she said flatly.

"It won't take more than a minute," Kathy said quietly. "Are you still in love with Donovan?"

Althea stopped breathing for a second. When her breath came, she was haggard. "Why, you . . ." she began viciously, then stopped and put one hand up to her eyes, shutting out the light. There was such a violent jab of pain behind them that for a moment she felt she might vomit. When she could speak, she said behind the shelter of her hand, "Damn you, what do you mean by asking me such a question? Is it any of your business?"

"I have to know," Kathy said unsteadily. "It's very important, Althea. Do you—or have you stopped?"

Althea's hand came down. She glared at Kathy. "Why is it important?"

"It just is."

"You mean there's a reason I should pull out my heart for you to step on again? What's the matter, have you been going to bed with him and now he's got you knocked up and won't marry you?"

Kathy's face was white, but her voice remained soft. "I've been to bed with him once and I'm not knocked up as far as I know." She saw the hate fade from Althea's face and the dreadful hurt take its place, and she had her answer.

Althea turned away. "No," she whispered.

"I had to tell you to find out."

"You've been to bed with him!"

"Once."

"Once." She said it as though it had been hundreds of times. "Why are you telling me?" Her breathing was ragged. "You've been in love with him all along, haven't you? I knew it. Something kept telling me so inside but I wouldn't listen, I didn't want to listen."

"No."

"No? What does that mean?"

"I don't love him," Kathy said, her voice low. "I thought I did." She was painfully honest about it. "I thought I loved him, but after we—well, now I know I don't love him. I've done a terrible thing." She saw how thin Althea had become and was shocked because she hadn't noticed it before. I haven't been looking at her, she thought. I've been afraid to look at her, ashamed to look.

Her voice grew stronger. "He doesn't love me," she said clearly.

Althea's shoulders moved slightly. "He doesn't love anyone, then," she said.

"I wouldn't know about that," Kathy said. "But I told him something and if it isn't true, I think you should let him know."

"What did you—"

"I told him you weren't in love with him, that you loved Larry Denning."

"You told him *that?*"

Kathy flinched but went on. "I believed it when I told him. That's why I asked you a moment ago if you were still in love with him. I'm not trying to be snoopy. I'm trying to do something right—for the first time. You think I'm bragging about going to bed with him? Oh, no, Althea, no, no!" Her voice became fierce. "Listen to me. I do not love Donovan, he does not love me. Does that mean anything to you?"

"You told him—"

"I thought it was true. It's gossip all over the hospital. That you and Larry are wildly in love."

"You told him—"

"You fool!" Kathy said, stamping her foot. "What difference will that make if you still love him? All you have to do is tell him so, because *you're* the one he loves! Do you understand?"

"Sure, sure, he loves me," Althea said as if to a child.

Kathy saw the glaze in her eyes. "You don't believe me," she said sharply. "Why?"

"I didn't say I didn't."

"Althea, please, go to him. Go to Donovan," Kathy said desperately. "Let him know you still love him."

Althea looked at Kathy. Her eyes were hard and glittering, her expression set. "So you went to bed with him and you didn't like it. Maybe you'd like to try out several guys before you decide just what you do like. How about Larry? He really knows how to take care of a girl!"

"I'm only trying to help you," Kathy said, choking.

"Sure, sure. Thanks, but I'm doing very well indeed. Just take care of your own flower bed, Kathy."

"Tell him—tell him, Althea. Let him know."

"You mean Donovan? Let him know what?"

"That you love him."

"Here we go again." Althea had all her stuff picked up and looked around once. "How about taking over here so I can go, huh?"

Kathy was filled with despair. She had made a mess of things again apparently. It probably would have been much better if she had said nothing to begin with; but how could she make amends if she didn't start some place? She felt the soreness between her legs, and it was like a sharp blade slicing into her conscience.

"Donovan Macleod loves you," she said shrilly. "Doesn't that mean anything to you?"

Althea stared at her for a second. "Coming from you—no," she replied, shaking her head. Then she walked to the door and let herself out.

After a moment, Kathy sat down at the desk and pulled the ledger closer. She looked at it without seeing it. She was conscious of a dreadful feeling of futility, as though there wasn't much point in struggling because the struggle was so worthless. What had she tried to do with Althea anyway?

Help her? Or be mean and cruel? Certainly she hadn't accomplished anything with her sordid little confession.

Suddenly Kathy realized where the real trouble lay. She still wasn't willing to go all the way. She had to start with the beginning, with Sarah Smith. Nothing could be mended or patched until that was out of the way.

She had known it all along, of course, because it had never really left her mind; it was always there under all her desires and hopes and fears. How many times had she told herself what had to be done, she wondered, and still she had not done it?

Abruptly she had the answer. *Why didn't she write about it?* Write? Of course. She would write it all in a letter to Donovan. Why hadn't she thought about it before? All at once she felt relaxed, almost cheerful. Perhaps she would be sent to prison—she didn't know, she didn't care. It would be such a relief to have it out in the open that anything in the way of punishment would be inconsequential.

She glanced up and looked in both directions through the safety-glass window in front of the desk. At either end of the hall were wards, but the patients were bedded down for the night now and only several white-capped women could be seen, sitting in little groups in front of their ward doors. They were not watching her. They did not care if she was crying like a baby; they were only interested in whether they could stay awake during the night ahead. Seeing them so absorbed, she calmed herself, found some scratch paper in a drawer, got out her pen and began to write. When she finished, she folded the letter, slipped it into an envelope and wrote "Donovan Macleod" across the front, then dropped it into a pocket. In the morning she would give it to Madge, who was now out of pack and back at her desk in the little room between Donovan's and Larry's offices. Madge would be only too happy to deliver the letter to Donovan. After that, she would have to wait.

CHAPTER 38

ON THE THIRD FLOOR of Rehabilitation, Millie and Ruth sat as usual in the hall between their wards. They had just finished checking their patients; Ruth had settled down with a Western, and Millie was crocheting. She was making a doily for the little table she used for her telephone. Crocheting was a new art to her, so she worked slowly and with great care because Ruth had told her that if she let her thread pull too tight, the doily's shape wouldn't be right.

"How come you like them Westerns?" Millie asked.

Ruth shrugged. "Don't know. Never give it a thought."

"I like true stories, m'self. Specially the ones about young people, the ones where the girl gets herself in trouble but the boy makes it right in the end. You know, them kind." She was thinking that perhaps she liked them because her life had been that way so long ago, although she had never told this to Ruth. So long ago, she thought, with a little sigh. She had been thirteen. She'd had only five periods when it happened. . . . She counted stitches, her mouth moving without sound.

"Yeah," Ruth said. She looked up at Millie. Why did she like Westerns? she wondered. Was it because they carried her completely away, talking about places and situations she knew less than nothing about and using words with such a rich, hefty sound? "My husband was always readin' 'em," she said, as if that explained most of it.

"Your husband?"

"Yeah. He came from Arizona. I don't mean he was born there. He was born in Brooklyn, but his dad had some kinda disease—asthma, I guess—so they moved to Arizona when he was just a baby. He usta tell me he grew up on a horse."

"He did?" Millie was enthralled. Ruth's husband had been a cowboy. It sounded unbelievable, her friend married to a real, live cowboy once. "How come he didn't stay there?"

"He should have, I guess. But if he had, I'da never met him."

"How did you meet him?"

"He was hitchhiking east and he got a ride with a trucker. They was coming through this way and they stopped in town for something to eat and it was a cold day. I was waiting for my bus to come to work. You know that corner where Lacy's Drugstore is now? Well, that usta be a little eatin' place. So I was in there, keeping warm, and here these two guys came in, one a regular old trucker, whiskers and all, and the other—" Ruth stopped, her finger holding the place in her book, her eyes staring dreamily at nothing.

"Go on."

She shrugged again, looked down at her book. "Well, the other was a young fellow. He—smiled at me. I guess I musta smiled back. Anyway, he never went on. He stayed and got a job and we was married."

"You never had no kids, didja?"

"Never really had time. I was kinda careful at first. You know, we wanted to get started, get our home and everything, and I knew what to do on account of working out here. Then he was drafted and that was it."

"You sorry now? I mean that you didn't go ahead and have a kid?"

Ruth was silent a moment. Then she stirred. "No," she said flatly. "What would I have done with a kid?" Sorry? God, she had never stopped being sorry that she didn't have something of Bill's.

"Funny, ain't it?" Millie said. "You losing your husband like that and here we've had another war since then."

"What's funny about it? Them politicians gotta do something to keep up the high cost of livin', don't they? Besides, it's the only legal way to kill anybody."

"They don't mean it that way," Millie said mildly. "They wanta keep things safe for people."

"Hah!" Ruth said and went back to her book.

Millie sighed. She wished she understood Ruth better. They were real friends, the kind you find only three or four times in all your life. But she felt she didn't do enough for Ruth. She would have liked to figure out some way to make Ruth happier. It came to her that she had seldom seen Ruth smile, and she had never once heard her laugh out loud. Being so held in like that wasn't good for folks, she thought. Then her mind went back to the thing that was chiefly in her thoughts.

"Ruthie," she said, "how about us going to that inquest day after tomorrow?"

Ruth glanced up, her eyes trying to focus. "Huh?"

"That inquest," Millie repeated patiently. "How about us going?"

"I thought . . ." Ruth sat up in alarm. "Now, look here, you gonna do what you promised you wouldn't do?"

"No, course I'm not!" Millie said indignantly. "I just wanna go t' hear what goes on. You know, it'll be quite an experience. I never been to one of them trials. Ain't you kinda curious?"

"No."

"No?"

"I ain't never curious about seein' what happens when some poor devil's gettin' the works."

Millie moved uneasily. "Well, I never thought about it that way."

"You think it's any different than when some o' these charges start slappin' patients out here? I remember one ward I worked on when I first came here. It was a male ward with a lotta drags, old men, some of 'em blind. There was one, Kennie Sims, the charge kept him strapped alla the time 'cause he'd roam around and bump into things and hurt himself. So he usta go to the toilet right in his chair. He'd open his pants and first thing you know, we'd hear this noise like a hose running and the charge'd jump up and run over there and slap that old man—my God, how he'd slap him! Then he'd holler at another patient to mop it up and

262

come back and say Kennie did it just to get attention. And it mighta been true. But I wanna ask you something, Millie. How could Kennie go to the toilet unless somebody unstrapped him? And how could he find his way less'n somebody took him?"

"Oh, that wasn't right. That was terrible."

"Sure. Of course it was terrible. That charge didn't wanta be running around all day, unstrapping them old men, taking 'em to the john, bringing 'em back and strapping 'em up again. And he didn't want the rest of us doing it 'cause it might set a bad example. We'd all be working insteada sitting around the desk, swapping dirty jokes and gossip. Animals. That's the way most folks look at each other. What can I do you for? What am I gonna get out of you? What're you worth t' me? Nobody ever thinks in his heart, What can I do for you, how can I help you."

"Some of us do," Millie protested. "Not everybody's like you say, Ruthie."

"Well," Ruth said, looking at her friend, "not you, Millie. I didn't mean you."

"No, there's lotsa good people. You, for instance. And Doc Travis—"

"Me! I wouldn't give anybody the time of day," Ruth scoffed.

"Doc Travis," Millie went on doggedly, "And that Miss Leslie—I figure she's kinda nice. There's lotsa people that's kind and goodhearted, Ruthie."

"You ain't gonna talk me into goin' to that inquest, Millie. I just ain't gonna go. Beside not carin' to see that Blayton get it in the neck, I need my sleep. And so do you."

"Well, I kinda thought I might go," Millie said stubbornly.

"All right. You go. But you better remember to keep your mouth shut, you hear?"

"Oh, I ain't gonna say anything."

"Just be sure you stick t' that, Millie."

"Oh, I will, I will." Millie looked at her crocheting. "I ain't hankerin' t' lose my job," she added, and started counting again.

In a tavern, on the south side of town, Margaret and Walter sat in a back booth where the light from two fluorescent pink circles was dimmest, and nursed vodka and Coca-Cola, mixed.

"She was all set to let me go, then she backed out," Margaret said bitterly. She had very much wanted to attend the inquest and could not understand Lucretia's attitude. There were plenty of supervisors to watch over the main office and let both herself and Lucretia go to the inquest. She knew why she was being kept on duty. Lucretia did not want to let the town know there was someone else in Nursing Personnel almost as important as herself.

"Don't worry," Walter soothed. "She won't be able to tell you what to do much longer—if what you say is true."

"Of course it's true. Dr. Herrington told me in so many words that I was doing just exactly right in coming to him and letting him know how addled she's gotten. He could hardly believe me at first, but I had the book that I write everything down in and when he saw that—the figures and the times, down to the minute, every little thing she's ever done—he was really impressed. He took it and studied it as if he'd never seen anything that clever before. I'm awfully glad you told me to start keeping a record of everything."

They smiled at each other. "Your daddy's a smart boy," he said, reaching over to pat her hand.

"I know."

They sipped their drinks.

"But I'd still like to go."

"You won't miss much. It'll turn out to be just a formality."

"You think the M.E. is just doing it to needle the hospital?"

"I think he's trying to get his name in the papers. He's got no business calling an inquest."

"That's what I heard. Are you going?"

"No, tomorrow's the day I open bids for the next three months' supplies for the hospital. Of course, it's pretty cut-and-dried, because I already know who's going to get our business, but legally I'm supposed to offer the bids at a staff meeting. What I actually do on Jubal's orders is to pick out the bids he wants accepted and submit only those."

She didn't understand this and didn't want him to try to explain it, because her drink was making her a little fuzzy. "My, I'm getting warm. You'd think they'd have a cooler in here."

"They do. Can't you hear it running?"

She listened. "That? I thought that was a refrigerator."

"Could be. Want another drink?"

"I guess not. You want me to walk out of here or be carried?" She giggled at him coyly.

For a moment he was almost nauseated. My God, he thought, do I have to look at that for the rest of my life? Then he remembered that what she had from the waist down was not too bad, and, after all, he wouldn't be able to see her face in the dark. He guessed he'd be able to take it once she became head of Nursing Personnel and they were married. With her salary and his and a few kickbacks he got from various sources, they'd have it made. And if her looks got too much for him, he could get a girl with a pretty face for a little off-duty pleasure. He had a sudden vision of himself trying to lift her solid weight and carry her out to the car.

"Why don't we go, then?" he said.

"Sure, why not." Her glance was meant to be inviting but only succeeded in being a leer. Her classes would have been shocked to see the prim Margaret Rich look so lecherous.

They got up and wriggled out of the booth. He left some money on the table and took her arm, pretending concern because she pretended to stagger. "Oh, my," she said. "I don't believe I'll ever make it."

On three drinks, he thought grimly. You either make it or I'll leave you where you fall. "Sure you can," he said intimately. "Besides, we got business outside, remember?"

"What kind of business?"

"Monkey business."

She made funny sounds in her throat and blushed. "Hurry, hurry," she whispered, forgetting to stagger.

"I'm hurrying," he muttered in her ear. "Unless you want to do it right here."

"Walter!" she gasped. The place was almost empty, so it didn't matter that they were two people no longer young who were behaving in a very silly manner.

As soon as they were in the car he put his arms around her and kissed her, opening his mouth and exploring with his tongue. Now he could forget that she was large and florid and very unpleasant at times. In the dark like this she was just a female with comfortable hips and a way of gripping him between her legs that showed she had waited a long time for him or any man to come along. When he started the car to drive to their favorite trysting place, he was wondering comfortably how soon Jubal would heave Lucretia out and put Margaret in her place.

CHAPTER 39

THE NEXT NIGHT was close. Kathy felt its oppression and wondered irritably how it was possible to feel the summer heat so easily in an air-conditioned building. She had stopped by Donovan's office to give the letter she had written to Madge, who solemnly promised that she would deliver it to Donovan as soon as he returned from his ward rounds. It had been a long day, Kathy thought. She had waited patiently for something to happen, either a call to go to the main office and face Lucretia Terry or one from Donovan. Because of her apprehension she had slept badly. Now she was stupid with fatigue, with a long night to face, and a hot night at that.

She reread what Althea had written in the ledger, noticed a comment on Edna and began to think about her—unstable, paranoid, morbid, catatonic at times, hallucinated, brutal and vicious when disturbed—in fact, with nothing to be said in her favor. She had regressed so far into her schizophrenia that she responded to nothing but drugs or shock therapy. Kathy agreed with the rest of Canterbury—Edna did not belong in Rehabilitation.

For a moment Kathy wondered what kind of woman Edna would have been had her childhood been different. Suppose her mother had loved her and wanted her the way mine loved and wanted me, she thought, and she had felt secure and safe and had had things like other girls have, spending money and a boy to carry your books home from school and getting to go to the show every Saturday. I went every Saturday, she remembered with a twinge of nostalgia. With Bettymae Redwine and Stephenie Bornschien. Poor Edna.

She looked at her watch. It was really too early to check the wards, but at least she would be doing something, and she could use Edna's condition as an excuse. She began to make the rounds, explaining to the charges that she was checking early because of a highly disturbed patient on one of the wards.

When she came onto Ward Five and entered the office, Ruth stood up respectfully. Her shoes and cap were still on because she never took them off until after the first ward check. She looked so composed and dignified that Kathy felt apologetic. "I'm early," she said, patting her forehead with a handkerchief.

"An hour," Ruth agreed. "Hot, ain't it? I'm sorry but I just started writing my report. It's nowhere near finished."

Kathy seated herself. "That's all right. I'm checking early because of Edna. How is she?" As she spoke, she pulled the ward's record book into position so that she could quickly glance through it.

Ruth looked down at the top of Kathy's cap. A newly made supervisor could be something of a trial to the attendants who were old-timers in Canterbury, but Kathy was an exception. Not that she didn't hold with regulations, Ruth thought. She certainly did that all right. But she was kind and polite and didn't deliberately try to find something wrong in order to make the office think she was efficient. "Edna? Oh, she's asleep. At least she was when Millie Higgins helped me check at eleven. She seems t' be well sedated. Guess all that sodium luminal finally took hold. I didn't have to give her the amytal." Her hands went into her pockets and came out empty.

Kathy noted the movement. "Go ahead—smoke if you wish," she said, uncapping her pen.

Ruth brought out the pack with relief. She had picked up the habit lately out of sheer boredom. As she lit her cigarette, she thought about Edna's conduct during the day. She hoped Edna's activity would not rate more than a reasonable amount of attention. If it did, it would mean work for somebody. Mainly me, Ruth thought silently, knowing she was not in the mood for extra work. She hadn't been in a mood for anything since taking charge of Ward Five. For the first time in her sixteen years at Canterbury, she felt that there was no point in taking her job too seriously. No one would appreciate what she did now because no one had in the past. She might as well be like so many of the other attendants in the institution. Go easy on the work, avoid responsibility, take home her share of hospital loot, nap when possible, even slap patients when she felt they had it coming.

She wondered what she could say to relieve Kathy's anxiety about Edna before it resulted in work which might otherwise be avoided. "You're probably wondering why the afternoon shift wrote up all that stuff, ain't you? Well, you know how it is. The day people want the office to think they got all the problems. So they write up these long, windy reports which read big, only they don't mean a thing. Makin' mountains outa molehills, that's what it is."

"This is Edna's standard pattern," Kathy said soberly, well aware of what lay behind Ruth's remarks but choosing to ignore it.

"Sure," Ruth agreed with what she hoped was a complacent attitude. "Edna blows her stack all day long. But what I'm trying to say, she puts on this show for the day people, then settles down at night to sleep like the sweetest baby ever born."

Kathy began to copy the report into her own record book. "Edna should be in restraint tonight," she murmured abstractedly.

"The new regulations, Miss Hunter. What's a person gonna do when it says right on the bulletin board downstairs that no Rehab patient is to be confined in restraint or seclusion by the night shift unless by direct order of the attending ward physician? That's Terry's latest, you know. It's all that Thorazine and Serpasil they're giving. Terry must figure that tranquilizers are gonna be the answer to all of Canterbury's problems."

"Tranquilizers do help, Ruth. They're solving a lot of problems. For the patients as well as for the staff."

"But not without a little something from us attendants," Ruth said bluntly, sensing that she could say this without fear of reprisal.

Kathy looked up at her. "Good care, food, therapy, kindness, affection—and tranquilizers," she observed gently, then returned to her writing. "Who's on duty tonight?" she asked.

"Dr. Cortwright. Not that it means anything. Person never can find him. He's always at some motel with some woman who ain't his wife." Ruth's contempt was obvious.

Kathy was not diverted. She chewed on the tip of her pen as she studied what she had written. There was a problem here and somehow she must handle it wisely even though she was inexperienced and was not actually too sure what she should do.

"That afternoon shift sure gives me a bad time," Ruth grumbled. "The morning people upset the afternoon people and then they gang up on me. From what they wrote, Edna really had herself a time. Yet when it comes time for them t' go home—all six of them—what do they do? They flip off the cuffs and belt, unlock the door to Edna's room, and leave me holding the sack. Me, all by myself. Eight people on the morning shift, six on afternoons and only one at night. How do you like that? I gotta do all the worrying. What's the office afraid of—that we night people might sneak a little shut-eye on our shift? Or is it because we don't have to give baths and shampoos and count silverware and see to it that the floors get a good polishing and so the other shifts are just plain jealous? So they gotta do something to keep us in a tizzy all night, huh?"

It was a familiar complaint. Each shift thought the other had it easier. Kathy liked Ruth and understood her viewpoint, but she was also the supervisor of the entire building. She was responsible for the welfare and safety of several hundred people; she did not want to make any mistakes.

"The day people are only doing their job, too," she said.

"Sure," Ruth said, her voice dripping disgust. "But if what they said about Edna is true, why is she down there sleeping like a lamb right now?"

"Edna's far from being a lamb. When she's really disturbed, she's one of the most dangerous patients in Canterbury. I wish she weren't here. She shouldn't have been assigned to this building."

"You know why that happened, don't you? She used to be

on one of the untidy wards, but Terry had her transferred because she's the day supervisor's cousin."

Kathy lowered her eyes. We're gossiping, she thought. I should not stoop to it. She pushed at her hair, which felt heavy and hot. "What medication is Edna getting?" she asked tiredly.

Ruth sighed. She bent and fished out of one of the drawers the doctor's order sheet on Edna. "Thorazine," she read off rapidly. "T.I.D. Two hundred milligrams. Sodium Luminal, IM, three ccs, P.R.N. Restraint and seclusion, P.R.N., A.M. shifts only." She placed the sheet in front of Kathy. "A.M. shifts only," she repeated pointedly.

Kathy nodded. "She's had her Thorazine and sodium luminal?"

"Plus shock therapy this morning after the first tantrum."

"That should hold her through the night," Kathy said. "It certainly should. Did you say you have an amytal order also?"

"By word of mouth from the afternoon charge. She said I was to give Edna sodium amytal if she was still upset when I made the first check. But she wasn't. She was asleep."

Ruth replaced the order sheet among the others and turned her attention to Kathy. "I don't think I'll have any trouble with Edna tonight, I honestly don't. Edna likes me—as much as she can like anybody, Miss Hunter. I always been nice to her. I let her go to the toilet or get a drink of water any time she feels like it. I always say there ain't no point in being mean to these patients for doing the things they do when they can't help themselves."

"But you're careful?" Kathy said quickly.

"My goodness, of course I am. I sure ain't afraid of anybody, but I never go down the hall alone. Never. I know better'n that." Ruth's tone was injured.

Kathy looked through the thick security windows of the office and into the ward parlor beyond. It was dimly lit, empty, silent. She did not doubt that Ruth meant exactly what she said. She was not afraid of the patients. The patients and the silence. She was an old-timer, and they all felt the same way. Ruth had probably worked so many years in the institution that she had lost the ability to sense the difference between the comfortable, brightly lit office with its shatterproof glass and a metal door which could be pulled hastily shut and locked by a flick of the wrist, and the silent parlor outside or even the dark corridor going down between the small rooms where insane women slept or moaned or wept and cursed. Ruth had begun working in Canterbury when the job paid fifty dollars a month and the wards were almost primitive. Naturally she was not afraid on a fine ward like this one in such a luxurious building. What had it been like when the pay was fifty dollars a month? Kathy remembered the things she had heard. Pitched battles every day. An employee's life then was not worth a thin dime if she turned her back to the patients. Every day buttons were ripped from their uniforms and hair pulled from their scalps. The attendants learned early that a brutal slap stopped many a fight in time. The best employees were stout, heavy-bosomed, large-armed and beefy. By contrast, here was Ward Five, which required the strength of only one employee at night. No wonder Ruth was not afraid of the too-quiet dimness and the unlocked doors to the patients' rooms.

Young and inexperienced as she was, Kathy knew exactly what would happen. She would leave certain orders to be followed and Ruth might carry them out to the letter, but she would probably handle her ward in whatever fashion she decided was most convenient. She could do it because there was no one to spy on her activity. She might even close and lock Edna's door, leave it that way for the better part of the night, then unlock and open it before the morning shift came on duty. She would certainly take off her shoes and her cap before long. She might use ward paper to write a letter and stuff a bar of soap into her handbag to take home. She would not check her ward alone—not because by so doing she would be breaking the most stringent of hospital regulations for night-duty employees but because she liked the company of her friend, Millie.

Kathy shut her eyes. She could almost see the two women, flashlights in hand, stepping softly down the corridors once every hour throughout the night and looking into the rooms to make sure everything was all right, looking into Edna's room. She opened her eyes with a little jerk. I wish I could be sure she'd lock that door, she thought. But she didn't dare tell Ruth to do so without a direct order from a doctor. She did not have that much authority.

Why am I so worried about Edna? she wondered. Is it because I'm tired and upset and it's so damn hot?

She reviewed what she had read. Edna's day had begun quietly enough with a good breakfast. At eight-thirty she took a bath and shampooed her hair. She made her own bed and tidied her room. Later she was given a pencil and stationery. Apparently she just stared at the paper. At ten o'clock she picked up a heavy oak chair and brought it down across the top of the table where she had been sitting. The chair crumpled and the table overturned. Before she could be reached by the nervous attendants, she had run to the nearest panel of glass bricks and had begun beating on them with one of the chair rungs.

The morning charge stated in her report that there was no reason for Edna's behavior; she wanted it clearly understood that Edna's disturbance did not stem from anything done or said by the morning shift. The day supervisor, Miss Horne, had just made her first ward check and had stopped to speak to Edna. Edna answered quite civilly. The cause of her outbreak a few moments later was therefore unknown.

The afternoon charge wrote that Edna had been in reasonably good contact again when Miss Horne, the supervisor, checked the ward at two-thirty. She was still somewhat confused from the electric convulsant therapy ordered for her by Dr. Macleod at ten-thirty but was sitting quietly on the ward porch. Miss Horne examined a cut on Edna's hand, caused by the broken chair. She stated that the injury looked inflamed, ordered it rebandaged and left. A few moments later, Edna went berserk again, attempting to choke a nearby patient. It took most of the personnel from Wards Five and Six combined to get Edna into full bed restraint and to give her six grains of sodium luminal by intramuscular injection. In spite of the drug, she spent the afternoon working her bed around her room by thrashing against her restraints. She screamed at intervals and deliberately vomited her food and oral medications.

Without putting it into so many words, the afternoon charge obviously felt it would be a grave error to take Edna out of restraint. However, she removed the cuffs and belt at Edna's bedtime, had her escorted by the entire ward personnel to the shower room for a bath and then back to a freshly made bed. Edna was calm by then, but Kathy did not know that the charge had said exhaustedly to Ruth when she gave up her keys, "I hope to God you have a better time with that damned Edna tonight than we did today! You can have this ward and welcome to it. I hope nobody looks for me to show up tomorrow, because I'm going to take the day off and stay in bed. God, what a time we've had with that woman!"

Ruth watched Kathy evaluating what had been written about Edna and was glad she hadn't repeated the charge's parting remarks. No indeed, she thought grimly. If there was one thing she still knew how to do, it was to keep her mouth shut. If Kathy knew what the afternoon charge had said, she'd never believe that Edna could be as high as a kite all day, yet, once she was settled in her bed and asleep, could be a lamb all night. When Kathy rose from the desk chair, Ruth picked up her flashlight and followed her quietly down the hall to look at Edna, now sleeping quietly in her room.

CHAPTER 40

THE INQUEST WAS HELD in a municipal building referred to by the townspeople as the city auditorium. Actually it was only a large gymnasium with a small stage two steps high, baskets for basketball at either side and benches against all the other available wall space. The windows were set high in the walls and there were double doors on either side of the stage. It was used by the town's one high school, by the town whenever it was needed for something special—such as a touring concert—and by various church groups ambitious enough to stage Christmas or Easter pageants. The fifty-dollar rental fee demanded by the town council went to the custodian of the building, who used the money to replace burned-out light bulbs and windows broken by high ball shots, to rent folding chairs and to fire up the furnace in winter. He seldom had much left of the money to pay himself for sweeping out the place and dusting the benches, but he was reasonably satisfied because, as he said, at least he was in on everything that went on in town.

The meeting was set for ten o'clock. At eight o'clock, Bud Nappy—two generations back it had been spelled Napiecinski—walked in and looked around.

"What in hell do you think this is going to be?" he asked Milsworth Greer, the custodian.

He made him remove the chairs and speaker's platform from the stage and pull the cheap burlap curtains, cutting off the stage entirely. Then he helped reshuffle the chairs until a space had been cleared in front of the stage, after which he and the old man carried in from the hall a battered desk used for ticket sellers, placing it to face the chairs, its back against the stage. The chairs for his six jurymen were set in a row at the right of the desk, and the only other chair besides his own was one at the left for his stenographer.

"I thought you wanted it up on the stage where everybody could see what's going on," Milsworth said, quavering.

"I don't give a damn who sees what's going on," Bud retorted. "This isn't a girly show. It's an inquest."

"Yessir."

"I'm going out for a drink. Don't open those doors until nine-thirty, you hear?" Then he added, "Don't open them until I tell you to."

"Yessir."

Muttering to himself, the custodian shut and bolted the

doors and Bud went across the street to a tavern, where he downed two Scotch-on-the-rocks in quick succession. Then he drove to the jail to get the deputy and his prisoner. He intended to be back at the auditorium before the crowd gathered, but when he got there the hall in front of the doors was full of people. They let him and the other two men through without much comment. Milsworth unlocked a door, let them in, relocked it hastily.

"No, sir, no, sir," he could be heard saying on the other side. "Nobody goes in there until I get the go-ahead sign. Them's m' orders and I'm sticking to 'em."

In a few minutes the District Attorney arrived, edged through the crowd and was permitted to enter the auditorium. At nine-thirty the six jurymen made their appearance. They were dressed in their best business suits, with clean white shirts, ties and freshly polished shoes. They all looked solemn, and the two trash haulers looked a little desperate. They had been told by their wives to keep their hands out of sight because they hadn't been able to get their fingernails clean in spite of repeated scrubbings. All six were allowed to pass, and almost immediately behind them came Bud's stenographer, a middle-aged, waspish woman who was thoroughly enjoying herself. She had two shorthand notebooks and a bunch of pencils held together by a rubber band in one hand and a purse the size of a small suitcase clutched under the other arm. The pencils had been sharpened so vigorously that their points looked needle-fine. Beginning to look irritated, Milsworth let her in, then relocked the door.

"Stop your shoving," he shouted. "Ain't nobody going in there until Bud Nappy says so."

At five minutes to ten, there was a sudden silence and the crowd parted to let Dr. Herrington and Lucretia Terry through. They were followed by the editor in chief of the town's newspaper, who was doing his best to look as if he had not come with Jubal and Lucretia but had wandered in by accident. Dogging his footsteps was a cameraman with all his equipment. They, too, were allowed to enter the auditorium, but almost immediately the deputy came to tell Milsworth to open the doors and fasten them back. It was hotter than hell already; what was he trying to do, cook everybody? Muttering to himself again, Milsworth let the crowd in and did not try to keep any semblance of order, or tell them to go by twos, as he would have had it been an ordinary affair with an ordinary audience. To hell with them, too, he told himself. What did they think he was, a janitor? He had half a mind to go down into the basement and start banging on the pipes. At the last minute, he had a change of heart and brought out his special chair, padded with old cushions, and planted himself at the edge of one of the fastened-back doors, where he would be sure to get what air was stirring.

The crowd settled quickly. Bud looked it over carefully, guessing that the only people who hadn't come were those who just couldn't get away from their jobs or who were out of town. He had hoped there would be a large crowd. Surely there would be one person among all those faces who would know of something to Blayton's advantage and would be willing to come forward with it.

Neither he nor Riley had succeeded in getting Jim to talk except to admit that in self-defense he had struck the blow that had killed Dr. Andreatta. The reason? No reason. He didn't know why. Maybe the doctor was crazy; maybe he didn't see so well in the dark and thought Jim was somebody else—God knows why he did it. He was no mind reader. That doctor had come at him with what looked like a knife, so he had hit him over the head with his shotgun. That was Jim's story.

The jury sat in their six chairs and tried not to look important. Actually they were a little uncertain as to how they did feel. They were supposed to listen to all the evidence given and then decide among themselves what they thought should be done. It was a grave responsibility having a man's life placed in their hands, no matter what he had done. They wanted to do the right thing.

The District Attorney was uneasy. He fidgeted in his seat, cleaned out his pockets, cleaned his fingernails, blew his nose. He had promised his friend Bud that he would not hold Jim for a criminal trial if Jim's story could be proved beyond a reasonable shadow of doubt, but he could already see the story headlined across the newspaper's front page: COLLUSION BETWEEN MEDICAL EXAMINER AND D.A.! They'd finish him and his career if things didn't go to suit Jubal Herrington. Why was Bud so determined to save Jim's hide? he wondered. Riley patted his neck with his handkerchief before he put it away and wished a little forlornly that someone had seen fit in the past to have air-conditioning installed in the auditorium. Of course, the place wasn't used too much during the summer; still, it was going to be a hellishly hot day. Already he was sticking to his chair. He turned to stare briefly at Jubal and Lucretia sitting left front in the semicircle of chairs, let his glance touch Rufe Tabor, the editor, sitting several seats away, and then swung back to look at the jury. How in hell had Bud accomplished that? he thought. Well, he hoped he had accomplished as much in the way of witnesses for the defense, or he would soon be looking like a complete fool.

In two chairs apart from all the rest sat Jim and the deputy. Jim was staring at the white lines painted on the floor. The deputy had his legs crossed and stared at the windows high in the walls. He was wondering why old Milsworth never opened the windows. There oughta be a little breeze up there; might help to cool things a bit. Maybe Milsworth didn't like to climb that high any more. Couldn't blame him for that, of course. A fellow his age could fall real easy, maybe break a hip. Then where would he be? Why, out in Canterbury, of course, stuck out there the rest of his life. It was an unpleasant thought to the deputy. He knew people who were poor and helpless and had to go to Canterbury because they couldn't afford regular hospitals. They died in Canterbury, locked up on wards. No, sir, he didn't blame Milsworth one bit for not opening those windows. But it was hot. He had forgotten to put a clean handkerchief in his back pocket, so he sat, feeling the dampness forming between his collar and his neck and hoping it didn't show. He hoped, too, that the inquest would be short. It ought to be; they didn't have a thing, really, to make it long.

Halfway toward the back, Millie sat in one of the narrow chairs. She wished she had nerve enough to occupy two, because the slat edges of the one chair pressed with painful sharpness against her thighs. She hadn't bothered to go to bed when she got off duty, knowing that if she once fell asleep even the alarm clock might not arouse her. She had changed from her uniform to her second-best dress, a flowered print that was as cool as anything she owned. She had put on a hat, too, thinking it might hide the fact that she hadn't had time to do anything to her hair. She was nervous and tense, wondering one moment what business she had being there when she needed all the sleep she could get, the next moment filled with a secret deep sympathy for the white-faced defendant. She had promised herself she wouldn't remember what she knew about Mary Elsie, but that was like telling herself the sun wasn't shining when it was and so hot that the pavement out in front of the building was spongy to step on. You couldn't make yourself forget things when they had been as shocking as what had happened to Mary Elsie.

Jim looked at the floor because he could not bear to look at all the faces staring at him, and thought about Mary Elsie. He remembered their honeymoon: it had been five days long, all the time off he could get. They hadn't wanted to waste one moment of it and there wasn't much money, so they went to a motel on the edge of town, not letting anyone know, of course. After they parked the car and unloaded it, they went inside and pulled the door shut. They didn't come out except to go over to a nearby coffee shop and eat, although they had never once been really hungry the whole five days, except for each other. We were so young, he thought, we didn't know anything, we had to learn everything. But it was like nothing either of them had ever dreamed of, not just doing what they did but the being together, knowing they had every right to be together and would be that way the rest of their lives. The rest of our lives, he thought, staring at the pattern of white against the gloss of hard lacquer on the wooden floor. As far as he was concerned, his life had ended with Mary Elsie's, and that had happened a long time before her actual death. Now he did not care what happened. He had told the police and Bud Nappy that he had killed Andreatta in self-defense because he didn't want them to know the whole story. He couldn't bear to have the town knowing and talking about what had happened to his Mary Elsie.

Bud rapped sharply on the desk. He was thinking that he had stuck his neck out and he was not quite sure why. He was out forty bucks, and Rufe Tabor was all set to give him a sneering, uncomplimentary writeup in his biased, two-bit newspaper. The six men on the jury were going to wonder what had possessed him, making them come out in this heat to see him make a fool of himself before most of the town. He hated to think about calling on Jim to testify, because while he insisted his motive had been self-defense, he acted as if he had enjoyed every moment of the clubbing. Certainly the doctors who had taken care of Andreatta weren't going to paint a very pretty picture. But the very fury of Jim's act had been what impressed him most. The town did not have much of a criminal element; it was too small, too countrified for that. A lone thug after someone's billfold would have grabbed and run, not stayed to kill his victim. He must have had a reason. He wasn't the kind of man who hated someone just to hate them; he was neither that dedicated nor that bigoted. Or even that ignorant. Jim Blayton was just an ordinary sort of fellow, getting along on a lower middle-class income and apparently very much in love with his pretty wife, who had surprised all her neighbors by losing her mind. I wish I had more to go on, Bud told himself uneasily, more than just this feeling that Blayton had a reason to do what he did.

He pounded with the gavel several moments before the crowd settled into silence. Then he got to his feet, rubbed one hand over his chin where stubble was already beginning to defeat his morning shave, and put the other hand into a pocket. There was a slight interruption and he turned his head impatiently as a man slouched in past Milsworth in his chair by the door to find himself a seat toward the rear of the room. It was Mike Stewart, late by five minutes. Only a few there knew him and Bud not at all. Bud waited until he was seated and pounded once more on the desk.

"All right," he said. "Let's have it quiet in here. I guess you can all see I don't have a mike set up and I'm not going to shout to make myself heard. You'll just have to listen." He put both hands in his pockets. "Now first I want to explain why we're here. This is an inquest. It has not been called because a crime was committed. We all know a crime has been committed. This inquest is for the purpose of determining whether the crime was justifiable—in other words, whether the defendant sitting here"—he pointed with an elbow—"committed said crime for the reason he states, which is self-defense, or whether he committed said crime without justification and deserves to be bound over for a criminal trial by jury on a charge of willful murder." He took one hand out and gestured toward the six men. "This is an inquest jury convened in accordance with the laws of the State of Dakota," he went on. "These men are here to decide which it shall be and they are free to ask any questions at any time. That man sitting over there is your District Attorney, Mr. John Riley. Most of you probably know him. We do not have a lawyer for the defendant because he has refused the services of one. If this jury decides he is to be bound over, the court will appoint a lawyer for his defense whether he likes it or not."

He paused and looked around, then flung out a hand loosely. "There are the two doctors who took care of the victim, Dr. Miguel Andreatta. They may or may not testify—it all depends. Now if there is anyone in this audience who wants to speak up with anything he knows that might have a bearing on this case, please stand up when you feel like it and you will be sworn in to testify. I have to admit—" he took out his handkerchief and mopped his face—"I have to admit that we don't have much to go on, and some of you are probably wondering why in hell we're having this inquest, if you'll pardon my language. Well, after we get started, maybe you'll figure that out. Now the crime was—" And he went into details that they all were already familiar with and to which they listened pleasurably in spite of the heat, getting a vicarious thrill from a crime that sooner or later might make the newspapers from coast to coast.

One by one, Bud called his witnesses: the policeman who was the first to see Jim stumble into the police station, his clothing soaked with blood from his gashed arm; the sergeant who took down his confession; the police surgeon and his nurse who had worked on the injured arm; the ambulance drivers and intern who had gone after Andreatta. Finally he was down to the one witness who had seen Jim that night, the woman who lived in the house in front of which he had parked his car. She was elderly, had a shapeless figure and sharp eyes. Her testimony was brief and said nothing in Jim's favor. Yes, she had seen the defendant. He parked his car right in front of her driveway. She never used it, but she was going to tell him off, only before she could get her door open he was out of his car and going down the street, and he was carrying a club. A club? Well, it looked like a club to her. It was long and thick and he put it under his arm as if he didn't want anyone to see what he was carrying.

The shotgun lay across the desk with the burlap bag it had been wrapped in. One of the jury, the retired school principal, requested Bud to wrap the gun in the sack and stick it under his own arm, which Bud did. "Now," said the principal, eying the witness sternly, "was that what you saw? Just like that?"

The woman stared, then nodded triumphantly. "That's exactly it," she cried. "You can see for yourself. It looks like a club."

In the dark, it very well could. They all had to agree to that. They watched the woman return to her seat, their faces solemn. A man had no business running around in the dark with a shotgun, their faces said.

Nervously, Bud put Jim in the witness chair. "Mr. Blayton," he said, politely but not too much so, "why don't you tell us why you were carrying a shotgun wrapped in burlap the night Dr. Andreatta was killed."

The room was quite still as Jim lifted his head to look at Bud. After a moment he said, his voice surprisingly clear, "Why, I couldn't lock my car and I wasn't about to leave my gun there for somebody to come along and steal. The gun ain't new, but it oughta be worth at least twenty-five bucks."

The jury nodded. Half the crowd nodded. The answer made sense. Most of the men in the room owned guns. They went hunting in duck season and deer season and sometimes out of season. They took care of their guns, cleaned and oiled them and kept them in leather cases or carefully wrapped in burlap.

But at this point Dr. Herrington stood up. Instantly every head turned in his direction. "May I ask Mr. Blayton a question?"

"Certainly," said Bud. Then to his stenographer: "No need to swear him in. He's not making a statement, he's asking a question."

"Mr. Blayton," Jubal said, his voice also loud and clear, "are you quite sure that on the night in question you were not planning to kill somebody? I ask this because I believe you were planning exactly that. I believe you were planning to kill me."

There was a startled buzz throughout the room. Bud swung his face from Jubal to Jim. "I don't believe you have to answer that question," he said. "If you answer in the affirmative, it will incriminate you and you've already pleaded self-defense." Turning back to Jubal, he said reproachfully, "That was not a fair question. You're trying to influence the jury."

"I do not withdraw it, sir," Jubal said testily. "This man is a murderer. He struck down a man in cold blood and I will not see him go free without making a protest. What kind of justice do we have in this town where such things can happen without fear of punishment?"

"Now, look here. No one has said anything about not punishing this defendant. This is not a trial jury. We are merely trying to establish the facts and you aren't going to help any by throwing up a smoke screen. This defendant says he was attacked by Dr. Miguel Andreatta and he has the injury to prove it."

"I would like to take the stand."

"All right, sir. All right. If that's the way you feel, step right up here. Jim, you're excused. Go back to your seat. Now, Dr. Herrington, just be sworn in by my stenographer here . . ." But he watched apprehensively as Jubal was sworn in.

"Do you solemnly swear to the truth of the testimony you are about to give at this inquest, so help you . . ." She chanted it and Jubal followed with a mumble, his hand on the big Bible she carried in her suitcase-sized purse.

"What now? Bud wondered. Well, he had asked for witnesses, hadn't he? Now it was up to him to see that they were honest and did not try to pull any hokey-pokey. He clamped his jaws grimly as Jubal sat down in the chair Jim had just vacated. Then he looked at the Bible now lying on the desk. How many people believed in what the Bible had to say? he thought. These days, at least. By God, they'd better tell the truth, he told himself. If he caught just one of them lying, he'd wrap them up but good in their own lies! "All right," he said, his voice cold and hard. "Just what was it you wanted to tell us?"

CHAPTER 41

WHEN KATHY WENT OFF DUTY the morning of the inquest, she barely spoke to Althea as they traded places.

The morning before she had given her letter to Madge to

be delivered to Donovan. Then she had spent an anxious, futile day waiting for something to happen. And then the problem of Edna was added to the rest of her troubles, although, as if from contrariness, Edna had slept quite peacefully. Like a lamb, as Ruth said.

Nevertheless, Kathy had been uneasy and worried and the night had seemed unending. Now she was too tired to care whether she even got as far as her room in Residence. She was sure she could have slept on one of the benches on the lawn. When she stepped through the outer door of Rehabilitation she saw Mike leaning against the bricks.

To be certain not to miss her he had been waiting for some time. "I didn't see you yesterday," he said, his voice a little reproachful.

She had deliberately avoided him, feeling sure he would know somehow what she and Donovan had done the night before. Mike's eyes were sharp and he loved her. He would be able to tell easily that she was different, that she was not the same girl he had known a day earlier. She did not want him to know what had happened.

"Hello," she said. "What are you doing here?" It sounded foolish, but she was tired as well as unnerved by his sudden appearance. He had never before waited for her outside Rehabilitation.

"I didn't see you yesterday," he repeated. "So I wondered whether something was wrong."

"Why should something be wrong?"

"You tell me. Is something wrong?"

"Of course not." She began to walk down the sidewalk, turning her face away from him. She was so tired she was trembling.

He fell into step. "Where did you go yesterday?"

"Where did I go?" She wondered what to tell him. "I had an errand to do."

"Why didn't you call on me? You need your rest."

"Rest?" What was that? "No," she murmured. "I couldn't. It was something I had to do—myself."

"I looked for you. I walked all over the damn grounds."

"Oh? I climbed in somebody's car and went to sleep. That's why you didn't find me."

"When I don't get to see you—even for a few moments—the day drags. It's a thousand years long."

"I'm sorry."

"You should be. You're the cause of it all."

"Yes."

He sighed. "How about it today? Will you marry me?"

She did not even smile. She plodded along, her head down, her eyes half closed.

"Kathy!" he said, alarmed. "What's the matter? Are you sick?"

"Sick?" she said, not looking at him. "Of course I'm not sick. I'm never sick. I haven't been sick since I was nine and had the measles."

"Were you awfully sick then?"

"Yes. I almost died."

"Darling."

She stumbled. He took her arm hastily. "Let me carry you. You can hardly see where you're going."

"Don't be ridiculous. What would they think?"

"What would who think?"

"Everybody." She managed to lift one arm and wave it. "The hospital, the patients, the charges—"

"Who in hell cares what they think?"

"Me."

"Why? They aren't watching what you do."

"Somebody's always watching what somebody else does. They find out."

"Find out what."

"Things."

"Silly," he said and picked her up bodily.

"Put me down."

"Of course. Right away, darling."

"This minute."

"This minute." He walked steadily. "You don't weigh more than a couple of feathers," he said. "See, I'm not even panting."

"Now who's silly?" She felt as if she had passed into a dream world.

"I am. Silly in love with you."

"Put me down," she said again.

"I can't," he said. "Your eyes are shut. You wouldn't know where to go."

"I can walk, I can walk." It was so pleasant to be carried, she thought. She had never felt quite so safe and protected. "Don't you believe me?" But she did not open her eyes.

"No." When he looked down again, she was asleep. He carried her all the way up to her room, gently laid her on the bed and very carefully removed her shoes. But he did not stay, because this time the house mother was in her chair and left it to climb the stairs behind him and wait on the next to the top step until he came back out of Kathy's room.

"Sick?" she whispered in a loud stage whisper.

"No," he said, the bemused expression still on his face, and went out without an explanation.

Curious, the house mother climbed the stairs again and

went to peer into Kathy's room, but all she saw was a figure with tousled hair and rumpled uniform deep in sleep. "Humph," she said, disappointed, and went back to her chair. Through her window she observed Mike striding off across the grass. "Going to the inquest, probably." Everyone who could was going; she wished she could, too. But she knew better than to leave with so many of the night-duty nurses asleep upstairs. "Hah!" she snorted, thinking about them. "Just waiting for me to turn my back so's they can sneak men up to their rooms. That Kathy Hunter! She didn't fool me one bit. Pretending to be asleep. I know what would have been going on if I hadn't been here when that young fellow brought her in. Carrying her like a baby. Hah! His baby, no doubt." Satisfied that she had saved the honor of Nurses' Residence, she picked up her fancy work and began counting stitches and rocking at the same time.

Madge heard the tiny crackle of the paper in her pocket and slid one hand in, feeling the smooth glaze of the envelope that held Kathy's letter to Donovan. Yesterday morning Kathy had given her the letter to deliver, stressing its importance. Give it to Donovan as soon as he comes in, she had said. Madge's hand fastened over the envelope protectively. I couldn't, she thought defensively. I never did get to see him. She had a parole, of course; she could have gone over to his apartment. She could have left the letter in his box. But Kathy hadn't said to do that; she had said, "Give it to him as soon as he comes in," and she had meant when he returned to his office. He had not come back before she left for her supper.

It was an honor to be given an errand to do; it made her feel special and responsible. Madge clutched the letter almost ferociously. She was not going to follow Dr. Macleod all over the grounds trying to give him Kathy's letter. She was going to do just as Kathy had ordered—give it to him when he came into his office. Those were orders and she knew how to obey orders. Just like having a boss in an office. The boss told you to address circulars or to mimeograph this form or to copy that memo, seven pages of it, one glossy and six carbons, so you did it; you did it exactly as ordered and very carefully, and you made no mistakes because bosses didn't like mistakes. A good stenographer always tried to please her boss, always.

Madge took her hand out of her pocket and patted it on the outside possessively. The letter was safe. She would guard it with her life. Then Dr. Denning came in. Her face cleared magically, and she forgot the letter.

"Good morning, Doctor," she said brightly.

"Hi, Sugar," he said. He did not look happy. He looked very gloomy. But he smiled for her benefit.

He walked through her cubicle, opened Donovan's door and glanced in. "Not back yet?" he asked, looking back at Madge.

"I haven't seen him since day before yesterday," she replied.

"Oh." He stood indecisively with his hand on the doorknob for a second, then closed the door and went toward his own.

"Maybe he's gone to the inquest," she said brightly.

He shook his head. "I don't think so. Neither of us can go. Too many residents on vacation." He did not add that he would not have gone in any case.

She saw he was about to leave and said quickly, "What will they do to him? That Jim Blayton, I mean. For killing poor Dr. Andreatta."

He hesitated. He hadn't liked Andreatta, had despised him in fact. But should he tell a patient what he really thought? "It isn't a trial, Madge. It's just an inquest. I wouldn't be surprised if they turned him loose."

"You really think so?" she asked shrilly. "That mean man?"

"He wasn't mean—just terribly upset and confused," Larry said quietly.

"They shouldn't turn him loose. He's a murderer!"

"I suppose he is." He turned away from her shocked look and went into his office, forgetting her immediately.

Last night Althea had refused to see him or even talk to him. When she came off duty, she had avoided him by taking a roundabout way over to Residence, then she had gone upstairs and locked herself in her room, refusing to answer knocks, refusing to come to the telephone.

"I'm not in to anybody," she had told the house mother through her locked door. "I have a headache. Go away."

The house mother quoted her exactly to Larry and added a little slyly, "She's not been feeling well lately. You don't suppose something could be wrong, do you, Dr. Denning?"

Bitch! he thought. "Nothing's wrong," he said, forcing his voice to be steady and cool. "Miss Horne's been working too hard lately."

He hadn't missed the implication. He almost wished Althea were pregnant. It might settle his problems. But Althea wasn't pregnant, he was sure of that. She showed none of the symptoms of pregnancy. What she did show was far different and terribly disturbing. He wanted to do something quickly to help her, but what could he do?

God, what a mess he had made of things! Yet, he hadn't

planned it that way. He had been honest in thinking that his love was great enough for both of them. Was it great enough for him to give her up?

He stood at the window in his office and stared at the sunlight flooding the lawn in front of the building. The beginning of another hot day. I called her seven times last night, he thought. She was there but she wouldn't answer; she wouldn't even come to the phone. Evidently Donovan hadn't made a move yet. What in hell has he been doing? Where's he hiding? I called his apartment last night almost as many times as I called Althea.

I could go over to Rehab right now and see her, Larry thought. I could go over this very minute. She'll be on duty. But we can't talk. There's no privacy. I can't kiss her—and I'll want to kiss her. I won't be able to help myself. So I'll feel like a heel and she'll be stiff because she'll know the Rehab people will say something about it later.

His thoughts turned to Donovan. He could contact him through the hospital switchboard, of course, but that would be so obvious. Dr. Denning paging Dr. Macleod. Althea would hear! Nor could he sit in his office all day, waiting for Donovan to return to his. His services were needed. As he had told Madge, too many residents were on vacation; he must substitute for them.

He sighed. Tonight, he thought. He would see Althea if he had to break down her door. And damn Donovan!

CHAPTER 42

JUBAL HERRINGTON HAD BEEN TALKING for five or six minutes. He had explained the hospital's need for trained doctors. Now he was ready to conclude his thunderous little speech. "No one in his right mind—" He paused and glared at the audience. "No one in his right mind could believe that this crime is justifiable," he said. "Dr. Andreatta was a small man physically, a delicately-boned man. He weighed one hundred and forty pounds. Can any of you believe he would deliberately attack a man weighing—" he glanced scornfully at Jim—"weighing at least one hundred and eighty pounds, perhaps more? Can any of you believe that?"

He turned to the six men of the jury. He held up his hands. Everyone looked at his hands. "A physician's muscles are not particularly strong. Only his hands are strong and his ability to stand the sight of blood and pain and the miseries of others. He has to be able to stand that before he can help those who suffer. Believe me, gentlemen, Dr. Andreatta did not attack this defendant. I say he was defending himself."

There was a brief silence. Bud moved uneasily. "Any of you fellows want to ask Dr. Herrington anything?"

The druggist leaned forward. "I'd like to ask him a question."

"Yessir. Go right ahead."

"My name's Greene, Jonathan Greene. I own the Acme Pharmacy down on Sycamore. I guess most of the folks here know my place, leastwise their kids do. I've got a very popular soda fountain. Well, I know something about doctors and such and I know that a doctor always keeps his tools in a sterilizer. What was this Andreatta doing with a scalpel in his pocket?"

All eyes swung to the desk where the scalpel lay beside the shotgun. "A very good question," Bud said quickly before Jubal could answer. "That's one of the main reasons I feel this inquest ought to be held. What was Dr. Andreatta doing with that—that thing in his pocket? I asked myself. It —well, I tried it on a chunk of wood. Oak. Guess you all know how hard oak is. And it sliced off a sliver just like that wood was butter. Now I call that a very sharp instrument and certainly nothing to be carrying in your pocket. Why, a fellow could sit on a thing like that and get himself permanently lamed."

There was general laughter. Jubal jumped to his feet. The laughter subsided. "I thought you were called a *medical* examiner!"

"Yessir," Bud said mildly. "But I was elected to this job. Do you want to answer Jonathan's question or one of mine?"

"There is no reason I know of why a doctor shouldn't carry a scalpel in his pocket if he chooses to do so."

"As far as I'm concerned he can carry it in his hat, but you'll have to admit it's a mighty queer thing to do."

"I carry instruments in my own pockets occasionally. Even professional men forget these things, Mr. Nappy."

"But you're a surgeon, Dr. Herrington. Was Dr. Andreatta a surgeon?"

Jubal spluttered. "I refuse to answer that, sir. Andreatta was qualified to do anything." Then he glared at the druggist. "Have you ever made a mistake as a pharmacist? Put the wrong stopper in a bottle or mislabeled a box?"

Jonathan flushed but his gaze was steady. "No, Dr. Herrington, I don't dare make mistakes. If I made mistakes, somebody might die."

Several spectators gasped.

"I didn't know there was anyone alive that perfect," Jubal

said harshly. "So perfect you never make mistakes. If you'll pardon me, I say that's a lot of hogwash, sir. We all make mistakes."

"I have yet to find out about the first one I've buried," Jonathan retorted grimly. "Yes, everybody makes mistakes of one kind or another, but when you're mixing drugs for people to swallow, that's not the time to make mistakes. That's the time you're as careful as hell!"

"Now, look," Bud interposed. "Quarreling won't get us anywhere. I certainly believe Jonathan when he says he doesn't make mistakes. Far as I know, there's never been a single complaint about his drugstore in all the years he's had one, and that's been quite a long time. I remember when he had his first store down by the Thaxton flour mills, because I used to run errands for him, and later when he moved up on Sycamore. I don't believe there's a person in this room that's ever felt Jonathan didn't know what he was doing when he filled a prescription. On the other hand, I can't say I believe Dr. Herrington wouldn't be telling the truth about doctors forgetting to take instruments out of their pockets. But it still seems a very strange place to carry one of those things. What I mean is, if a doctor is using one, wouldn't he be wearing a surgical gown and, when he got through cutting, wouldn't a nurse take his knives and his gown and his mask? She'd see to it that the scalpels and tweezers and so on were put back on their tray. So how would it be possible for this scalpel to get into Andreatta's suit pocket, a good suit, one he was wearing when he went into town for something special?"

"You're making a mountain out of a molehill," Jubal said. "The suit was not special. I have it on the word of competent authority that it was an old suit, even a little baggy, that he only wore when he was making his rounds. That's probably why the scalpel was in his pocket."

"Of course, I can understand that," said the retired postmaster. "But he wasn't making rounds when he got killed, was he? I understood he was returning to the hospital and had just gotten off the town bus."

"We never question where the resident doctors go when they are off duty," Jubal said coldly. "They aren't in prison, you know."

"I just wondered."

"If he was wearing an old suit, maybe he was slumming," the insurance agent murmured. "That could explain the scalpel."

Jubal looked livid and Bud said hurriedly, "Now, you know that can't be so. We've got no slums in this town, not even a first-class red-light district."

The school principal said, "Will you have your stenographer go back and read that part where Dr. Herrington said something to the effect that he believed he was the one supposed to be killed?"

"Why, sure." Bud nodded at his stenographer, who in turn cleared her throat nervously, flipped several pages over, found what she wanted and read it aloud in a dry, breathless voice.

"That's it, that's what I wanted. Dr. Herrington, why did you make that statement?"

Lucretia stood up. "I think I can answer that as well as anyone," she called out. "If Dr. Herrington will let me trade places with him—"

There was a general craning of necks and mutterings from the audience. "Well, I don't know." Bud looked at the D.A. perplexedly. "What do we do here? Is it all right for her to clear up someone else's statement?"

"Oh, I think so." Riley drawled. "If Dr. Herrington says it's all right and agrees as to the truth of what she says. No point in being too formal about this. All we're trying to do is let the jury arrive at some definite conclusion so they'll know how to bring in a verdict one way or the other."

Jubal was glad to sit down. He had reached a point at which he could no longer trust himself to speak without antagonizing the jury, and that was the last thing he wanted to do. He went back to his seat and listened to Rufe Tabor's whisper over his shoulder. "What a dumb ass that Bud is. Will I ever make him look sick in my editorial tomorrow!"

"No," Jubal said. "He's dumb like a fox. He's going to get Blayton off. You'll see."

"But why? What kind of an ax has he got to grind?"

"No ax. That scalpel. He can't understand that scalpel."

"So what? Blayton had a gun, didn't he?"

Jubal shrugged and Tabor settled back in his seat. Lucretia had been sworn in and now was seated in the witness chair.

"Now, Miss Terry," Bud said, teetering on his feet and running a hand abstractedly through his hair. "Mr. Marble here used to be principal of our high school, Thaxton High School. He's retired now, but he keeps up with what's going on. Mr. Marble wants to know why Dr. Herrington thinks he was supposed to be the victim the night of the crime. You said you could explain that. Will you do so?"

Lucretia had worn a uniform, feeling it would establish her position. She sat stiff and narrow in the chair, her angular face bleak. "Mr. Nappy," she said crisply, "you are very careful to avoid certain terms, aren't you? For instance, you keep referring to it as the night of the crime. Why don't you say the night Dr. Andreatta was murdered by Jim Blayton?"

"Well, now," Bud said apprehensively, "we can't call it murder until the jury decides that. It was a killing, all right, but if it was justifiable, it was manslaughter and that's something else again." He looked at the District Attorney, who nodded slightly. "Anyway, Andreatta didn't die that night. He died the next morning, right?"

"What difference does that make? You're still quibbling. Jim Blayton clubbed Dr. Andreatta and that's a fact you can't get around, although you've certainly tried to."

There were a few snickers from the spectators. Bud frowned. "Miss Terry," he said gently, "you're putting me on a spot. Okay, I can take it. But you're up here to tell Mr. Marble why you folks at the institution think Dr. Herrington was supposed to be clubbed down by Jim Blayton over there instead of Dr. Andreatta. Believe me, Miss Terry, I never saw a young fellow who looked less like he wanted to club anybody, let alone somebody as important as Dr. Herrington. Suppose you go ahead and give us your version of this affair and I won't interrupt even once."

"You've been very clever, Mr. Nappy, very clever, but I, too, can take it." She stared at him disdainfully for a moment, then shifted her body to face the jury. "Which one of you is Mr. Marble?" When he nodded, she leaned forward, her eyes sharp. "Mr. Marble, what do you know of Canterbury?"

His stare was puzzled. The audience was silent. "I'm sure you know something, but perhaps not a great deal," Lucretia said, her voice carrying throughout the room. "So I will tell you a little about the institution that hires a great many of the people in this town. Every hospital must have certain regulations. A mental hospital very much so. It is absolutely essential to enforce these regulations for the safety and well-being of the patients as well as the employees. Some time ago, Jim Blayton's wife, Mary Elsie, was admitted to Canterbury as a patient. I won't reveal the details of her condition because we never make such disclosures publicly, but if Mr. Nappy cares to clear the auditorium, I will tell the jury exactly what Mary Elsie's trouble was." She waited.

The members of the jury shook their heads and Bud said, "It's all right, Miss Terry. You go right ahead. If necessary, you can tell them later." Then everyone looked at Jim, sitting as though in a trance, his face paper-white.

Lucretia said, "Thank you. Now. One Sunday afternoon, Mary Elsie was visited by her husband. During the course of that visit, a regulation of the hospital was violated. It was of such a nature that we realized we could no longer keep Mary Elsie as a patient. Consequently, Dr. Herrington signed the papers necessary for her release and Jim Blayton took her home. I, Dr. Herrington, others have never doubted for one moment that Jim became very angry over his wife's dismissal. We believe that he brooded over the matter and eventually decided to make Dr. Herrington pay for what had happened. To a man like Jim, such payment would no doubt consist of a terrible beating or something of that nature. It is obvious that Jim was on his way to do violence to Dr. Herrington and was intercepted by poor little Dr. Andreatta, who received the punishment intended for Dr. Herrington and was clubbed to death. This is the sincere belief of all of the staff at Canterbury and also why we feel that Jim must be held for a criminal trial. He is a murderer, Mr. Marble."

The room buzzed with whispers. Bud grabbed his gavel and banged heatedly. "Look here. We've got to have silence. We can't think with all that racket going on." The noise subsided slowly. He stopped glaring and turned his attention to Lucretia. "You said, Miss Terry, that the defendant here decided to punish Dr. Herrington for what happened. What exactly did happen?"

Her hesitation was brief, almost unnoticeable. "Mary Elsie . . . died."

"Died? Did you say died?"

"Yes," she said shortly.

"Well, now, I didn't know that." Puzzled, Bud looked at Jim and then everyone looked at Jim.

"It had nothing to do with Dr. Herrington," Lucretia said, her voice sharp. "She died after she left the hospital. But Jim must have blamed Dr. Herrington, and if he had been the one to get killed, I could have understood that. However, it wasn't Dr. Herrington, it was Dr. Andreatta who was killed. So you see there was no reason for it. It was a senseless thing to do, to club down an innocent man for nothing at all. If you let this killer go free, you are all committing a crime as bad as his. Who knows? Someday he might decide to kill again."

Bud stood behind his desk, feeling a sinking sensation in the pit of his stomach. Jim Blayton's wife dead! Why in God name hadn't he said something about it? Because of course that was the reason he had killed Andreatta. Bud saw the picture clearly. But now it was too late to regain the jury's sympathy. Not one person in the room would be willing to accept what must have really happened. No doubt Andreatta had been the wife's personal doctor. Not for an instant did Bud believe that Jim had killed anyone but the man he had planned to kill. Bud looked around the room and wondered desperately what he could do. He was still teetering, hunting frantically in his mind for straws to clutch at. He realized that if Lucretia went back to her chair and said nothing further, the jury would be ready to wind things up and get away from the heat of the room as fast as they could. But what could he do or say to stop them?

Lucretia gave him a triumphant look and stood up. "Was that what you wanted to know, Mr. Marble?" she asked, turning her face toward the jury. She saw that they looked a little abashed and went back to her seat without waiting for Marble's nod.

"Well," Jonathan said, glancing at the others, "don't see that there's much left to this case. Sounds pretty cut-and-dried now. What do the rest of you think?"

One of the trash haulers cleared his throat. It was an apologetic, meek sound but made them all look at him. "There's something here that ain't quite clear t' me. I usta work out there, you know. Canterbury, I mean. I sure wouldn't want my wife t' be a patient out there. The food's good, of course, and they got regular doctors as well as them other kind and everything's kept real clean. But they lock the doors tight. You can't get in without a pass, you can't take anybody out without one. Don't you kinda think we mebbe oughta find out just what made this Jim Blayton so sore when they wouldn't keep his wife? I mean, I'd been tickled t' death if I'da been in his shoes. It's sure lots harder getting out than getting in, if you know what I mean."

"Maybe he's a tightwad," the insurance agent said. "Maybe it cost him dough to keep his wife at home."

The postmaster looked down his rather long nose. "Don't be an ass," he said distinctly. "The defendant should have picked on somebody his own size when he decided to maul people around. As far as I'm concerned, he's a killer and ought to be hung. Let's get this thing over with and all go home. What do you say?"

Riley hunched himself down in his seat, wishing he could make himself invisible. He avoided looking at Bud. Rufe Tabor sat behind Jubal and swelled a little. He turned to his photographer. You can start taking pictures in a moment, his eyes said. Jubal mopped his face and began to relax. As far as he was concerned, he couldn't get back to the hospital fast enough. At least they had air-conditioning there. The heat in this place was terrible. Must be a hundred at least. He avoided looking at Jim Blayton. Lucretia sat perfectly still. She felt nothing, neither the heat nor the dull ache in her uterus.

In the back of the room there was a stir. A figure was standing. "Sir!" Millie Higgins said hoarsely. "Sir, I'd like to say something." She looked around wildly as faces swung in her direction.

The room was as hushed as though everyone had been

stricken dumb. Only Bud was alive, jerking himself from behind the desk and coming forward to the first row of seats. "What did you say?" he shouted.

She was silent from fright. She could only stare back at him.

"Speak up, lady!" Bud cried.

Someone placed hands on Millie's broad back and shoved. She stumbled forward, righted herself. Another pair of hands pushed her and then another. Unable to protest, she was propelled forward, her mouth working but incapable of uttering a sound. Finally she was within Bud's grasp.

"Come on, come on," he kept saying, his ugly, stubborn face assuring her that she was safe, that she didn't have a thing to fear.

He put his arm around her shoulders and steered her toward Jim. "You know what this is, don't you? It's an inquest and this is the defendant. He's been claiming that the night he killed Miguel Andreatta he was only defending himself, so if you have anything to say that will help clear this all up, we'll be mighty grateful, the jury and myself and Mr. Riley here, the District Attorney. You see, we haven't been quite sure whether Jim's been telling the truth."

He kept pushing her until she stood directly in front of Jim and had to look down at his white, set face. Then he stopped talking and they both were looking down, the room behind them utterly silent. For a moment, Jim gazed up, his face expressionless. That same moment she stared at him. When she looked around at Bud, her fear was gone.

"Yes," she said. "I got something to say. I certainly do have something to say."

Bud grabbed her, whirled her around. "Wait. Let's get you sworn in. I want this all legal. I want it in the testimony records. Here—you just stand right over here. Put your hand on that book."

"Look here!" Jubal roared from his seat. "This woman is an employee of the hospital. She has no right being here to testify!"

Suddenly the room was in an uproar. Bud reached for his gavel. He banged and shouted until order was restored. "Once more," he said, his eyes glittering. "I'm going to tell you once more. You make that kind of racket again and I'll have you all thrown out of here. Which means you'll probably miss out on something that's beginning to sound like it might be about the most interesting thing ever to happen in this town. Do I make myself clear?"

There was an instant hush. Bud turned to Jubal. "I don't believe you understand what an inquest is, Doctor. Anybody is free to come up and testify, one or a dozen. Makes no difference whether they work for you or not."

Lucretia got to her feet. "If this woman testifies, she won't work for us any longer!" she said icily.

It was the wrong thing to say. The crowd looked at her, disliking her instantly for this display of power and authority. Bud felt his heart lift. They had played right into his hands, this doctor and his head nurse. He turned to Millie.

"Now, you've got nothing to worry about," he told Millie. "If you've got anything to say, this is the time and place to say it. If you don't say it, you might never forgive yourself. Know what I mean? Soon as my stenographer swears you in, you sit in that chair and think real carefully just what you want to talk about and then you'll find it comes real easy. After all, if you know something that might save this defendant's life, no job would be worth not telling that, would it?"

She was a fat, shapeless woman. Her shoes were neatly polished but run down from long use. Wisps of hair strayed untidily around the edges of a faded, ancient hat. Her dress was sleazy, obviously a five-ninety-eight from the bargain rack in Sterling's department store. But she looked at him steadily, and there was a dignity about her that was untouchable.

"It won't be easy to tell. It's almost too terrible to talk about. I don't know whether it'll do anybody any good, him most of all." Her glance moved to Jim and back to Bud. "But you're sure right about one thing. I'd never forgive myself if I didn't tell it, because it's something I should have told a long time ago."

She turned and looked at the roomful of people, then she looked at the jury. She bent her head and listened to the hush. She shrugged a little. "I don't think there's a man in this room wouldn't have done what Jim did," she said, and turned back to be sworn in.

CHAPTER 43

"You NUT, you crazy nut!" Ruth said. "They won't even let you in here."

"Nobody told me not to come," Millie said doggedly. "I figured I'd keep right on coming to work until somebody says I'm fired."

She and Ruth were walking up the sidewalk to Rehabilitation. After the inquest was over and she had gone home, she had waited the rest of the day for the telephone to ring, but it never had. She had not even gone to bed but had taken what she called cat naps on the lumpy sofa in the living room. If the phone rang, she would be sure to hear it there, so she had waited nervously for an order to report to the office. Then, when it never came, and daylight was finished and a very faint touch of coolness was setting in, she decided there was nothing to be gained by waiting. She would go to work just as if nothing had happened. The next move was up to Lucretia Terry and Dr. Herrington, not her.

However, she was dreadfully tired—from sitting so long in those stingy chairs, she told herself, or else trying to sleep on the sofa. Every time she moved she almost fell off, it was so hard and narrow. And Ruth had scolded her without mercy, calling her every kind of name for what she had done, making her want to cry, because she hadn't done wrong, she knew she hadn't. Getting up in front of that crowd and telling the truth had been the only right thing she'd done in a long time. Ruth oughtn't to make her feel so cheap about it; she felt bad enough remembering the whole miserable experience and knowing that her job was finished. Maybe Miss Terry hadn't called her on the phone; maybe she'd be allowed to finish out the week, even the month. But the job was over; she knew that because she could still see the way they had looked at her, Terry and Herrington. And she had looked right back. She had dared to defy them.

"You'll see," Ruth said bitterly. "They'll meet you at the door and give you your walking papers."

She was angry. She did not want Millie fired. She didn't want anything bad to happen to Millie. She had grown to love Millie the way close sisters love each other or mothers love children. She had even made a will, leaving everything she had to Millie. But that wouldn't be worth a thing until she was dead, and since they were so close in age, Millie might die first and never know that Ruth had loved her enough to do such a thing. To Ruth, charity wasn't worth a damn if you had to make a production out of it.

"I told you, didn't I?" she said bitterly. "I told you over and over. Keep your mouth shut. You'll only get canned for your trouble. My God, Millie, don't you have any sense at all?"

"Well, I don't care. It got him off, didn't it? What I said. You know something, Ruthie? They—they clapped when I went back to my seat. I could hardly believe my ears. The people on either side—two ladies, they was—they said, good for you, good for you."

"Millie! Those two ladies gonna pay your bills, huh? They gonna make the payments on your house and the taxes?"

"I don't care. You—you don't understand. I hadda do it."

"You hadda do it. You hadda get up there and shoot off your mouth and throw away a perfectly good job. I knew I shoulda gone along when you asked me. I knew you'd get into trouble."

They had finally reached the front doors of Rehabilitation. "Well, here we are," Ruth said heavily. "Here we are."

They stopped and stared at the heavy doors uncertainly, as though somehow there must be an answer to everything in the panels of glass and structural steel.

"Okay," Millie said, making a desperate effort to hide her uneasiness. "What are we waiting for? We'll be late if we ain't careful."

Ruth turned to look at her. "You mean that matters now?" Her voice was incredulous.

"It matters far's you're concerned, don't it?"

"Oh, Lord!"

"Well, no point in you getting in the doghouse, too, is there? Maybe—maybe you oughtn't t' act like we come together. Why don't you go in kinda by yourself, huh? You know. We can speak but don't act—well, chummy, if you know what I mean."

Ruth's look turned to one of pure disgust. She gripped Millie's arm and punched the bell that would bring someone with keys to let them in. "Goddam you!" she said. "I did come with you and I'm gonna stay with you. Like I shoulda this morning. You need a wet nurse about like a week-old baby. Get this through your thick head. I am your friend and no goddam old Lucretia Terry's gonna put a stop to that. I wouldn't stop being your friend for all the jobs in all the hospitals in every state in the union. Nobody can go through trouble alone, Millie—nobody. I know."

Millie could not speak. She had tried hard to keep from knowing how afraid she was, almost as much afraid as she had been that morning when she stood in front of that whole roomful of staring faces. Yet it had ended the right way, hadn't it? At this moment it was just as clear in her mind as though it were happening again.

She had been sworn in; she was seating herself in the witness chair. The jury was watching her. Bud was prancing—she could think of no other word for it—prancing like a horse just finished eating his oats. The crowd was rubbering like mad. Rubbernecks! she thought. In a minute she'd hear the rubber snap. Lucretia and Jubal were like icicles, all stiff and frozen and white. They—they ain't much different from the patients, she thought, bewildered; staring like they didn't have good sense, most of them! Then she was a little ashamed. I was staring, too, she remembered. Just like everybody else.

That Bud! You'da thought she had given him a Christmas present, the way he looked at her. Calling her "Mrs. Higgins," just like she wasn't dirt poor and had to work for a living! It helped her most of all to get over the worst part of her story, telling about what actually happened in Mary Elsie's room that night she had seen Andreatta in there, especially when the jury and the District Attorney started asking questions. "Mrs. Higgins!" You're Mrs. Higgins, a taxpayer. You help to support schools and city government. You count. Believe us, you count.

He got mad, too, that Bud did. He said that if the District Attorney had known about Andreatta, he probably would have sent him to prison.

But the crowd! Hanging on every word that came out of her mouth! Even when she was so ashamed, the words had to be dragged out by Bud almost by force. How clever he'd been, talking, talking, then suddenly slipping in a question that she answered almost before she knew a question had been asked.

"Mrs. Higgins, suppose this Mary Elsie had been your daughter. Just suppose she had been. Here's this young, pretty girl locked up in a room. She can't get out, can she?"

"Of course not. She's not supposed to get out."

"But anybody can get in—isn't that what you said? Anybody can go into her room?"

"Anybody who turns the doorknob. The doorknobs are on the outside of the doors."

"So you went down the dark hall, you saw the light, you looked through the little window in the door and you saw Dr. Andreatta. Tell the jury again. It was Dr. Andreatta you saw and it was Mary Elsie's room he was in."

"Yessir. He was in there. Both of 'em. And naked—naked as newborn babies."

"Yes, naked as newborn babies. But not babies, not babies at all. A mature man, a young girl old enough to be married, an obsessed girl, who masturbated on the furniture, didn't you say?"

"Yessir," said Millie, her voice low, her face averted in shame.

"How long did you watch these two naked people?" Bud's voice cut through the deathly silence of the room.

"Not long—long enough." Millie had to stop and reach for breath.

"Long enough for what?" Bud roared.

"Do—do I hafta say?"

"Yes, yes!"

She lifted her eyes to the jury. "He did everything he could," she whispered, her breath in agony in her chest. "First he did it the right way—I mean, like folks usually—" She stopped and swallowed, and saw that they knew what she meant. "Then he—he—" She gagged and sought for control.

"Then he committed abnormal acts!" shouted Bud, striding up and down. "He committed the acts of a depraved animal, isn't that what you mean? Isn't that what you're trying to tell us?"

"Don't put words in her mouth," commented Riley from his seat but without much emphasis.

"Yes," Millie whispered. "I—I couldn't watch any more. I—it made me sick at my stomach. I ran—I ran down the hall."

Bud looked at the jury and then at Riley. "Does that sound as though I put words in her mouth? Does it?"

"No," Riley said, shrugging.

"No," said most of the jury.

Then that silence, that terrible, terrible silence, like nothing she could think of. Jubal and Lucretia sat as though turned to stone. What could they say? They hadn't known? Who would believe that they did not know what went on in Canterbury?

The crowd. Shocked, thrilled, avid for details, identifying themselves subconsciously with something wanton and horrible, reacted to Bud's indignation and the District Attorney's cold condemnation. Good enough for him, he got what was coming to him, was now their collective opinion about Andreatta's death.

The jury was calm about it. "Don't see any reason to prolong this," Jonathan Greene said, the other five nodding. "Guess we all feel the same." He looked at them for confirmation he knew he did not need. "Clear case of a fellow taking care of his homework, far as we can see."

"Self-defense?" Bud cried.

"There's a point here—" Riley began but he didn't have a chance.

The jury members stared at him coolly. "Self-defense," they said together.

"Oh, well." Self-defense, justifiable manslaughter—was there too much difference here? As long as the verdict was unanimous, he might as well string along. He guessed the hospital wouldn't say anything, especially after their own employee's testimony. "We might as well acquit. Does anyone move for an acquittal?"

"I do so move," said Jonathan, not looking around this time.

"Okay. Direct acquittal it is, then."

And it was over. Millie went back to her seat, sat down, saw that everyone was up, beginning to mill around. The women on either side bent over her. "Good for you, good for you," they said.

Bud came back, pushing, ignoring outheld hands. "Wondered where you went to. Come on up here. They want to take your picture."

"No, no!" she almost whimpered. "Just lemme go home. I hafta go home." She was going to be sick very soon.

"Sure, sure. You did a fine thing, Mrs. Higgins. This town won't forget it, believe me." He shielded her from the camera. If she didn't want her picture taken, then by God she didn't have to have it taken. "You go straight home and get some rest." Then he went back to Jim, crowded back behind the desk, staring with enormous eyes at the hands that thrust themselves at him to be shaken. As though he had earned a reward!

"Get me outa here!" Jim gritted.

"You bet," Bud glowed. "You're a free man. No reason you shouldn't leave anytime you want to."

"Get me outa here!" Jim was panic-stricken.

"I'll help him," a voice said at Bud's elbow. "I've got a car outside." It was Mike Stewart, still shaken from the turn of events. He could guess what Jim's reaction at the moment must be, the horror that people finally knew what had happened to his wife. Yet surely there was relief now that he could escape from everything.

By using a kind of football formation they made it to the car. "Good luck," said Bud, his face very sober, his eyes dark with sympathy.

"Come around if there's anything I can do," said Riley.

Behind them were others. "You lose your job at the mills, you come to me," Jonathan said.

Mr. Marble interjected, "He won't lose his job. What're you talking about?"

"Where to—your home?" Mike asked.

Panic swept into Jim's face. "No, they'll all be there, all them people! Anyway, I got no home. It's up for sale."

Mike stared at him somberly. "How about the recruiting station?" he said suddenly. "You ever thought about that? The naval recruiting station?"

There was a deep hush, a moment of concentrated thinking. "Yeah," Jim said slowly. "Yeah. Maybe that would be all right."

"You want me to drive you there?"

After another silence Jim nodded. "Yeah," he said. "You might as well."

He did not look at Millie Higgins, who was standing on the curb, watching him.

In front of Rehabilitation's doors, Millie waited. As long as Ruth felt the way she did, she wasn't alone.

She felt Ruth's tight clutch with unbelieving gratitude. Not a penny saved! Catastrophe! Yet as long as Ruth was there, someone who cared, she guessed she could take it.

Then not a word was said. The two women were let in by an attendant who yawned and said she was glad it was getting time to go home.

The supervisor had nothing to say either. Not a word.

"Tomorrow," Ruth said when they got to their wards. "They're probably short of help tonight. You'll hear tomorrow."

"Probably," agreed Millie, but with a little surge of hope. Maybe they weren't going to fire her. Maybe they *needed* her.

CHAPTER 44

JUST LIKE LAST NIGHT, Kathy thought. I came on duty, we barely spoke, she went off duty, I read the ledger. Edna was upset, Althea had said, and she was still menstruating. And there was a full moon.

Kathy read the ledger again, four pages written up on the day's activities, one page for seven wards, three pages for Edna Horne on the other ward. Ward Five. It hardly seemed real, Edna doing the same things all over again, breaking a chair in the morning, trying to choke a patient to death in the afternoon, settling down finally in the evening. Shock, sodium luminal, angry attendants. Donovan coming, ordering shock—she thought of Donovan with a little inner stab, because tonight the name meant so little. What had he done about her letter? Why wasn't he doing anything? Perhaps he felt there would be no point in doing anything after all this time.

She would have to check early again and she hated that, too. She was supposed to check at certain specified times, and she was not supposed to change a schedule set by the office. Of course, the office granted a certain amount of leeway, but if anything went wrong they would demand an accounting of every minute of her night. Still, she felt she could not afford to disregard the warning unconsciously written into the ledger. What if Edna did sleep like a lamb at night? What if she had seen that with her own eyes the night before? This was another night, and with mentally disturbed people there were no valid rules.

If I didn't think about myself so much, these things probably wouldn't seem so sinister, she thought angrily. I'm the one who's disturbed and upset.

Also, she was thinking about the inquest and Mary Elsie and Dr. Andreatta. All afternoon and evening gossip had been running riot about the inquest and how it had ended. Of course a lot was added to it that hadn't been said, but Mike had been waiting for her when she walked over to the cafeteria for her supper and he had told her the facts, watching her so intently that she hadn't eaten very much. He finished the story and then put his hand over one of hers.

"You're thinking about this morning, aren't you? Well, nothing happened. You went to sleep before I got you up to your room, but Mrs. Robinson and her eagle eyes kept me from doing anything improper, like undressing and then crawling into bed with you, which is what I very much wanted to do."

"Okay," she said breathlessly.

"Sorry. Don't know why I say things like that. I mean them, of course, and you know I mean them, but crudeness shouldn't be confused with romance. How long did you sleep?"

"I woke up at three. The best sleep I've had since I started nights, really."

"But you're tired and you feel you should be rested. I know. Sometimes the less sleep you have, the better you seem to get along."

"Yes."

They were silent a moment. "Maybe you just don't eat enough," he said gently, looking at her barely touched plate. "And drink too much coffee," he added.

"I need a dog," she said. "I could put my plate down on the floor when nobody's looking, and he'd clean it up for me."

"I'd like to think you need me. You need a husband and a home and several kids with my health and your good looks."

"You never told me that before."

"Really, Kathy. You never fished before." He watched her flush. "You're beautiful, darling. Every inch of you."

"Well, I certainly asked for that," she said helplessly.

"Will you do something for me tomorrow?"

She eyed him warily. "What?"

"Will you ask for tomorrow night off? There's a ballet coming to the local theater and I want to go. I've seen it before—it's an English ballet movie in color. I think you'd like it. I did, enough to want to see it again. We could go to dinner first. There's only one performance, just like a concert.

Eight o'clock. How about it?"

It was crazy, but suddenly she did want to go. She hadn't been to a movie in a long time.

She looked at him, her eyes bright. "I'll try," she said. "I mean I'll ask."

"First thing in the morning?"

"First thing."

"Good! I'll get tickets."

Now she was not sure of anything. Meeting Althea had done it, that glacial stare penetrating her thoughts, troubling her. Well, right now she was going to check Rehabilitation, all four floors. Maybe she'd check four times instead of twice during the night. Maybe she'd even call up Mike, ask him to come over and keep her company. She'd do something, anything.

She grabbed up her things a little wildly and left her office. She checked the other wards first, leaving Five and Six for last, Five where Edna slept, Six where she must give an envelope to Millie, containing a notice of dismissal.

That, too, she realized, was part of the reason for her disturbed emotions, having to be the one who must let Millie know that her services were no longer wanted in Canterbury. Although the note was unsealed, she hadn't read it as most supervisors would have done, reasoning that it was their prerogative to know what it said, because she couldn't bring herself to have any part of what was being done to Millie. It isn't fair, she thought. I shouldn't be the one to tell her she's fired; someone in the office should have that responsibility. When she reached the third floor on her rounds, she unlocked the door of Five and grimly let herself in. It seemed easier to cope with the problem of Edna than the problem of Millie.

It's like seeing an old movie again, she told herself as she entered Ruth's office, Ruth getting up promptly and standing aside for her to sit down at the desk. Even Ruth's expression was the same as it had been the night before, dignified and composed and just faintly curious, while she herself was apologetic and muttered something about being early again. Almost the identical words. An hour. Hot, ain't it? Sorry, the report's not finished, nowhere near finished. Then on to the discussion of Edna, the problem of Edna, Edna sleeping like a lamb. It was almost eerie.

Edna's pattern for the day had been almost the same as the day before, her medication the same, her therapy, her reaction. Now they would find her sleeping peacefully in the last room at the end of the corridor.

There was one slight change in the conversation between

Kathy and Ruth. "Too bad she's way down here," Ruth whispered after they had walked the length of the corridor and were standing in Edna's doorway. Ruth's light pointed toward the ceiling where the glow could deflect downward yet not disturb the sleeping patient. Immediately Ruth realized how her remark must sound and added in haste, "But Miss Horne, the day supervisor, ordered it. Miss Horne said Edna would probably sleep better away from all the noise up front, the doors banging and toilets flushing and all. Course, there's no doubt about Horne—Miss Horne—knowing what to do for her own cousin, I guess, putting Edna way down here and all."

Kathy saw the point of the change. There was always a lot of noise toward the front of any ward where patients were permitted to get drinks and go to the toilet. Naturally, the ends of the corridors were quieter. Still, after two such disturbed days as Edna had experienced, was it wise to let her sleep so far from supervision?

She looked around, observing the massive steel fire-exit door directly across from Edna's room. A small light gleamed on the wall above the door. The light was not bright but it spread a faint, pink glow across Edna's bed. Kathy stared uneasily as she listened to Edna's heavy, regular breathing. Why should the pink light be so disturbing?

"I could move Edna," Ruth said with what she hoped was just the right amount of reluctance. "Switch beds, you know. Millie'd be glad to help me."

Kathy caught the reluctance. Move this patient, wake her and hope she doesn't go off into another tantrum? Takes six to eight women to handle her, remember, six to eight—

She shook her head. Edna was sleeping. It would be silly to wake her.

"I'll admit I don't like her being down here so far from your office," she whispered. "But she does seem to be heavily sedated." Curiosity stirred. "Did you shut her door last night?"

"Of course not!" Ruth whispered indignantly.

"Well, I'll get an order for you to do it tonight. A seclusion order is all we need, then everybody will be safe. It would be silly to disturb her and the rest of the ward as well by moving beds around at this time of night when the other would take care of everything."

Ruth's relief was almost tangible. She turned off the flashlight and the two women returned to the office. Kathy scrawled her name and the time of her visit in the ward book and prepared to leave. "Remember, don't go down the hall alone until I call you about a seclusion order on Edna," she cautioned.

301

"Oh, never!" Ruth said, both politely and emphatically. As soon as Kathy was out of sight, she slipped off her shoes, pulled off her cap, settled herself in the desk chair, cigarettes and matches handy, feet propped on the edge of an open drawer and the telephone pulled close for the hourly call to Hazel, the night switchboard operator. This was the way she planned to spend as much of the night as she could, her chin sinking solidly to her chest, yet still able from somewhere in her subconscious to reach out a hand and pick up the receiver each hour to report to Hazel.

The similarity of Edna's two days had not struck her with any force. She had thought last night, like tonight, that she was in for a bad time. Changing patients from room to room at night wasn't any joke. Either it meant moving beds with all the lights turned on, or cleaning units before changing patients from one bed to another. A lot of work any way you looked at it. Probably not a patient would have gone back to sleep if Kathy had insisted on its being done. But Kathy had been sensible and come up with a better solution. A seclusion order would be just the thing. Why did she ask me if I shut Edna's door last night? she wondered. Did she think I'd go ahead and do it on my own without an order? Well, it's an idea at that. Why didn't I? Why don't I right now?

But she was too comfortable to move. Nice little Miss Hunter, she thought sleepily. So thoughtful and considerate, actually making a person feel important and worthwhile. "Like my opinion was every bit as good as anybody's," Ruth said aloud.

Unhappy, too, she thought. Maybe she needs a boy friend. All girls need boy friends. All us women need men, she told herself, her chin sinking finally to her chest.

Kathy did not stay long on Six. She checked the ward with Millie after reading the ward book, and when they returned to the station she placed the envelope on the desk without comment. She knew that she should ask Millie if she wanted to discuss the letter or receive any advice about the matter, but after she saw the look of hopelessness in Millie's eyes she could not bring herself to say anything.

After the first deep shock of seeing the letter, Millie composed herself. She politely escorted Kathy to the ward door, unlocked it to let her out and shut and relocked it. Then she returned to her station, her steps slow and plodding and reluctant. She did not want to read the letter. She sat down at her desk and looked at the white envelope out of the corner of her eye. Maybe if she just didn't pay it any attention she would suddenly discover she had imagined it, that it wasn't really there. Automatically she glanced up at the ward clock.

In a little while it would be time for her and Ruth to check their wards. Ruth would notice the letter right off. You couldn't hide anything from Ruth, not if you were her friend, because she was that way; she looked out for her friends; she was always wanting to know if things were right or not right; she even pried a little bit. Millie stopped thinking for a full second. Then she shook her head. It was no use. She couldn't keep on stalling. She might as well get it over with and read it. And hide it, put it away. Why not? Ruth wouldn't have to know tonight. Tomorrow would be time enough to tell her.

She read the note, then reread it. Her notice. One sentence stuck in her mind. "Above all qualities, loyalty in an employee is essential and you are sadly lacking in that quality."

Yes, she thought bitterly, she was not loyal. She had told.

CHAPTER 45

WHEN SHE GOT BACK to her office, Kathy moved restlessly about. She was more worried than ever. She had realized suddenly how very young and inexperienced she was. She would probably not know how to handle an emergency if one arose. The knowledge that she was responsible for the welfare of so many people was almost appalling when it was balanced against the cold fact of her inexperience and youth. To relieve her anxiety she tried to concentrate on something outside her job. There was Mike's invitation to a movie and the way he had carried her upstairs and put her to bed. There was his faithful, daily proposal. But she felt no relief.

It was Edna who was causing the trouble, Kathy realized. Edna was very dangerous, very volatile, and the night was hot and charged with currents of tension. But Edna was disturbed last night, Kathy thought, and nothing unusual happened. She had spent the night peacefully sleeping just as Ruth had promised she would. Tonight she was the same. But the danger was still there. Kathy was certain of it, and she felt ashamed and confused because she had been staring at the telephone for the last five minutes. She knew that Donovan was the logical doctor to call for Edna's seclusion order. She had no right to take chances, to be careless with her job, just because two evenings ago she had forced herself on him by deliberately undressing in his bedroom and inviting him to go to bed with her. Was that a good reason to ignore the warning about Edna she read in the records?

Regardless of what he would think, she had to call him.

Taking a deep breath, she reached for the telephone and lifted the receiver. When Hazel answered, she asked for an outside line and then dialed Donovan's apartment. She was listening to the ringing at the other end when there was a click and to her astonishment a woman answered.

Before she could stop herself she said, "Dr. Macleod, please," and waited, feeling foolish, to be told she had the wrong number.

But the voice returned with superb composure. "Dr. Macleod? Of course. Just a moment." Then there was another click and Kathy realized the connection had been broken.

She sat immobile from shock for several seconds. Althea! She had just heard Althea's voice on Donovan's telephone!

She didn't know which shocked her more, having the connection broken or the realization that Althea, at long last, was back in Donovan's untidy living room with its stacks of books and magazines and its general clutter. Althea and Donovan together at last! She wouldn't have believed it if she hadn't known that husky, throbbing voice so well.

Her next sensation was one of fantastic relief, fantastic because it had never occurred to her just how she would feel if Althea went back to Donovan. This must be the answer to her letter! This must be the first thing Donovan had done after reading it. He had set things right between Althea and himself! If so—if so, he wouldn't be too harsh with Kathy, probably.

She felt as if she had received a last-minute Presidential pardon. It's not over by a long shot, she thought, tears in her eyes, but I can see daylight for the first time. She stood up dizzily, took Edna's folder and turned toward the file cabinet. Then she came to her senses and sat down again. She must be out of her mind, she thought incoherently. She hadn't done anything yet about Edna. She had the folder out because she intended to study it. In spite of the abrupt feeling of intoxication and headiness, there was no reason not to study it. Edna was still there. Determinedly she opened the folder and forced herself to begin reading. She turned the pages hurriedly, wanting to finish them and get them out of the way. Then to her surprise she realized that her attention was being caught by a sentence here, a word there. She began to read the reports very carefully. And it began to seem to her that there was a pattern, almost a plan, in Edna's madness.

For a full minute she sat motionless. No, the story she had just read was peculiar but there was nothing that couldn't stand examination or couldn't be explained in a rational way. When a certain time of the month came around, Edna always got upset. She wasn't triggered this time by someone clever enough to know what it took to set her off.

But instantly a sharp thought pressed. How do I know it's Edna's period? It isn't mentioned on her daily chart. And the hospital insists that we keep careful record of such things.

A weary, hopeless confusion took the place of her former excitement. Had she discovered something peculiar in Edna's story or had she imagined it? She looked at the wall clock and saw that it was her usual time for checking the wards. In less than five minutes she would ordinarily be unlocking the door to Ward Five and walking in. She had never varied the pattern of this check until last night and tonight, when she had just done it on a whim. Nobody could have guessed that she was going to change her routine.

She put her head down and pressed a forefinger into each temple. Think, think! What is there about this business of Edna that makes you believe something is wrong? Is it because you aren't too sure she really is menstruating, or is it because she's become upset in identically the same way for two successive days? Why should that indicate anything out of the ordinary? Edna's insane, she follows a pattern. But the nagging worry was there and she couldn't get around it, couldn't find reason in it. The pattern seemed right, but she had been taught that no two outbursts from any patient were ever completely identical.

Edna was triggered! she thought in horror. In a few moments—the time when Kathy was supposed to be checking Ward Five—Edna would be ready and waiting for her. There simply was no other explanation for all the odd little things done and written into the records. *But what about Althea! She isn't in the building. She's in Donovan's apartment!*

Althea doesn't have to be in the building, Kathy said to herself.

She set things up before she left. That's all she had to do! And Edna isn't even in restraint. She's free as a bird to do whatever comes into her mind!

But why you? How could it possibly be you?

Because there's a chance, even if it's a remote one, that I might be handy when Edna starts to explode!

Then why didn't it happen last night?

Because Edna wasn't quite ready. It took two days to make her ready!

Ruth! she thought.

Kathy clawed for the telephone. "Hazel!" she gasped. "This is Kathy Hunter again. Send help! Fast! Yes, yes, help! Ward Five! I haven't time to explain."

She dropped the receiver and rushed for the elevator.

Hazel would alert all the wards in the building, and attendants would converge on Ward Five as fast as humanly possible, but she did not dare wait for them.

She fumbled for keys, damning them and all locks because her fingers were so stiff with terror that she could not find the right key, much less get it quickly into a lock. Then as if to add to her terror, the elevator was somewhere above and had to come down before she could use it. It seemed to take an eternity in spreading its doors apart and in closing them after she got inside, and another eternity to reach the third floor. Dear God, she said half aloud, don't let me be too late!

CHAPTER 46

A FEW MOMENTS EARLIER, Ruth lifted the receiver of her telephone, waited for Hazel's routine "Yes?" and said without enthusiasm, "Ward Five, Ruth Ellison speaking."

This duty out of the way, she ground out her cigarette and went to the toilet. When she washed her hands, she discovered that the water was only lukewarm and wondered whether it would eventually run hot enough to make a cup of instant coffee. Leaving the tap open enough to permit a small trickle through, she returned to her desk for her flashlight and padded off the ward to join Millie on Six.

They always checked Millie's ward first since it had two untidies who usually needed dry bedding. Millie could not relax as long as she had the discomfort of clammy, wet beds to think about, and Ruth didn't care which ward got the first check.

They found one damp bed, which they changed swiftly, disposing of the soiled linen afterward in a laundry bag. Then they washed their hands and went to Five.

Ruth stepped along briskly. The ward was quiet, the night reasonably young. She had no medications to give until five in the morning. With any luck she would have ample time for a good rest. She reached Edna's room a few paces ahead of Millie, who was checking another cubicle, and went inside, her flashlight pointed at the ceiling while she observed the mound in Edna's bed. The covers were high but the incongruity of this on a hot summer night did not alarm her. Even the deep silence, the complete lack of noise, did not seem ominous. If Edna were not snoring or breathing audibly, it only meant that she was still deep in her sedation.

Ruth stared long enough to convince herself that she detected respiratory action in the mound. Then she lowered her light and turned. At that moment a pair of thin but incredibly strong arms reached out around her neck and pulled furiously tight. Dumfounded, she tried to swerve and only succeeded in losing the flashlight. It dropped without sound onto the bed.

Her first thought was instinctive and protective. *Millie, Millie, don't come, get away, get away!* She meant that Millie should not try to help her because it would be too dangerous. But almost with the thought, Ruth realized that she could get no sound past the grip on her throat.

She was on the edge of panic, yet she still did not fully understand the moment's reality. What was happening just could not be possible. She had stepped into a nightmare of some kind. It must be a game! Of course! Edna was playing a game. If she had chosen a poor time for it, it was only because time meant so little to her. Sure, sure, that was it: Edna wanted to play. She was lonely. But how could she convince Edna that a game could go too far when her power to object was cut off by a stranglehold on her throat? She began thrashing and twisting, fighting for breath, but Edna on her back kept thrashing and twisting with her, apparently able to anticipate her moves while the thin arms grew tighter and more merciless.

She filled with frenzy. It wasn't the pain from the iron grip that bothered her as much as the way her tormented lungs ached for air.

Then she went from frenzy to full terror, gagging and struggling against the terrible pressure on her throat. The blood began to pound in her head and ears. Now she wanted Millie to come, not to endanger herself but to distract Edna long enough to save her.

Vomit came into her throat but it stayed just at the edge of the iron band. A thick, syrupy lassitude began to creep into her hands and feet. There was a hot dribbling of urine between her legs.

As the pounding in her head turned into a continuous, rushing roar, her silent shrieks and pleas ended. The thrashing and jerking of her limbs became convulsive. When her tongue began to push out between her teeth, she was no longer aware of the transition from conscious muscular activity to the paroxysms of approaching death. If she had had one last thought, it might have been that it had taken a dreadfully long time to die.

Several steps away, Millie's attention was caught by a gentle thump. Mildly perplexed, she moved to Edna's doorway. While her eyes were straining intently into the gloom, her fingers reached automatically for the light switch. She saw Edna standing on the other side of the bed with Ruth lying on the floor at her feet. At the sight of Ruth's ravaged face Millie was filled first with bewilderment.

Then came the impact of the shock. Her face turned the color of gray putty, but she did not scream. She couldn't scream because it was as though a fist had been rammed into her mouth. She stared at Edna, at the expressionless eyes. She wanted to scream with pure fury, to jump on Edna and carry her to the floor and gouge out those black eyes, to stamp with her feet until Edna was ground into a mass of blood and gore. That's all Edna was fit for. She was only fit to be mashed to pulp. In this moment Millie was insane with her rage, savage with it.

Then the moment passed and she came to her senses. Whatever she felt like doing to Edna in that bitter surge of hate would not undo Ruth's death. It might spoil all decent sorrow forever. When she wept for her friend, she might find herself crying also for this crazy creature who had never had a chance to be a friend to anyone nor had ever had a friend herself. Why, I can't hate Edna, she thought bewilderedly. She ain't to blame. She don't know what's she done. She *can't* know!

Now she realized she must start thinking, and fast. She did not dare to gather Ruth up in her arms. If she made one out-of-the-way motion, she would live no longer than Ruth had. But she must live. If she were dead, who would see to it that Ruth was given a decent burial? Who would be there to mourn? She wasn't concerned for her own life or own burial. That would be the least of her problems if she were dead. But Ruth—who cared about Ruth? Who gave her a single thought?

Here was danger, deadly danger, this crazy Edna who was always wanting to beat something with a chair rung or choke somebody to death with her hands. With her hands, twisted and useless-looking from scar tissue, that were as strong as hemp rope.

The incredible thought came to Millie that this was finally her punishment. She had put Harry to sleep because she hadn't been able to endure the sight of his suffering any longer, but it hadn't been her right to do such a thing. That lay with a higher power. Now Ruth had been taken from her and in such a terrible manner that she would know forever and forever whose right she had stolen and used. You really knew the depth of hell when someone you loved was made to pay for what you had done.

Yet she had to stay alive. She had to take care of Ruth. Proper care of what was left of Ruth. Ruthie, she thought with a sick shuddering beginning in the pit of her stomach. Ruthie, my friend!

The tears began rolling down her face and she couldn't summon up the concentration to decide what to do. Edna hadn't moved. She stood in exactly the same position, even to her outstretched hands. Her eyelids were wide apart and unflickering.

"Get back into bed," Millie whispered through lips that felt like iron strips around the opening of her mouth. "Back in bed, you hear? You'll catch cold."

She used the phrase unconsciously, then realized she had said it and even how ridiculous it sounded to be giving such admonishment to a mad woman on a hot summer night. But Edna didn't know the seasons any longer. She lived in a world of her own. The muscles in her cheeks twitched at Millie's words, but she did not move.

She can't hear me. I ain't getting through to her, Millie thought apprehensively. "The Lord is my shepherd, I shall not want," she said aloud. She couldn't recall the rest, only this beginning, but she said it over and over in a soft mumble. "The Lord is my shepherd, I shall not want"— over and over, like the drip from a broken faucet. The sweat ran steadily down between her breasts and down the small of her back. She was only faintly aware that she was sweating or that she was mumbling.

Edna, she thought, didn't you hear what I said? She stopped her muttering and said aloud, "Get back in bed, Edna."

Involuntarily she looked at the bed. The bed looked as though it held a body. It was too much; it was the final straw. Millie knew she had to discover the meaning of the mound. No terror was high enough or wide enough to stop her from finding out what was hidden in Edna's bed.

She tried a slow, careful step. Edna did not move. She tried another step. Still Edna was motionless. A third step and Millie was close enough to the bed for her purpose. She let one hand come away from her side but so carefully it scarcely seemed to move. She managed to get two fingers on either side of a little fold in the top cover. With the two fingers she pulled and slipped and eased until an inch of bedding had been shifted. Then she saw all she needed to see. A tightly rolled blanket had been used to create the deceptive mound in the bed. Edna had done this to her blanket and her bed. Edna who was as crazy as they come had craftily rigged the bed to make it look occupied! Anyone who looked at the bed in the dark would have believed the bed held a living, sound-asleep body.

Careful, careful, Millie thought hazily. This Edna ain't so crazy after all, maybe.

"Why, it's just an old blanket, just an old blanket!"

Stunned, she looked at Edna and swallowed. Did she

believe that Edna was really smart enough to think up such a thing? Never in God's earth—never! But what was she to think?

"You fixed that real nice," she stammered.

She swallowed again and stared at the glazed eyes. I got to beat her to the door, she thought wildly. I gotta get outa here before she gets me! The saliva flowed thickly into Millie's mouth.

"So nice," she whispered heavily. "Like it was your dolly, your baby. Whoever showed you such a trick?"

She stared despairingly at Edna, at the shining, depthless eyes, and knew it was no good. She would never make it, she would never get out of the room alive. Someone else would have to bury Ruth and shed tears beside her grave. She would never get to do it because Edna was poised, tense, waiting, her hands already beginning to spread and lift.

The second I take a step, she'll be on top of me, Millie thought. I've only got one advantage. I'm facing her and the light's on. But in spite of knowing the advantage, panic surged in sick waves. It was judgment, judgment! Judgment for Harry, and all the bars of soap and hospital towels and cans of food taken home and the blankets given to old, sick women when Charlotte Range had expressly ordered her not to pamper old, sick women. It was getting up before practically the whole town and letting everybody know some of the things that went on in Canterbury—judgment for all of it!

She pulled in all the breath she could and bunched her muscles, calling on every last ounce of her courage. Her eyes never left Edna's face. Another second, another second, then give it all you've got, she told herself. Then Edna lifted her arms high and Millie's heart gave a furious lunge and almost stopped beating entirely. The next second she heard an unbelievable sound—the turning of keys in distant locks.

Millie almost screamed. She could have fainted from the abrupt, sudden release of muscles as the terrible tension between her shoulders relaxed. She was dizzy and nauseated, but she stood without moving until six people burst into the room. Then her broad body sagged until she was kneeling heavily over the body on the floor.

Kathy was the first one of the six women to enter the room. Silently she knelt beside Millie. She was too shocked and horrified to speak. She saw instantly that Ruth was beyond help. Ruth would never need either help or pity again.

Swiftly the other women surrounded Edna. In a matter of seconds they had her flat on the bed, her wrists and ankles cuffed and strapped to the frame of the bed. They were neither

310

rough nor cruel. They fluffed her pillow, placed it neatly under her head and drew the sheet over her body to her armpits. They unrolled the blanket, squared and folded it and returned it to her bedside stand. Then they took her bedspread, stretched it flat on the floor and stood in a silent, absorbed circle around Ruth for a moment before they carefully lifted her and placed her on the spread. Finally they looked at Kathy, still kneeling beside Millie. When Kathy indicated by shaking her head and looking up at them mutely that she could not speak, they took the spread by its corners and slowly pulled it and its burden out into the hall.

Just like that, Millie thought dully. One minute we was coming down the hall, Ruthie and me. Now she's going back and she's dead.

She put her hands over her face, her nose showing between the palms, her mouth open but making no sound while a flood of tears ran through her fingers. Kathy, still kneeling, put her arms around Millie and thought from a depth of terrible weariness, What are we doing here on the floor?

Edna looked at the two women on the floor near her bed. The small, dark one resembled someone or something she tried to recall from a remote, very dim past. Unconsciously she pressed against her restraints, but they did not yield. After a second or so, she gave up. Her tensed muscles relaxed. Then the two women got up and left the room, the dark one passing from sight last by turning out the light and closing the door.

CHAPTER 47

EARLY THAT SAME EVENING, Donovan opened the door of his apartment in answer to a short, timid ring. He stared in confusion at Althea waiting in the hall. What in the world! he thought incoherently. For a moment he felt he must be imagining her presence, because he had been thinking about her all day and now it was as if she had simply materialized at his doorstep.

Tardily he asked her in and then, because he was disturbed by her presence, he ran around clearing books and papers from the couch and opening a fresh pack of cigarettes for the dish that was always empty on the coffee table. After all this time, Althea was in his living room again. He took one of the cigarettes, then hastily returned it to the dish when he noticed how his hands shook.

But he need not have been concerned. She was not watching him particularly. She moved hesitantly to the seat he had cleared, determined to stay, and after a moment he realized that she wanted to talk but was having even more difficulty in beginning than he was.

"It's been a long time," he said, because it seemed to him that it had been.

Then she looked at him. "Oh, no," she said, shaking her head a little. She stripped off her gloves and put them with her purse on the coffee table. She looked at the cigarettes. "May I?"

He took two cigarettes from the dish, lit them and gave her one. He took a deep breath, trying to maintain a calmness he did not feel.

"Thank you."

"May I fix you a drink?"

"Would you?"

"What would you like?"

"Anything."

He stumbled out to his little kitchen. Why had she come? Did she know that Larry had been to see him about her? That they had discussed her quite frankly?

He set out two glasses and took ice cubes from the refrigerator and reached into the cabinet for bottles, splashing bourbon and soda in on top of the ice cubes in the glasses.

He began to feel a quiet, secret glee. She was here, she could not escape him. He could sit down opposite her and feast his eyes on the sight of her and then he could tell her everything that had happened and how he had been in love with her from the very beginning. And if she said one word about Larry, either in protest or apology, he would not listen; he would close her mouth with his. If she knew about Kathy, if Kathy had told her, he would be honest. He would confess that he had simply lost his head. There was nothing strange in that; many men had experiences they were ashamed of when they lost control of themselves. Surely she would be able to understand that.

He got a spoon and stirred the drinks, then carried them into the other room, handing Althea hers. She was sitting with one hand over her eyes. When she took the hand away to accept the glass, she blinked as though the light hurt her eyes.

He lifted his glass. "What the doctor ordered." He tried to smile as he said it.

She bent her head. "Very good."

"It's not too strong?" he asked anxiously.

"No."

"Good."

Her eyes avoiding his, she sipped her drink. After a while she did not look quite so strained and white. He watched her and felt himself relaxing. Where is my professional manner? he wondered. Why don't I ask her why she's here? But still he could not bring himself to start the conversation.

"How are you?" he asked at last.

Her face lifted. "What?"

"How are you?" he repeated.

Her eyes were a little wary. "All right, I guess. I have these headaches."

He did not really hear her. He stared into her eyes and then he looked at her glass. "It's empty," he said and held out his hand.

"Just half this time."

"All right," he agreed.

He took both glasses back into the kitchen.

He heard the telephone ring and took an impulsive step, then turned back to his mixing. Althea would answer and call him, if necessary. He listened with his head bent, but she did not call out. Wrong number, probably, he thought, and was glad because he did not want anything to interfere with their time together. He carried the glasses back into the other room and set them on the coffee table. She was gone.

Bewildered, he searched the apartment. She might be in the bathroom, he thought. But she was not. And the apartment was not big enough for anyone to hide in. Was she playing a game with him? Suddenly he was angry at her, his dignity offended. But no, she had obviously wanted to tell him something, something important . . . It was no time for games.

He sat down on the couch, picked up his drink, and drained it, annoyed at himself and suddenly worried. It was just ridiculous! One moment she was here; the next, she was gone.

He looked around the room again. Her gloves and her purse were still on the coffee table. Donovan knew enough about women to be sure that she would come back for them. Grimly, he picked up her drink and sipped at it, looking from time to time at his watch with growing impatience.

Then, suddenly, the front door opened and she walked in, looking even more flushed and nervous than before.

"Where have you been?" he asked.

Her eyes were glazed, as if she were not looking at him, as if he were not there. Then they suddenly snapped into focus.

"Out," she said. "I just stepped out. I wanted—I wanted—to get a breath of fresh air. I felt faint . . ."

"Faint?"

"Yes. I—I haven't been feeling well lately. I've been having migraines . . . I thought you could tell me what to do."

Was that all she had come for, to get medical advice? He was a little confused. "I—well, you'd have to come to my office for a check. Blood pressure and so on. How long have you had them?"

"For weeks. My blood pressure is all right. As far as I know, everything's all right. Blood count, urinalysis, sputum test—I seem to check out just about the way I should for my age. But these headaches—"

"What have you been taking for them?"

"Phenobarbs."

"Who prescribed them?"

"I—I get them through a friend."

"Do they help?"

"At first—not really."

"How are your eyes?"

"I've had them checked, too. My vision is very good. But when these migraines attack, I'm—well, almost blind."

"Of course. You would be. And nauseated."

"Yes."

"But phenobarbital. I don't like that. What made you think you needed that?"

"I had to have something. When an attack begins, I'm almost out of my mind," she said softly.

He leaned toward her. "Tomorrow," he said sternly, "don't go on duty. You come over to Surgery and we will run some tests."

"Whatever you say."

"Let me see your eyes." Obediently she lifted her face. He leaned closer, put his hand under her chin and tilted her head toward the light. Her eyes looked at him for a second. Then her eyelids swept down as though she were afraid of his searching scrutiny. He could feel her chin trembling in his hand. Abruptly he dropped his mouth to hers. When he lifted his head, he saw the agony in her face. It filled him with unbearable pain.

He pulled her into his arms and held her against his heart. He forgot the way he had ravaged Kathy. He forgot everything but the reality of holding her. Her arms slipped around his neck; her mouth came eagerly to his this time. He asked no forgiveness and made no apologies as he undressed her. Not for a moment did he feel shame.

"Althea!" he whispered once because she did not struggle or even pretend to struggle. He heard her sigh, a sound like those children make when cradled tenderly in a parent's arms after a time of terror and hurt. The agony he had seen in her face was leaving. All the crying and heartbreak, the shame and degradation were slipping softly into nothingness. He did not know how he sensed this, but he knew it was taking place.

The telephone rang. They heard it, but only remotely, as though it had no connection with them in any way. It rang steadily for several minutes, then it stopped.

He was amazed at her ravenous hunger and his own unfaltering passion. He wondered vaguely if the flame would leave as it had come. If it did, would he again be the stupid, muddling fool he had been, full of conceit and vanity, playing at being God? He must always remember this flame and pray that it would never die, because it made a radiance everywhere, and he could not bear to think what it would be like without the radiance.

The flame soared fiercely as he possessed Althea.

"I've got to find her," Larry muttered to himself as he ran along the path leading from Nurses' Residence, where he had been told by Mrs. Robinson that Althea was not in her room. The shocking news about Ruth Ellison's death was out now, and he wanted to be the one to tell Althea what had happened. He felt that he could somehow mitigate the shock. He had called Donovan's apartment and got no answer, but when he reached the long building which held the private apartments the hospital assigned to its staff, he glanced up and noticed a soft glow in the window of Donovan's living room. It could mean that he was not there and had left a lamp on; it could also mean that he had just returned. Perhaps he had been out with Althea, or at least knew where she could be found. He decided to enter the building and go up to Donovan's apartment. Once upstairs, he moved along the hall until he reached the right door. Then he put a thumb on the bell button and leaned against it.

The clamor inside became so insistent and determined that Donovan finally stirred. He was not particularly alarmed, only a little angry that at a time like this someone should so insistently disturb him. He covered Althea with his coat, pulled on his trousers and stumbled to the door. Then he gripped the sides of the door frame with his hands so that Larry, standing with his thumb still pressing the button flat, could neither see past him nor step into the apartment. The precaution was unnecessary. Larry was too upset to notice Donovan's dismay and confusion or his disheveled appearance.

"Where have you been?"

"Why, here."

"Is your telephone out of order?"

"Not that I know of. Was someone trying to get me?"

315

"The office has called you a dozen times. I've called you I'm looking for Althea. I've been all over this damn institution." Larry noticed Donovan's peculiar expression. "You mean you haven't heard about it yet?" he asked incredulously.

"What are you talking about?"

"Althea's cousin on Rehabilitation," Larry said thinly. "She committed a murder. Just a short time ago."

"What!"

"Edna Horne. She killed someone."

Donovan was dumfounded. He recalled Edna vividly and the shock therapy he had ordered for her the last two days. "How—"

"The office tried to get you but finally gave up and called me. Somebody official had to examine the body. And now we can't find Althea. Terry thought she might be with me, but I haven't seen her for two days. I was coming by here and I saw your light so I thought perhaps you might know. You should have your telephone checked. It must be out of order. I've looked everywhere for Althea, but she seems to have vanished. The office needs her signature on some papers, and of course they want her to know as soon as possible what's happened. She's Edna's only living relative, I guess. You know how Terry can be. She doesn't give a damn about the other fellow when she wants to get something over and done with."

Donovan swiftly pulled the door shut, with himself out in the hall. "Kathy!" he said hoarsely. "Is she all right? She wasn't—"

"She wasn't there on the ward when it happened. Ward Five."

"Well, who got killed, then?"

"The charge. Woman named Ruth Ellison. Strangled."

"My God!" There was a moment's silence. "What did you do—I mean, what did you order?"

"Relax. Edna's down in full restraint and four attendants from Geriatrics are stationed on the ward to keep the peace the rest of the night. Kathy Hunter's down in her office trying to explain to Terry how it all happened. And I'm hunting for Althea. Oh, yes. Edna was already strapped down when I got there, but I gave her a slug of sodium amytal anyway. Figured it would make her a little easier to get along with tomorrow."

"Good idea. Just the thing."

"So everything's all right except for Terry riding that poor little supervisor's back. But where the hell is Althea? I've got to find her." He looked harassed. "I want to be the one to tell her what's happened. She's had so much to put up with." He stopped and stared at Donovan with a frown. "I suppose you wish I'd make up my mind, don't you?" he asked harshly.

"Haven't you yet?"

"I don't know, I don't know."

They looked at each other, Larry baffled and unhappy, and Donovan with the annoyed expression of a man who obviously wants to break off an unpleasant conversation.

"All right," Larry said angrily. "I just thought I could help her in some way."

Donovan said the first thing he could think of. "Have you gone to the library? It's open quite late because of the night shift, you know. Perhaps Althea is doing some research. There's some new material on insulin therapy." The lie did not come easily, but Larry did not notice.

"Funny," he said, thinking how strange it was that there should still be something he did not know about Althea. "I don't believe she ever told me she used the library. Okay, thanks. I'll run over there. Thanks for the tip." He swung around and was off down the hall and out of sight before Donovan could move.

Donovan opened the door and went back inside. Althea was still on the couch, but she had dressed. Her face was so gray that he knew she must have heard Larry's news. He wondered how she would feel about her cousin.

"I'm sorry," he said shortly, coming to sit down beside her. "That must have been something of a shock. I didn't get the door shut fast enough. How do you feel?"

She didn't answer, just stared at him.

"Poor darling," he murmured, taking her hands. "I told you. I'm sorry. But it's over and done, something that can't be helped. You won't be blamed just because she's your cousin, you know."

She shook her head. Her lips parted a little. "Kathy," she whispered. "It wasn't Kathy—"

"Didn't you hear that part? No, it was the charge on Ward Five, the ward your cousin's on. She's the one that got—oh, darling, don't look like that. Don't look so terrified and crushed. It wasn't anything that could be stopped. It was just one of those bizarre things. You've studied schizophrenic patterns enough to know how something like that can happen when it's least expected to happen. People like Edna can't always be controlled."

A peculiar sound came from between Althea's parted lips. At first he could scarcely believe his ears, then he realized that the sound was indeed what he had first thought. She was laughing. Recognizing hysteria, he took her by the shoulders and shook her. Poor darling, he kept saying, my poor darling!

She knew his hands were clutching her, but she was no

longer there with him. The pain that had penetrated her skull as she listened at the door was now unbearable. But there was a blinding light around her and just outside that was dark world into which she was going to run and run until the pain could never catch up with her again. There was something red in the darkness, like dancers, but she was not afraid of that; she was only worried that she might not get started in time to keep ahead of the pain. Something was screaming at her, sharp, jagged sounds that went up and down like the oscillations on a heart graph, and she had to escape that too, because the points of the sounds were driving into her forehead as though they were nails. She got up and began running toward a muddy, violent darkness.

Actually, she never left the couch, and the screaming came from her own throat.

Donovan released her shoulders and stood back, as Althea began to scream. God above! he thought incoherently.

It was as if she had suddenly turned into Madge or any one of a dozen other patients he could name.

CHAPTER 48

WHEN THE SOFT KNOCK CAME, Mike was in bed but not asleep. He had been going over the story of the inquest in the evening paper and was outraged at the whole article, which was heavily biased, giving the impression that the jury had been composed of stupid people who did not know much about judicial procedures—trash haulers, the author of the article wrote with barely concealed contempt—the hand picked jury of a Medical Examiner who had never finished his medical-school training. The author did say, however, that while Bud did not know much more about the practice of medicine than most housewives did, he certainly knew how to sway public opinion.

After Jim Blayton was escorted from the building by an unruly mob of well-wishing cohorts, he was whisked from sight in a car driven by an unknown man and later it was reported that he had left town rather than face those townspeople who were not in sympathy with his crime or the jury's verdict. According to Dr. Jubal Herrington, Superintendent of Canterbury, where the murdered Dr. Andreatta was in residence, the hospital deeply regrets that the jury, the Medical Examiner, and the District Attorney saw fit to set an acknowledged killer free, and it is to be hoped that this deviation from a norm of justice will not set a precedent for future such crimes as so often happens when these deviations become known to the general public. . . .

Clever, very clever, Mike thought. Now the town would begin to forget that Jim had been terribly wronged. They would only recall that a gory crime had been committed. Then they would wait fearfully for the next bludgeoning to take place. Eventually they would be thankful that Jim was gone. It's just as well that Jim has joined the Navy, Mike told himself. He wadded up the paper and stuffed it into the wastebasket near the head of his bed. Then he heard the knock. He looked at his watch and saw that it was a little past midnight.

"Just a minute," he called, getting out of bed and fumbling for his robe. He didn't bother with slippers but walked barefoot to the door and opened it.

It was a mousy woman whose thin, intense face was familiar, but not until she spoke did he remember where he had seen her before. She was the stenographer who worked for Donovan and Larry. She was also a patient. He hesitated, wondering whether it would be considered proper to invite her into his bedroom.

"I'm in a hurry because I've got to get back before someone finds out I'm not in bed," she said brightly. She was very precise about it, as though she wanted to be sure he understood every word. "You're Kathy Hunter's friend, aren't you?" She held something clutched to the breast of a purple housecoat decorated with overlapping circles of gold rickrack, a garment that she had probably made herself. Her eyes stared at him with blurry hopefulness, and when he nodded because he couldn't think of anything to say yet, she brought her hands down and he saw that they held a bedraggled letter.

"I want you to have this," she said. "It's not supposed to be for you, but I want you to have it anyway. I want you to read it."

She thrust the letter toward him. He noticed that it had been opened. The night light in the hall was dim, but he could plainly see the ragged edges where the envelope had been slit.

He pulled back a little. "If it's not for me, why should I read it?" he asked, stalling for time while he tried to understand her behavior and decide what he should do about it.

"Somebody's got to read it," she snapped. "But not the one who's supposed to have it. I've been carrying it around trying to make up my mind." By that time she had forced it into his hand. "You gonna take it and read it or not?"

He turned it over reluctantly and made out the name of Donovan Macleod written across the face. "This belongs to Dr. Macleod. Where did you get it?"

319

"She gave it to me. Kathy Hunter. Asked me to see he got it."

"Well, why didn't you?"

"You read it and you'll know why I didn't."

"Look here, we're not supposed to be reading other people's mail. Didn't you know that?"

"Look here, yourself. I know a lot of things. You see any stamp on that letter, huh?"

He shook his head.

"All right. What's illegal about reading a letter that's got no stamp on it? You just tell me that."

"But it's addressed to—"

"Yes, I know. To Donovan Macleod. Well, let me tell you something. Maybe I'm a patient out here, but I still got a brain I'm not crazy, not by a long shot. After what happened just a little while ago I know exactly what's going to happen next. Dr. Macleod's gonna take up with that fancy Althea Horne and that'll drive Dr. Denning away from Canterbury. And that will be terrible, it'll be the most terrible thing to ever happen." She stopped and looked as if she were about ready to cry.

Mike's head was ringing with confusion. "Calm down, calm down and don't raise your voice like that. You want to wake up the whole building?" He grabbed her arm and pulled her into his room. Damn the proprieties! he thought. There was something here he had to find out about.

"Now. Start over again. Just what are you talking about? Take it slow and try to remember I don't know a thing about any of this."

"Well, I don't know," she said, hurt but a little pleased somehow to be in his room. "You don't act as if you even care about somebody getting killed tonight. Maybe you're happy about things like that."

The hand holding her arm shook her. "Killed?" Mike said tensely. "What do you mean?"

She stared at him intently for a moment. "You mean you haven't heard, you really haven't heard?"

He swore, then said tightly, "Haven't heard what?"

She shook his hand away. "No need to be nasty. After all, I am a lady even if this does look sort of peculiar, me coming here and all in my housecoat. But you know how it is. They take away our clothes at night, so I didn't have anything else to put on."

"My God, lady, I wasn't swearing at you. I was just— swearing. It didn't mean a thing."

"And my name's Madge in case you're interested. Madge."

He controlled himself with an effort. "All right. Madge.

A very pretty name. Now look, Madge, why don't you tell me what this is all about like a nice—Madge?"

Now that he was going to be nice and take her seriously, she relented. "Okay. I'll tell you all about it. One of the charges in that new building, Rehabilitation, was killed tonight. Don't ask me how I found out because we have a sort of grapevine out here and I wouldn't want to get anybody into trouble."

"Rehabilitation?" he stammered.

"That's the place," she replied cheerfully. "It was Ruth Ellison got killed and it was Edna Horne did it. It was an awful battle, I heard. They fought all over the place and it took ten women to get Edna down into restraint and everybody got scratched and bitten and kicked. My, I wish I could have seen it!" Her dull eyes took on a little glow.

"But . . . Kathy! What about Kathy Hunter?"

"Oh. Well, nothing, I guess. This letter's from her. It don't have anything to do with tonight. She wrote it a couple of days ago, I guess. I'm not really worried about her. It's Dr. Denning I'm thinking about."

Mike was sure that in a moment his head would explode. This infuriating woman! "Where in hell does he come into this?" he snapped.

"There you go again." She shook a finger at him. "Naughty, naughty. Well, you see it's like this. When Dr. Macleod reads that letter, he's going to get all worked up about Althea. But Althea is Dr. Denning's girl. Only that letter says that Althea wants to be Dr. Macleod's girl. So then, what happens to Dr. Denning? Don't you see it at all?"

He shook his head, almost past speech. "Well, you should. Dr. Denning's going to get all upset," she said triumphantly. Then her face abruptly altered; she looked sad and helpless. "Then he'll go away. He won't stay here at Canterbury any more," she almost whimpered. "And I don't want him to go away. Whatever will I do if he goes away?" She put her hands up to her mouth and shook her head. "You don't know what it's like not to have any friends or anybody who cares about you. It's terrible, terrible!"

"But—yes, I understand all that, all you've said so far. But what connection is there between that and what you say has happened on Rehabilitation?"

She wagged her finger again. "That Edna Horne didn't go to kill anybody on her own planning. She hasn't got that much sense. Why, she's about the craziest female patient we have in this institution." She had swiftly changed from unhappiness to self-importance. "Somebody told Edna what to do," she whispered eerily. "Somebody told her. Maybe her own cousin told her what to do. They're talking about it on all the wards. So you've got to do something. You've got to read this letter and then you'll know what to do because this thing isn't over, all this killing business. As soon as Edna gets it into her poor, empty head that she didn't kill the right party, she's going to try again. You'll see. She'll try to kill the person she was told to kill in the first place and she'll do it, too. She's strong. You just don't know. It took fifteen women to get her back into restraint—why, maybe they haven't got her down yet. Maybe she's still chasing everybody around. Oh, I wish I could be there to see what's going on!"

"All right. I'll do something," he said. "First, before you go—" because, of course, you're going, aren't you? his voice implied—"how did you get off that ward you sleep on?"

"Oh, I'm glad you said that. Here. It's to go with the letter."

He stared down at the ring of keys she had pressed into his free hand. "What in the world is this?"

"Keys. All of them." She flung out her arms. "They'll unlock every door in the hospital except the elevators on Rehabilitation. That's a master set. All the doctors carry those and the supervisors carry them. Suppose you're wondering how come I got them, huh?"

"How did you get them?" he asked softly.

"I took them. Right out of Dr. Macleod's desk drawer. He had three sets in there. Guess he thought they were absolutely safe. He doesn't know what a girl can do with a hairpin, does he?"

"Apparently not. But when he does—"

"He won't miss them for a long time. I took all three sets. How do you suppose I get out whenever I want to, huh?" Her expression was sly. She stared at him for a second. "Now, look. When you get through with whatever you're going to do, you take those keys over to the office. Understand? We can't have crazy people getting hold of those keys and running loose all over the place, can we? So you turn them back to the office before you lose them. Don't worry about me. I still have two sets."

Suddenly it came to him that part, at least, of what she was telling him must be the truth. "Why do you think Dr. Denning will leave Canterbury? Tell me again, Madge."

"Oh, goodness." She was getting impatient and anxious now to be gone. Soon the charge would check the ward she slept on and perhaps find out that her bed was empty. "It's all perfectly simple. The police'll come and they'll find out what that Althea's done and they'll arrest her—you know, put her in jail. So then Dr. Denning'll leave. Wouldn't you in his place? If you got your heart broken, would you stay around where it happened? Now I ask you."

"I guess not."

"Okay. Can I go now?"

I didn't ask you to come, he thought, watching her turn and flounce away as if she had abruptly become afraid of him. He closed his door and looked first at the keys and then at the letter. He turned it over. There was no date, because, of course, it had never been posted. Someone had expected it to be delivered by hand, obviously. Would Kathy do such a thing? He could scarcely believe she would, but then how would he know unless he read it?

Should he read it? What gave him the right to read a letter belonging to someone else and written to someone else? But he had to know—to know if Kathy would ever be free to love him. He took out the letter and unfolded it.

It was a rather long letter, but it took him only a few moments to scan through it the first time. The second time he read more slowly. When he finished, he knew at last about Sarah Smith. He also knew about Kathy's experience with Donovan the night before. His eyes filled with tears thinking of the courage it had taken to write such a letter.

The last part of the letter was the most important part to Mike. He read it over and over, filling his mind with its meaning.

> *I let you do something I shouldn't have but it was because I thought I loved you. I didn't realize until it was all over that I hadn't loved you for a long time. I think I must have been afraid to say to myself that I no longer loved you, because it made what I did to Sarah so much more terrible and pointless. But I have to tell you now, Donovan, because we can't keep on tormenting Althea and making her life such a hell, you and I. You must let her know that she is the one you love—because she is, isn't she? And I will begin by letting her know that I do not love you and that you do not love me. You see, when Mike Stewart is around, I almost stop thinking about you and Sarah and Althea entirely. I just think about him and what it must be like to be a decent person again, somebody who likes to do things for others, not do things to them. If I could live it all over, I'd cut off my two hands before I'd ever harm anybody. Such an easy thing to write, I know....*

Mike folded the letter and slipped it into the pocket of his robe. Then he stood thinking for a moment. Madge had read the letter. And tonight she had deliberately hunted him out. Why? Had someone really been killed in the building where Kathy worked? This night of all nights? Tomorrow she promised to take the night off so we can go to a show, Mike thought. Wouldn't it be ironic if something happened tonight?

He felt a flash of fear. Because of the letter and the patient coming to his door to deliver it as she had, it was somehow Kathy who had now become the victim of a terrible tragedy. He began to dress as fast as he could, half scolding himself for being so susceptible to suggestion. When he had his pants, shoes and shirt on, he dashed out of the room leaving the door open and took the stairs three steps at a time. He reached his rented car to discover the only keys he carried were the ones given him by Madge, so he ran on instead of going all the way back and upstairs for the car keys. It was a black night, but he went through it like a cat and pulled up, winded, at the corner of Rehabilitation just as a group of people emerged slowly from the front. Even at that distance and with the only light coming from high over their heads, he recognized some of them as they got into parked cars and drove away. Obviously Madge had been telling at least part of the truth, because what but an emergency would bring Lucretia Terry, Walter Sturgis, Margaret Rich and others to Rehabilitation at this time of night?

He felt faintly relieved. Kathy had not been with the group, so she must still be in the building. He waited until all the cars had gone on around the curving driveway and out of sight behind other buildings, and then he stepped quickly along the side until he reached the doors. Just like a housebreaker, he told himself grimly, still panting from his run. He tried the keys carefully. He didn't care if it looked like housebreaking; if he could get inside he was certainly going to do so. He intended to see with his own eyes that Kathy was all right. When he found the right key, he unlocked the massive door, pulled it open and ran into the foyer.

CHAPTER 49

THE MORTICIAN and his assistant left first with Ruth Ellison's body. Then Lucretia and her party went away. They left Kathy sitting at her desk with a splitting headache, trying to recall everything that had been said.

There was to be a staff inquest to determine exactly why Ruth's death had occurred. Lucretia had refused to accept any explanation Kathy had offered. She had scrutinized each detail of the tragedy again and again until Kathy was ready to scream with horror. Margaret had stood behind Lucretia and offered little sly questions of her own. Yet with all their hints and accusations, they had not been able to shake her story or force her to change any part of it. She could remember that much clearly.

Walter Sturgis had ended the questioning by stating, rather surprisingly, that he believed every patient in Canterbury was entitled to one bit of mayhem toward an employee, considering what was ordinarily done to the patients. Why didn't they all go back to bed, since Ruth was dead and Edna was down in restraint and behind a locked door? Jubal hadn't put in his appearance, had he? It was perfectly clear how he felt; he felt the whole business could wait until the light of day. He wasn't going to let a little thing like a charge getting choked to death keep him from getting his sleep.

Lucretia gave him a long, frozen stare. She gathered all her papers and records together and swept out, leaving Kathy alone in her office. Before the group had finished locking the doors on their way out, Kathy was writing something on a sheet of paper pulled hastily from a drawer.

When she dropped the pen, she picked up her flashlight, glanced once with a strange expression at what she had written and went to the elevator. There was no hurry, but she still felt a sense of pressure and anxiety. When the elevator reached the third floor, she got off and went in to talk to Millie, because she could not do what she was planning without Millie's help. She found Millie lying on a couch, staring at the ceiling with a wounded, bitter look. Millie did not apologize for being caught in such a position. She could have explained that losing a job and her best friend on the same night was about as much as a woman could take. She wasn't too sure why she hadn't already gotten her things and gone home, where she could at least cry in decent seclusion. It was habit that made her stay. But she sat up, and Kathy sat down beside her

Kathy put her hand over one of Millie's and then she began to speak. When she finished, Millie pulled back and looked at her resentfully. What a story! she was thinking. In the first place nothing would have gone wrong if this silly girl had checked the wards at the proper time. Now she had come upstairs to start things all over again, saying she was the one supposed to have been choked to death by Edna, when the stupidest fool in the whole institution would know that Edna choked people because she liked to choke people.

Suddenly she noticed how Kathy's hands were twisting together, exactly the way one of the patients on her ward twisted her hands together. That was little Jenny, who had been in the car crash. Millie always went down the hall to Jenny's room when she began crying, and she would take Jenny into her arms just like she would have a baby and rock her a little bit and then tuck her back into bed with her soiled, ragged Teddy bear. Jenny would always go right off to sleep. Now here was Miss Hunter, a nurse, a supervisor, trying to tell Millie a perfectly crazy story and looking and acting like Jenny. The way with the hands, the wild look in her eyes, even the same stubbornness as Jenny's.

"Why, I do believe you mean every word you're telling me. You really believe somebody's trying to kill you!"

"Yes."

"But it don't make sense, Miss Hunter. It just ain't possible there'd be somebody mean enough to make that poor Edna wanta do—do what she did."

"But it did happen, didn't it?"

There was a little silence. "God, yes," Millie said simply. "To my best friend. Ruthie." She said the name on a deep sigh.

"So that makes me responsible and I've got to do something."

"No, no! You can't give bad for bad or it turns right around and eats you up like rot in a piece of fruit."

"I didn't ask for it to be done," Kathy said. "But when it has been done—and you know how it was done—you can't let it keep on. You've got to do something, no matter what happens afterward."

"Sure, I know that. That's what I mean, myself. Only you can't do it the way you're talking about."

"What other way is there?"

Millie stirred uneasily. "Well—well, you could talk to Miss Terry, couldn't you? Tell what you think and show her how it says right in Edna's chart—"

"I could talk to Miss Terry, but you didn't, did you?"

"You mean—" Millie looked stricken—"you mean what happened to that Mary Elsie?" She stared miserably at Kathy. "I—I couldn't. I just couldn't."

"So the evil went right on because nobody stopped it. Right?"

"Oh, Miss Hunter, I think that's mean to say."

"I think so too. I'm sorry I had to say it, but I wanted to make my point."

"But I woulda gone to the office, only I just knew it wouldn't do any good." She looked imploringly at Kathy.

Kathy nodded. "I could go, too, and they'd laugh at me."

There was quite a long silence this time. "Are you sure you're not trying to get even about something?" Millie whispered finally.

"No," Kathy said steadily. She rubbed her face with her hands, then looked intently at Millie. "I'm always making a mess of things. You know, some people are that way. They just do everything wrong in spite of the best intentions in the world. Well, I seem to be that kind of a person, so I suppose this—this effort will be no different. But I can't help myself. I've got to do it. Oh, I'm not going to tell anyone that I believe Althea is to blame for tonight. Not that, Millie. I only want to prove to the office that Edna must be taken out of this building, that she will always be dangerous, especially around people who in any way resemble her mother."

"What did her mother look like?"

"Me."

Millie's jaw dropped. "Honest t' God?"

"Yes." Kathy stopped twisting her hands and leaned toward Millie. "Now, Millie, I want you to think hard. Was there anything you heard just before—just before you got to Edna's room that didn't sound just—well, right?"

Millie concentrated. "Well, before the—the thump—you know, when she—when Ruthie fell, there was this little noise. I don't know. Didn't give it much thought then, but seems to me when I think about it now that it didn't belong. You know, it shouldn't have been there. Now, I'm not saying I really heard it, maybe I just think I heard it. Only, if there was this sound—which I sort of think there was—I know I've heard it before. You know?"

"I'm sure you heard it. You must have heard it or you wouldn't think you had."

"Am I making sense? This sound—well, it's like one you hear every day, so you get kinda used to it. You know, the sound is there, so you don't really listen. You just know it's there. Like the refrigerator door going open and shut or the bathroom door." She stopped. "Oh, dear," she said helplessly, "why can't I put it into words? A sound like that, you hear it so much you don't really give it a thought until like right now when it could be so important, you want to remember and you can't!"

Vexed, she bent her head as if magically the words would come. "Such a little sound," she said. "A hiss, sort of. I just can't think for the life of me."

Kathy caught her breath. "Could it have been the—fire-exit door? You know, the gadget that makes the door go shut automatically?"

Millie's vexation changed to awe. "Why, that's exactly what it was! The fire-exit door going shut!"

"You see?" Kathy said, her voice very low.

"But—but—" Millie's face filled with shock. "God help us!" she said unsteadily.

Kathy looked down at her hands. "Now it's I who can't believe it." Her voice sounded bewildered.

Millie stared at her. "Well, you gotta remember this is all your idea to begin with, you know."

"She couldn't have been in this building," Kathy said slowly, as though she were talking to herself. "In spite of how it looks. When I called Donovan to get a seclusion order, she was there in his rooms. She answered the telephone."

She tried to picture the location of the building that housed the doctors. Was it close enough to Rehabilitation so that someone could go from one to the other in just a very few seconds? If so, then Althea could have left Donovan immediately after Kathy's call and got to Rehabilitation in time to be responsible for the sound Millie had heard. I'm sure she put Edna in the mood to go on a rampage, Kathy thought, but I'm not sure just how she did it.

Millie studied Kathy. It had been a terrible day and night, she thought. She didn't know whether she could stand much more. Along with all her feelings of guilt, now she had this to worry her.

"Look," Millie said. "Why don't we just forget all this? I don't know what you got in mind, but I'd be willing to bet all I got in my sugar bowl at home that it won't work. What you first mentioned doing—it's too dangerous. It would be downright wicked for you to take such a chance."

"You mean you don't care why Ruth was killed?"

"Don't say that! Don't ever, ever say that! I—I can't begin to tell you how much I care. All I'm saying is that you got no call to make a fool of yourself just to stop Edna from doing the things she does. What difference does it make now, for God's sake? Ruth's gone, ain't she? Won't nothing bring her back—nothing."

"Next time it will be someone else."

"Maybe there won't be no next time."

"You don't know that."

"You just march yourself over to Terry and tell her what you think steada trying to get yourself choked to death!"

"We've been over that before."

"I tell you, you just don't make sense. What exactly will it prove? Tell me that. What will it prove?"

"That Edna hates women with dark hair and that she goes wild when she hears the word 'fire.'"

"When you're laying down there in her room with your eyes popped outa your head, you think the office will take my word for what you proved?"

"Yes."

"Ah, you must be crazy!"

"No. I wrote it all down on paper and left the paper on my desk. The office will believe that."

"What does it say?"

"That Edna hates dark women. Her mother was dark. That Edna becomes maniacal when fire or heat or something being scorched is mentioned in her hearing. Her mother used to burn her with matches and make her put her hands against a hot stove. Things like that."

"Nothing is so important you should deliberately needle a woman as crazy as Edna just to prove all that. You ain't kidding me. You're trying to find out if Edna accidentally killed the wrong party." Millie stared searchingly into Kathy's face. "Are you trying to commit suicide?"

The little smile Kathy tried to achieve made her look ghastly. "Not really. But if you don't help me, it'll come to that."

Millie found she could not take her eyes away from Kathy's white face. After a long moment she said, "All right. Maybe you don't know it, but you got me over a barrel when you look like that." Her breath caught in her chest. "Whatever comes of it, I won't be around after tonight. I lost my job, you know. Funny, ain't it? I tried to help that fellow out— you know, that Jim Blayton. I did, too. But I got canned for my trouble. Now tonight my best friend's gone. Guess the best thing to do is just take it, kind of, and not keep asking why did it all have to happen. Just like I had to stop asking why my husband had to get cancer and die by inches. You can lose your mind easy if you keep on asking yourself why things happen like they do. Sometimes it's best to put all your questions away until you're all alone, maybe getting ready for bed, and then bring 'em out and spread 'em out nice and neat for God to look over. Even when He doesn't say anything you can hear, you feel a bit better, sort of. It's kind of a *caring* feeling."

"Caring?"

"Maybe that ain't the right word. Cared for—maybe that's what I mean."

Kathy shut her eyes. "Cared for," she whispered. "That's right. Cared for, caring."

Millie swallowed. "Okay. What do you want me to do?"

Then Kathy told her. They examined their watches to make sure they had the same time, after which Kathy left Ward Six. She entered the minor surgery which served both Five and Six, stepped through a side door and was on the landing of the fire exit for Five.

Millie waited in her office, a dozen thoughts jabbing at each other in her mind. Ruth was the center of them, but Harry and her mother were there, as well as Ruth's Bill. At least there was one thing, Millie thought. They had nothing to worry about any more, while she didn't have anything but worries. Soon she wouldn't even have a house to live in. And no cats. It took money to feed cats.

A picture of Charlotte Range flashed into her thoughts. If Charlotte hadn't done what she did, Ruth would still be alive, Millie told herself. Rotten inside, that Charlotte. Yet, rotten or not, Charlotte was doing all right. She still had her job.

Millie looked at her watch. "I'm the world's biggest fool, I do believe," she muttered, getting to her feet. She stiffened her shoulders and plodded through the connecting hall to Five. Unlocking the door quietly, she eased it open enough to see the white caps of the four women left in charge of the ward by Terry. They sat in the parlor, looking nervously down the dim corridor. She watched them a second, then began to stamp her feet and make sharp cries of distress. Startled, they jerked out of their chairs and came stumbling frantically to find out what was wrong. They saw Millie in the hall, her cap off, a button missing from her uniform, a wisp of hair falling out of her net and across one eye. She shouted something about a quarrelsome patient. They followed her without question; apparently it did not occur to them to leave at least half their strength on Ward Five.

They were more than a little relieved when the quarrelsome patient was reached and found asleep. Immediately gossip welled. God, what some of these patients could do! Scaring a person to death, almost. Anybody remember that Beverly Whipple? She got hurt on detention, y' know. Patient kicked her. Phlebitis, the doctors said. They kept on cutting her up until she got sick and tired of it and died. And how about that schoolteacher patient, that Lorraine somebody? She was gonna have a baby but lost it when her husband committed suicide over some stinker of a showgirl. So she got put in Canterbury and she was really crazy. She just up and pushed the charge on her ward down a whole flight of stairs. You remember that, don't you? The charge got up, walked about from here to that chair and dropped dead. Right in front of all us girls. God, we never had anything shock us as much as that, honest! Embolism. Sure, you know how fast that kills a person.

Millie kept her eye on her watch. She had promised Kathy she would lead the women back onto Five after a full eight minutes. In eight minutes, Kathy hoped to accomplish what she had in mind.

Millie was unlocking the door to Five when the scream came. High, thin, terrified, it split the air into shocked little

330

slivers of sound. The women jolted to a stop and put groping hands toward each other.

"God above, what was that!"

Millie did not wait to explain. She flew into action and left them standing openmouthed. Conscious of only one thought—that she would be too late because she was too far away—she tore through the door and across the parlor. Her body forgot its age as she ran down the dark corridor. She did not know or care whether she was followed by the women. She was not aware of the darkness. She only knew that she had to get to Edna's room. She prayed that she would reach it in time.

CHAPTER 50

KATHY STOOD ON THE LANDING outside the fire-exit door to Ward Five and looked at it. On the other side were four, perhaps five steps across the hall to Edna's room. She took a deep breath and unlocked the door, making as little sound as she could, pulled it open and went past it into the hall.

The door began to make a soft hissing sound as it slowly swung shut. She listened to the sound and knew that it had been what Millie had heard.

She put out a hand and kept the door from shutting completely. Resting against the jamb like that, it could not automatically lock itself, and all she would have to do to escape through it would be to push her way out.

She turned her back to the door and looked around. For the first time she realized how dark it was down at this far end of the hall. The light above the door was about the size of a large red eye, and the glow it created only emphasized the gloom below.

She began to feel that she was doing something pointless and that she would have proved nothing after she had finished doing it. The darkness was unfriendly. She had to force herself to remember the curious matter of the rolled blanket that Millie had discovered in Edna's bed, so cleverly placed that it looked like a covered, sleeping body. And then two days of similar behavior on Edna's part, so much alike that they seemed artificially stimulated.

She stepped across the width of the corridor and turned the knob of Edna's door, then moved quietly to the bed and looked down. Edna was breathing heavily and regularly, and little bubbles of saliva puffed rhythmically at the corners of her parted lips. She was sleeping soundly, but Kathy could not help wondering how long she would stay that way once somebody started unfastening her cuffs and straps.

She tried to visualize the restraints in the dark. Removing them would require a delicate touch, and already she was shaking. It made her stomach turn to realize how impossible it would be to unlock the straps and remove them from the loops without arousing Edna.

But somehow it had to be managed. In order to do what she planned, she had to reproduce the same circumstances that had existed when Ruth was killed. Otherwise she was wasting her time. And making a fool of herself, she thought unhappily.

She stood quite still for a moment before she began to work on the straps. This can't be really happening, she was thinking. It's too horrible and frightening. But she bent over the straps, unlocking them one by one. Carefully, carefully, she eased them out of the loops. Edna stirred once and groaned. Kathy almost fainted with fright, but finally the job was done; the straps dangled from the bedsprings and the cuffs were placed softly on the nightstand.

Now she could straighten up. She steadied herself against the stand and used the flashlight for a quick look at her watch. She was amazed that only two and a half minutes of the time she and Millie had agreed on had passed. It did not seem possible.

That left her five and a half minutes, she thought, daubing at the sweat on her face. Now came the part she hated to think about, but the most important of all, the part that had to be done to prove anything, to verify her suspicions. She leaned over the bed and said above the ragged pounding in her chest, "You are a wicked girl, Edna."

It sounded utterly theatrical and ridiculous. But Ruth was dead and that was not ridiculous. She forced herself to try again. This time it came a little easier.

"You are a wicked girl, Edna. You have been very bad, so you must be punished. Do you hear me? You are going to be punished and I will use fire, Edna. Fire. Listen to me, Edna, listen. You know what fire is, don't you? Don't you, Edna?"

The pink glow from the red eye outside stretched across the bed. Outside the glow, the room seemed to waver with monstrous shadows. Kathy shivered and kept her eyes away from the shadows and on the bed instead. "You killed your mother, Edna. Why, why? Didn't you like her? All she ever did was to punish you when you were bad and you were bad so often, weren't you?"

There was a slight movement from the bed. Kathy persisted. "Can you hear me, Edna? Do you remember how it was when you were a little girl? You were always being punished by your mother. With something hot, remember? The stove, matches, hot water. Remember how your mother would make you put your hands against the stove and how she would light matches and hold them against your fingers and how she would pour hot water into the palms of your hands —do you remember all those things, Edna?"

"Do you remember me, Edna? I look like your mother. I'm short and have dark hair and my eyes are dark just like your mother's were. Who knows? Maybe I am your mother, come back to punish you, to burn you with fire. Remember how your mother used to burn you, Edna? Remember?"

This time there was a definite change. The thin, scar-twisted hands lying where they had been held by the restraints on the edge of the bed twitched slightly. Kathy observed the movement. "Fire!" she said quickly. "It hurts terribly! You were just a little girl when she began to burn and scorch and blister you. Every time she looked at you, she must have wanted to torment or hurt you in some way. She wanted to make sure that you would be very good, very perfect. So she did cruel, vicious things to keep you good. How could you be bad? You never had a chance to be bad! Still, she was always saying you needed to be taught a lesson, and fire would teach you best of all because that's what you'd get in hell. Oh, I can just hear the terrible things she said to you!"

Kathy's voice was filled with indignation. For a second she had forgotten what she was trying to accomplish while she visualized the wicked brutality of Edna's mother.

She came to her senses with a start. Her voice turned cold. "Why did you hurt Ruth, Edna? Did someone tell you I was your mother? Did someone tell you that just a short time ago? I was your mother and soon I would be coming down the hall and into your room? Only instead of me it was Ruth. But you went ahead and did as someone told you to. You killed the person who came into your room because she was going to burn you?"

Sweat poured profusely from Edna's face. In the dim pinkness, Kathy could see its gleam. "Who told you what to do?" she asked harshly. "Someone must have, Edna. Someone said, Get up, wait in the dark, grab whoever comes into this room! Because it might be your mother who's coming to hurt you. Isn't that the way it happened?"

Edna's breathing became harsher. Kathy leaned closer. "Whoever told you what to do is someone you like and trust, and you like and trust that person because it's someone you've always known. That person showed you how to roll up a blanket and put it under the covers. Maybe yesterday— or the day before—that person showed you how to fix your blanket. And you remembered and did the little trick tonight, didn't you? Who told you what to do? Who told you how to fix the blanket?"

Edna's hands slowly began to move toward each other and Kathy's mouth went dry. "Who told you what to do?" she insisted, her voice unconsciously becoming high and shrill.

The hands curved and shot up like grotesque claws. Kathy jumped. She had to wet her lips with her tongue before she could go on. "Tell me!" she choked. "Tell me, tell me!"

Suddenly she could stand it no longer. She fell on Edna's shoulders, shaking them in fright-inspired fury. "Tell me!" she screamed. "Who makes you do what you do?"

Edna came out of the bed and onto her feet with a convulsive muscular explosion. She groaned hideously and Kathy tripped backward against the doorjamb. She saw Edna swaying drunkenly and enormously large in the gloom and she panicked. She ran through the doorway and stumbled across the small space of corridor to the fire-exit door. Her feet seemed bound to the floor with lead, making the little space an obstacle course of insurmountable agony.

She reached the door and shoved with desperate urgency, and then filled with horror when it did not give. It had closed and locked itself. Now it could be opened only by a key. She hunted frenziedly for the keys.

She shook the door, shook and pounded again and again, terror sweeping over her in waves. Then she hunted again for the keys, but now it was her fingers that she couldn't control. She found the keys but her fingers couldn't separate them and pick out the one that unlocked the door. She lifted one foot and kicked the door as hard as she could. The pain in her toes as her shoe came into violent contact with the door's hardness seemed to affect her frozen hands. Kathy began to scream.

The tall figure came on, arms outstretched, the fingers on each hand spread like bent tines on giant forks. In the pink light, Edna's facial contortions were terrifying. There was monstrous hate in her fixed gaze. Her broad, bare feet moved crablike, her lean hips swaying from side to side with a curious and repulsive undulation. Saliva dripped in streams of mucus from pulled-back lips down to the front of her shapeless, muslin gown.

Kathy stopped shrieking. She watched Edna's hands lifting. Distorted and bent with scar tissue as they were, they still looked vital and imperishable.

In a moment I'll faint, Kathy thought. I won't feel it when she puts those hands around my neck and starts to choke and choke.

What's the matter with me? Why did I do all this? Edna's

just insane, that's all—she'd kill anyone. Why doesn't Millie come?

She slid down to the floor.

In Kathy's office on the first floor, Mike was looking around perplexedly. He had passed three women sitting in the hall outside, but two of them had been napping and one was so absorbed in counting stitches in something she was knitting that she did not bother to glance up; as he unlocked the door to Kathy's office and let himself in, she kept right on counting as though she hadn't heard a thing. Possibly she realized someone wearing trousers had come in the front door and gone on into the supervisor's office, but probably she associated him with all the activity of the evening. He was strongly tempted to go back out into the hall and ask her where her supervisor had gone to, then he thought better of the idea. If one of the charges had met death as Madge had claimed, the woman in the hall would no doubt try to give him a full account of all that had happened and include as much of her own imaginings as she dared. He felt he would prefer to get his information from Kathy.

He entered Kathy's office. He could almost see her directing the affairs of the building from here on her nightly shift. Was it here that she had written the letter he had put into his back pocket?

He went over and sat down in her chair. It was a snug fit. He enjoyed the snugness, sensing how Kathy's hips must fit themselves to the chair's embrace. Then he noticed the sheet of paper almost touching his hand as it lay on top of the desk. He noted Kathy's signature at the bottom first, then his eyes shifted to the beginning.

> *Edna Horne must not be permitted to stay on Rehabilitation. She is a detention patient. I firmly and sincerely believe that she is very dangerous and will always be dangerous and that unless she is kept under constant, heavy sedation, no employee who is short and dark in coloring, who smokes or otherwise uses matches in any way, will ever be safe near her. Edna's mother was short and dark-haired and terribly brutal to Edna, wholly responsible for Edna's present condition. This is a fact known to all who study Edna's medical history. Furthermore, I believe that Edna did not purposely kill Ruth Ellison. Edna made a mistake. She intended to kill me. Why? I look like Edna's mother, probably. How do I know that Edna can differentiate like this? I don't know. I only believe. Signed. . . .*

Mike jumped to his feet, stuffing the note into the same pocket that held Kathy's letter. What in the hell was Kathy up to now!

He vaguely remembered ward numbers, although whether it had been Madge who had mentioned them or Kathy herself he was not sure. He turned in the direction of the door that led to the elevators, then realized belatedly that he had no key to the elevators and that the information had come from Madge. He looked around and saw the other door with the red light. It was not locked. He stepped through and stared up the well of steps leading to the top floor. This was the fire-escape route for the east side of the building. He knew that he must get to the west fire-escape route. He went back into the office and on out into the hall. At the other end, past the three women who were now sitting erect and staring at him with alarm, he saw the other door with its familiar red eye. Without giving the women a glance as he ran past them, he reached this other door and went through without hesitation. Now he was on the west side of the building and the third landing of these stairs should lead directly into Ward Five. He went up, three steps at a time. On the third landing, he halted briefly to catch his breath. He was facing a massive, metal door with a bar lever across the approximate center.

He could hear nothing. He touched the lever and saw that it was a mechanism by which to open a door that would automatically lock from the other side. He pushed down on the bar and the door moved enough to let him know it was unlocked. He grabbed and pulled, the heavy door coming open reluctantly. The light from the landing shone through to combine with a faint glow from another red eye. He saw a tall woman standing stiffly with outstretched arms, a glazed, set expression on her face. She did not move when the door opened. Catatonic! was Mike's first thought. Then he saw the small, dark mound in the gloom around her feet and knew at once that it must be Kathy.

He reached for her frantically and almost immediately Kathy stirred, struggling upward, her face white and dazed and momentarily uncomprehending as she groped for support. He had taken her into his arms and was trying to stand when, without a sound, a warning of any kind, Edna was on his back, jerking with that vicious, incredible strength. He staggered, thrown off balance, and Kathy fell away.

For a second Kathy was rigid with this new horror. She could not understand how Mike had come to be involved with Edna, but she had felt his hands and arms for a brief instant. She lurched forward and caught at one of Edna's arms. The arm swung free, striking her on the side of the face and knocking her to the wall. She lost her balance, oppled and lay still for a moment. Then she got to her feet, her heart beating furiously with the effort.

She could feel blood running from her nose and was sure it must be dripping down the front of her uniform. She groaned and lost consciousness.

CHAPTER 51

KATHY OPENED HER EYES and stared upward. There was something familiar about the bleak white ceiling, but a moment or two passed before she could orient herself. Of course, she thought, I'm lying on the couch in my office. But why?

She tried to sit up and discovered that she was too sore and stiff to move anything but her head. She managed that and saw that someone was sitting on the floor, leaning back against the couch.

"Well!" she said faintly.

Mike looked around quickly and passed a hand over his bruised face. "Hi," he said.

"Oh—Mike!"

He turned himself over onto his knees and put his arms around her. "Honey, honey, it's all right, believe me, it's all right!"

She was safe, they were both safe. Tears began to run down her face. "I—I'm such a fool!" she wailed.

"More or less," he agreed.

She felt sodden inside with shame and despair. "What happened?" she asked, sobbing.

"Why, you turned that patient loose and she took off. I mean she tramped on you."

"No, no, not that. I remember that—"

"You mean when did I get in the fight?"

"Yes."

He was silent a moment, looking down at her. "Let's just say I got there in time, huh?"

"Mike!" she whispered, suddenly agonized with the realization that he might have been badly hurt. "Are you all right?"

"Well," he said judiciously, "I think I'm going to have a black eye. See?" He showed her, gravely.

She swallowed convulsively, wanting to touch his bruised face, yet too sore to lift her arm. "Edna?"

"Back in full restraint plus seclusion."

"Does the office know?"

"Know what?"

"That I—I—"

337

"The office has gone home and to bed, I presume," he said blandly. "Right after their first visit here. Is that what you're stuttering about?"

"No."

"Oh." He considered her thoughtfully. "Well, I have here in my pocket a note you left on your desk. No one has read it but me. Upstairs, our good friend Millie Higgins is explaining to four scared women that the exercise you and I had with Edna Horne was merely routine and not even worthy of mention in the log—or whatever you call that daily and nightly record thing."

She shuddered. "It isn't funny!"

"No, not funny. I just wanted you to know that Millie is your friend and that she doesn't intend letting Canterbury and Lucretia Terry know about this latest fool stunt of yours. As far as she's concerned, there's been enough damage done tonight. She thinks you're very brave. Furthermore, as she also said, she does not work for Canterbury, come the dawn, so why should she feel obligated to the hospital any longer? Beholden was the word she used, I think."

Suddenly he put his face down against hers. "What if I hadn't come here tonight?" he whispered thickly. "Kathy, Kathy, if anything had happened to you, what would I have done!"

She began to cry again. She cried convulsively, hurting with every sob but unable to stop herself. Carefully he eased one arm under her, lifted her and slid himself underneath so that she was resting in his arms and lap. "Darling, darling!" he kept whispering, holding her against himself as if she were a small, unhappy child. "It's all right," he crooned, kissing her hair, her cheeks, her eyelids, her tears. "Everything's all right now. Believe me, darling. Please believe me. It's all right."

When she could catch her breath, she turned her wet face against his neck. "Oh, Mike, you don't know—you don't know. I wrote him—"

"Who?"

"Donovan—I wrote him—"

He listened to the misery in the soft, reproachful whisper and was silent a moment. Then he said quietly, "He didn't get your letter, Kathy."

She became very still. When she tried to sit up, he wouldn't let her. She had to keep her shamed and flushed face against his neck. "What are you talking about?"

"Your letter. Madge didn't deliver it as ordered. She gave it to me."

"Oh, no!"

There was a long silence. "Did—did you read it?" she asked in a choked voice.

"Would you hate me if I did?"

"Oh, no, no! I—it would be the other way around."

He looked down at her. "Why?"

"Why?" She looked away hurriedly. "I—just think you might not like me if—" She faltered.

How could she think his love might be so shallow? he was tempted to ask. He hoped she would never think of asking him why he had come to Rehabilitation this night. Just in case, he'd better be working out some reasonable explanation.

"I didn't read it," he lied without expression.

In front of the main office building, the cars that had just left Rehabilitation separated. Lucretia turned hers in to park it in front of the building and the rest drove on. The picture of Margaret and Walter in the same car filled her with helpless anger, and she waited until their lights were out of sight before she got out of her car. Then she was almost bent double as a sharp pain twisted cruelly back and forth in her pelvic region. She gripped the door handle until the pain began to ease, then she walked up to the building, entered and went to her office.

Only a few people were in the building. A bored attendant herded several patients who were mopping and dusting and polishing. Hazel was alert at her switchboard, and a few nurses drifted in to study posted schedule sheets, yawn and drift out. Two male supervisors were talking and smoking in one of the side offices, but otherwise the place held that feeling of suspended time and effort that ordinarily belongs to night duty in hospitals like Canterbury.

Lucretia lit her desk lamp with one hand and with the other went into a pocket for cigarettes. As she did so, her fingers touched a small metal box. After a little hesitation, she pulled it out and placed it in front of her on the desk. Without opening it, she visualized the two capsules it contained. She had been carrying the capsules for some time. One was enough for the use she had in mind, but she kept two in the box in order to feel assured that when she was ready for what they could do, it would be swift and certain. She didn't like to attempt any task and not succeed.

She lit a cigarette and realized that her hands were shaking. It was shock, she supposed. She thought about it bitterly. Putting Edna on Rehabilitation against everyone's advice was her second great mistake. The first, of course, had been to let Walter get away and Margaret take over, even to the announcement of their engagement. Two such mistakes were enough to destroy her. Now she would always be suspicious of her own judgment. She was rapidly reaching the time when she would no longer be able to conceal her pain.

Her thoughts traveled back through the whole disastrous evening until they reached the morning's inquest. Here she did not feel so much that she had made a mistake as that she had faced a situation she could not handle. She was honest in believing that the hospital's good name must be protected at all cost and that in not revealing what she had long suspected about Miguel Andreatta she had been serving the best interests of everyone concerned. She could have told Bud Nappy and his jury that Mary Elsie Blayton was actually better off dead, since all she had to look forward to was institutional therapy for the rest of her life. She could have mentioned that Andreatta did not always violate his patients; quite often he was very successful in helping them.

But she had kept still. The jury had been sympathetic to Jim's predicament; they had identified themselves with his position and they had set him free.

We do what we can, she thought bleakly. It's not humanly possible to be perfect.

She pulled out a sheet of paper, pushed the metal box to one side and began writing. *Dear Margaret,* she wrote. She stopped and looked at it. Why did she call Margaret dear? She hated her with a deadly intensity! But she did not change what she had written. Instead, she pushed the pen back and forth steadily.

As you may have guessed, for quite some time I haven't been well. One of these days, perhaps soon, I am going away while I can still do so with dignity and self-respect. I do not desire to emulate the behavior of those patients on Female Terminal who are dying of uterine cancer. My reason for writing this is to spare you the shock of hearing from outside sources that someone else, not you, has been chosen to take my place. She is no one you know, a registered nurse and therapist from Johns Hopkins, very highly recommended, and selected for my position by even higher authority than I possess, although I will not deny that I was able to partially influence this choice. Knowing that you have planned to step into my shoes, I assume that you will be quite disappointed. All I can say is that I honestly believe my shoes would never have fit you, Margaret. No doubt you will find much in your coming marriage to Walter Sturgis to solace you and provide compensation for what might otherwise prove a heavy cross indeed. I wish I could have been able to do more for you, but I have always felt—and always shall—that the employees of Canterbury must be caretakers in the truest sense of the word. If I have failed to be one, my opinion is still unchanged. However, I think you will agree that if I did fail, it wasn't because I didn't try. . . .

She signed her name, folded the paper and slipped it into an envelope, sealing and addressing it before she tucked it away in a drawer. She did not intend to have it delivered. Just found.

She started another letter, addressing it to Walter. Then she hesitated. She could say, "If you had been half a man and married me as you promised, perhaps I would still have life ahead of me, wonderful, exciting, vital life instead of the death I face." But such words would neither shame him nor make him particularly uncomfortable. What he would hate would be the knowledge that the woman he did intend to marry would never sit in Lucretia Terry's seat of authority. He would often remember with regret the pay check Margaret had never managed to earn.

She tore up the sheet. She did not feel triumphant at thinking how disappointed and chagrined he would some day be; instead, she felt very tired and lonely. The pain in her abdomen nagged at her like a toothache. It was dull much of the time, but it was always there. When the sharp twists came, she could hardly bear it.

She returned the metal box to her pocket. Turning off the light, she left the office.

I'll have Elizabeth write up a report tomorrow on this business of Ruth Ellison, she thought, stooping a little as she walked because of the pain. She was just too tired to do it herself.

In a car parked in dark shadows behind the hospital laundry, Margaret and Walter sat comfortably relaxed. Walter was wishing she would suggest they call it a night. He was satisfied for the present and it was late. In fact it would soon be dawn. He glanced at the drab brick building on his left. It sprang into activity at about five every morning, and he had no desire to be caught parked behind it with a woman in his car. Especially Margaret. After they were married, he would have to admit to his involvement with her, but until then he didn't even want to think about her except on certain occasions and preferably when it was dark enough so that he couldn't see her face. He moved restlessly and she glanced at him with an inquiring expression. He still puzzled her most of the time, but she didn't know why. At times he was passionate and aggressive, but often he seemed restless and uneasy. Perhaps he was just trying to get used to the idea that anyone as intelligent and well-educated as she was could be so competently responsive. But surely he would realize that she must know something about such things, since she studied them all the time. Or did he? Surely—surely she hadn't shocked him, had she? The thought made her feel a little complacent and superior.

"Turn on the light," she said.

"What?"

In answer, she reached over and clicked on the overhead dome light.

Alarmed, he sat up. "What the hell! You want somebody to see us?"

"Who cares!" she returned elaborately. "I've got something to show you."

He looked around apprehensively while she dug into her purse. When her hand came out, it held a large white card. She balanced it in front of his face. "Nice?"

"What is it?"

"Oh, dear." She sighed for his stupidity. "Just about the most important thing in the world to us. Look closely."

He squinted and shook his head. "Too dim."

"Our wedding invitations. Isn't it lovely? I'm having two hundred and fifty printed. They won't be cheap. Feel. Embossed. The most expensive. But nothing's too good for us, is it, Walter?"

He turned off the light hastily. "Sure, sure," he said. At that she was right. As head of Canterbury's Nursing Personnel, she'd earn enough to be able to afford the best. It was a pleasant thought. He started the car. "Gotta get you home," he mumbled. "Don't want you getting sick. Won't be too much longer, you know."

"No, it won't." She settled back, still holding the cardboard square in one hand while the other went to a breast, cupping it firmly but with a sensuous delicacy. "Thanksgiving Day," she murmured, watching his profile as it began to show clearly in the first, faint light of early morning. Her expression was sly and a little hungry. "A little more than four months."

CHAPTER 52

THERE WERE SEVERAL PEOPLE in Jubal's office when Larry arrived there in answer to Jubal's summons. He saw Althea the instant he stepped into the room. She was sitting in a straight-backed chair near the window and did not look around.

He glanced at the others. Behind Althea stood Margaret, her face even more flushed and disagreeable than usual. On Althea's far side stood Elizabeth, an anxious, closed expression on her face. Donovan stood near Jubal, and Dr. Barth and Dr. Tolliver, two of the older staff members, were behind Jubal's desk.

They look like a congregation of wardens, he thought. What was all this about and why was Althea here? Was it in connection with Edna and Ruth Ellison's death?

He began fumbling in his jacket in a search for cigarettes, a device he always employed when he wanted time to think. But before he could get his pack out, Donovan came over with both cigarette and lighter.

"Thanks," he said, staring directly at Donovan.

"Not at all." Donovan looked away quickly.

Larry inhaled deeply, thinking, What gives with this bunch? Is something wrong?

Jubal cleared his throat. His face showed strain. "I think we're all here. Close the door, will you, Larry?"

Jubal waited until Larry had turned back, then stepped out in front of his desk and began to talk. "We have a problem. I think everyone here knows about it except Denning."

He sounded deeply disturbed and Larry had a strange, brief premonition. Have I made Althea pregnant? he thought. He glanced in her direction, but she did not move. For a moment he was tempted to ask for swift and sure information, then he relaxed. He could only wait until the problem was explained or clarified in some way.

Jubal walked three steps forward and three steps back. Each time he turned, he seemed more distressed. "I don't—I can't—I can't recall that this has ever happened here before in Canterbury. It simply lacks precedent, and that makes it al the more difficult to arrive at a reasonably satisfactory solution."

Larry felt a momentary flood of relief. Thank God, at least it couldn't be Edna and her unpredictable violence. Ruth Ellison was not the first employee in Canterbury to meet death at the hands of a patient.

"I don't believe it will be difficult, Herrington," Barth said. "Unless we let it be difficult. We have every facility—"

"Jubal is referring to the lack of relatives, I believe," Donovan said quickly. "Someone who would agree to be responsible for the commitment. You know, there are certain formalities which must be observed unless we want to go to the courts."

"At least the hospital can't be blamed for this," Margaret said thinly.

Whatever it is, the hospital can't be blamed, Larry repeated silently. *What is it the hospital can't be blamed for?*

He began to study them, one by one. As he searched their faces they looked elsewhere. When he reached Elizabeth, she was the only one to return his look openly and honestly. He was startled to see that her eyes were full of tears.

"It's the purest form of regression I've ever had the good fortune to observe," Barth said. He was a short, fair man and relied heavily on bluntness and what he called a direct approach.

Jubal scowled at him. "Good fortune? Not good fortune in this case, Barth. What a way to put it!"

"Regression," Barth repeated stubbornly. "From the onset. We'll be able to do comprehensive research from now on until she begins to curl into the fetal position."

"Ridiculous!" Tolliver said sharply. "We'll give her every possible test and follow immediately with the therapy indicated. Perhaps even a lobotomy. It could be that we still aren't too late. I've seen many cases where prompt therapy achieved remarkable results."

Margaret nodded, her florid features looking oddly triumphant. She was there because Lucretia hadn't felt well enough to face a new ordeal. Elizabeth put one hand on the back of Althea's chair and averted her face. Althea did not move.

The monstrous knowledge struck Larry. *Why doesn't she move?*

He edged past Jubal and Donovan until he stood near Margaret, and still Althea did not turn her head to look in his direction or to look at anyone. Now there was a sudden, complete silence in the room. They were all watching him.

"Althea . . ." he said hesitantly.

Elizabeth moved quickly for her age. She placed herself between him and the chair. "Dr. Denning, perhaps you should be told what this is all about by either Dr. Herrington or Dr. Macleod before you see—" She broke off unhappily and glanced imploringly toward Donovan.

"He doesn't know," Donovan said in a low voice.

Larry turned toward the rest. "Know what, for God's sake?" he said loudly.

Jubal cleared his throat loudly. "It happened very suddenly," he began.

Donovan put out one hand. "Let me tell him," he said, his face haggard. "It was the—the night Ruth Ellison was killed. As Jubal says, it—it happened very suddenly. She— Althea—went into a catatonic trance." He said it sickly and with a terrible effort, as though he could still scarcely believe what he knew was true. "There was no previous warning that

I know of. That's a hopeful prognostication in itself. I can only believe it was caused by shock when she heard what her cousin had done—and, of course, for shock there is something we can definitely do."

With a stiff jab of his arm, Larry pushed Elizabeth aside and stepped around to stare down at Althea. Although he had known in his subconscious mind what he would see, shock and horror held him fast. Like a picture revealed by a sudden, strong light, everything that had happened in the past few weeks flashed through his thoughts.

Jesus God, what have we done to her!

"There was plenty of warning. It's been coming on for weeks—weeks." Ever since you shamed her in front of the hospital, he wanted to shout at Donovan.

As if he realized what Larry was thinking, Donovan shook his head. To agree could mean that he, too, had done his share in creating this terrible situation. "No," he said, drawing one hand nervously across his face and down along his neck.

"Yes," Larry said distinctly. *You and I have done this dreadful thing!* his expression said.

He stumbled around to stand between the others and Althea, shielding her. Through a haze he stared at them. You, too, all of you, he thought. *What will you do!*

"So now you'll all make your little diagnoses and you'll prescribe your therapy," he said hoarsely. "You'll lock this girl up on a ward and dress her in a denim sack. You'll regiment her, of course—you'll regiment every monent of her living death. As she gets progressively worse, you'll let some sadistic attendant slap and cuff her around. Maybe you'll even let her get pregnant by another Andreatta with his nose smelling out all the females in heat. You'll talk about new drugs and you'll experiment and you'll analyze but you'll never waste one bit of honest love!"

He halted and sucked in a ragged breath. "If she ever comes to her senses long enough to know what's going on, and she happens to hang herself from a bar in a window or from the framework of a shower stall, you won't like it but it won't ruin you. You'll say we did the best we could, we did the best we could." He shook his head and there was a long silence. "Ah—you make me sick!" he said quietly.

Now he was shaking so hard that his teeth chattered. Their faces, at first full of shock and dismay, were changing to concern. "You're overwrought, naturally," Tolliver said almost gently.

Larry swung on him. "Why naturally? Because I worshiped the ground she walked on? Because I took her to bed whenever I could?" he asked furiously.

Their concern turned to alarm. "Believe me, Dr. Denning, we'll take very good care of her," Tolliver said stiffly.

"Believe me, you'll never get that chance, Dr. Tolliver!"

"Now see here!" Jubal said. "By what authority—"

"My own," Larry said intensely. "I have every right. She's my wife." He told the lie without a qualm.

Donovan was horrified. Didn't Larry realize what he was doing? The fool could ruin his whole future! Then he remembered that Larry had once told him about getting a marriage license and carrying it with him all the time. How did he know that it hadn't been used?

"Don't do anything foolish, Dr. Denning," Dr. Barth said crisply.

Larry looked at him. "You mean like keeping her with me? I want her with me, Dr. Barth."

"But she's custodial! You can't begin to give her the care she'll get here in the institution."

"I may not, but I'll be the judge of that." He bent and lifted Althea to her feet, his face humble and tender. Slipping an arm around her waist and turning her toward the door, he looked at and through them.

Shocked, but unable to keep from sounding malicious, Margaret asked, her mouth twisting, "She won't be much of a wife, Doctor. What will you do when she becomes dangerous?"

Instantly he turned and stared at her. "Do you really care?"

Her face flaming, she stepped back.

"Where are you going?" Jubal asked.

"You'll find my resignation in the top drawer of my desk. I made it out a day or two before Mrs. Ellison was killed."

The day he came to me about Althea, Donovan thought with shame. He turned away, unable to bear the contempt he saw in Larry's eyes.

Larry did not add that he had not sent in his resignation because he had not quite decided that he could endure being away from Althea. A long time ago he had received an offer from Darby, a West Coast hospital comparable to Canterbury, but he had not regarded it seriously. Jubal began to splutter. "But you—you'll need a job! It's no simple matter to take private care of a deranged woman. You'll have to hire competent help and pay for medications out of your own pocket."

Now was the time to tell Jubal—all of them, in fact—that he would not be without a job. But why bother? Why relieve their feelings? Without troubling to answer Jubal, he guided Althea past Donovan and out the door.

After a long moment, Jubal said angrily, "It seems we've come to a pretty pass when the superintendent of a hos-

346

pital as large as this one cannot command the respect and attention which are his proper due!"

He stared around belligerently but no one had anything to say.

The next day, a little before nine in the morning, Larry glanced around his room before he left it for the last time. He was leaving the room just as it had been assigned to him —neat but empty.

Downstairs, he went around to the driver's side of the car, opened the door and slid in. Then he turned to stare intently at Althea, sitting on his right. She looked straight ahead through the windshield with expressionless eyes. Already her soft beauty was dulled. Her hair had lost its satiny, golden luster; her breath had become a little fetid. She had acquired a mannerism: she clasped her hands together and rubbed her thumbs back and forth across each other. Unless he thought of some way to stop it, she would continue doing this until her thumbs became dangerously raw.

He took one hand away from the steering wheel and laid it in her lap, palm up. "Put your hand in mine, Althea," he said. He repeated it several times. When she did not respond, he reached out and separated her hands, gripping one of them firmly. He drove that way for many miles. "Like this, my darling," he said softly. "Like this, all the rest of our lives."

CHAPTER 53

THE MORNING that Larry and Althea drove away from Canterbury, Kathy met Mike outside Rehabilitation. Her face was still white from the shock of what she had heard. Mike's expression was grim. They walked in silence away from the building.

"I can't stay on," she said suddenly. "I just can't, Mike." When he didn't answer, she turned her face toward him. "Didn't you hear me?" she asked desperately.

"No."

"What?"

He looked around, saw a bench and pulled her toward it. She sat down unwillingly with him facing her. "Look," he said quietly. "What have you got to gain by pulling out?"

"I—what do you mean? There's no question of gaining something."

"Then what are you trying to prove?"

She looked away and shook her head. "It's just that I—I can't bear to think about it," she replied, her voice low.

"It makes me feel so terrible."

"Yes?"

"Don't you see? I'm to blame—me, me!" She put her head down and pulled at a piece of Kleenex until it was completely shredded.

He sighed, took the tissue out of her hands and flicked the shreds off her lap with the tips of his fingers. "Kathy, I'm going to tell you something and then let's never talk about it again. Okay? When you keep on going over and over something, you don't accomplish a thing."

He gripped her arm so that she had to face him. "Now, you listen to me," he said. "I've agreed with you that you did a hell of a thing back there, but what I can see, and you can't, is that you were honest. You did it because you loved somebody. Then you tried to straighten it out but you couldn't."

"I didn't try hard enough. I didn't go all the way."

"Perhaps," he agreed. "On the other hand, maybe that was something you simply could not help. We all have limitations, you know."

"How can you stand me, Mike!"

He shook her a little, lovingly, tenderly. "Listen to me, Kathy. It's over, all of it. You've got to stop thinking about it. Honey, people need each other. I need you, you need me, those patients need us."

"Wouldn't you like me to quit and go away with you?"

"No," he said promptly.

"Mike!"

"I don't want a little kid. I want a wife who's adult enough to face things."

"I thought you loved me."

"God!" he said and sighed. He picked up her hands and kissed them, first on the back and then the wrists and finally the palms. "There's more than one side to love, Kathy."

Her eyes were shut. "I know," she whispered, tears beginning to run down her cheeks. "You're right, Mike. I have to act like a silly kid because I've been doing it so long I can't seem to stop doing it."

All the rest of her life she would have to live with what she had done, but he was right: she must stop talking about it; she would have to grow up.

He looked at her wet face. "There's just one thing," he said gently. "Do you still think Althea was trying to kill you?"

After a long moment, she shook her head. "I—I guess we'll never know. But it isn't important now. The only thing that matters is that she gets well."

Her face tilted up to him. "Mike! Will—will you wait for me?"

"You mean there could be a doubt of it in your mind?"

He began to grin. "I'll be right in the front row, watching you walk across the stage to get that diploma."

"I'll probably stumble and fall when I go up to get it," she said with a little hiccup.

"You better not," he said, his grin spreading, "or I'll come up and lay you right there on the stage in front of everybody."

"Goodness!" she said faintly.

He took her into his arms. "There are probably much better ways of showing approval, I suppose," he murmured. "But at the moment, I can't—I simply can't think of any."

It was also the day after Ruth's funeral. Millie sat in a downtown lawyer's office. She had received the lawyer's telephone call right after the funeral, almost as soon as she had got back to her house from the cemetery. Ruth Ellison had been his client, he said, and could Millie come down to his office in the morning, as there were some matters of importance he wished to discuss with her?

She heard the lawyer say that Ruth had been a moderately prosperous woman, a property owner, which was incredible enough; but when he kept insisting that everything had been left to Millie, she simply couldn't believe him.

"It's true, Madam," he said. "She left you everything."

Ruth had owned three pieces of property. There was the house next to Millie's, all clear, paid for; there was a small store building, occupied by a thriving radio and television business which paid a handsome monthly amount for the privilege of using the building. There were a few acres on the edge of town with a good house and fixtures. Fixtures, the lawyer explained, were barns, chicken houses and fences.

"It's all yours, Mrs. Higgins," said Harold Fenn patiently. "Now, don't tell me all that property won't come in handy."

"I won't say that," she stammered, looking at him with troubled eyes. "You know I lost my job. I told you that right off. I guess I just don't want to believe what you're telling me on account of it means I maybe traded Ruthie, sort of, for what she gave me."

"Nonsense. That's no way to look at it."

Her fat shoulders lifted in a heavy sigh. "No, I guess not. But it sure seems funny when I think how I can't run over next door like I used to because Ruthie won't be there any more."

It was too bad, of course. A real tragedy. But time would take care of her sorrow as time had a way of doing. To divert Millie, he showed her that the income from the store alone was more than she had been making every month on her job. If she rented the house next door and acreage with house, she could easily make the payments on her own home plus taxes and upkeep, and her living expenses as well. As soon as her home was clear, she could begin to save.

"Or you could sell something," he suggested. "Say, the acreage. You'd get enough from that to completely pay off your own mortgage. Then you could live off the rental of the other two properties." He added that he had a buyer for the country place if she cared for the idea.

"Good prospect," he said. "These people have wanted the place a long time. Mrs. Ellison knew about them but she never seemed at all interested in discussing a sale. Evidently she disliked them personally. Of course, their credit rating was poor some weeks back, but they've come into some money recently—a matured insurance policy, I think. I should explain that they came to me right after the—the tragedy and wanted to know if the property would be put up for sale."

So many things coming at her, Millie thought in confusion. It was hard to keep them straightened out. "Sure, sure," she muttered abstractedly. "Don't know as there's any point in hanging on to something when you can't use it yourself. Three pieces of property besides my own house. I can't rightly believe it. Sure can't live in all of 'em." She looked around his office helplessly. "Why do you suppose these people want to live outside o' town?" something impelled her to ask. "Can't they buy anything else?"

"The man's not well, not well at all. A spot on one lung, I understand. The woman thinks she could keep on working and he could sort of farm the place. You know, be outdoors most of the time in the fresh air and sunshine."

There was a moment's silence as something began to penetrate Millie's confusion. "You say Ruthie didn't like these folks? Why not?"

He scratched his head. "Ah . . . I can't really say. Just an impression I had."

"Where'd they work?"

"Why, right now they both work in Canterbury, Mrs. Higgins."

"Canterbury?"

"Yes."

"Supervisors?"

"He is. She's an aide, I believe. And a charge on one of the wards."

"Day shift?"

"Ah . . . yes."

Her eyes squinted at him as her thoughts churned. She was thankful that she could go on looking pleasant and not show that she had guessed the identity of the people who

350

wanted to buy a little house and five acres on the edge of town.

"Well, I'll tell you, Mr. Fenn," she said finally. "If these people are willing to come and talk business with me personally—oh, you'll get your commission, of course—why, I'll see what I can do. I'm not saying I'll sell, but we can sure talk about it."

He thought that was fair enough and that he would let the people know right away what she had said.

They came to her door. She asked them in but did not ask them to sit down. When the silence became unbearable, she told them that they could buy the property on the edge of town.

"Only, not for cash," she said quickly. "I have another plan. I'll have Mr. Fenn draw up the papers, all legal and foolproof. Your payments'll be as small as possible. I want this to last a long, long time."

The man rubbed the back of his neck. They had hoped to pay it off fast in order to save as much interest as possible.

"Small payments," Millie said smoothly. "And real cheap interest, interest as low as the law allows. Paid to me every month. The first time you miss meeting me to give me the payment, I'll give you back all your money you've paid in up to that time and we'll call the whole thing off."

What did she mean? they asked.

Just what she said. "Sure, it'll take a long time to pay it off, but what have you got to lose if the interest's small? Goodness, it shouldn't come too hard for one of you t' meet me at a certain place and hand over the payment while I'm writing out a receipt, huh? Believe me, you'd be mighty foolish not to take me up on the proposition I got in mind. All you gotta do is sign on the dotted line that you'll do just like I want about this and you can move out there tomorrow."

They were silent a moment. Unable to control his curiosity, the man said, "What kind of a gimmick is this? Where would I have to meet you?"

"Not you. Her."

The woman became angry. "All right," she snapped. "You've got some damn silly scheme in mind, but I'll go along just to hear what it is. What's behind all this hocus-pocus?"

Millie said softly, "You both meet me tomorrow at my lawyer's office and we'll have this all made legal and—"

"I know—foolproof! But where is this place I have to meet you to make the payments—this goddam mysterious place?" The woman's voice was loud.

"My goodness, haven't you guessed?" Millie said.

Charlotte Range became very still. Then her face darkened and her husband put out a warning hand. "You're kidding, of course," he said hopefully, but Charlotte said thickly, "You must be crazy!"

Millie folded her hands across her stomach. For a woman with a heavy body, she looked majestic at the moment.

"Well, I don't know." She shrugged. "But it is my property. And if you want it, you'll have to meet me every month at my friend Ruthie's grave—Mrs. Ellison to you—so's you can give me your blood money right there beside her bed in the dirt. What's the matter? You afraid you'll hear her turning over when she knows you finally got something she didn't want you to have?"

Charlotte and her husband backed toward the door. "Goddam you!" Charlotte shouted. "There's something wrong with your mind!"

"Maybe so," Millie agreed calmly. "But I happen to be the charge on this ward. You want the property, you know the terms."

They left hurriedly. She went to the window and watched. Then something happened that made Millie push her nose closer to the window in order to see better. Charlotte's husband began coughing. He coughed so hard that he had to stop and bend over with Charlotte supporting him, anxiety sharp in every motion she made. Millie kept her nose against the window until they had both staggered on down the street and out of sight.

She stayed at the window for a long time because she was too ashamed to move. The scene had brought Harry back to her as clearly as though he were actually right there in the room. It was plain that Charlotte loved her husband just as much as Millie had loved Harry. Charlotte wasn't all meanness and toadishness, Millie thought. It wasn't right to mistreat her just because she had the upper hand for a change.

I shouldn't have done it, Millie thought, shaking her head. Two wrongs don't make nothing but two wrongs. We all got our problems. We should be helping each other when we can. Why, look at me! Here I am, acting like I was almost too good to breathe, and all on account of I got a windfall. Do I deserve it? Do I deserve it any more'n Charlotte Range?

She had an impulse to run after Charlotte and her husband and let them know she had changed her mind. But deep inside she knew they would be back. She'll be cross. She'll say nasty, uncalled-for things, but she'll be back. I can take care of it then.

She went out into her kitchen and stooped to smooth Georgie's fur. Then she glanced out the little window over the sink and across into Ruth's back yard. Well, for heaven's sake! she thought. The rose hedge was beginning to leaf again. It hadn't been destroyed after all.